# ALL'S FAE

## THAT

# ENDS FAE

Guardians of the PHAE
Book Three


ROWAN DILLON


GREEN DRAGON PUBLISHING

Published by Green Dragon Publishing
Beacon Falls, CT
www.GreenDragonArtist.com
All rights reserved.

# Pronunciation Guide

Below is a list of some of the words and names in the story that are in other languages:

Anú—(AHnoo) A goddess of pre-Christian Ireland. Sometimes conflated with Danú.

Balor—(BAHlore) A chieftain of the Fomorians

Bealtaine—(BELLtehna) "May" in Irish, also an ancient festival

Beannacht—(BANecht) "Blessing" in Irish

Bintou—(bin-TOO) A Malian name

Bláithín—(BLAheen) An Irish name

Bran mac Máelmórda—(bran mahk malMORdah) A 10th century Irish chieftain

Caoimhe—(KWEEveh) An Irish name

Cé a ghlaonn orm?—(CAY eh GHLAYon ORem?) "Who calls me?" in Irish

Ciara—(KEE-rah) An Irish name

Cú Chulainn—(koo KHUHlinn) A demi-god/hero of pre-Christian Ireland

Dáil Éireann—(DAWil YAIRinn) The Irish Parliament

Dáil—(DAWil) The lower house of the Dáil Éireann, the Irish Parliament

Dia 's Muire duit!—(DEEah smweerah ghwit) "May God and Mary be with you" an Irish greeting

Dia daoibh—(DEEah ghweev) "May God be with you" an Irish greeting, plural

Dian Cécht—(DEEun KAYecht) A healer god of pre-Christian Ireland

Draoí/Draoíthe—(DREE/DREEheh) Priest/priests of pre-Christian Irish religion

Dún Ailinne—(doon ALinyeh) A sacred site in Kildare, Ireland

Éire—(AYreh) Another name for Ireland

Éist—(EESHT) "Listen" in Irish

Emain Macha—(AWen MAHKah) A sacred site in Armagh, Northern Ireland

Ethniu—(ENyoo) A goddess of pre-Christian Ireland, mother of Lugh

Fomorians—(foeMOReeuhns) Beings who lived in Ireland before the Tuatha Dé Danann

Gaijin—(GUY-ZHEEN) "Foreigners" in Japanese

Go raibh maith agat—(go rahv MAH a-get) "Thank you" in Irish

Hiroki—(hih-ROW-kee) A Japanese name

Kami—(kaMEE) Deities venerated in Shinto

Lugh Lámfada—(LOO lavFAHda) A god of pre-Christian Ireland, Lugh of the Long Arm

Lúnasa—(LOOnasa) "August" in Irish, also an ancient harvest festival

Macha—(MAHkhah) A goddess of pre-Christian Ireland

Manannán mac Lir—(MAHnahnahn mahk leer) A sea god of pre-Christian Ireland

Matsuri—(MAHTsooree) A prayer of gratitude to the ritual of Nature

Mo chroi—(mow KROY) "My heart" in Irish

Mo leanbh—(mow LANuv) "My child" in Irish

Oghma—(OWmah) A god of pre-Christian Ireland

Omoikane—(ohMWEEkaNEH) A Shinto god of wisdom and intelligence

Poitín—(pohCHEEN) An Irish alcohol, moonshine

Qacha—(KAH-chah) A Mongolian name

Ráth Cruachan—(rath CROOkhen) A sacred site in Roscommon, Ireland (Rathcroghan)

Róisín—(row-SHEEN) An Irish name (little rose)

Tá failte romhaibh—(taw FALLcheh ROWuv) "You're welcome" in Irish, plural

Taoiseach/Taoisigh—(TEEshekht/TEEsheeh) Head of government of Ireland (singular/plural)

Teachta Dála—(TYOKHtah DAWlah) An Irish legislator

Teachtaí Dála—(TYACKtee DAWlah) A member of the Dáil Éireann, the Irish Parliament

Tuath—(TOOah) A tribe or family group in Irish

Tuatha Dé Danann—(TOOha day DAHnen) Deities of pre-Christian Ireland

Uisneach—(ISHnock) A sacred site in Westmeath, Ireland

Wəlastəkwewiyik—(woolLAStwoWIig) "People of the beautiful river," native tribe in New Brunswick and Maine

# Prologue

When the magnetic poles shifted, the world panicked. However, much like the millennium bug in 2000, the feared difficulties failed to manifest, and everyone relaxed.

At first.

Within months, a small percentage of people developed special talents. A famed opera singer reached impossible octaves. An Olympic swimmer grew fins. A famous glass artist could manipulate molten glass with his mind.

People changed. They grew. They *evolved.*

In time, a center formed to care for and educate these people, dubbed the Unhidden. The Protectorate for unHidden Advancement and Education (PHAE) was headquartered in Ireland and combed the world, searching for these new talents. Many of them came to PHAE to learn how to harness their growing powers.

Anna, who had power over water; Max, who commanded the winds; Hiroki, with the power of persuasion; Komie, who could command plants to grow; Bintou, who could read any language; And Qacha, who could control fire.

But before they could finish their training, they were attacked.

Several groups formed an alliance against the Unhidden to fight their progress. The Pure Earther Movement (PEM) developed a plan, obtained weapons, and executed a multi-pronged attack on Ireland. Bombs were planted in several cities. And while they were able to prevent parts of the attack, the bombs in Galway and Dublin were detonated, killing thousands of people.

In the aftermath, the Unhidden helped to heal the survivors, but the bombs contained more than just explosives. They spread several weaponized diseases.

As they scrambled to find a cure, the Unhidden came into contact with ancient gods and goddesses from the Irish pantheon.

The world began to polarize, some seeing the Unhidden as heroes and others seeing them as evil. Both the PHAE and the government of Ireland agreed to work with them to fight against the disease rampaging across their population.

But they may have agreed to more than they should.

# Chapter One

"Do not look upon this world with fear and loathing. Bravely face whatever the gods offer."
– Morihei Ueshiba

**Latest CNN Update:** *The double scourge of pneumonic plague and weaponized anthrax continues to ravage not only Ireland, but several other known concentrations of Unhidden population, including the United States, Iceland, Siberia, Peru, Japan, and China. As a result, PHAE headquarters in Ireland have issued a blanket lockdown for all PHAE enclaves.*

*Certain state governments have insisted upon lockdowns, regardless of the PHAE's orders. However, the PHAE continues to work with those governments to come up with a workable solution for those affected.*

*Some enclaves are also defending from physical attacks from splinter extremist groups. Ireland, the largest concentration of the PHAE population and the location of the group's world headquarters, has sustained the most damage due to several bombings in June. A coalition of several extremist groups, the Pure Earther Movement, or PEM, took responsibility for those attacks last month.*

*Other locations are now doing their best to withstand sieges, guerrilla attacks, and insurgencies. We have not verified that the PEM are behind these other attacks.*

*However, without the resources of a national government, these enclaves are having a much more difficult time defending themselves. The compound in Peru, thought to house approximately two hundred Unhidden, has already been overrun.*

*Initial reports indicate some of the PHAE personnel escaped, but the remaining forty members are unaccounted for. Anyone with information on these missing individuals is urged to contact the Peruvian Ministry of the Interior or the Ireland headquarters of PHAE.*

**Bintou:**

Bintou Sissoko couldn't move a muscle as Lugh, the ancient Irish god of light, art, magic and, well, everything, traced his finger along her jaw. Her skin burned at his touch, a heat that shot straight down to her belly, a burning desire that she fought against with every fiber of her being. And yet, she didn't want him to stop.

Abruptly, he turned away from her to face the assembled Dáil, the legislative body of the Republic of Ireland.

He raised his arms in an expansive gesture, a broad smile on his face. "My friends, welcome! Welcome to this, the first new day of an amazing new age. I look forward to working with each and every one of you!"

Thunderous applause greeted his opening words and he beamed, his skin glowing with its own light.

"I am here to outline an ambitious plan we have crafted with the help of these delightful maidens of PHAE..." He gestured behind him to herself and Ciara, and Bintou rubbed at the goosebumps on her arms. She forced herself to stand straight, shoulders back, though she despised being on display.

"Our first step has already begun..."

Now that he was no longer paying attention to her, Bintou could breathe again, and her muscles trembled like jelly. It took every ounce of self-control not to collapse after that roller coaster of adrenaline.

She didn't love Lugh. In truth, she didn't even like him. But his ridiculously over-the-top beauty and heart-melting smile still reduced her to a quivering mass of hormones, despite herself.

"We shall embark tomorrow on a historic mission to the metropolis of London, in your United Kingdom, to meet with leaders from many modern countries, to see how we, the ancient gods, may work together with humans for the betterment of us all."

In truth, Bintou would much rather spend time amongst ancient scrolls and manuscripts, as she had with her job in Mali. But she'd been assigned to translate for this shining god.

In his few weeks in this time, Lugh had gained fluency in both English and modern Irish with remarkable speed, but he still needed her to translate. He had issues with unusual accents and regional slang, and any modern language other than English or Irish.

As Lugh finished his speech to enthralled applause, Bintou escaped the room and the building, her duties finished for the day. Skirting the ever-present protestors outside, she slipped into the underground bunker headquarters for PHAE, the Protectorate for unHidden Advancement and Education.

She hurried down the concrete halls, her footsteps echoing against the walls. Most of the residents were off on missions, so she reached the sanctuary of her office and rooms without encountering anyone.

Once alone in her own space, she shut her eyes and stood with her back against the cool, concrete wall. The offices were sparse, but they'd become her home over the last few months, ever since she left Mali at the invitation of her ex-lover, Ibrahim.

She didn't love Ibrahim, despite traveling to a different continent for him. She used to, but then he'd left her with barely a word, and she'd spent two lonely years trying to get over him.

Bintou *had* loved Martin, and still did. But Martin had died, and she hadn't been able to save him. In fact, she'd probably killed him.

She let out a rueful laugh and now that her heart had finally calmed and her rational mind took over, she sat at her computer. The Malian woman gave a few nervous glances around the empty room, despite knowing full well she was alone.

Over the last few weeks, Bintou's puzzlement at the gods' actions had grown. She didn't know exactly why they were here or what they wanted, and something in the back of her mind screamed that she was missing some essential hint.

She couldn't outright ask them, but she might find clues in what they've done so far. Therefore, she'd been compiling a list of all their actions, no matter how small. Once that was complete, she'd search for a pattern and form a hypothesis to be tested.

Her talent was to read or speak any language. However, years of analyzing ancient documents, searching for patterns and interpolating motives, gave her tools to analyze the actions and words of these ancient gods.

Besides, research might keep her mind off Lugh and his searing touch.

After a few hours, Bintou leaned back and stretched her arms, staring at her screen. Nothing seemed to fit into place.

In the last few days, she'd interviewed everyone she knew, but it still didn't seem like enough. She couldn't discern any strong patterns yet. She dredged her memory for any other incidents she might have forgotten.

Hiroki had excellent recollection and filled in several things Lugh had spoken of while addressing the Dáil. Masaaki, Hiroki's friend from college, added a few more.

Even Ciara, the PHAE liaison who had helped them ever since their arrival to Ireland, filled in some gaps. And while Bintou had been hesitant to approach Ibrahim to help, Ciara urged her to ask him.

Ibrahim had never really needed encouragement to think well of himself, but a bit of flattery always worked wonders. She snorted to herself at the thought of Ibrahim's self-image needing any sort of support. Still, his contributions had helped flesh out her list.

Despite all that, the pattern didn't work. She was missing something.

Maybe she could head out to the west coast to speak with Anna? Since Anna had command over water, she'd been apprenticed to Manannán mac Lir. Anna might have lots of details about the Irish god of the sea. But would she be willing to pass on that information?

Anna had a brother, another Unhidden. But Bintou couldn't care less what had happened to Joel. He'd betrayed them several times over and could fall off a steep cliff. She rarely thought ill of anyone and was an avowed pacifist, but in his case, she'd make an exception.

She'd completely lost track of where Qacha had gone. Perhaps the Daughter of Fire was on the west coast, as well.

Why were they actually here, awake, in the modern day? *How* were they here? Had the same phenomenon that wakened Unhidden powers like her own opened a portal to let them manifest? They were helping the Unhidden, and the Irish people in general, but to what end?

Most cultures who still held onto a strong tradition of Other Folk, like the faeries in Ireland or the *Huldafolk* in Iceland, had a higher percentage of Unhidden in their populations. Would any of the *yumbo* appear in her native land of Mali? Maybe the Byrnes could help, with Colin's deep knowledge of folklore.

Bintou let out a deep breath, saved her file, and closed her laptop. Her eyes were burning holes in her head. She needed sleep before she could make any sense of the data she had, or even make plans to obtain more.

Tomorrow would be soon enough to ask Ciara about visiting the Byrnes. For now, Bintou sought out her bed, a cot in one of the two rooms. She crawled in under the warm wool blanket. The hotel they'd been staying in was still in shambles. She didn't mind this cot so much now that they had thicker mattresses.

But it was lonely without Martin here.

**Bintou:**

The next morning, after much argument and cajoling, Ciara had convinced Lugh to eschew his linen tunic hemmed in gold and wear more modest, modern garb for this press conference.

She sent for a tailor, who came quickly, followed by an assistant wheeling a rack of Italian business suits. Lugh had scowled at the selections. "This is what modern men wear for formal occasions? They are so dull! There are no colors."

Clearing his throat, the tailor began his spiel. "I assure you, these are made with the finest of materials, in the Italian cut and style—"

Lugh cut him off with an upraised hand. "They look much too binding. I do not like them."

Bintou placed a hand on his arm. "Please, at least allow them to measure you for one. A properly fitted suit looks good."

Lugh considered her plea, and finally gave a curt nod. The tailor and his assistant took measurements, offered several suits as options, and Lugh finally settled upon the one with the flashiest fabric. Nothing less than the best would do for this flashy, vain god.

But was it considered vanity when he obviously was a superior specimen of the species?

Now, standing in front of the Irish press corps, Bintou hid a yawn, wishing she hadn't stayed up so late staring at the computer. Her eyes still ached and felt gritty with sleep.

She stood behind the podium and to one side. News cameras were trained upon the speaker. She glanced to her left at Ciara, both of them arrayed behind Lugh.

He was a warrior, a master at all the crafts, and a king. Together with this god, they would first give a press conference, and then embark to London on a diplomatic mission.

In appearance, Lugh would have felt at home on the front of western romance books, his impressive chest bared, with long, golden curls flying free in the wind. On such a cover, she'd be clad in some medieval European gown with bright colors, her head back as he kissed her neck or something equally melodramatic.

Bintou dragged her mind away from that image. She'd never been attracted to the muscle-bound type. Ibrahim was tall and thin with skin darker than her own. Martin, being of Jamaican descent, also had dark skin, but a more solid construction. This god should be on the cover of a weight-lifting magazine.

She stared at her feet. She really must stop thinking about his physique. But her gaze strayed to him as he spoke. He constantly paid her compliments, almost courting her, and they worked closely every day.

Lugh had been granted designation as the representative of the Tuatha De Danann to the government of the Republic of Ireland and the PHAE. He was authorized to act as their mouthpiece and make agreements on their behalf. As a result, Bintou was assigned as his translator.

Few people spoke Old Irish fluently, and she was the obvious choice. Sure, several scholars spoke the language, but some of them had only a vague notion of pronunciation and might not have a firm grasp of jargon.

Most of them worked in the antiquity department of Trinity College or University of Dublin, and were content with their scholarly pursuits.

Her knowledge of the language was due to her magical talent, and therefore hadn't been tarnished by misunderstanding, outdated idiom, or a millennium of mistranslations or Christian slant.

That scholarly life still called to Bintou. She longed for the quiet, peaceful afternoons in the archives, working through a translation of ancient text. But she'd deliberately given up that life and her job at the University of Sankore in Mali.

Did she regret that decision? Some days, absolutely. Bintou craved the smell of ancient papyrus, antique books, and the dusty silence of the university library. Other days, she embraced this most exciting time to live. Exciting and dangerous.

But leaving Mali meant she'd met and fallen in love with Martin. And she wouldn't trade that for all of Ibrahim's misogyny or Lugh's arrogance. She clenched her fists in grief and concentrated once again on Lugh's speech.

The god had now finished his brief farewell speech. Now they must travel to meet with several world leaders in London.

While Ireland was under quarantine, they underwent intense testing and six days of isolation. Therefore, Bintou and her companions were granted permission to travel to this summit. They'd even brought Dian Cecht to testify that none of the travelers harbored any contaminants. The god of healing had pronounced them plague-free.

They took a private jet, and Lugh had been delighted with the transportation. He studied each aspect of the plane, despite the flight attendant's insistence that he remain seated. Instead, he took her hand and bowed low over it, kissing her knuckles while staring into her eyes. "My dear lady, you are most enchanting. Will you show me all the wonders this magical craft can offer?"

The flight attendant blushed and glanced to one side, while Bintou shoved down a twinge of jealousy. What did she have to be jealous about? She wasn't Lugh's lover and had no wish to be. Still, it felt odd watching his charm from the outside. He wielded his power like a physical weapon.

Did the god have some sort of charm magic? Of course, the gods had magic. That's part of what made them gods. Still, that notion made her both angry and curious.

After the plane landed at Heathrow, the UK Foreign Secretary and Princess Beatrice greeted them on behalf of the royal family.

Lugh bent over Princess Beatrice's hand, his sultry smile full of confidence. "You are the most enchanting creature I have yet met."

However, the princess retrieved her hand and gave a polite nod. "Thank you for the kind greeting. I am pleased to meet you, and I welcome you to the United Kingdom of Great Britain and Northern Ireland."

She must be well-used to flattery from attractive people in her position. Lugh looked momentarily nonplussed, but he recovered quickly.

Next, they were led to a fleet of limousines and driven through the city streets and the Mall, escorted by the Household Cavalry. Union Flags and the PHAE flag decorated both sides of the road, and crowds of people lined the street, like at a parade. Bintou waved with the others, feeling like an actress in a movie.

They finally stopped at 10 Downing Street to meet with the Prime Minister. The simple black brick building was reassuringly somber.

Bintou was already exhausted by the time she was permitted to sit in the meeting room. Her feet ached and her clothing chafed. The jet cabin had been unusually warm, and she still wasn't used to European clothing. She'd finally obtained some clothing that had the European style but with her favorite bright colors, but they still fit oddly.

All this meeting and greeting wore on her, but Lugh looked as bright and chipper as always. He exuded his charm on everyone. For a moment, she was envious of his inhuman energy and aplomb.

Lugh spoke quietly with the Prime Minister, an older woman with gray hair pinned into precise curls. His English had improved impressively in the last week, as they'd concentrated on English lessons.

Bintou let out a snort, recalling her last "lesson."

Lugh had asked her, "What does *not in a million years* mean? Surely this is not meant to be a literal time period?"

"No, it's hyperbole. That means—"

He waved a hand. "I'm aware of that term. I am acquainted with the very Greeks who coined the word."

Now finished with the Prime Minister, Lugh raised his hand, his gesture for her to join him. Bintou pulled herself to her feet and stood one step behind the god.

He spoke to her in Old Irish. "This delightful woman would like to invite us to dinner. Is there an acceptable way to decline? I wish to explore this amazing metropolis."

Bintou swallowed. To turn down the Prime Minister would be horribly rude and a social gaffe of the highest degree. But how to deny a god? She hadn't yet gotten the knack. "It would be more politic to accept and ask her to arrange a formal tour tomorrow."

"Very well."

He rose abruptly, giving the Prime Minister a shallow bow. "I accept your invitation. Will you arrange for a tour? I ache to explore your wondrous city."

The prime minister gestured to her secretary. "Of course. Giles, can you please make arrangements?"

"I shall see you at dinner." Lugh turned to leave, and the attendants scrambled to open the door. Bintou rushed after him with an apology to the Prime Minister, whose frown showed her displeasure.

When she caught up with Lugh in the hallway, Bintou touched his arm. "You ignored the protocols for leaving. We told you what you were supposed to do."

He waved her away. "I was bored with her conversation. She is all form and no substance, with a face full of bitter lemon. I will go explore the entertainments of this amazing and exciting city now."

"But the Prime Minister said she'd arrange a tour tomorrow."

"I will go now."

Bintou glanced back at Ciara, who only shrugged. How does one contain a god intent on mischief? She had no wish to foment disaster.

The summer afternoon was hot and muggy. Bintou was used to heat, but Mali wasn't muggy. Ireland was muggy, but rarely hot. The ever-present concrete must make a difference. The constant car exhaust added to it.

Before they'd walked more than two steps, Lugh turned to ask the guard at the entrance to the Prime Minister's house, "How can I obtain transport around this metropolis?"

Bintou placed a careful hand on Lugh's arm. "Shouldn't we wait for Giles?"

He shook his head. "I wish the unadulterated tour, not the one carefully arranged by a politician."

Lugh strode down the pavement, passing an old red phone booth covered with stickers promising sexual phone calls.

The guard coughed and nodded to the street, where a black cab idled. Bintou touched Lugh's arm to get his attention. She'd had enough world knowledge to take the lead here, at least. She'd traveled extensively, both at home in Africa and here in Europe.

Between herself and Ciara, they got Lugh inside the back of the vehicle. Bintou sighed with relief as the cool air-conditioning hit her face, drying her sweat.

Lugh slapped his thighs and spoke to the driver in his booming voice. "Take me around the city, good man!"

The man's cockney accent sounded so thick that Bintou had to concentrate to understand the words. "Wouldja like the full ci'y tour, then? That'll be £120 each, for a total of £360. I'm afraid I 'ave to ask for payment up front, you see. Too many passengers do a runner as the tour is almost over."

Lugh raised his eyebrows at Bintou, who shrugged, as she had no local currency. They both looked at Ciara, who rolled her eyes and handed over a credit card. "It's a business expense, so I'll need a receipt, please."

The driver completed the transaction, handed her the card and the receipt, and pulled into traffic. "Now, we'll start with the Tower of London, then there's a guided tour of Westminster, and the price includes a Thames River Cruise. You can also upgrade to get a ticket on the London Eye. I recommend that one for sunset, see, as that's the best way to see the ci'y. It'll be a clear evening, from all reports."

He pulled up to a low curtain wall, one Bintou recognized from photographs. The cabbie waited in his car as Ciara and Bintou led Lugh to the Tower of London.

His eyes grew wide as they approached the entrance. "This is a strong ringfort. The masons must have been most skilled. How long has this structure stood?"

Ciara used her public tone, the one she used when speaking to the press. "The central tower was built almost a thousand years ago, but I'm not sure about the curtain walls. Many hundreds of years, at least."

Lugh stared as they walked through the main gate. Several people gaped as they passed, but Bintou was getting used to the spectacle a living god made, even if spectators had no idea who he was. His skin glowed, even in full daylight. A few tourists gave him a second glance, but he paid them no mind.

The god turned around as he walked, almost in a dance, taking in all the surrounding sights. An enormous black raven cawed behind him, hopping toward the god. He knelt with his hand out, and the bird hopped onto his open palm.

When he rose, a beefeater wearing a colorful red uniform approached him. "We ask that people not touch the birds, sir. Can you please put the raven down?"

Lugh gave a solemn nod. "I shall, of course, respect them. Ravens are sacred." He delicately replaced the raven to the ground, but then the bird flew to perch upon his shoulder, giving another caw.

Giving an avuncular smile, the god cocked his head. "It appears this bird has chosen me. Should I deny him his choice?"

The guard gave a sigh. "Just don't leave with him, please. He must stay within the walls, as the prophecy demands."

The god frowned. "Prophecy? I was unaware your people heeded prophecy. Tell me the terms."

Taking a deep breath, the beefeater chanted a well-practiced speech. "It is said that the kingdom and the Tower of London will fall if the ravens ever leave the fortress."

"Then I shall, of course, be cautious not to break this *géas.*"

The guard backed away but kept an eye on them. Bintou stared at the bird who glared back at her with beady black eyes and keen intelligence. She didn't like that one bit, but could scarcely say anything.

As they entered the central White Tower, Lugh's companion clung to his shoulder, occasionally fluttering his wings or letting out strange noises.

When Lugh spied the first full set of armor, complete with helm and foot armor, he let out a surprised exclamation. "This is amazing craftsmanship! I could barely do better myself! Where is this master craftsman? I must congratulate him and discuss his technique." He glanced around as if the blacksmith were hiding behind the armor.

Ciara clicked her tongue. "I'm afraid that suit of armor was created in the 16th century, five hundred years ago. The artist has long since died."

Lugh's face fell. "Your human lives are so heart-breakingly ephemeral. I will speak to Dian Cecht about improving that. Such artistry should not be limited to a few short years of creative life."

A chill ran through Bintou's blood at that declaration. Did she really want the gods tinkering with their lifespans? Even if they could, that seemed a dangerous gift at best.

As they exited the ringfort, Lugh carefully removed the raven from his shoulder and placed him on the grass. "This is where we must part, my new friend. You must remain in your home. But I will see you again someday, I vow to you."

They visited several other sites, including Westminster Abbey and Big Ben. Lugh craned his neck up at the tower, fascinated by the giant clock, but seemed impressed most by the differing styles of architecture.

Then they visited the Royal Regiment of Horse Guards. The troops were doing parade practice as they entered, and Lugh practically jumped up and down in excitement. Bintou had to stifle a giggle at his enthusiasm.

One guard rode his horse to greet them. "I'm informed that you are visiting dignitaries from Ireland. Welcome, visitors!"

Lugh did not return his greeting, but instead, stared into his horse's eye. Then, he placed a gentle hand on the horse's nose.

The guard pulled on the reins. "I must ask that you not touch my horse, sir. Thank you."

Lugh ignored him. He didn't touch the horse again, but still stared into the beast's eyes. The horse gave a whinny, shook his head, and reared up. With some difficulty, the guard held his seat. The horse reared again, higher, and this time, the rider tumbled to the ground with a surprised grunt.

Two more guards rode quickly toward them.

The horse, now free from his rider, gave another whinny and launched into a gallop around the parade ground. The two horses approaching them halted abruptly, whinnied, and reared up.

Bintou's heart raced as she leveled a glare at Lugh. "Are you doing this? Stop it, now!"

He raised his eyebrows, the very picture of innocence. "I have done nothing against the rules. The horse merely agreed with my assessment."

As the two approaching guards were also dumped to the ground, she spoke in a fierce whisper. "What assessment?"

"That they are noble beasts, and to be used as mere vehicles was an insult to their dignity."

Bintou shut her eyes and counted to ten before she yelled at him. She needed every shred of patience she could get. "And urging horses into a rebellion is playing within the rules?"

The god lifted his chin and squared his shoulders. "I heard nothing against such an action when we entered."

She rubbed her temples. "Please, you must stop them now."

"I do not wish to."

With a glance toward Ciara, who was patiently trying to placate the guards, Bintou placed a hand on his arm. "Please, Lugh. I would appreciate it very much."

Something in the god's attitude. He cleared his throat and walked to another horse, one still trying to dislodge his rider.

This guard pursed his lips and opened his mouth, but Bintou shook her head to forestall his protest. Lugh looked into his horse's eyes, and the animal shook his head, but didn't rear up. Instead, he let out a squeal.

The other riderless horses–there were twelve, now—squealed back, slowed to a trot, and returned to where their riders stood, clustered around Ciara.

Bintou spoke with quiet sincerity in Old Irish. "Thank you, Lugh."

They escaped before the god caused any further mischief. He kept glancing back at the horses, but Bintou pulled him out the door and back into the waiting cab.

Their final stop that afternoon was the London Eye. Lugh stood at the bottom of the giant Ferris wheel and stared up. "This is truly a wondrous construction! What is its purpose?"

Bintou gave a snort. "Purely to show off engineering skills. And to offer people a fantastic view of the city. Shall we climb aboard?"

Lugh's eyes grew wide. "We are to climb to the top?"

"In a way. We get into one of those transparent capsules and the wheel turns so each group of passengers can see from the top."

He shook his head. "This must have been expensive to construct. And simply to offer entertainment? Astonishing."

Lugh wore a huge grin as they led him into a capsule. Then he stroked the clear material and placed his face against the surface. "This is a majestic place. It is worthy of us."

Ciara and Bintou exchanged an amused glance as the pod rose gracefully into the sky. Lugh exclaimed about the sights and marvels of engineering while Bintou took a much-needed rest on the bench.

Despite being in the taxi most of the time, they'd been tramping all over London for several hours, and she heartily wanted a nap away from people. And away from babysitting an ancient Irish god.

When their ride on the Eye ended, Ciara gave the cabbie instructions for the Savoy Hotel.

**Anna:**

Anna glanced surreptitiously at Carlos as he drove to the hospital. She'd been dead set against going to see Brendan. After all, he'd been a jerk, so why should she return? The PHAE only wanted to use her, just like Max had warned them all.

But if Brendan might have been just acting nice to her because it was his job, he wasn't the only manipulator. Carlos had used Brendan's illness to lure her away from Manannán's apprenticeship.

Still, something deep inside her needed to see Brendan. Anna needed to reassure herself that he was still alive. That, despite the ridiculousness of the notion, that her rejection hadn't caused his death.

Carlos came with her, leading her down the corridors. The stink of illness tickled her nose, and she stifled a sneeze. She didn't want to be here. She wanted to be in the clean ocean breeze, playing in the waves, not here in this soulless place filled with dying people.

For a moment, she almost bolted, but Carlos kept a grip on her shoulder and squeezed.

As they entered the room, she caught her breath. Brendan had been tall, solid, with dark hair to his shoulders. Now, his hair hung in greasy, stringy clumps and he looked so incredibly pale and thin.

He wasn't awake, but she sat beside his cot and held his hand. So many emotions rushed through her. Guilt, pain, regret, hope, and maybe even love.

When she gripped his hand in both of hers, a power flowed between them. Icy cold yet still soft. Something within him still called to her. A flicker of recognition of their souls, perhaps.

Finally, the nurse came and told them that visiting hours were over. Anna didn't want to let go of Brendan's hand. Carlos was barely been able to drag her away.

Three visits later, Brendan was actually awake when she entered. His voice was faint, but as soon as she sat and took his hand, he forced out two words.

"I'm sorry."

Anna gave him a wan smile and a nod. She wasn't certain what she should say in response.

He coughed and spoke again. "I was a jerk, and I shouldn't have been so jealous."

Anna kissed his lips, forgiving him instantly, and a wide smile spread across his face.

But each time since then, he'd been either out of his mind with fever or resting. Anna couldn't bring herself to interrupt his sleep. His body needed time to heal.

And despite Brendan's importance to Róisín or Anna, Dian Cecht had the job of healing most of Ireland, and that took precedence. That didn't mean Anna had to like it.

**Bintou:**

After returning Lugh to his suite, Bintou tried to nap, but couldn't quiet her mind. Instead, she called Ciara and they met for a drink in the hotel lounge.

Amidst the mahogany walls covered with prints and memorabilia and the green leather booths, they put their heads together, trying to hash out what the gods' end game might be.

After Bintou ordered her drink, making sure they understood that she didn't want any alcohol, she shared what she'd discovered so far with the other woman, bringing out her list and analysis. "If you look at what Lugh said there, and Macha's mention of world leaders here, it's possible that they have designs larger than Ireland."

A lone guitarist sat on a stool on a dais across the room, tuning her instrument. Ciara sipped her Old Fashioned and pursed her lips. "Definitely worrying, but still not enough to make sense of. We need to talk to Unhidden in other enclaves. We've heard, so far, of the wakening of several pantheons. Chinese, Japanese, Siberian, Incan, Aztec, and of course, the Irish."

Bintou tapped her paper as the hotel waiter brought her a fizzy drink, clear but with a pink tinge. She took a sip and decided she liked it. "Don't forget the Greeks."

"Oh, yes, can't forget them. But they just showed up and disappeared again, didn't they?"

Bintou shrugged. "So the media reports. But I'm not counting on them for accuracy."

The guitarist began testing the microphone, tapping it and making sounds. "Right. Who else?"

With another sip of her Shirley Temple, Bintou said, "Hawai'i. And Norse gods have appeared, haven't they?"

"A few of them. North Norway, mostly. A couple in Iceland, but they seem less powerful than those in Norway. I think they're organizing together. The Finnish and Sami gods seem to be keeping their own counsel."

"Interesting. Could they have less power due to being, what, off-shoots? Copies?"

The woman with the guitar started playing a Spanish-style guitar melody. Ciara gave a shrug and raised her voice. "I'm not sure how it works. I'm not sure they know how it works. Or if there's a logic at all to them. We're still not even sure why they're all coming to life."

The Irish woman gave a shrug. "It's got to be due to the magnetic shift, but did that trigger it, or did the Unhidden do something to open a portal? Or are they both by-products of some other event?"

"Isn't that what the PHAE researchers are trying to determine?"

"Sure, but I'm not happy with their lack of progress."

Bintou leaned back, cradling her drink in her hands. "But what can we do about that? We aren't scientists. We aren't genealogists, nor geneticists. We're diplomats, organizers, translators, and healers. Shouldn't we stick to where our talents lie? What's the term, *stay in our lane?*"

Ciara let out a deep breath and scowled at her cocktail. "Yes. I know that's what we *should* do. But I've never been particularly skilled at staying in my lane."

With a chuckle, Bintou sipped her drink. "It sounds like you wish you had more control. That you are the only one who might do things right. But that isn't true. Other people are competent, even talented. Don't you have Unhidden on the research team? It's literally their talent to help."

Ciara wrinkled her nose. "Their talent, yes, but not necessarily their training. The world is full of talented people without training who get nothing done."

She needed to change tactics, otherwise Ciara would end up spiraling into a morass of self-doubt. "What's your power again? Suppressing other talents? I don't see how that would be of particular help in research. No, you're best here, where your human talents *and* training are of use."

Ciara peered up at her. "*Human* talents. That's dangerous phrasing."

Bintou clenched her teeth, remembering the angry protestors and their call for *pure humans.* "That's a fair point. But *non-Unhidden talents* sounds so cumbersome. *Pre-shift talent?* Even *natural talent* is a problematic phrase. Maybe *vanilla human?* That still sounds insulting."

They both finished off their drinks in silence, alone in their own thoughts, until the server came to refresh them.

Once the server brought new drinks, Ciara asked, "So, let's use some of my all-important training. What are we aiming for? What does success look like for us?"

Bintou stared at the fizzy drink in her hand. "If Lugh meets the world leaders, doesn't create some international incident, and we sign treaties with each of them to work with their local gods, would that be a success?"

Ciara downed half of her cocktail. "That might open up a whole new era of diplomatic service."

"And the worst result could be diplomatic disaster, global war, and total chaos."

The guitarist in the corner finally finished her Spanish guitar tunes and launched into a folk tune. Ciara and Bintou fell silent, each in their own thoughts.

They still needed to request aid without quite asking for it for Ireland's PEM problem. Terrorist groups were attacking other countries, but the bulk of them had been in Ireland.

Due to being neutral in World War II as well as being an island nation on the western edge of Europe, Ireland had very few physical defenses. They'd always relied on world resources for any serious threats.

Which is why they were now finessing those world resources by trotting out a living, breathing god.

As the musician finished her song, the hotel waiter asked if they wanted more drinks. Ciara nodded and handed him her empty glass. Bintou asked for hot tea to replace the over-sweet Shirley Temples.

Bintou prepared her tea, then waited for it to cool enough for her to drink. She didn't particularly care for this Earl Grey, but it seemed ubiquitous here. Mediocre tea was better than no tea.

She needed something warm inside. The hotel lobby was too air-conditioned, to the point of freezing, and her clothing, perfectly suitable for the muggy day, was too thin.

Ciara took a sip of her drink. "I've barely ever had a chance to use my talent, you know. Really only once, outside of testing and training. When we brought Joel in."

Bintou didn't want to hear about what they did to Joel, so she remained quiet. Then a thought occurred to her. "Would your talent work on a god?"

A light of both curiosity and intrigue shone in Ciara's eyes, along with a shadow of fear.

**Bintou:**

Bintou woke, unsure of where she was. This wasn't her room in the Dublin bunker. Nor was it the hotel rooms in Dublin, before they were bombed, or her room on the Byrne farm. She'd lived in too many places lately. Then she remembered the trip to London. After rubbing her eyes, she let out a yawn so wide, her jaw cracked.

Her dreams had been fragmented and vaguely disturbing, but she couldn't put her finger on any one thing or a scary part. Just general unease.

She rose and took a shower, choosing a professional western-style outfit. Noises from the next room suggested Lugh had also woken and was being dressed.

They'd brought several men to act as attendants for the god, which relieved her of that duty. She'd feel highly awkward helping him dress, and surely Ciara felt the same.

Back in Dublin, they'd had a fierce battle convincing him to wear modern clothing. But finally, he'd agreed to try shirts and slacks. But he looked as awkward as Bintou felt in the western styles.

Today, Lugh was to meet with the assembled world leaders. She must look and behave her best, and she prayed that Lugh would do the same. They'd meet with Presidents, Prime Ministers, and leaders from China, France, Canada, and India.

Lugh planned on offering the services of the ancient Irish gods as a liaison to their own culture's gods. Bintou still couldn't figure out how autonomous each pantheon was, or if they were all working together. Her inquiries so far had met with vague answers.

Once everyone emerged from their rooms, they descended to the ground floor, and Lugh marveled at the elevator mechanics. In the lobby, they met their handlers for the day, a diplomatic concierge charged with getting them to the right people at the right time and versing them in the proper protocols. Once again, they piled into limousines, this time to Buckingham Palace.

As they circled the Victoria Memorial, Lugh made them stop. "Which goddess is this? I do not recognize her."

Bintou remembered Colin's stories of how much the Irish had suffered during Queen Victoria's reign and pursed her lips.

Ciara wrinkled her nose. "She's not a goddess, Lugh. She's a queen, who ruled this country over a hundred years ago."

"A mortal woman? But she is surrounded by angels."

One of their handlers cleared his throat. "She is greatly revered."

Once past the statue, they pulled in front of the gates to Buckingham Palace, and Lugh stared at the gilded architectural wonder that was the palace of the Monarch of England.

Once they entered the black and gold iron gates, the Irish god turned slowly, taking in the Neoclassical architecture. "So, *this* is a temple to their god?"

Ciara shook her head. "No, this is the home of their human ruler, the Queen of England, Elizabeth II. If we have time later, we can bring you to St. Paul's Cathedral, if you are so interested in the English God."

Lugh shook his head. "Not the modern god. The ancient ones. I'm more interested in the temples to the gods these English worshipped before the Christians took over. Woden and Thor, Brigantia and Cernunnos."

Ciara let out a noncommittal noise. "I don't believe they have any temples to those gods in London, Lugh. But now we are in the Queen's house, so we should keep our focus on her."

As they entered, he glanced up at the gilded bannisters and down at the red carpet. "She must be a mighty war queen, to have amassed such incredible wealth!"

Bintou stifled a giggle as they were led down a hallway with walls covered in painted portraits. "She certainly is a strong leader, and she served in World War II, driving ambulances. But I wouldn't exactly call her a war queen."

With a scowl, Ciara said, "Tell that to the separatists in Northern Ireland or the Falkland Islands."

Lugh cocked his head. "Tell me the tale of these battles."

Ciara shrugged and glanced over her shoulder. "This isn't the time or the place. We've got to get to the dining hall. I'll tell you the stories later."

They entered a chamber with many people milling about, waiting for lunch to be announced. The world leaders had been speaking amongst themselves, but everyone grew silent when Lugh entered.

Once he was announced, Ciara introduced him to several people, but they must have been the last to arrive, for luncheon was announced within a few minutes.

They entered the dining hall and Bintou halted. So far, she'd avoided taking in the grandeur, in the interest of keeping Lugh moving along, but now, she had to stop and take in the lush décor.

Red carpeting was mirrored in the sideboard, covered in gold plates. Enormous oil paintings hung on either side of the room, and a royal dais stood on one end for the Queen's table, also backed in red. Everything else was in cream with gold accents. A half dozen chandeliers lit the space, and the table glittered with plates and cutlery.

As Lugh sat between the President of India and the Prime Minister of Canada, Bintou concentrated on the nuance around the room. Last night, she and Ciara had created game plans for Lugh's unpredictable nature, disaster scenarios, and exit strategies should everything go horribly wrong.

Bintou watched him carefully throughout each course, but he seemed to be acting reasonably. She was pleasantly surprised that he remembered their lessons on which utensil to use with which course, how to address each leader, and for a wonder, he broached no forbidden subjects.

As soon as the lunch dishes were removed, Lugh stood to address the attendees. Bintou shot a glance of alarm at Ciara. This was unplanned, against protocol, and they had no idea what he was about to say. Ciara gave a bare shrug.

Lugh gave the assembled dignitaries a wide smile. "Thank you all for meeting me and welcoming me to this, a most lavish feast, in a hall fit for the Queen of the Tuatha De Danann. While I am not the king myself, I am spokesperson for the king of our people, our all-father, the Dagda. He is the Good God, the mighty one, the fertile one."

He paused and received a smattering of applause. "It is on his behalf that I bring you salutations from our people. And it is with his blessing that I invite you to a similar feast on our homeland of Éire."

Bintou dared to breathe. This didn't sound so terrible. Certainly, they could host a feast for visiting leaders, and that would even help the PHAE's reputation worldwide. It might even offer an opportunity to learn more about other gods and what they'd been doing.

"Come to our halls this time tomorrow, and we shall host an epic feast!"

The color drained from Ciara's face. Bintou pulled at Lugh's arm and hissed to him, "Lugh! We need time to plan such an event! At least a week!"

He shook off her hand without glancing at her. "I am told that I am hasty in my invitation. One week from today, we shall host this epic feast! I shall consider anyone who declines this invitation to offer insult upon our house."

The Irish god sat with a smug expression. Ciara covered her face with her hands. Bintou's anxiety kicked into high gear and she whispered in Lugh's ear. "You must offer them a way to decline gracefully. Many of these leaders are extremely busy with running their duties and may be halfway across the world by next week."

He turned to her, confusion on his face. "Then they can travel back, by that magical conveyance you brought me here upon."

Bintou stood and smiled at the surrounding people, her heart fluttering at addressing such an assembly. "Please, our guest has only recently learned modern English. The invitation stands, but of course there will be no hard feelings if you are unable to attend."

Her knees about to buckle, she sat again. Lugh paid no attention to her and was examining the silver dessert spoon.

Bintou let out a deep sigh of relief and Ciara took a long drink of her champagne. Then the Irish woman grabbed someone else's champagne and downed that, too.

**Róisín:**

Róisín drifted in and out of the clouds, soaring like Max did on the winds. She didn't know how she got there, nor how she'd ever return to the comfort of the earth beneath her feet. In truth, she didn't care. She just wanted to ride the wind.

Like a harmonious choral production, she sang as she dipped and wheeled through the air. White, fluffy clouds caressed her skin, cool condensation embracing her.

Is this the love that Max felt for the skies? This silent soaring through the heavens he so craved? If so, she understood his obsession.

Something called her name in the back of her mind. A tiny buzz, niggling her bliss like sandpaper across silk. Róisín tried to brush it away, ignore it, drown it, but it kept returning with louder and more irritating insistence.

"Almighty and Eternal God, You are the everlasting health of those who believe in You."

She covered her ears, trying to block out the voice intruding on her bliss.

"Hear us for Your sick servant, Róisín, for whom we implore the aid of Your tender mercy, that being restored to bodily health, she may give thanks to You in Your Church."

Róisín tried zipping through a darker cloud, heavy with rain. She emerged soaked but the voice still hammered at her peace. And yet, something within it called to her heart. The words? The voice itself? It was familiar to her soul.

"Through Christ our Lord. Amen."

Róisín moaned and shifted, the voice calling her back to herself.

"Róisín? Róisín, can you hear me?"

She finally recognized the voice in the center of her heart. The first voice she'd ever heard, even before she was born. The voice of home. Mam's voice.

It wasn't within Róisín's power to ignore her mother's voice. All her childhood memories were linked to that voice.

With great effort, Róisín dragged herself away from the paradise of the skies, the soaring wind, and the velvet caress of the clouds. She slammed back into her body, pain and exhaustion enveloping her.

Wrenching her eyelids apart, she blinked, trying to focus on the utterly mundane surroundings. Her old room, at her parents' farm. Pale blue walls, white ceiling, and a teenage heartthrob poster of George Michael still stuck to the wall at a rakish angle. "Mam?"

A warm hand clutched fiercely hers as her mother's worried face came into view. "Róisín! Oh, thank Christ our Lord, you're back."

Róisín throat hurt as she croaked out, "Mam... you're here?"

Her mother tilted her head, her eyebrows raised. "Well, of course I'm here. Where else would I be, *mo pháiste?*

Róisín cracked a smile. "You haven't called me that since I was a wee girl, Mam."

Her mother's expression softened as she caressed Róisín's cheek. "Ah, well, I've been thinking about you a lot these last few days. And your childhood."

"Few days? Mam, how long have I been ill?"

Glancing over her shoulder, her mother looked apprehensive again. "Long enough. The doctor did what he could for your physical injuries, but he couldn't do much for your mind."

Róisín struggled to sit up. "My mind? Physical injuries? Mam, what happened to me?"

Her father came into view, a frown marring his face. "Do you not remember a thing, now?"

Shaking her head, Róisín tried to pull up the details, any details. "I remember a mob. Angry people with signs and banners. Something about Max abandoning me." She wrinkled her nose. "Then, lots of dreams about flying, screaming, but those might have been half nightmare. Then, I woke up."

Perching on the edge of her bed, her father patted her arm. "And you're safe and sound here, especially now that you're awake. We'll call the doctor, so, but you'll see for yourself that most of the scratches have healed."

Startled, she examined her arms and saw fading bruises and half-healed cuts. Róisín must have been out at least a week. At least she could finish the healing with her Unhidden talent now that she was awake.

An older woman poked her head in. "Did I hear Róisín's voice? Is she awake?"

Her father grinned at Nokomis, the native woman from Arizona. "She's awake. Can you ask Fiona to bring tea and broth? Róisín needs to regain her strength."

Komie flashed a grin and disappeared. Her mother squeezed her hand tight. Róisín squeezed back, grateful to be home and safe.

Even in her mind, she'd had a rough couple of weeks. Snippets of scenes flashed into her memory, images and voices. Joel's face, contorted in rage and smug satisfaction. Writhing vines. Hatred and pain.

She couldn't make sense of it all, not yet. For now, she concentrated on sipping the tea her little sister brought and sipping spoons of chicken broth. The warmth felt so wonderful.

Even that effort drained her energy. She needed to sleep and to heal. Pulling her healing power up through the earth and into her own body, she finished off the half-healed bruises and cuts. A torn muscle in her shoulder. Rope burns around her neck. Her twisted left ankle. Each of these pains faded away as she fell once more into a deep sleep.

*Physician, heal thyself.*

**Tiberius:**

Tiberius Wilkinson slammed his hands on the mahogany conference table so hard, it shook all the glasses. "I don't give a rat's naked ass what you think, Charlie! I need better information!"

Charlie shrank back from the red rage on his boss's face. Not that it was unusual for Tiberius to lose his temper, but his second-in-command had great skill at redirecting any blame from himself. This time, his finesse hadn't worked. "But T, that *was* good information. At least, it was good when we got it from our operative. Things are changing fast over there."

Tiberius growled and threw his notebook against the wall. He'd never throw anything that would do damage. Besides, he had paid too much for these offices to mar the carefully chosen sage green paint job. And he was damned if he was going to let his temper reduce the value of the space.

The lights flickered as he tried to calm himself. "Now, look here. You need to get me a proper report. One with details I can rely on. Details I can act upon. This," He shook the printed report in the air, "Is prime-A bullcocky. What the hell are you talking about with this Macha woman?"

Charlie's voice grew meek. "She's a goddess of war?"

The lights flickered again, and several people in the board room glanced up, as if expecting a power outage. But the sky outside was clear with the Texas summer sun shining through the windows. Nothing less than a full hurricane should mess with their robust power grid.

Tiberius placed his hands on the table and leaned forward as he gritted his teeth. "A goddess. Of war."

Charlie, evidently too nervous to speak, gulped and nodded.

Shutting his eyes, the head of the American Branch of the Pure Earther Movement clasped his hands behind his back and stalked to the plate-glass window. He gazed out at the Houston skyline.

He'd memorized this view, having lived in this city all his life. This was his home, his heritage, his heart. Not just the city of Houston or the state of Texas, his beloved Lone Star State, but all of the great and powerful United States of America.

And he was damned if he was going to let a bunch of upstart satanic magicians take any power away from him. Sure, they worked out of Ireland, but branches of this ridiculous, dangerous cult were popping up all over the world.

The Houston branch had wormed their way in his neighborhood six months ago, right next door to his office. And one rainy day, one of those evil sycophants had destroyed that office with an explosion.

People he loved had died in that explosion, and that was something he could never forgive.

The explanation given to the public was that this guy, this Unhidden talent, was still getting used to his power, but Tiberius knew the truth. These Unhidden were downright dangerous, and he'd since made it his mission to keep them from getting control over his city. Or the country. Or the world.

He'd sunk his considerable oil fortune into the PEM, a movement which had already built up a lot of steam.

Once he started financing their efforts, the organization had exploded onto the world scene. At first, he was a silent partner, content to let others hold the reins. Tiberius hired a competent staff and directed them to organize protests and legislation changes everywhere, especially here in the United States.

But it wasn't enough. He needed to reach them in Ireland, at the heart of their operation.

His predecessor organized the initial attack, a submarine attack in the night. That had gone horrible and resulted in a regrettable failure. The man who'd organized that fiasco had resigned from leadership in shame and faded into obscurity.

The next attempt was reasonably successful, smuggling several dirty bombs into the island nation, and some even exploded. But the man who organized that one had been killed by his own plagues.

And this still hadn't destroyed the PHAE.

Now Tiberius was in charge of the PEM, and he didn't mean for them to fail a third time.

He'd had even traveled to Ireland and run the local protestor organization for a few weeks, getting the feel of the land, how things worked there, and who he could rely on. He met with local organizers, including a few of his sleeper agents. But in the end, he'd had to beat a hasty retreat as the authorities circled in on him.

But if he was going to succeed, he needed data, not fairy tales. And Charlie was only giving him fairy tales.

He took a deep breath and turned back to his boardroom, to glare at the five people sitting there. "Let's start from the top. Who's currently in charge of the PHAE? What's their command structure like?"

**Max:**

When Róisín finally woke, Max was delighted, but worried. She might have healed her cuts, but there were still deep bags under her eyes, and she still needed time to heal.

But, in a classic move, after just two days, she announced that she'd wanted to seek out Dian Cecht and help him with his healing tour through the country. Max didn't like that in the slightest.

As the Irish woman sliced brown bread for their breakfast, Max perched on a stool, cradling his coffee mug in his hand. "You still need to rest, darlin'."

She pursed her lips but didn't look at him. "No. I need to get out of here. Mam is practically smothering me."

He scowled into his coffee cup. "Just because you're fretting under your parents' care, doesn't mean you're healed enough to go haring around the countryside. And that god has no sense of human frailty, remember? He practically chewed you up and spit you out the last time."

The Irish woman wrinkled her nose as she sliced more bread. "I'll heal well enough. That's literally my superpower, remember?"

Max made a rude noise. "And how many times d'you think your body's gonna recover from that sort of thing? Trust me on this. I know body trauma. And mind trauma. Hell, I'm practically a walking trauma machine. Insert your coins here, get your pain there."

He grinned to take the sting from his words, but Róisín kept scowling. She cut a few more slices, then put the remaining half-loaf into the breadbox.

After she pulled the butter from the refrigerator, she turned to him with a solemn expression. "Max, I thought you understood me. I'm a healer. I need to heal. My country is ill. Cases are spreading all over Ireland, not just in the bombed cities anymore. I *need* to help. It's part of my nature. God gave me this incredible ability to help more than anyone else can. It would be incredibly selfish for me to pamper myself while others die. It might even be a sin."

Her father, Colin, shuffled into the dining room while reading a book. The Irish man halted, glanced up from his pages to his daughter and then to Max. He placed his bookmark before setting the book down. "For what it's worth, I agree with Max. Your mind needs to recover just as much as your body, young lady."

Róisín rolled her eyes and took a bite of her bread. Max swirled the dregs of coffee in his mug and decided that Colin made a good ally but wasn't adding much to the conversation.

Then Michelle entered the kitchen and the atmosphere cooled considerably. She sent Max a narrow glare, but he was able to return it with a clear conscience. This time, he'd been on the side of reason. How had that actually happened? He didn't know, but he was going with it for the moment.

His hostess had a severe dislike for strong drink and strong language. But he'd added no whiskey to his coffee this morning, and he took pride in that. And while he'd needed both in droves before Róisín regained consciousness, now that she'd mostly recovered, his need had eased.

Not completely gone, but it shrank enough that he could survive with only a slight nag of need.

Michelle offered him a slice of bread, but he waved it away. "Good morning, Maximilian. Did you sleep well?"

He gave her a pleasant nod. "Well enough. No more than the normal nightmares, at least."

Róisín furrowed her brow. "I thought you'd stopped having those?"

He let out a bitter laugh. "I've never stopped having those, darlin'. Not for over forty years. But some nights are worse than others. I had a light load last night."

He lifted his coffee mug in a salute, but the Byrnes all exchanged meaningful glances. He wondered what all that had been about, but he kicked back the mug, draining the last of his morning joe down his gullet. Then he hopped off the stool and poured himself another dose.

Black coffee cured many ills. Or at least shoved them into a box for a while, long enough to get on with the day.

Colin clasped his hands in a scholarly gesture. "Róisín, I realize you are a woman grown now, and capable of making your own decisions."

The younger woman pursed her lips. "And it's about time, too, Da."

He cleared his throat while Max took a sip to hide a smirk. The girl had learned a lot of sass since he first met her. But he didn't want Michelle to catch on to his approval. Nor to assign him the blame.

Her mother pressed her lips together in a thin line. "What your father is trying to say is that we still worry about you. We'll always worry about you. You're our eldest child, and our dear daughter. And you must admit, you've never had a solid grasp of your own physical limits, now."

Róisín clenched her fists and her voice grew quiet. "My physical limits, is it? You make it sound like I'm suffering from some deformity, Mam."

Her tone had every marker of the first shots across the bow in a grand battle. Max glanced at the back door. If he moved really slowly, he might escape before the cannons were lit.

Colin straightened his spine. "A deformity? My dear daughter, that was a horribly ableist thing to say. We've raised you better than that."

Róisín deflated, her shoulders slumping. "Ah, crap. You're right, Da. I'm sorry."

Michelle barked out, "Language, Róisín."

Max slid off the stool carefully and inched toward the back door. If he could get into the garden, he might not get hit by the shrapnel.

The younger woman rolled her eyes again. "See, this is what I need to escape from. You're both wonderful, and I love being home. But I also need to get away from the constant surveillance. Can't you just let me be, for once?"

Michelle opened her arms wide. "We did! And look at the state of you now!"

Róisín stared at her for one long second before stalking out of the kitchen and through the back door.

Max had made it halfway, and decided he'd better make a run for it. He darted to the door, reaching the handle just as it slammed shut.

Fumbling to open it again, he shoved his half-full mug on the counter and escaped into freedom.

Max spied Róisín sulking on a garden bench next to the roses. She leaned forward, with her face in her hands, elbows on her knees.

He sidled up to her, but she flashed him an annoyed glare. "You aren't helping, you know."

"Aye, I'm well aware of that, luv. But I want to help now. How about if I switch my stance? I support your need to get away?"

Róisín narrowed her eyes. "Oh? And in return for what?"

He flashed her a sly look. "You're learning how things work, darlin'. I'm proud of you. In return for letting me go with you, so I can keep an eye on how much that Irish god bloke drains you. But you need to promise me you'll actually listen when I insist that he pulls back on the throttle, eh?"

A scowl crept across her face. "What, and move from one surveillance to another? No, thank you."

Max gave a shrug and a half-smile. "But it's different when I watch. I only care about what your healer god does, not what you do."

Róisín didn't answer right away, but finally she gave a curt nod. "Fine, then. I'll take you along as my babysitter. But you'll behave, yes? No binges?"

He gave her a half-smile and patted her on the arm. "Luv, if you haven't noticed, I never binge when you're around."

# Chapter Two

"Better than worshipping gods is obedience to the laws of righteousness."
– Buddha

**Max:**

As Max and Róisín walked into the Ennis General Hospital ward, everything was oddly silent, as if the entire room held their collective breaths. The scent of antiseptic and blood filled the space. Machines beeped in discordant rhythm.

The intern, Ekon, who'd been Róisín's helper and friend, stood next to a hospital bed in the children's ward, surrounded by a crowd of people. He held his hands out in front of him, palms down, with his head back and eyes closed. He looked like an evangelical faith healer calling for the Holy Spirit to heal a sinner.

Which wasn't far from the truth.

Obviously, the ancient Irish god of healing, Dian Cecht, inhabited Ekon's body. Ekon was a young Nigerian man who'd worked with Róisín in the Galway University Hospital after the bombing and had even developed a crush on her. But when the healer god had used up all of Róisín's energy and abandoned her body, the god had switched to other volunteers, including Ekon.

The god then traveled from town to town, across Ireland, using the bodies of volunteers to perform his healing magic and discarding them as they were used up.

Róisín fumbled for Max's hand, gripping it tight. "When Dian Cecht was inside my body, my consciousness went into hiding. I huddled in some back corner of my mind."

Max swallowed and glanced at her worried face. "Were you even aware of his actions?"

She shook her head. "Not until he left me and went into someone else, after he burnt through all my energy. And then he'd use that person on and go to the next. And so on, and so on."

Ekon's body glowed with Dian Cecht's power. Swirling lights formed above the beds. The onlooking doctors, nurses, and press let out a communal gasp. The girl on the bed, perhaps ten years old, arched her back and let out a screech.

A woman fell to her knees, grasping the girl's hand.

The lights danced in a spiral, getting more complex as Dian Cecht first hummed, then sang a single note, filling the hospital ward with vibrations.

Max's skin itched, and he rubbed his arms, trying to smooth the goosebumps. Róisín squeezed his hand. *Am I reassuring her or is she reassuring me?*

As the god's voice grew louder, Max's head throbbed. He let go of Róisín's hand to cover his ears. Everyone else did the same. Just when he thought his head was about to burst, a thunderclap slammed through the room.

The child's body relaxed, and Dian Cecht let out a satisfied sigh. He lowered his hands, opened his eyes, and lifted his chin in a haughty expression. "I am finished. Physician, perform your tests. You will find she is quite healed."

Crumpling on the floor, the mother let out an impassioned sob. Her daughter opened her eyes and the surrounding press gasped. A man with an enormous camera on his shoulder let it drop to his chest until his companion elbowed him in the ribs, and he lifted it back into place.

Dian Cecht strode to the next hospital bed, but Ekon's body stumbled. He grasped an intern's shoulder for support. "This body grows weary. I must use a new one." He glanced to either side, but both of his support personnel had dark circles under their eyes.

Then the god glanced around, catching sight of Róisín. He threw his arms wide,. "My first apprentice has returned to me! This is delightful. Come to me, Róisín. You are forgiven for your defection. I welcome you back into my good graces."

Max grabbed for Róisín's arm, but she was already running into the embrace of the ancient Irish god, or at least, into Ekon's embrace.

The arrogance upon the intern's features was surreal. Max had spoken with Ekon several times, and the young man had a disarming humbleness, a quiet, gentle soul. He reminded Max of a spiritual leader amongst the aboriginals near his home in Coober Pedy, someone at home with himself in the universe.

But when Dian Cecht inhabited the intern's body, his entire demeanor changed. Arrogance and imperious demand obliterated the humble quiet nature of the host.

Just like Róisín's face changed when Dian Cecht possessed her body. Max hated to see that, but he had to admit, Róisín's natural healing talent made her much more suited to withstand the god's power than Ekon and the other vanilla volunteers. She had more strength, and it took much longer to use her body up.

Max still hated it, and he was determined to keep the god from burning her body to a crisp with his inhuman zeal. Max had no idea *how* he'd make sure the god left, but he still vowed to do so.

Even now, as she embraced the shell of the intern with genuine affection, Max saw a shimmer that heralded a transference of the god's essence. Ekon's shoulders slumped, and Róisín's straightened. Her face glowed with more than the morning sun coming through the hospital window.

Other interns caught Ekon just before he collapsed and quietly carried him out of the ward, presumably so he could sleep off the effects of playing host to the ancient Irish god of healing.

Now, Róisín's lovely face took on a hard edge, full of arrogance and demands. Her gaze fell upon Max, who straightened his own spine. "Ah, I remember you, Son of the Wind. You have brought my apprentice back to me. You will find, Maximilian Hurley, that the gratitude of a god is no small thing."

Max gave a nod, not wishing to give an inch. But he'd already been on the shit end of a god's resentment, and still had the bruises from that tussle. Gratitude had to be a hell of a lot better than *that*.

Ignoring the crowd of onlookers, who watched the exchange with intense interest, Dian Cecht cocked his head. "I understand that you have gained the enmity of one of my compatriots."

Grinding his teeth, Max answered, "Aye, but that's not a discussion I wish to have right now, mate. Can you just get on with your job, here, and save the chitchat for another time?"

"If that's your wish, I shall do so." The god turned to the next hospital bed and the press camera followed his every move.

**Róisín:**

Róisín both loved and hated hosting Dian Cecht. She hated it because she lost any control over her body, her thoughts, and even her memory. When the god entered her mind, she fled whimpering into a dark corner of her brain, cowering with fear and loathing against the god's awesome power.

On the other hand, she reveled in the incredible sensation of healing power flowing through her muscles, an exhilarating sensation greater than anything she'd ever felt.

Róisín had no idea if the joy was worth the fear. And each time she allowed him in, a part of her felt chipped away, never to return. How many pieces could she lose before he subsumed her? Would she ever heal enough to get those parts back? Or was she forever fractured?

Even considering all that, though, the healer within her couldn't refuse him. People needed to be healed, he was the most powerful healer around, and she was his strongest vessel.

Róisín watched from behind her own eyes as Dian Cecht approached a hospital bed. Another patient with both anthrax and pneumonic plague. The teenage boy's face dripped with sweat, and he moaned in his sleep. Dian Cecht thrust his hands out, palms down, as he'd done so many times before.

As he called up his healing powers, they flowed through her body, singing with the voices of a thousand angels as it rushed into every vein, artery, and capillary. It tasted sweet, like the purest sugar, and yet spicy like cayenne. All her nerves tingled with intense pleasure as the healing burst through her hands and into the boy.

The god's cries caressed her ears, musical notes of a world-class orchestra. Every note turned to liquid, an almost sexual pleasure as she writhed in that tiny corner, eager to lick up every drop of pain and power.

Róisín gasped as the dregs drained away, crying out in her tiny prison, craving more, always more, like any addict. She sobbed, bereft of her fix as this ancient energy trickled to nothing. Despair engulfed her being and her inner self curled into a ball to cry.

Dian Cecht used her legs to walk to the next hospital bed to do it all over again.

After the tenth ride on the roller coaster of his magical healing, her soul stretched thin, strung out with this cycle of pleasure and pain, of fullness and emptiness. Light flashed outside of her vision, like a thunderstorm on a dark night. Even though she tried to shut her soul away from the effects, it still washed through her.

Eventually, she yanked her consciousness away from Dian Cecht, and her mind finally slipped into a troubled slumber as the healing god strode to yet another patient.

But Róisín's ability to shield herself was imperfect, even in sleep. Her dreams swung from nightmares to erotic dreams like an insane pendulum.

It seemed like weeks later when she finally struggled back to awareness. Dian Cecht voice rumbled through her, but his words didn't penetrate her fog. Max shouted angry words, staccato pounding against her skull. Róisín hauled herself out of her corner now that the enthralling healing magic had stopped.

The Australian's words filtered into her tiny cell. "It's time to switch, mate. Róisín's got dark circles under her eyes, and new lines on her face. Look in a mirror, you bloody rat bag. You're killing her! And then where'll you be?"

Dian Cecht breathed in deep, straightening Róisín's shoulders. "I am now aware of the humans' frailties, Maximilian Hurley. I will not end her life with my use of her body."

"Then get the hell out of it, *mate!*"

"The other volunteers are not yet sufficiently rested to assist. Her power makes her a stronger conduit for me, and she can survive longer. She is also more comfortable to reside in."

Róisín peered out of her own eyes, and Max's face had grown red in his rage. He balled his fists and got into the god's face. "I don't give a damn tuppence for what's more comfortable to you, mate! Get the hell out! Why can't you manifest your own damn body like the other gods? Are you less powerful than them?"

Rage flowed through her blood as Dian Cecht took umbrage to Max's words. Then, something different happened, something she'd never felt.

A new power rushed through her, tingling in her blood and bones. It drained away, like when Dian Cecht moved from her body to another's, but something else had been added. A hum, a rumbling, a chime in her inner ear.

As the tingling faded, a figure formed next to her, a shining presence as tall as Max. Amorphous, smooth, it glowed and thrummed with power, hers and Dian Cecht's. With each heartbeat, energy drained from her and into this new form. Pulsing, flowing, throbbing with new life, new magic.

Just as the last shred of life was about to drain from her body, the world turned black and Róisín collapsed into Max's arms.

**Max:**

Max stumbled back from the glowing form, but when Róisín's body crumpled, he leapt forward to catch her. She was heavier than he expected, dead weight. Frantically, he searched for a pulse, a heartbeat, anything to reassure him that she hadn't died.

He pressed his fingers against her neck, the way they'd taught him in the war, decades before. There, beneath his fingers, he felt a faint flutter. He heaved a sigh of relief and almost collapsed himself.

Dragging Róisín to an empty hospital bed, he ignored the Dian Cecht's shining new body. Once he got her prone, covered, and was confident she could finally rest, he spun to discover what he'd goaded the god into creating.

A man stood with his hands on his hips in a power stance, his feet wide. Everyone stared with their mouths agape, silent and frozen. As features formed beneath the light, it shifted into a lined face framed by curly blond hair and beard. His long hair was mixed with gray streaks. An older man, the personification of wisdom.

Dian Cecht held up his arms, his skin still glowing with preternatural light, a beacon to the entire ward. Folks crowded around him, several falling to their knees. One woman murmured prayers and bowed her head.

The healing god wore a long white robe. *He's like something out of the damned Bible.* Max wondered if that was a conceit to appeal to modern fables, or if he'd worn this back in ancient times. After visiting countless Catholic hospitals, Dian Cecht must have seen pictures of Jesus. Every hallway had at least one Sacred Heart on the wall, along with images of Saint Brigit, the Blessed Mother, and who knows how many other random saints.

Had the god consciously created this form to look like the son of God? Macha hadn't done so, but she'd manifested without the benefit of all those visual examples. And she didn't seem like one interested in impressing others, nor one to cater to someone else's ideals. Dian Cecht seemed more addicted to human vanity and accolades.

Then again, maybe he'd misjudged the god. Dian Cecht had actually listened to Max and left Róisín's body. Could he have formed some scrap of a conscience? Or was he just tired of being hassled about it? Either way, Róisín was free, and Max counted that as a win.

In his newly created human form, the god placed his hands on the heads of his two closest worshippers. Again, a very Jesus-like action.

Max scowled, but if these idiots wanted to worship this bloke, so be it. He did heal the masses. Wasn't that one of Jesus' miracles? People had worshipped gurus for pretending to heal, and this guy actually *had* the powers.

Dian Cecht moved to the next hospital bed, his flock following him like hungry lambs. Trained doctors and nurses were turning into mindless sycophants. Max shook his head with utter disgust and returned to Róisín's side.

Someone he didn't recognize was kneeling beside her, holding her hand. One of the interns, perhaps. Was she already awake? She usually slept for hours after hosting Dian Cecht.

Max stopped a nurse, asking him to set up an IV. The man glanced at Róisín and wrote something on his pad. At least some professionals weren't so enthralled by the new messiah that they ignored their jobs.

Believing his duty done and Róisín in good hands, Max strode toward the door, intent on getting something to eat. However, something stopped him and he turned back.

Sure enough, Dian Cecht was gliding toward Róisín's cot, pushing the intern out of the way, and Max clenched his teeth.

The god laid his hands over her. A warm glow flowed through his hands and Róisín arched her back. She didn't scream, but moaned and thrashed her head, perhaps too exhausted for more.

When the god released her, she fell back, the bed bouncing. Her eyes flew open, her gaze darting around the room. Dian Cecht turned to Max. "Maximilian. You were correct to suggest I take form. I can feel the power of belief flow through me with increased intensity. I will offer my appreciation to you. Come closer."

Max glanced toward Róisín, and she nodded encouragement. He took a few steps toward the god. He didn't like this, not one bit, but turning down a god might be bloody dangerous.

The god of healing placed his glowing hands upon Max's shoulders. Sweet, salty energy zapped into his muscles. Years of ache and weariness shed away like water off metal.

His shoulders straightened as his lower back stopped hurting. His knees no longer stabbed with pain. Even his old rotator cuff injury felt better. The god's magic dug into his body, his mind, maybe even his soul, making his heart race.

As he breathed in, the power tickled his brain. Like the buzzing of bees, it jumped around in his mind. Max pulled away from the god's grip. "Oi! What the hell are you doing now?"

Puzzled, Dian Cecht peered at him. "You have injuries in more than just your bones and blood, Maximilian. You have damage to your mind. I can heal that."

He stepped back, his hands held up. "No bloody thank you! I don't want any damned god messing around in my memories! Just keep your bloody mitts away from that!"

But what if the nightmares were silenced? No, he didn't want anyone in his brain. He might lose memories he wanted. Max could never do anything that might erase Trina's smile.

The god pursed his lips. "If that is your wish, I shall not complete the healing. You may keep your pain, if you are so enamored of the damage."

Dian Cecht flung the double doors open with a wave of his hand, not even touching them, like Moses and the Red Sea, and his flock scurried after him.

As the last minion disappeared, Max knelt by Róisín's side and held her hand. "Róisín? You're awake. Are you okay?"

She gave him a wan smile. "I'm tired, but well enough. Thank you, Max." Her stomach growled and they both stared at it. She let out a chuckle. "Evidently, I'm also ravenous. Can you find me some lunch? A half a cow, maybe?"

Max gave her hand a squeeze. "A nurse is getting an IV, but I can find something for your gullet." He ran off in search of some food. He bumped into the nurse wheeling an IV and grabbed his arm. "She woke up. I'm getting her some food. She probably doesn't need that now."

The man scowled at him. "I'll make my own determination, thanks very much."

Max shrugged. "Please yourself. Where's the cafeteria, mate?"

He hurried off in the indicated direction. After several long corridors, he spied someone carrying a food tray, and made a beeline to the door they came through.

Max entered the bustling cafeteria, peering around. A big sign with an arrow showed where he could order food. He peered at the offerings, wanting to get the best thing for Róisín. Tomato soup would be hot and nourishing, but the chicken burger would be more substantial. He'd get both, and whatever she didn't eat, he would.

Laden with his tray of soup, sandwich, and a few cookies, along with two plastic cups for coffee, he grabbed cream and sugar for her. He drank his own black, other than whiskey.

For a wonder, considering the stress of the last few hours, he didn't even feel the craving. Which was good, because he didn't have his flask with him. He didn't even remember where he'd left it.

Max backed out of the cafeteria, tray in hand, and returned to the hospital ward where Róisín lay. As he entered, someone was kneeling next to her cot. No IV line was set up, so the nurse must have listened to him.

As he set the tray down, he noticed Róisín's limbs jerking. The man next to her cot was holding a pillow on her face. Max grabbed the man's shoulder. "Oi! What the hell are you doing?"

He wrenched the man away, sparing a quick glance at Róisín, but her eyes were open. Shoving the other guy against the back wall, he knelt next to her. "Róisín?"

She coughed a few times and waved him away. "I'm fine, Max. I'm fine."

"Right." Then, he spun to confront the guy with the pillow, the one he'd assumed was an intern earlier. "Oi, mate, what the hell did you think you were doing there?"

The young man was about Róisín's age and stared at him with glassy eyes as he wrung his hands. "She's *his* favorite. I want to be his favorite. I can't be his favorite if *she's* still there for him."

*Bloody hell. So, this was how it was going to go.*

Max grabbed his shirt and pulled him within inches of his face. "You can bloody well shove off, mate. If she gets hurt, you get hurt, understand? Get the hell out of here!"

He pushed the man several times until his back was against the door. One more shove and Max pushed him through. The attacker shuffled away in the direction Dian Cecht had gone.

**Hiroki:**

The world was silent.

At least, that's what it seemed like to Hiroki. Deep under the concrete bunker in Dublin, where he seemed to be spending every minute of his life now, Hiroki missed the homey sounds of his flat in Tokyo. The whoosh of tires in the rain. A neighbor shutting their door. Someone singing karaoke in the bar downstairs.

He sat on his cot in the simple room, a single candle burning on the side table. Staring at the candle, shutting out the surrounding darkness, he concentrated on the words Oghma had taught him, the ritual designed to call his teacher. Hiroki eagerly anticipated the lessons tonight and was looking forward to learning fascinating new things. Each time they met, he learned more.

The chant spoke of learning and laughter and memory. Sorrowful expressions of inevitable sadness and reveling in playing the fool. Hiroki didn't like the words, as he hated feeling foolish, but he knew they were part of the code to call the ancient Irish god of communication.

After the third chant, the candle flared once, twice, three times, and Hiroki knew his call had been heard. He stood to properly greet the god. While Oghma didn't insist on obeisance, Hiroki felt it would be dishonorable not to accord him proper ceremony.

A glowing mass formed in the middle of his room. The mass coalesced into human form, and when the glow faded, Oghma stood before him, his hands out like Jesus in many paintings.

"You have called me, apprentice. Do you seek knowledge?"

"I do, Oghma. Will you teach me?"

"I will."

Now that the greeting ritual was complete, Hiroki grinned. "What do you have for my lesson tonight?"

The god cocked his head and studied him. "You have learned well the techniques of speech and rhetoric so far. Would you like to learn something a little different?"

Hiroki opened his arms wide. "I would learn whatever you wish to teach me."

"Then I will tell you of my own family. Sit, and I will share."

Sitting cross-legged, he listened as Oghma spoke. "My father is Elatha, and my mother is Étaín. Have you heard of them?"

Hiroki shook his head. "I have only heard of the gods who have manifested so far in modern times. Macha, Lugh, Manannán, and Taranis."

Oghma let out a snort. "Taranis. He is not really one of us. He is of the Gaulish gods, and has elbowed his way into our manifestation. Manannán is displeased with his actions."

Hiroki's eyes grew wide. Fighting amongst the gods?

"I also have two sons, Delbaeth and Tuireann. Tuireann, alas, is long dead. There is a tale of that tragedy, a tale too long to relate to you tonight."

"Will you tell the tale another night? I should like to hear it."

Oghma gave a kind nod. "I shall certainly do so, though it pains me to speak of him. I tell you of my family so I can show you the ties. Tuireann's mother is Brigit, and she is also manifesting in the modern world, though you may not have met her yet."

"I haven't. What is she the goddess of?"

He let out a long laugh. "What isn't she? She has poetry and healing, protection and smithing. She is inspiration and flame. She is a skilled blacksmith and sings with the night. She brings in the spring on a cold winter's day."

As Oghma spoke, his face lit up with an actual glow, shining in the dark room, and Hiroki realized he spoke as one would of a lover, full of passion and dedication.

He wanted to meet this Brigit, this goddess who inspired his own patron so strongly. Would she accept him into their family?

**Caoimhe:**

As Caoimhe stood her watch on the Waterford Lighthouse, her mobile phone chimed. She pulled it out to see who was calling.

The wind tried to push her over, but she kept her grip tight on the red handrail. The sun had already dipped below the horizon, and twilight enveloped the coastline. She shivered, despite her woolen wrap.

Under Macha's direction, she'd worked with the other *draoi* to create cooperative defensive and offensive spells all along the coast. They practiced both with and without the goddess' assistance, to ensure they could stand up against an attack even if Macha weren't around.

The number on her phone wasn't a call, it was a drill signal.

Suppressing a shiver, Caoimhe rang the lighthouse bell, the signal to begin the drill. As the other *draoi* took their stance and drew energy in, she did the same.

Pulling power from the earth, the air, and the sea, Caoimhe dug deep into the bones of the land, tingling through her blood. Her skin buzzed and itched.

The goddess wouldn't deign to lend her power for mere practice, so they were on their own. Caoimhe could feel the difference, but she knew how to compensate and redirect.

Opening her eyes, she followed the line of *draoi* with her vision out of focus. That way, she could sense the shining barrier they formed. The priest to her left, on the next headland, shone bright in the deepening dusk. A gossamer fabric of power draped across his body and past him to the next priestess, almost invisible in the distance.

On her right, an American witch, Morgan, stood tall, their power radiating in a shining beacon. Past them, a tarot reader perched on the rocky shore.

She'd organized this network to cover the entirety of the southern shore of Ireland. Caoimhe only wished she had enough personnel to guard the entire island. But only so many true powers existed, so they concentrated on the coastline facing Europe and England.

The Unhidden didn't quite work within her network, though she grudgingly admitted they'd been helpful, and there was some overlap between talents. This protection of their land was a privilege and an ancient duty, to keep the enemy from the emerald shores. Caoimhe meant to keep it strong.

As the leader, she had a contact number for the Central Command of the War Council in Dublin. This group had hastily formed in the last few months, consisting of representatives from PHAE, the governments of the Republic of Ireland and of Northern Ireland, through the United Kingdom.

Something pushed against the net. Like a spider in the center of a web, Caoimhe felt it poke. Nothing penetrated the barrier, and might have been a fluke, but she sent her awareness along the line like a telegraph, questing the closest practitioner. *Is this an attack?*

The answer came back. *Unsure. Investigating.*

Again, pressure tickled her, in a different place, ten kilometres further down the line, west toward Dungarvan. Again, Caoimhe sent a query about the nature of the incursion. Again, her people sent back an answer of *Unsure. Investigating.*

Sirens wailed, the sound penetrating her skull, bouncing around like a pinball. Caoimhe clapped her hands over her ears, trying to dampen the painful klaxon. At the same time, she sent an alarm through the network. *All hands alert! Possible attack! This is not a drill!*

She got acknowledgements from all but one of her *draoi*. Morgan, just next to her, gave no answer. Caoimhe glanced down to where the American witch should have been, barely a spot in the evening light. Someone stood there, but they wore a different shape than Morgan. Heavier, bulkier, taller.

The klaxon wailed again. Dark spots on the water came toward the shore. Boats, and not just a few. At least fifty dark spots dotted the black ocean.

Caoimhe let out a long breath. Go time. She drew in her magic and called to her patron goddess.

*Macha, hear me. We need your help. This is not a drill. We need your help* now.

Once upon a time, Caoimhe would have chanted an ancient prayer to call the goddess. She'd have repeated the prayer nine times, and then maybe received a slight tingle of acknowledgement, and considered herself privileged for that response.

After working with Macha's physical manifestation these last few weeks, they were more or less on a first name basis now.

Caoimhe had become the goddess's human representative, and the only one able to call her at will. Well, her and that woman from Arizona, Komie.

Despite her initial dislike for the woman, Caoimhe didn't begrudge Komie access to the goddess. The native woman had gotten plenty of grief from working with Macha. Working directly with the gods wasn't a pure blessing.

But now, someone was attacking Ireland. This was exactly the sort of mayhem that Macha reveled in. Battle. Defending her land. Killing the enemy.

A deep smile crept across her face as Caoimhe felt the goddess respond to her call. Each time her heart took a beat, the goddess's footsteps drew closer. The *draoi* could feel each step in her muscles, the shaking of the earth beneath her feet.

A light sparked in the north, pulsing in time with those footsteps. Not the sun, not a headlight, not a candle, but divine light.

Macha, one of the three *Morrigna*. Goddess of the land, fertility, kingship, horses, and war. Macha, come to collect her harvest. The heads of the slain. The acorns of battle.

A surge of pride, tinged with both confidence and fear, rushed through Caoimhe. She'd finally stand beside her beloved goddess in battle. A moment to treasure for the rest of her life.

Her hand strayed to her sword, fingers curling around the grip. She'd endured smirks at carrying this ancient bronze gladius, but now she wore the smirk. She would smite her foes in battle, like in the ancient tales, and defend her land with her very body.

As the divine light grew closer, Caoimhe tried again to count the boats in the water below. She gave up at sixty, as the darkness swallowed them. They winked in and out of creeping evening fog. None of them carried lights, as that would be foolish in a night raid.

She did wonder at the low-tech attack. Had they no other resources? No air support? Were they just throwing what they had, like a modern-day Omaha Beach invasion? Or was this just distraction from another attack?

With that notion in mind, she sent an urgent text to Central Command. Their portion of the island also lay vulnerable, and they had considerably more weapons to combat any incursions.

Of course, the UK representatives had only promised to defend the shores of Northern Ireland, but that was less coastline her people needed to defend.

After Caoimhe sent her text with all the details, she glanced over her shoulder. Whoever had replaced Morgan was now gone. The space was empty. Her net had a gaping hole.

Macha came closer, her form visible within the ball of light. Instead of joining Caoimhe on the lighthouse gallery, she approached Morgan's spot.

Caoimhe hoped Morgan wasn't hurt. They were friends, and she enjoyed their company immensely, even if they were American.

A burst of light exploded on the shore below Morgan's spot. Then another. And a third. Tiny, silent explosions.

Caoimhe didn't know if they were part of the invaders' attack or Macha's defense. Through her network, she sent another query. *Source of light?*

The answer came from several of her *draoi* at once, pride welling within each one. *Macha.* It became a chant, a mantra. *Macha. Macha. Macha.*

Her own heart pounded with pride until the lights stopped. Ten flashes and now nothing. She still spied dark spots on the ink-black sea, boats strung along her beloved shore.

Macha's light, which had burnt bright along the cliffside, faded to a spot of nothing. Only a red after-burn lingered in Caoimhe's vision.

Had Macha failed? Was the goddess banished? Had Morgan been taken? Caoimhe didn't know, but she couldn't wait around to find out. Rage and fear bubbled inside her blood, and Caoimhe used that power to bolster their waning shield, to mend the hole in her net.

Power buzzed with renewed energy, pulsing along her web. She made her own light now, a faint glow along the tendrils of sentries, around the entire southern coast.

One boat came close enough to be seen in that faint light. The sentry nearby, the tarot card reader, flashed once, twice, and a third time, then burnt out like a dying light bulb. Caoimhe couldn't tell what happened, but she could no longer feel that person in the network.

Her heart fell and her blood grew cold. She tried to raise her power again, but she'd used all her resources already. Caoimhe tried to call upon Macha for more help, but she received no response, not even a flicker.

And the boats kept coming closer.

*Latest CNN Update: As more reports of individual attacks upon PHAE enclaves come in, some are regrouping to form defensive compounds. The Helsinki and Oslo groups have both relocated to Akureyri, on the north coast of Iceland, making use of a system of caves in the nearby mountains.*

*While those members of the Unhidden located in Sweden have stayed in place for now, it's possible that they will join their Scandinavian compatriots in the more defensible location.*

*The Copenhagen contingent, however, have contacted the Berlin office and requested sanctuary.*

*While Iceland is notable for having no standing army, they do maintain a small navy and robust Coast Guard. It is believed that those refugees relocating from other countries have brought military equipment from Finland and Norway to bolster their firepower.*

**Róisín:**

Róisín gasped awake, unable to get a breath. Something covered her face. She shoved at it, but it pressed down harder. Wiggling to get free, to pull in precious air, she let out a whimper. Her voice was muffled and weak.

Suddenly, whatever covered her face disappeared, and she sucked in a sweet breath of fresh air, deep into her lungs. Róisín sat up and coughed into her hands, wheezing in and out. She had a hard time pulling in air, but after several gulps, she relaxed into normal breathing.

Max rushed over, his face flushed and sweat on his brow. She choked out in a rough voice, "Max? Are you okay?"

He sat next to her bed and patted her hand. "I'm grand now, luv. Just a bit of housekeeping that needed doing. You?"

"I'm fine. I could do with some water, though."

He reached under the cart beside her, handing her a plastic bottle. She drained half of it and choked again. After patting her on the back, he glanced back over his shoulder towards the ward door. "You don't sound all that fine to me."

Róisín waved away his concern. "I'm fine, I'm fine. Still starving, though. Did you get that soup? I'm just glad to get some rest. Hey, did I imagine it, or did Dian Cecht do something different this time? It felt strange when he left me."

He rolled his eyes as he moved the wheeled tray to her, though the tomato soup was no longer steaming. "You could say that, sure."

Róisín raised her eyebrows as she ate a spoonful. "Then say that. I mean, tell me what was different."

Max gave her a wry smile. "He formed his own body. Like, manifested it, straight out of thin air, like Macha and Taranis did. And light, lots of light. He looked like a bloody Christmas tree with dancing fairy lights draped around him."

If Dian Cecht created his own body, he wouldn't need to use hers. Which meant she'd finally get to rest long enough to fully recover. It also meant that she'd never again feel that exquisite combination of pain and pleasure when he worked his magic through her. Her elation dropped to despair and back again. "Wow. What made him try that?"

Letting out a chuckle, Max said, "I bloody dared him to do it."

"Oh? Do tell."

He stared at his feet. "The bastard tried to heal me. I mean, that was fine and all for the cuts and bruises, and my knees haven't felt this good for years. I don't even feel my rotator cuff injury. But bloody hell! Then he started tinkering in my mind."

Róisín tilted her head. "Your mind?"

"He started poking around, lighting up memories, all sorts of shit. I told him to get the hell out. That's what started the, uh, heated discussion."

Róisín studied the Australian man. He'd been through a lot in his life, that much she was dead sure of. He had lots of trauma to deal with, things that made him drink to forget.

Since she'd first met him, she'd been subtly working to heal that trauma. She'd started with reducing his need for alcohol, then sanding down the rough edges of his worst memories.

So far, it had been working. He'd cut down on the self-destructive drinking, at least whenever she was around to *encourage* him. Now guilt over her heavy-handedness crept over her. If Max really didn't want to be healed, what right did she have to force it on him?

But if Dian Cecht had barreled in where she had been so carefully laying gossamer paths, well, no wonder Max felt so violated. "Tell me, why are you so against being healed? Do you not *want* a healthier mind? Or is it just because he didn't ask permission?"

He shook his head, refusing to meet her eyes. "I don't know, darlin'. A man gets used to his pain, aye? It's almost a comfort. Something I'm familiar with. In a way, it's part of what makes me myself. If someone takes that away, what's left? I wouldn't recognize myself in a mirror. I know how to deal with the pain I have."

Róisín snorted. "Through a bottle of aged brown liquid, yeah. Just like my grandfather did."

He lifted his gaze and scowled at her. "You sound awfully judgmental all of a sudden, darlin'. I've never heard that from you before."

She let out a deep breath. "I didn't mean it like that. I'd like to help you heal, if you'll let me. I promise I'll be gentler than Dian Cecht."

Max shot to his feet and paced around the hospital ward. "I don't want *anyone* in my head, luv, not even you. Nobody, no way, nohow. I've got plenty of ghosts living there already."

Róisín rolled her eyes. "At least let me try. How hard can that be? Look, it's half-done already. All I have to do is gather the threads together and finish off the healing—"

He spun and glared at her. "Christ on a piece of toast, I thought you understood me. Now you just want to fix me like any other self-important sheila I've ever met!"

She caught her breath, her heart racing. "Max! You can't mean that!"

"I can and I do, luv! Now kindly fuck off out of my life." Thunder boomed outside as he stalked away from her. He put his hand on the door, glanced back at her, and then at the door again. Instead of leaving, he paced back and forth in front of the ward doors, like a caged cat.

Róisín hadn't paid attention to the weather, but sunlight had been streaming in earlier. Now dark gathering storm clouds loomed ominously above. A flash of lightning almost blinded her. Had Max called up the storm as he got angry?

Another roll of thunder rattled the windows. The vibration traveled up the cot and into her bones. She stared at Max as he paced, his fists clenched. His agitation *must* be causing the storm, but she hadn't heard him speak to the wind at all. Didn't he normally talk to them out loud? "Max?"

He halted and spun to face her. "What?"

"I think you're causing chaos outside."

Confused, he glanced at the window, then grew pale. Without a word, he shoved open the ward doors and ran down the hallway.

Grumbling under her breath, Róisín flipped the sheets off and got to her feet. Her legs buckled, but she gritted her teeth and tried again until they held her weight. Then she picked her way through the ward doors, following in Max's wake, thankful she still had her own clothes on.

As soon as she exited the hospital, icy wind slapped her in the face. She let out a gasp. *This is July! Why is it so cold?* She gripped the red brick wall of the hospital to keep her balance.

Her gasp made Max turn around, his hair escaped from his ponytail and dancing in the fierce wind. "Róisín! What are you doing, ya mad Sheila? Get back in bed!"

She gritted her teeth and held tight to the wall. "I will not! You need to calm yourself or you'll bring this storm down on all of us!"

Thunder cracked again, making her jump, and a whimper escaped her lips. She'd never liked thunder, and to be outside in this gale, exposed to danger, stole every bit of her courage. Still, she wouldn't leave Max like this.

"Get inside, Róisín. I've got to deal with this myself. I don't need you to meddle anymore."

Róisín clenched her jaw. "Max, I wasn't meddling. I was *helping*."

"It's the same fucking thing, darlin'! Just stop it. Leave me alone!"

Lightning struck the tree next to Max, flaring with an enormous crash and burning so bright, Róisín had to turn away. When the brightness faded, flames licked the leaves, a burning bush in the pouring rain.

She was wet, cold, and exhausted, and wanted nothing more than to curl up in a warm bed and sleep for a week. What the heck was she doing out here in a furious storm, arguing with a madman bent on self-destruction?

But the healer in her wouldn't abandon him. Not when he obviously needed her more than ever. Not when part of this was her fault, for meddling with his healing in the first place. She stumbled away from the wall, trying to get close enough to grab his arm. She couldn't heal him without touching him.

Max stared at the sky as she inched closer. Róisín didn't want to startle him. He seemed so skittish, like a colt. Thunder boomed again, and fear shot through her. Just a few steps more, and she could heal his pain. Surely, he couldn't protest healing his physical body.

She grasped his upper arm and pulled on her power, but nothing came through. No tingling, no ecstasy, no power, nothing. Not even warmth.

Max glared at her with an expression of disgust. "What do you think you're doing? I told you to get back inside!"

Then, his hair stood on end and his eyes grew wide. Róisín stumbled away just as lightning struck his head. His entire body lit up like a fake Hallowe'en skeleton. Róisín was shoved back by the impact and skidded on the wet pavement.

She stared at the Australian man as his body jerked and fell next to her. The lightning disappeared and the world turned dark again.

**Hiroki:**

Sitting in their bunker office under the Dublin streets, Hiroki glanced first at his best friend, Masaaki, then over to Bintou. Ciara stared straight at the computer monitor, her mouth agape in amazement.

The news announcer spoke as they watched in stunned silence. "I repeat, reports are coming in that the PHAE enclave just outside the Siberian city of Omsk has formed a force field against the outside world."

The picture grew fuzzy, and the sound crackled before the announcer resumed. "At this time, we have no details on how they've built this barrier seemingly overnight, nor what its capabilities are. More to come as we investigate these questions."

Hiroki leapt to his feet and started pacing. Ciara took a long swig of some cocktail she'd called a zombie. It sounded horrible to Hiroki, but he had to admit he could use the kick of a shot of whiskey. It might calm his racing thoughts and warm his blood.

How had the Siberian PHAE formed a shield? Was it scientific technology or Unhidden power? The news footage showed an enormous dome, cloudy rather than opaque, glowing with a heartbeat-like pulse, with threads of sparks tickling the surface. No one had reported any attempts to penetrate, but it didn't look like it would treat intruders kindly. It reminded Hiroki of a lantern zapping mosquitoes.

Masaaki chugged half his Coke. "Ciara, has headquarters heard from the Siberian group at all? Did they know what was planned?"

The tall Irishwoman's eyes were glued on the screen as a drone image panned out, showing that the dome covered at least ten square miles. "Nothing. At least, nothing that they've shared with me. They could be keeping any information confidential. I'm only the liaison with the Irish Unhidden. Foreign Affairs are a different group."

As they watched, a sharp whining cut into the transmission. The talking head returned, her hand on her ear. "We've got a breaking story coming in about the Siberian enclave. There seems to be a bogey heading towards it. I think we've got visual verification of that. One moment..."

Her image disappeared, and a shaky view of the dome filled the screen. A small, red light shot toward the cloudy substance in a ballistic trajectory. It looked like it came from the city of Omsk itself.

The sullen light whined as it got closer to the surface of the dome. Just as it struck, an explosion boomed and the drone camera shook. When the plume of smoke cleared, the dome appeared unscathed. The light had disappeared.

The dome had some defensive ability, after all.

Hiroki let a smile escape. He hated bullies, and the attackers had shot first without asking questions or trying to negotiate. There'd been no time for a diplomatic solution, just the missile, and their missile failed.

In real terms, that meant the PHAE group in Siberia suddenly had a much stronger negotiating position. Now they had a valid complaint against the Russian government, as well as proof of their defenses.

At the same time, things might get worse for all the PHAE.

He turned to the others, and they were all frowning at him. Bintou asked, "Hiroki, why are you smiling? People are dying there."

Hiroki shook his head. "I'm not smiling at the death. I'm smiling at the justice."

She leapt to her feet. "Justice? You call this justice? How can you even say that?"

Ciara clicked her tongue and shook her head. Even Masaaki wore a frown. Did none of them understand? A true friend would understand. But he didn't know how to explain, so he stayed silent.

Bintou pursed her lips and stared at him a long moment more before turning back to the screen.

The smoke from the bogey was joined by a second. Then a third and a fourth. Soon, dozens of missiles had hit the dome, but none seemed to penetrate the barrier.

The drone camera zoomed in, and then out again, unable to get a clear picture of any missile actually hitting the dome itself. Then it panned over to the city of Omsk. Black smoke billowed from several large buildings.

Ciara's face had turned unusually pale. She sucked down the rest of her drink.

Masaaki stalked to the minifridge and yanked it open. He cursed and grabbed the only thing left, a bottle of cider. He opened it, took a swig, grimaced, and then chugged the rest.

Hiroki considered asking Bintou if she still had Martin's flask, and if she'd refilled it with whiskey. But reminding her of her dead boyfriend wouldn't be kind. Still, the warm burn of strong drink would help relax his own anxiety.

Bintou clasped her hands tight against her stomach. "Are those PHAE bombs? Or PEM?"

Ciara shook her head. "I have no way of knowing. I pray to God that they're PEM, not us. But one can only poke a tiger so many times until they bite back. The PEM may have just discovered this truth."

A larger explosion rocked the transmission, and just before the screen went black, fire filled the frame. The announcer returned, her finger on her earpiece. "Our transmission has disappeared. We'll try to reconnect and report further information as it comes."

Hiroki clenched his jaw as Ciara rose, went to the filing cabinet, and pulled out the bottom drawer. She returned to the table with a bottle of Bushmills. Without a word, she poured four measures in plastic cups, one each for her, Masaaki, Hiroki, and Bintou.

Bintou pushed hers away with a shake of her head. "You know I do not drink, Ciara. It is forbidden by Allah."

Ciara pushed it back. "This is medicinal. Think of it as taking a drink in honor of Martin."

Masaaki took her shot and said, "I'll drink on her behalf."

Bintou clenched her jaw and tears glistened in her eyes.

Hiroki cradled his shot with grateful hands. He downed it and relished the warm fire that burned his throat, the oaky taste that tickled his nose. His skin tingled, like it had when he'd met the god, Oghma.

He wondered what the god was doing now, or if he knew about these attacks. Were the gods involved in some way?

Oghma hadn't really told Hiroki much about the plans of the gods, just about what he needed to do to help. And Hiroki ached to help them, to gain their approval. If his father refused to be proud of him, then Hiroki would need another family to be proud of him.

Oghma had told him how to do that, and he meant to make it happen.

**Max:**

Everything hurt and he couldn't move.

Max was no stranger to pain. Pain was more like an old friend, something comforting and real. It meant he was still alive. He'd known physical pain, mental pain, and emotional pain his entire life. His grandmother used to wallop him when he crossed her.

As Max got older, he'd been taught that the pain meant she cared about him and wanted to raise him right, even though he didn't realize that nuance as a child. He'd wailed to high heaven every time she smacked him across his arse with the peach switch.

In Vietnam, he experienced agony with every bomb they commanded him to drop, with every strafe of an enemy village.

For a brief time, that pain had been salved with Trina's smile. Her love and laugh had made everything better. And then he'd destroyed that, too. The pain of her ruined, burnt body disintegrating in his arms haunted the rest of his days and most especially the nights.

He created his own pain.

None of this was anything to the pain that now gripped his muscles, bones, and blood.

Max let out a moan, a crackling shadow of his voice, ripping through his throat like sandpaper on iron nails. Someone knelt beside him with cool, gentle hands on his chest. Then a sweet, precious soothing power flowed through him.

Then it was gone.

Róisín's voice cried out. "Let me heal him! You've almost killed him!"

A booming voice rattled his ears. **"He has defied me yet again. He dares to call upon my own storm and expects to escape the consequences."**

Max recognized the voice instantly. *Bloody hell.* Taranis, the storm god. Taranis hated him.

Róisín's voice shook with stubborn fury. "You will not harm him again. Do you hear me?"

**"And who are you, to command the god of the skies?"**

"I am Róisín Sarah Byrne of the Ó Brioin, descendant of Bran mac Máelmórda, King of Leinster and I am an acolyte of Dian Cecht. And you will listen to me."

The pride and strength in her tone made him so proud of her. She was finally standing up for herself. *Good girl.* The fact that she had to do so to protect him, though, filled him with shame.

Max thought he must be imagining things, but the god of the skies actually hesitated before thunder boomed across the heavens again.

Slowly, Max lifted his hand and wiped the rain from his face. It was instantly soaked again, but at least he could blink his eyes open to watch her standing defiantly over him, facing the roiling, booming sky. Her body was tense, but as Taranis had no physical manifestation to focus on, her glare darted back and forth.

**"I do not see Dian Cecht in you."**

Róisín lifted her chin. "Well spotted. You're perceptive, for a god. He finally figured out how to manifest his own body. It's the polite thing to do when someone is speaking with you."

Max chuckled at her barbed hint. As if Taranis would recognize anything so subtle. From Max's interactions with the god of thunder, he didn't exactly have a good grasp on subtext or manners. Not that Max was a shining example of either.

**"How am I to trust you are his acolyte?"**

Just as Max turned onto his side and keep the falling rain from getting into his eyes, Róisín threw up her hands. "You should be able to see his touch on me. He's used my body a dozen times to heal others. Surely that's left a mark even *you* can see!"

Max held his breath. She was taunting him dangerously close to insolence. Max had learned the price of sassing Taranis and had gotten his ass kicked for it. Multiple times.

**"I see nothing."**

"If you can't see it, how am I to trust you are actually the god of the skies?"

Now he hissed a whisper. "Róisín! Be careful? He can destroy you!" It only came out as a strangled croak, and he coughed several times.

She spared him a glance, then a wide smile crossed her lips. Was she taunting a god on purpose? The Róisín he knew was modest, cautious, and mature. This didn't sound like any of those.

Another voice boomed behind him, deeper and stronger than the thunder god's. **"Taranis. Stop being an arse."**

**Anna:**

The song of the sea tugged at Anna's mind. She'd almost forgotten that feeling, that distant call of the ocean waves.

Once she'd become Manannán mac Lir's apprentice, that tug usually heralded his arrival. But he'd given her a month's leave to help Carlos and the rest of the PHAE defend Ireland against the PEM. A part of her regretted that leave, and her soul ached to be in the sea. But the month was far from over. Why would he be calling on her now?

She turned to the Miami man as he peered at a circuit board mounted to the wall. "Carlos? What is it?"

His Unhidden talent with anything electronic had made him in high demand after the bombings. These last few weeks, they'd visited each water treatment plant in County Dublin.

She purified the water while he fixed the electronics. Her ability to hold water let them clean out tanks, redirect flow, and whatever else they needed. "Hmm?"

"He's calling me."

Carlos blinked a few times, focusing on her face. "Who's calling you? Blondie? Elvis? Jesus?"

Anna let out a chuckle. He did make her laugh. "No, silly. Manannán."

With a frown, he slammed the circuit box shut, then dusted his hands. "What the hell does he want, then? He promised you a free month. We're only a few weeks in."

She shrugged. "I don't know, do I? I can hear him calling." She turned toward the west whence the call came. Staring into the distance didn't do much good, as only the modest skyline of industrial Dublin lay before her.

The tallest buildings here were cathedrals and the Guinness Storehouse tower. Her native Rochester didn't have particularly massive skyscrapers, but they had more than Dublin.

Even without any details behind the call, she could still tell exactly from which direction it came and would easily be able to find him. But she didn't have Max's ability to ride the wind, so she needed a ride.

Carlos scowled as he followed her line of sight to the west. "We're done here, and that's the last one damaged by the blast. But Ciara asked us to complete an inspection tour around the country."

Anna rolled her eyes, turning back toward him. "Yes, I heard her tell us. And I'm also aware I made a promise to help PHAE. But what exactly am I supposed to do when he calls, huh? Ignore a freaking sea god? Do you really think that's a power move?"

He got to his feet and dusted off the knees of his jeans. "Well, it's up to you, of course, but I thought you wanted to visit Brendan again before we left Dublin?"

The light tone in his voice didn't fool Anna one bit. He might be jealous of her affection for Brendan, but he knew how to use it to make an argument. A twinge of guilt about Brendan stabbed her heart. "Yes, I want to visit Brendan."

"Fine, then I'll take you to visit Brendan. Then we'll figure out what to do next, together. Fair?" He lifted his eyebrows a few times, with a comical smile.

"Fair."

After helping dig out the rubble in Galway, Brendan had fallen ill to both weaponized illnesses, anthrax and pneumonic plague. Ironically, the person best able to heal him was his sister, Róisín, but Dian Cecht had kept her busy in the west.

Anna had begged Ciara to keep her near Dublin so she could visit him after each job. With this last Dublin plant dealt with, she'd finished everything nearby. She'd have to move on, and even though she realized it, her guilt kept hammering on her heart.

Anna crossed her arms. "Right. After Brendan, we can head west. Ciara must have a plant on her list in that area? Manannán's near Galway."

Carlos grimaced. "I was hoping never to see *that* place again. But fine, let me check the listing." He pulled out his tablet and scrolled down. "Sure, there's one in County Clare. Ballymacraven, it's called. What is that, house of the raven's son?" He grinned at his attempted translation.

Anna rolled her eyes again. "You're too silly. Raven's got to be a different word in the Irish, doesn't it?"

"Yeah, well, you can't blame a guy for trying. Irish is at least as incomprehensible to me as the ways of women are."

She pursed her lips as he collected his tools. "All set?"

"Yeah. Help me carry these into the car?"

All through the process of packing, getting supplies, and taking their leave, Anna avoided speaking with Carlos. By the time they got buckled up, he let out a deep sigh. "Hospital now?"

Anna kept her voice even. "Please."

Their awkward silence continued as Carlos navigated out of Dublin and to the Kildare hospital a half hour west. Those in the main city were still filled with bombing victims, so casualties had spilled out to the suburbs. Kildare was at least close enough that Anna had been able to visit every day.

Carlos usually stayed in the car. She didn't know if this was out of respect for her privacy with Brendan or out of jealousy. She wasn't certain she wanted to know.

Anna liked Brendan a lot. He'd been so kind to her when she arrived in Ireland, alone and frightened out of her wits. He'd helped her understand the limits of her talent with manipulating water, acted as teacher, protector, and confidante. They'd held hands, talked to each other, even shared a few sweet kisses.

But then they'd gotten into that stupid fight after staying at Carlos' B&B. She got along great with Carlos, and it was nice to talk with another American.

But then Brendan had gotten all jealous and demanding, and she couldn't deal with that. She'd had a bad boyfriend in the past who had gone stalker on her.

Therefore, she left him and went to go work with Manannán mac Lir. Away from people, away from Carlos, and away from Brendan.

Anna had thought about Brendan often, as she lived on the islands, far from any drama. She'd thought about Carlos, too. Carlos seemed to accept her as she was, never pushing her to do things. But then again, hadn't that been Brendan's job? To help her find her limits and the capabilities of her talent?

Which made her think that his affection for her was also part of his job, his duty to make her feel welcome and part of the family. That notion made her heart grow cold, and she couldn't let the idea go, no matter how kind he'd been to her. He didn't like her, personally. He just acted like it to bring her into PHAE.

But she still liked him. And maybe he *did* actually like her.

Anna entered the hospital, anxiety rising in her throat. A mixture of antiseptic and vomit tickled her nose. Two doors down, turn left. One more door on the right, then turn left again. Pale, sickly green walls reflected fluorescent light on everything. Third door down on the left.

Brendan wasn't awake this afternoon. She could tell as soon as she walked into his ward. His eyes were shut, and his head tossed back and forth.

A nurse wiped the sweat from his cheeks and looked up when she approached. "I'm afraid he's regressed today, Anna. He was lucid earlier, though, so he's still on the road to recovery."

"Thanks."

The nurse left as she took Brendan's hand and squeezed. She always felt so foolish talking to him, knowing he couldn't really hear her. At least the nurse was kind enough to leave to give her as much privacy as could be had in a busy hospital ward.

She sat on the stool beside his bed and spoke in a low tone. "Hello, Brendan. It's Anna. I heard you were feeling better earlier."

She waited as if he would respond, but when he didn't, she kept going. "I'm afraid I've got some bad news. I need to head west again. Manannán called me, you see. I'm still doing work for the PHAE, but there are some places in County Clare we can help, and that way, I can find out what he wants. But that means I won't be able to visit you each night. You know better than me, that's too long for a daily commute."

Anna waited for him to agree, but then felt silly and stopped. She so much wanted him to answer. She cleared her throat and rose, still holding his hand. "I'll call to find out how you're doing, if we can get a decent signal. Some of the damaged towers out west are repaired now."

She laid his hand on his chest and patted it. Anna wanted to say she loved him, but she didn't even know if that was true. Fond of him, definitely. And maybe, given time, she'd grow to love him.

She'd never been quick to give her heart, and they'd really only known each other a few days before the PEM attacks had thrown the entire island into panic mode. In the end, she settled on a safer parting. "I miss you, Brendan. Heal quickly."

She couldn't even promise him that she'd be there when he got better, not with all honesty. By that time, she might have returned to

Manannán's care, to live in the sea. Anna glanced out toward the parking lot, where Carlos awaited her in the car.

Or Carlos would capture her heart. She wasn't sure about that, either.

# Chapter Three

"We get stuck when we insist that God be both good and all-powerful."
– Barbara Ehrenreich

**Anna:**

As they drove along the M7 headed west toward the Ballymacraven Water Plant, they once again fell into an awkward silence.

Anna didn't know if she was their only source of rivalry between Carlos and Brendan, but she certainly played a part in it. Two men fighting over her was a new experience, and the modern woman in her screamed against the old-fashioned patriarchy of it all.

She couldn't deny that it felt sort of empowering, though. Anna hid her smile by staring out the car window at the passing landscape. Rolling farms turned to suburbs, which turned to urban sprawl.

As they passed Limerick, Carlos turned north. Fancy horse corrals faded into poorer farms and rocky hills, and then the rocky hills took over.

Carlos spoke for the first time in an hour. "This is the Burren."

She nodded, staring at the odd landscape, like something on the moon. "Colin Byrne told me about it."

He cleared his throat. "It's a weird place. I visited when I first came to Ireland. Camped out for a few nights with some other folks from the States. There are odd sounds on the hills at night."

She gave a chuckle. "Bears? Or something more along the lines of Colin's scary fairy stories?" After she said the words, her smile faded. Those scary fairy stories had turned real in the last weeks.

Actual ancient Irish gods coming to life and meddling in their lives. Helping them, for now, but at what cost? Silence descended upon them again.

They passed a church spire as they drove past a city. The sign read *Ennis.* Angry storm clouds swirled overhead, ominous, threatening. Did this country do anything else but rain? "How much longer?"

"About a half hour."

Suddenly, the call from Manannán yanked at her so hard, she jerked up straight. Carlos glanced over, his eyes wide. "What? What is it?"

"He needs me. Now."

Carlos angled the car to the pullover by the side of the road. Once the car stopped, he turned to her. "Brendan?"

She stared at him. "No, you idiot. Manannán. Who do you think has been calling me all this time?" Then, aghast at her snappish tone, she covered her mouth.

Instead of getting angry, Carlos chuckled and waved her horror away. "Okay, okay, I asked for that one. Where is he? Can you figure out which direction?"

Closing her eyes, Anna quested for her mentor's touch. Behind them? She turned toward the city of Ennis. "Back there, I think."

"You think? Or do you know? Trust your talent, Anna." He lowered his voice and spoke in a British voice. "Feel the force, padawan."

She let out a giggle. "Fine. I know. That way." She pointed toward the city center. Carlos gave her a saucy grin and pulled a U-turn as she stuck her tongue out at him. While Carlos may not have the quiet peace Brendan did, he definitely made her laugh. And laughter was good for the soul.

They threaded through suburbs and then city streets. Anna kept pointing periodically, listening to the inner call, wondering why they weren't going toward the coast. Manannán's voice hummed in her head now, a tuneless tone that made her skull rumble and her ears tickle. She rubbed at her face several times, wishing the vibrations would stop.

Thunder rolled and a bolt of lightning struck a church steeple as they drove by. The flash made her jump, but Carlos kept a firm grip on the wheel. The day had turned dark with the storm clouds.

Anna both loved and hated weather like this. Water called to her, and she loved dancing in the rain. Water made her skin less itchy, less painful, though to be fair, now that she'd grown scales along her arms and legs, the itchiness had eased a lot. The scales stopped short of her thighs, for which she was grateful. She didn't wish to become something inhuman.

At the same time, the startling boom of thunder always frightened the little girl deep inside of her and made her want to run and hide.

Carlos pulled past the Ennis General Hospital sign, and Anna noticed several things at once. Róisín, shouting at the sky. Max, lying flat on the ground. An angry face in the thunderstorm, complete with a flowing beard and lightning crackling in the eyes.

*This must be Taranis.* Manannán had warned Anna about him. A nasty god full of temper and impulse, with none of the constancy of the earth or the sea.

Max had tussled with Taranis before. Evidently, he was doing so again. He didn't learn easily.

As soon as Carlos' car screeched to a stop, Anna leapt out, rushing to kneel beside Max. Róisín seemed too busy facing down Taranis to stop to heal him.

While Anna was no healer, she might be able to keep him alive. As a swimming coach, she'd been certified in CPR.

She did a quick assessment. His clothes were scorched. His long gray hair, usually tied in a neat ponytail, looked like it had been teased for an Eighties music video, complete with a full can of hairspray, and the ends were singed.

She felt for a pulse in his wrist, just below the thumb, and felt a flutter. His skin was wet and freezing. "Max? Max can you hear me?"

He coughed, his entire body spasming as he spluttered and caught his breath. *At least he's breathing.* He croaked out in a breathy whisper. "I'm fine. Don't let him get me again, though."

She stood up next to Róisín, her fists clenched in defiance. In a fierce whisper, she asked the Irish woman, "What's going on?"

Róisín flashed her a frown. "I'm shielding Max from Taranis. That's pretty much all I can do at the moment."

The tug from Manannán came closer and Anna smiled. "No worries. Backup's coming."

*Latest CNN Update:* Reports are coming in of damage caused by the recent attack on the Siberian domed enclave of the PHAE. The nearby city of Omsk has requested Russia to declare martial law. So far, however, the Russian government has not granted their request.

The city has mandated evacuation of all residents. They are being moved to a quarantine facility to determine if any biological weapons were used with the missiles. We have found no reports on the Russian state-owned media about these attacks.

In related news, the Chinese contingent of the PHAE are reportedly joining with the Siberian enclave. We have not discovered how they are being transported into the dome.

The numbers of the Chinese group haven't been verified, but rumors have them at least two thousand members. They've previously kept a very low profile, as the government of China have declared anyone with Unhidden powers to be wards of the state and subject to internment in concentration camps.

*It's believed that most of those with such powers remained part of an underground organization to this point, and it's possible that underground organization has been instrumental in moving them to Omsk.*

*The PHAE headquarters in Dublin have issued a blanket statement that any Unhidden across the world who can escape their own country and wish to come to Ireland will be welcomed. They only have to find one of the PHAE enclaves and request refugee status.*

**Max:**

Both Róisín and Anna towered above him, protecting him. Protecting *him*. Max couldn't understand it and didn't like it one bloody bit. A wash of shame gripped his guts at two women having to fight for him.

At the same time, he realized how much his life had changed in the last few weeks. Two people *wanted* to fight for him.

Max had never had many delusions about himself. He was a right bastard, an arsehole, and chauvinistic as hell. In fact, he wore that persona proudly. His age and his past allowed him plenty of leeway, at least in his own mind.

Both women were like daughters to him, or maybe even granddaughters. Women and friends to be cherished and treasured. *Is this what true friendship feels like?*

He'd gotten precious little of that in his lifetime and didn't really know how to recognize it. Max knew the brotherhood of fellow soldiers, a strong, true bond, from Vietnam. But he didn't hang out with those blokes after the war was over. Too many memories to share the misery. Besides, many of them were dead and the others scattered throughout Australia, living in solitary holes for the rest of their lives, wallowing in their misery, reliving their painful memories. Or escaping them in the bottle.

But friends, true friends, those had always been thin on the ground. Which meant he'd better not squander those few fools who put up with him now.

Max struggled to get to his knees, rain still pouring down on his back. A hacking cough gripped him again, his limbs exhausted and tingling at the same time. *Damn Taranis and his damned lightning. How can I battle a fucking sky god?*

The ground trembled beneath his knees. He searched the sky for lightning to go with the thunder, but nothing struck the ground.

Anna and Róisín stared defiantly at the sky, feet wide and fists clenched. They hadn't spoken to Taranis in a while, so the tension just kept building. His skin crawled and his teeth itched.

Again, the ground rumbled. Max didn't like the possibilities crowding his imagination.

Did Ireland have earthquakes? Either that, or another god was coming. That could be a mixed bag. Some were decent enough, he supposed. Some were downright bastards like this Taranis bloke.

A third rumble. Through the sheeting rain, a blue glow formed at the end of the street, vaguely human-shaped, stomping toward them. With each step, the ground shook. Max struggled to his feet. He was damned if he was going to stay on his knees and let the ladies fight for him, not if he could stand on his own. He might have a shred of dignity left, after all, or even a crumb of chivalry. *Who'd a thunk it?*

Max might not be able to do shit with his wind while Taranis ruled the skies, but he didn't care. His pride insisted that he rise.

The blue light formed a massive male figure with blue skin and a beard that Neptune'd be jealous of. He didn't carry a trident, but starfish and other sea creatures were hitching a ride in his long, blue-white hair. Bloke had massive muscles, too, like something out of a Disney cartoon.

This must be Manannán mac Lir. Max turned to Anna as a smile crept over her face. The blue bloke stopped a few yards away, crossed his arms, and planted his feet wide. Then he glared up at the roiling clouds. His voice thundered across the parking lot. **"Taranis."**

**"You're out of your domain, Manannán."**

**"Everything water is my domain. Your domain is *made* of my domain."**

The storm clouds rumbled and flashed with what might have been anger or laughter. Max didn't know which and he really didn't care. What he *did* care about was getting the women out of harm's way while Taranis was distracted.

Another man joined them, someone Max hadn't met. Anna had talked about someone named Carlos. The new bloke turned to Anna and Róisín. "Let's make tracks while they duke this out, eh?"

Anna shook her head. "No. I need to stay in case Manannán needs me. He's the one who called me here."

The Hispanic guy gripped her arm. "Are you insane? You want to stay outside while two ancient Irish gods have a fucking celebrity deathmatch?"

Max liked this guy already.

A bolt of lightning cracked and struck the ground just on the other side of Manannán. The sea god glowered at the clouds. **"You dare to strike at me? You will know my wrath, Taranis!"**

Róisín's eyes darted back and forth. Max grabbed Carlos's arm. "Look, mate, if I take Róisín to safety, can you protect Anna?"

The Spanish guy's eyes grew wide. "Protect her? From two gods? No fucking way, man. I can shield her with my body, but that's about it. I don't have this kind of power. She's far more capable than I am at any sort of battle."

Out of the corner of his eye, Max noticed Anna stand straighter. Well, the bloke had a point. With her power over water, she was in her element in a rainstorm, and a war between the storm and the sea.

But he couldn't just leave her on her own. "Can you get her to safety, at least?"

Carlos placed a hand on Anna's shoulder. She stared up at the sky, and then toward Manannán. "Go with them, Carlos. I'm fine here."

He let out a snort. "You are not!"

She spun on him, her eyes flashing. "I. Am. Fine."

The other guy backed up a few steps. Instead of waiting to see how that little spat turned out, Max grabbed Róisín's arm and yanked her toward the hospital entrance. She resisted his efforts without even looking at him, still staring at the sky.

"Róisín! Now's our chance!"

She turned to glare at him. "You'd abandon your friends?"

A cold, sinking feeling hit the bottom of his stomach. "Anna can take care of herself far better than you or me, darlin'! Come *on!*"

He pulled again, but she jerked her arm out of his grip. "I'm not going anywhere. And if you want to go crawling to safety while they're defending you, then go! Slither into a corner!"

He gulped and glanced up just as another bolt of lightning came crashing down a few feet away. Max leapt back. "Bloody hell on a biscuit!"

Nightmares hammered on his memories, demanding to be let into the waking world. Memories of bombs, fire, and napalm. Memories of Trina's village. Of her body, destroyed and crumbling in his arms. The back of his mind screamed.

He couldn't let that happen to Róisín and Anna. And he couldn't handle that guilt on top of everything. He needed a huge drink. A whole bottle would be better.

Róisín turned and gripped his shoulders. "No. You do *not* need a drink. Get hold of yourself, Max. Be a man for once!"

Suddenly, a drink didn't seem all that important. Max stared up at the swirling clouds and straightened his spine, despite the yearning to run crying and screaming for shelter. He'd been slammed by Taranis before and didn't crave a repeat of the experience. That shot of lightning had bloody well *hurt*.

Despite his shaking knees and roiling stomach, Max took a deep breath and stood next to his friends. urge took his hand. He gripped Anna's hand on the other side, and Carlos took her other one.

As one, the four Unhidden faced Taranis, with Manannán mac Lir at their side.

**Anna:**

As Anna stood with her friends against the storm god, she drew in the surrounding moisture surrounding. Rain had been pelting down, and this was Ireland, full of humidity. She had plenty of material to work with, even being miles from the ocean.

Dimly, she sensed a river nearby, an inlet to the south of her, should she need more water.

Manannán rarely spoke to her in words. He'd just flash pictures of what he wanted in her mind. When he did speak, he tended to talk in her head rather than out loud.

Now, as she glared at Taranis, and considered his defiance of Manannán, Anna realized this might be a test of her apprenticeship. Would she be able to defend her mentor against another god?

A huge part of her screamed *no!* That this was far too much to ask of a half-trained Unhidden, a human with some trickle of fairy blood from some far-distant ancestry. But could that trickle be forced into a firehose?

Manannán was in her mind, images flicking through her imagination, but Anna didn't understand them. He showed her riding a wave up to the sky. That would only bring her closer to Taranis, bringing her into his physical reach.

But that would remove her from the surrounding city and would keep their battle from destroying thousands of people. *Fair enough.*

Anna gathered water below her, flowing magic through her body, forming a tower. She cried out to Carlos, to Max, to Róisín, to anyone within earshot. "Get to safety!"

Carlos clutched her hand, but she slipped away, leaving him on the ground. Her constantly renewing column lifted her up, up, into the sky.

Lightning struck next to her. Anna flinched, but she hadn't been the target. She glanced down to Max laying on the ground, smoke rising from his chest. Róisín and Carlos dragged Max away.

She must do this alone.

Higher and higher the column lifted her as she gathered its power inside her, the fantastic potential of water.

Water could do a lot of damage. The breathtaking majesty of the Grand Canyon proved that. But such wonders took thousands of years to create. Anna needed something immediately dangerous, something that could slice and cut.

Solid water. Ice. Hail. Sleet. Water shot with laser precision.

Beneath her feet, she peeled water from her tower and crafted it into a dart. A wicked, long weapon, like the lawn darts her dad had played with as a child. The tip was incredibly sharp, a point formed and held with magic.

Anna's column reached the height of the clouds. They loomed so close, she might reach out and touch them. Fear gripped every muscle in her body, but she was committed to this action. She must protect her friends and the city below. She had to show Manannán her power and prove she was a worthy apprentice.

And she had to wipe that smirk off of Taranis' taunting face.

Anger boiled in her blood at his smug expression. How dare he threaten her mentor? Her friends? How dare he threaten *her?* Using that anger, she made more darts and launched them at the thunder god to pierce his stormy eyes.

The first one hurtled towards the god's face and he blinked. He shook his head and glared at her. **"You are trying to hurt me."**

Anna tried to imagine what Max might say. She put all the confidence she didn't have into a sarcastic answer. "You just noticed? Aren't you the clever one?"

Taranis growled, thunder rumbling across the sky. Her knees buckled and she almost lost her balance. She sent three more darts toward his eyes and one up his nose.

Anna had no idea if these little toys could actually hurt him. Who could wound a god? And if he was really formed of clouds, rather than flesh, nothing she did would affect him. Unless her magical darts could get through.

Someone shouted from below, but she couldn't make out words over the rushing water. Anna spared a glance down, but rain obscured everything except Manannán's solid blue form hulking next to her column of water. She hoped her friends had gotten to safety.

Clouds boiled around her as Taranis' face pinched into anger. Had her darts even tickled him? She just made him angrier. Instead of another dart, she fashioned a spear of ice and hefted it in her hand. Aiming carefully, she flung the spear with the speed of a bullet.

As her spear hit his left eye, he yowled. Thunder rumbled like a freight train in her head. She clapped her hands over her ears and fell to her knees on the water column.

Anna's concentration flagged and the water level dropped. Her stomach flipped and for a moment, she panicked. The water tower wavered dangerously.

She gritted her teeth and gathered her strength again, restoring the tower to its former strength and height. Then she crafted another spear.

Anna flung it toward the thunder god, her magic willing it straight at his eye again. Once again, Taranis howled and the sky thrashed with his pain and rage.

With a wicked surge of glee, she crafted a third spear.

"Enough."

Manannán's voice cut through the thunder like a hot knife through butter. Without her command, the column of water descended. Her mentor cupped his hand around her, placing her gently on the concrete of the parking lot. **"You did well, apprentice."**

Anna glanced around for her friends, but they'd all disappeared. She hoped they were safe and sound inside the building.

The sea god glowered at Taranis. **"You have seen my merest apprentice give you pain. Do you doubt what I can do if I should so choose?"**

Only rumbling answered him, but the storm clouds seemed lighter and the rain eased. Anna hid her dismay at being described as his *merest apprentice.*

**"Leave us, Taranis. And do not disobey me again."**

**"You have no command over me! Only the Dagda can do that!"**

**"In this matter, I do. Go."**

*Latest CNN Update: The latest reports coming in from Lima, Peru show ongoing fighting in the streets. The PHAE enclave in Lima has obtained military-grade weapons and the government has reported that this enclave has risen up to take over the city.*

*However, the Peruvian armed forces have fought back with their anti-terrorist task force, and they seem to have superior weaponry. The Joint Command has coordinated their attacks and succeeded in quelling the insurgents.*

*In addition, they've put out calls to the surrounding nations of Argentina, Bolivia, and Brazil to assist in the insurgency. So far, those calls have not been answered.*

*Reports of a PHAE enclave in Hawai'i being destroyed by locals are still awaiting independent verification. We have a reporter on the ground, and they hope to call in shortly. We'll keep you updated as we hear more details.*

**Tiberius:**

As his second-in-command, Josiah, droned on about his latest project, Tiberius stared at the wall, seeing nothing. Everything he'd worked for seemed to be coalescing into a single purpose.

He'd used his father's wealth to invest heavily in the oil industry and he'd grown that nest egg into a great empire. Slowly, his focus moved to lobbying and political intrigue, wielding his wealth as power behind the scenes. And this latest development had shifted it yet again.

He was proud of what he'd built, but in truth, it was beginning to lose some of its luster. Sure, they were doing God's work, and nothing was more important than that. Their primary duty now, to rid the world of these satanic magicians who call themselves the PHAE, was a major project, a necessary step along the stairway to heaven.

He might not be able to complete the work in his lifetime, as thousands, maybe even tens of thousands of these wicked non-humans were hiding in every country. New ones were popping up all the time.

In fact, he'd just gotten a report that the Chief of Staff of the Texas Governor had developed some sinful talent. It wasn't even an impressive one. The ability to make his fingernails glow, or some stupid bullcocky like that.

Tiberius let out a sigh and nodded at Josiah's pause, giving him permission to continue his monologue. Josiah was a decent guy, heartfelt about his faith and determined to cleanse his town. But the man's monotone delivery made Tiberius want to yawn, and he didn't want to be rude to the guy.

Instead, he took a sip of black coffee. Darn thing got cold while he was listening, so he grimaced, and rose.

"T? Are you okay?"

He waved as he walked to the sideboard and the coffee pot. "I'm fine, I'm fine. You were saying?"

As he poured a new cup of coffee, he glanced up to his wall to read, for the thousandth time, the Bible verse his wife had cross-stitched for him.

*What does it profit a man to gain the whole world, yet forfeit his soul?*
*– Mark 8:36*

He chewed his lips and took a sip of steaming coffee, still staring at the verse. He didn't like how it seemed to speak directly to him right now. It had never been his favorite, but Doreen had insisted on him hanging it there. Now, with her gone, neither hell nor high water would get him to take it down.

And he hadn't gained the world. He'd lost it. All of it.

Six months ago, Tiberius had gone out in the field, giving a tour of their drilling facilities for investors. He'd been feeling on top of the world, certain of a fresh crop of capital coming in for his new construction in the shale segment.

As he strode confidently back to his office from the parking garage, he slowed, annoyed, at the police barricades. Then he smelled smoke. When the sunlight dimmed, he glanced up, and he saw the black cloud. His blood chilled and he hurried past the barricades, ignoring the shouting officers. After he turned the corner, the gaping hole where his office had been filled him with rage and dread.

Even then, he hadn't realized the full measure of this disaster. When the police tried to pull him back, he jerked away from their grip, yanking his phone out of his pocket and desperately trying to reach his secretary. The phone didn't ring. He only got blank silence.

Then he tried his wife, and it did the same thing.

Tiberius had turned to stare at the black hole, laughing at him, mocking his pain.

Only later did he find out all the details, after comparing notes with his housemaid, his wife's sister, and the school.

His wife had come by to visit with their daughter, Annie-Mae, and their unborn son. They'd arrived about ten minutes after he'd left to give his tour. If they'd just gotten there a bit earlier, he would have taken them along.

He might have waited, if he'd realized they were coming. But the new tenants next door had been making strange noises, and he didn't want his investors to hear too much and decide against him, so he hustled them out of the building earlier than originally planned. In so doing, he left his family to their destruction.

Everything that was good in Tiberius died that day, too.

He stared again at the cross-stitch bible verse and clenched his teeth. He remembered a scrap of conversation with that American operative in Ireland, Joel something-or-other. Suddenly, he spun, and Josiah halted mid-sentence. "I need you to start a new project for me."

"But what about the—"

He held up his right hand. "Put that on hold. Put them all on hold. I need this done first. A-plus priority. D'you get me?"

Josiah gave a tired nod. "I get you, boss."

**Komie:**

Komie woke, but she didn't feel rested. She'd been exhausted this past week, ever since she helped Max save Róisín from Joel's angry mob of idiots. She'd used all her power reserves, and a few she didn't have, to trap them with rhododendron roots.

Her older bones and muscles weren't as resilient as these younger folks. Still, after almost a week of enforced bedrest, she needed to face this world again. Or at least get up off of her butt and do something. Komie detested being idle.

*This world.* One filled with ancient gods and unruly magic. A world out of a fairy tale, a world of legend from the Time Before.

Despite being in the middle of it, Komie still couldn't quite grasp how much things had changed. Sure, people have always held unusual powers. Her own people, natives of Maine and New Brunswick, had always spoken with the land, trees, and wild beasts. They'd honored their ancestors and the Great Spirit. But now, the Great Spirit was talking back, albeit through the voices of these archetypal gods.

These gods weren't her ancestors, though. These Irish gods weren't of her blood. Then again, so many Europeans had colonized her homeland in generations past, she couldn't know for certain if she carried any of their blood. She might never know for certain.

She *did* know that her power had grown substantially after the magnetic pole shift, like so many others. Instead of merely encouraging plants to sprout and grow with her prayers to the earth as she once did, now they grew visibly, right in front of her.

As they did that night on the cliff, when she captured the mob. She shivered at the memory.

Komie had never liked violence and had made a stand against being weaponized by the PHAE, just as Bintou had. And yet when an evil, angry mob attacked, she'd defended herself and those she cared for.

Komie hadn't hurt anyone, she just silenced and immobilized them until the authorities arrived. She still felt soiled as they took Joel away, to be put into prison for the rest of his life. A normal prison this time, not some torture cell. She'd at least been reassured on that account.

Shoving her covers aside, Komie swung her feet to the floor, stretching her back to pull the kinks out of it. As comfortable as the Byrne's guest bed was, with its homemade crocheted coverlets, she needed to get outside. For the first time since that night, she needed a walk through the forest, to be amongst growing things.

After dressing, the native woman padded down the stairs. No one stirred in the big old farmhouse.

Komie had helped Róisín to recover her strength, through the time-honored traditions of nurturing the sick. Róisín was the one with the talent to heal others, not her, but she was a mother and a grandmother. She knew how to care for sick children, even if they weren't her own. But Róisín and Max had left yesterday after a big argument.

Mid-summer mornings came early in Ireland, and the sun was already rising. Glancing at the kitchen clock, she gave a half-smile. *Yes, just 5am now.*

She heated water in the electric kettle for her morning tea and gazed out the kitchen window to watch sunlight spreading across the sky in peach-colored rays across the deeper blue of early dawn. Komie let out a sigh at the sublime beauty as birdsong filled her ears. She lived for mornings like this.

With a warm mug of tea cradled in her hand, she walked outside to commune with the plants of the garden first. To a few, she gave a nudge or two to grow with more health and efficacy. Another, she caressed, getting rid of the hint of fungus on its silver leaves.

These tiny acts of her talent no longer drained her, a sign that her power was growing, or that she had learned how to use it more wisely.

After greeting the garden, she wandered into the woods behind the house, a thick stand of trees between the Byrne Farm and the River Shannon.

Komie had always loved the forest. In her ancestral lands in northern Maine, she'd been friends with the trees and bushes. She knew each grove, had a favorite birch glade, and often sat beneath that old gnarled oak on the hill, sharing its grumpy heartbeat.

When she followed her love-struck son, Mihku, to Arizona, to live with his new wife, she missed the lush green hills terribly. The rocky, dry desert soil resisted even her powers, but she still managed to scratch out a serviceable garden.

Then Mihku died in Afghanistan, and she was left with his widow and their infant daughter. Komie's heart twinged at the thought of her granddaughter, her beloved Tansy. But Old Tom had promised to look after her, and he sent her regular letters with their progress.

Maybe someday, after the drama subsided, she could send for Tansy, to live in this lush landscape among the emerald-green trees, so similar to her ancestral lands.

The surrounding trees rustled in the morning wind. Komie smiled up at them, patting a trunk and thanking them for being themselves. She stepped over a rhododendron root, also thanking it for help when an intruder tried to attack the farm.

That night had also been exhausting and fraught with peril. But it helped teach her what she was capable of. And that lesson helped her save Róisín later. That was twice that type of plant had helped her commit violence.

The root answered. **I am coming.** The faint strain of a harp plucked in her mind, barely discernible.

Komie had heard the plants talk. The trees had spoken to her, but not with words. Certainly not words with a deep, male voice.

At this point, she'd spoken with several of the ancient Irish gods. The first had been Anu, who had contacted her, helped her, lent her power, but never manifested.

Then, when she tried to call upon Anu for more immediate help, she found Macha, a goddess of both war and fertility. That apprenticeship had been fraught with danger and violence. A rocky relationship, to describe it mildly.

Macha, however, then moved on to work with her priestess, the rude *draoi* named Caoimhe. And to be perfectly honest, Komie welcomed that shift. She was uncomfortable with Macha's bloodthirstiness and demanding nature. She craved a partnership with a gentler power.

Now, someone else called to her and evidently, he was coming.

He, who? She resisted the urge to run into the house and wake Colin, the keeper of all the old tales. He'd have some idea who might be contacting her in the early dawn.

Komie tried to remember the names of any male gods in the pantheon from his evening stories, but there were too many possibilities.

Who else was there? Cuchulainn, the hero? But he was a demigod, not a true god, at least, that's what she recalled from Colin's tales. Lugh had already shown up in Dublin. And Anna had her sea god.

Komie's cup of tea was almost cool, so she drained the dregs and sauntered back toward the house. While she wouldn't deliberately wake Colin, she'd start cooking breakfast. The aroma of bacon often roused folks.

As the eggs, bacon, and tomatoes sizzled in the skillet, her plan worked. The twelve-year-old twins, Liam and Hugh, entered the kitchen, rubbing sleep from their eyes. Komie hid a smile and made plates for them.

Fiona, the youngest at ten, stumbled in next and she made a third plate. Finally, both Colin and Michelle entered, fully awake, showered, and dressed.

Michelle gave Komie a grin and tried to take the pan away from her, but Komie held tight. "No, no, I've got this."

Michelle narrowed her eyes and glanced at the cutting board where a chunk of bacon was set out, ready to slice. She picked up a knife, but Komie gently took it back while speaking in a firm voice. "Sit down and enjoy your breakfast. I've got it this morning."

By the time Komie finally prepared her own plate, the children had finished theirs and were washing the dishes. She turned to Colin as she sipped her second cup of tea. "Colin, might I have a word once you're done with breakfast? I have some questions about the lore."

His eyes lit up as any enthusiast did when questioned about their favorite subject. He shoved the rest of his breakfast into his mouth like his sons had, eager to finish and get talking. Komie hid a chuckle and finished her tea at a more sedate and reasonable pace.

When she'd finished her meal, she handed Fiona her plate with a grin and followed Colin down the hall.

Once they settled in the library, Colin sat at the edge of his overstuffed leather chair. "Well? Did something happen?"

With a half-smile, Komie nodded. "Someone else contacted me. One of the gods, I'm sure. But I have no idea who."

His eyes glittered. "Where? When?"

"This morning, as I wandered in the woods. A male voice, deep and perhaps older. More mature? I'm not sure how to describe it properly. He simply said, *I am coming.*"

"*I am coming*? Intriguing, to say the least. What were you doing, precisely, when he spoke?"

"I'd just patted a tree trunk and stepped over a rhododendron root." She suppressed a shiver at the memories that plant evoked.

He tapped his chin and glanced up at a wall of books. Suddenly, he leapt up and grabbed one with a green fabric binding. Flipping through it, he stopped at a page, running his finger down the words.

Colin then grunted, shut the book, and replaced it, pulling another one, all while muttering under his breath. "Male voice. Mature. Trees."

He grabbed a third book, searched several places, then replaced that one, as well. His eyes darted across the bookshelves, then his eyes lit up. "Aha! This might help."

The Irishman pulled out a more modern volume, with a glossy paperback cover. When he opened the index, he muttered, "Hmm. Cian, Lugh, Manannán mac Lir. Crom Cruach? I sincerely hope not. Donn? Maybe Goibniu, the smith god. Not with trees, though. Nuada of the Silver Arm? Oghma the sun-faced god? Oh!"

Colin glanced up. "Maybe the trees aren't the clue. Did you hear music when he spoke?"

Komie furrowed her brow. "Actually, I think I did. Maybe a harp or a lute? I'm no expert in music."

A wide grin spread across Colin's face. "It might just be possible."

She cocked her head. "What's possible?"

"It might just be possible that the god who called you was the Dagda."

Komie scoured her memory for mention of that god. Colin must have mentioned him in his nightly tales of Irish folklore. He sounded important. More like a title than a name, like The Chief or The King.

He was one of the *Tuatha Dé Danann*, that would be certain. Most, if not all, of the gods who had recently sprung to life were part of that group of ancient Irish deities.

Her faulty memory dredged up a tale about a magical harp, which would explain his association with music. But what did he have to do with the growing things that she had power over?

Colin closed the book with reverence. "The Dagda is a father figure god. He's a king of the *Tuatha Dé Danann*, and associated with strength, humor, wisdom, and, more importantly to you, fertility and agriculture."

"Fertility? A male god?" She narrowed her eyes. "First Anu, then Macha, now the Dagda. How many fertility deities do you have?"

Colin let out a chuckle. "Aye, it does seem counter-intuitive, doesn't it? Not many mythologies attach fertility to a man. But he has a few magical artifacts. Among them is the magical harp you must have heard, but also a bottomless cauldron. It fills again and again, no matter how much food is taken from it. Thus, he feeds the multitudes. There are several aspects to fertility."

"Ah, an allegory to Jesus and the loaves and fishes in the Christian mythology?"

He gave a shrug. "Similar enough, but tales of the Dagda predate Jesus by at least five hundred years. He mostly uses that during great feasts and during battles. The good news, and I mean that as the pun it is, the Dagda is also known as the Good God. He's well known for his good nature, humor, and generosity."

Komie gave a cynical half-smile. "Well, that would be a bit of a change from Macha."

Colin's gaze narrowed. "I'd be cautious of what you say about her. She doesn't take kindly to criticism."

This time, Komie let out a snort. "I'd gathered that much already."

"Right." He slapped his hands to his knees and rose from his desk, handing her the book. "This has a chapter or two on The Dagda. Feel free to read about him in case he should contact you again. Or do you wish to initiate a conversation? Your sweat lodge is still out back. You might use it for a ceremony."

She shook her head. "I'd rather keep that for speaking with my own ancestors but thank you. I do appreciate it. And I may use it to ask their advice, but not yet. Let me digest this information first." She held up the book.

As Colin left, she sank into the armchair and opened the book to the relevant chapter. The Dagda was, as described in the book, a god of immense power. He had a club, *lorg mór,* which could kill nine men with one blow, but the handle could return the slain to life. Powerful indeed, to bring the dead to life. Very few gods were accorded this power.

Then the ever-full cauldron, *coire ansic,* with a ladle big enough for two people at a time. And then his magical harp, the *Uaithne.* Its music could cause the seasons to turn.

This last was much more to Komie's taste than a weapon of destruction. The harp could also be used in battle, but one story told of its use to lull a great hall to sleep to accomplish a theft without violence. A useful tool, especially in times of strife. Perhaps she could work with this god, after all.

He also owned two pigs, one ever-growing, the other ever-roasting. And something about fruit trees always well-laden with fruit. This god definitely loved a good feast, and this jived with his aspect of fertility.

As she perused the tales, she noticed the Dagda was often portrayed as comical, even goofy. He bared his bum and dragged his enormous penis on the ground.

She smothered a giggle at the image of any deity being so silly. And yet, he didn't lose the respect of the other deities, for all his antics. The Navajo had Coyote as a trickster god, and yet he garnered enormous respect.

Komie read about his family next. Married to the Morrigan, of whom the Macha was one aspect. *Well, that's interesting. Did Macha tell the Dagda about me?*

Was that why he'd responded to her in the forest? He fathered a great many other gods, most with names she didn't recognize. Midir, Bodb Dearg, Brigit, Oghma.

Brigit sounded familiar. Colin had told a tale about the goddess morphing into a Catholic Saint at some point in her history. Hadn't Bintou spoken of Oghma? No, she'd talked about Ogham, the Irish written language, but that was probably named for the god.

Komie closed the book and massaged her forehead. She'd taken in enough knowledge from the tales for now. Anything more and her head would burst.

She repeated the details in her head, to cement them in her memory. Now, she needed to learn directly from him, if he was truly coming.

Komie returned to the kitchen, now empty of the breakfast contingent as they went about their morning chores. Komie glanced at the clock in surprise. She'd spent two hours reading about the Dagda.

Komie strode through the kitchen door into the backyard. She nodded at Liam and Hugh as they weeded their mother's garden. They waved at her as she followed the forest path with Colin's book in her hands.

This wasn't the first time she'd called upon a god. Even before she'd moved to Ireland, heeding the call of the Unhidden around the world, Nokomis Nicholas had spoken to her own ancestors all her life.

Komie followed the ancient ways, the ways of her people, and did not fear the old ones. She respected them and their power, but fear and respect weren't the same things.

Now, she must call upon someone else's ancestors for questions she wasn't even sure how to ask.

Finding a clearing surrounded by towering oak trees, she sat cross-legged, though her knees cracked and ached. The ground cover was springy and green, smelling of crushed grass. Everything around her was natural and teeming with sound, soul, and life.

Komie quieted her mind, closed her eyes, and breathed in the woods. Buzzing insects came as music to her ears. The rustling of roots in the loamy soil sang to her. The very thrum of the earth became one with her heartbeat.

Once the calm of the natural was in tune with her own soul, she pulled out the paperback book Colin had lent her. She turned to the page with a prayer to the Dagda and read aloud.

*I call to you, O Dagda, kindly one,*
*Generous god of many talents,*
*Father of all children good-hearted and strong,*
*Master of treasures beyond telling,*
*Your cauldron always flowing,*
*Your trees always heavy with ripened fruit.*
*To renew the withered tree, as to wither the new.*

*Upon your oaken harp, Four-Angled Music,*
*You play to bring the land to new-grown life.*
*In hand, you wield the hefty club*
*To take or give back lives.*
*O Dagda, god of many names, granter of many gifts,*
*Bearer of wisdom and holder of knowledge,*
*Worker of wonders,*
*You shield me in safety,*
*You bless me with bounty.*

As she spoke, the ground rumbled beneath her. It might have been the roots of the trees and bushes, it might have been the earthworms greeting her, or it might be the god himself answering her call.

Komie prayed for the latter, but cautioned herself for disappointment. Calling any god was difficult, especially one she had no earlier connection with.

A part of her hoped she would fail. Komie set that unworthy notion aside. Self-doubt had no place when dealing with entities of power, no matter how good-natured a reputation they might have.

The ground stirred again, rumbling and grumbling like an empty stomach when the aroma of a feast is on the air. Komie grinned at this appropriate imagery for a god of plentiful feasts.

A bountiful harvest, a thanksgiving, in the American colonist sense of the word. She pushed her distaste for that holiday away. Thanksgiving, in the United States, was a holiday fraught with bad baggage for native people.

Back to the presence, she sent an inquiry to the grumbling earth. "Who is there?"

**"I am coming."**

The same mature male voice from before. Closer now. Stronger. Full of virility and power. A booming voice of thunder and earthquakes.

Oak leaves trembled, something more than wind making them rustle and shudder. Komie dug her hands into the earth to feel how it responded to this new arrival.

The dirt sang in her hands, reveling in the coming god. She found relief in that, as the earth had good judgment. If it delighted in his arrival, perhaps she could, too.

Running feet and harsh panting came up behind her. She turned to see Fiona, eyes wide, and Colin close on her heels. The Irish man pressed his hand to his side as he gasped out, "Komie! What are you doing?"

She spoke in a calm tone. "I've called the Dagda. He's coming."

The rumbling under her grew to roaring. The earth itself bellowed a welcome to the Dagda as he burst through the earth in front of Komie, Colin, and Fiona. The child hid behind her father.

A young oak tree rose, growing rapidly into a mighty tree. The tree's branches stretched for the sky, reaching the size of its neighbors in seconds. Bark split into crazed vein-like patterns and new bark sprung into the gaps. Then this new bark sloughed off, leaving a massive man with deep red hair and beard.

Ethereal harp music surrounded them, both insubstantial and tangible. Melody caressed them, dipping up and down until finally dying away. Komie felt the absence of that delightful music like a physical blow.

Fiona buried her face in her father's chest as he clung tightly to her. She peeked out, her eyes wide. Colin's face turned deadly pale. Only Komie gazed upon the new arrival with something resembling calm acceptance.

**"I am come."**

Komie replied to the obvious with a dry tone and ignored the chance to make a dirty pun. "Yes, I can see that."

The tall man wore an off-white long tunic, his belly sticking out, and long autumn-leaf-colored hair and beard. He stared at her for a moment before letting out a burst of laughter.

With a half-smile, Komie gestured toward the massive hole in the clearing. "You might want to fill that in."

He stopped laughing, a confused expression coming across his face. As the Dagda glanced around, he noted the eruption of dirt, roots, and wriggling earthworms. He let out another chuckle and waved his hand. The earth reformed beneath him, and he stamped it a few times, then clapped his hands. **"You care for the earth, child."**

"I am not your child, but yes, I care for the earth. The earth is our mother."

**"Just so, just so. Very well. My daughter has told me of you."**

She raised her eyebrows. *Which daughter?* "And what, precisely, has she said?"

He crossed his arms and gave her a grin. **"That you have strength, and that I should be respectful of it. Macha is seldom wrong about such things."**

Komie wrinkled her brow, turning to Colin. "Daughter? I thought Macha was his wife?"

The laughter returned and the Dagda's voice boomed. **"Macha has been many things to me. Mother, wife, lover, daughter, sister. There are no static relations in our world, child."**

She straightened her spine. "I said I was not your child. While I may number far fewer years than you, you are not my ancestor. They lived and died on shores far from here."

He waved that away, almost striking an oak tree. **"We can discuss this detail later. I have come to be your mentor. And that, my chi... and that is no small thing. By what name do you prefer to be called?"**

"You may call me Nokomis." Komie preferred her nickname, but something about this god put her on edge, despite his amiable reputation and demeanor. He wasn't as full of sheer anger and prickles as Macha was, but still, something felt ragged.

She didn't know what it was, and until she understood, she needed caution. "How can you speak modern English?"

**"I have been listening."**

Colin gasped behind her, and she spun to see what had surprised him. Thousands of sparkling lights danced in the surrounding woods. Even in the late morning light, sparks of blue, green, and purple danced amongst the trees, swirling around the Dagda, getting tangled in his beard, and clinging to his tunic. He laughed again, waved his hand, and made them twist like a whirlpool.

Well, it would take more than a magician's light show to make her trust him. But for now, she'd listen. He might have a lot to teach her.

# Chapter Four

"All good fortune is a gift of the gods, and you don't win
the favor of the ancient gods by being good,
but by being bold."
– Anita Brookner

**Komie:**

The Good God asked to be shown around, so Komie took him through the woods and garden behind the Byrne Farm.

Komie and the Dagda spent the rest of the morning in a careful dance of ritual, politeness, and questions about modern life. Then he asked to see more.

She discussed the possibilities with Colin, and he agreed to take them on a driving tour. "Mind you, just for the day. We need to be back to help Michelle with supper."

When the Dagda emerged from the oak tree, he'd been almost eight feet tall. As the day progressed, however, his form had shrunk to a more manageable six feet, similar to Colin's size. His girth was still hefty and his old-fashioned tunic marked him as an ancient.

Colin offered to lend him some clothing for their tour, but holding his belly, he laughed. Now that his size had reduced, his voice stayed at a human level. "And what would a slim man like you offer to cover this amazing stomach? Nothing! Ha!"

He had to squeeze himself into the car seat, but once he did, he marveled at the vehicle. "This chariot has no horses? Amazing! I am impressed. Unless you have tiny horses hidden under that?" He pointed to the car.

Colin opened the hood and explained that while they called it horsepower, the engine made a series of tiny fires, and the power of these tiny fires made the wheels turn.

The Dagda stared at the engine. "Incredible! I must see more of this."

With a raised eyebrow, Colin asked, "I thought you wanted a tour of the area?"

The god clapped his hands. "Yes, I want that! First that."

After they climbed in and Colin drove down the road, the Dagda asked, "Are all farms as small as yours?"

Colin pursed his mouth. "Our family doesn't rely on the production of our garden. We earn money from teaching others to use their talents."

"Ah, I see. You are like bards. I thought I detected the soul of a *seanachie* in you. And there are larger farms over there. What are they growing? What's that tall cylinder?"

As Colin explained the wonders of modern farming technology, Komie studied this affable god. By outward appearance, he could pass for a man, perhaps fifty years old. Solidly built, tall, broad-shouldered, but with tinges of gray in his long red hair and beard.

He carried a thick, gnarled walking stick of dark wood. Could this be the club she'd read about? He didn't carry a harp, but she had heard music when he appeared. Maybe he left his magical items wherever he came.

As they turned toward Limerick, the Dagda frowned. Highway ribbons rose and fell as they approached the city. Then, as buildings came into sight, he growled, "What have they done to my beautiful countryside? What travesty is this? Where are all my trees?"

Colin cleared his throat. "Ireland lost most of its trees in the last thousand years. Centuries of clearing land for farming, building ships by both the Vikings and then the English, almost destroyed our forests. But

102

we're replanting them. There are several government plans dedicated to that."

The Dagda clenched his fists, and the car shook as he growled again. Komie silently urged Colin to drive away from the city, toward the wild places, lest the god react with violence.

Colin must have had the same notion, for he turned west. Soon, they were driving along a single-track road down the coast, seagulls crying above them and waves crashing against the cliffs.

The Irish god's frown eased into a sigh. As Colin pulled into a parking lot with a brown sign indicating a scenic view, they all climbed out.

Hands on his hips, the Dagda gazed out at the Atlantic Ocean. Boats dotted the Shannon Estuary, both pleasure craft and fishing vessels. A few brave surfers dotted the beach below.

Colin gestured with wide arms. "As you can see, the coast is mostly unchanged. We still treasure the land."

Komie wrinkled her nose. "True, the Irish haven't paved the entire island over, but I would hesitate to call them the best at preserving nature."

The god turned toward her. "Explain."

Realizing she'd put her foot into it, she straightened her shoulders, determined to stand by her words. "I am of the native tribes of North America, a continent west across the ocean. Our people have honored the land for thousands of years."

The Dagda raised an eyebrow and sat upon a low, stone wall. He gestured for her to continue her story.

"For hundreds of generations, my people have lived part of the land. We are the People of the Beautiful River. The *Gici Niwaskw*, the Great Spirit, created the land, the rivers, and the animals for us to care for, and they will care for us."

He placed a finger to his lips and cocked his head. "Where does your Great Spirit live?"

Komie cocked her head. "Within the land itself, of course. Where do you live?"

He let out a belly laugh and almost fell from his perch. Komie felt herself smile in response, and Colin was grinning like a loon.

"I like you, Nokomis Nicholas. You make me laugh, and that is also to be cherished. I appreciate your love for the land. Will you be my guide in this new time? I am eager to learn all that it has to offer."

She exchanged a glance with Colin and he gave a shrug. Then, she straightened her spine and turned to the god. "I would be honored to be your guide."

***Latest CNN Update:*** *"New reports are coming in about the PHAE enclave on the Big Island in Hawai'i. We're joining our reporter on the ground for more information. What's the situation, Shelley?"*

*"As you can see from the billow of smoke behind me, the PHAE enclave here has been destroyed. However, we have yet to confirm if this is an action by the locals, the PHAE themselves, an accident, or some outside agent. We haven't yet been able to discover if there were people inside the building at the time of the explosion."*

*"What sort of outside agent would have that kind of access?"*

*The reporter looked intensely uncomfortable, her gaze shifting to several places before she continued. "It is said that the goddess, Pele, has been seen near the building, and she looked as if she was on a destructive rampage."*

*"What are the legends about Pele?"*

*"The Hawai'ian Islanders refer to her as Tūtū Pele, the goddess of volcanoes and fire. She is the creator of the islands, which is true enough, for volcanic islands. She is a child of the Sky Father and the Earth Mother."*

**Qacha:**

As Qacha became aware of her surroundings, she catalogued sounds and scents. Birdsong. Wood smoke. Water lapping against a shore. Fresh-cut hay. Honey.

None of these made any sense to her. What did she last remember? A woman. No, not a woman, a goddess named Brigit. A powerful goddess, with thick arms and strong muscles, standing as tall as herself, clad in leather armor.

The Mongolian woman pushed herself into a sitting position, swinging her legs over. She was in a roundhouse with a thatched roof and a central firepit. The fire smoldered as a large bronze cauldron hung over it on a tripod. Something savory simmered in the pot, and Qacha's stomach rumbled. When had she last eaten?

Flashes of memory came to her. The endless time in that cell of darkness, madness, crawling creatures tormenting her. Had Brendan come to rescue her, or had she imagined him? She didn't even remember how she'd escaped.

And now she was here. She glanced out of the window, but the greenery looked much the same as anywhere in Ireland.

Her bare feet tingled as she stood, and she shifted balance until the blood flowed again. She peered into the cauldron and stirred it with a wooden spoon, unwilling to let food get scorched. Beef, garlic, onions, potatoes, sage, and rosemary. It should be ready soon.

Qacha crept to the door and glanced around, trying to find her hostess, but no one was in the glade. A wide, shallow river lined with reeds hugged the clearing. A rocky cliff hovered behind the hut, forming a box canyon. She really didn't see a way out of this.

This Brigit seems to have brought her to another jail. A far more pleasant prison than the last, but still a jail.

Movement out of the corner of her eye made her whirl, memories of those creeping creatures tickling her fear, but it was only a cat.

Then she narrowed her gaze, as the cat looked exactly like her own pet, Manol. But Manol should be safely on the Byrne farm, in Fiona's capable care. Qacha missed him and wished she was with him, away from this odd place.

She crouched with her hand out, as she would with Manol, to beckon him closer. The creature didn't move like a cat, and its eyes sparkled with intelligence. They came closer with cautious steps.

Qacha pursed her lips. "You are not Manol."

The cat-creature shook their head and spoke in a rasping voice. "That is true. I am not Manol. You may call me Beagan. It means small, and I am small."

Colin's stories about the dangers of trusting any fae creature kept her cautious. "Why do you look like Manol? I do not like it."

Beagan shimmered and changed into another cat-like form, not so similar to Manol's markings, and stood on their hind legs. "I thought it might make you more comfortable. I am sorry if I was wrong."

The corner of her mouth twitched, but she still didn't like the deceit. Beagan barely came to her knee, even standing on his hind legs. "But how do you know what Manol looks like? And why do you want me to be comfortable?"

The Fae creature gave a shrug, an odd gesture in a feline body. "I have been visiting Manol. Brigit asked me to check on him, to ensure he thrived and is being well-cared for. I like his company. He is pleasant to talk to. He misses you, though."

"Talk? What does Manol say?"

"He talks about you a great deal. He wishes you would come back. But the girl who takes care of him is nice, too. She pets him and squeezes him a lot. He doesn't mind the squeezing, because she brings many treats."

Now Qacha had to smile. Such simple pleasures from her pet. She was pleased that Fiona was taking good care of her cat, if this creature spoke the truth.

"Will you be seeing Manol again soon?"

Their eyes flicked around the clearing and their tail whipped a few times. "I will."

"Can you please tell him that I also miss him? I will try to return to him."

"I can pass on that message. But now I must go. I can never stay here long."

With a pop, Beagan disappeared.

*Latest CNN Update: We have received an update on the ongoing situation in Athens, Greece. We reported earlier that several gods from the ancient Greek pantheon, notably Artemis, Athena, Apollo, and Hera, had made themselves known in the Parthenon. They appeared as shining beings, twice as tall as normal humans, at the base of Mount Olympus.*

*However, their initial welcome by the local authorities resulted in a conflict. Modern military personnel surrounded the area, and the new-arrived gods attempted to fight them.*

*The local military held fast, and their modern weaponry gave them an advantage. The Greek gods have now evidently retreated to wherever they originated from. Reports of new activity on the slopes of Mount Olympus have not yet been confirmed.*

*Protests in Athens are reaching a heated frenzy, with people on both sides getting angry. Some are welcoming the ancient gods back to the world, while others are demanding their destruction. We will keep you informed of any further developments on this story.*

**Komie:**

Colin held the mobile phone to his ear, nodding several times. The Dagda looked at him with a curious expression. Komie could barely make out Ciara's excited voice.

Finally, the Irish man said, "Right, fine. We'll go now. Yes, right now. Should be there in a few hours. Yes, I told you, we're on the west coast. Not that I'm aware of. Right. Bye, now. Bye. Grand. Bye."

He let out a sigh and glanced up. "We're to go to Dublin. Ciara says that Lugh is insisting on it."

Komie furrowed her brow. "Lugh? Which one is he?"

The Dagda let out a belly laugh. "Ha! Lugh is a proper peacock, but he's usually in the center of things. By his own design, of course. But where is he?"

Colin glanced toward the car. "He's in Dublin, our capital city. That's about a two-hour drive."

"City? Two hours in that small carriage? I don't wish to do that."

Komie placed a hand on his arm. "A city is a large settlement, with thousands of people living in a small area. There are many wonders to be seen there, including tall buildings, a massive harbour, and many technological wonders."

Then she remembered his harp and smiled. "There's even a historic harp in the Long Library at Trinity, isn't there, Colin?"

The Dagda's eyebrows rose at mention of the harp, and Colin nodded vigorously. "Sure, and there is! It's our oldest harp, and we're the only country in the world to have a musical instrument as a national symbol."

Evidently, the promise of a harp convinced the Dagda to endure the two-hour drive, as he squeezed back into Colin's car. They passed horse farms and rolling hills, but after a while, the farms to either side faded into suburbs.

As they grew closer to their destination, Komie grew more nervous. If the Dagda had been upset at the modernization around Limerick, how would he react to Dublin? She didn't want to be in the car if he lost his temper.

As they passed Kildare, the Dagda said, "You have many people living in the country. I see horses and farms and many dwellings. The people of Eire seem to have prospered. How many live on the island now?"

Colin changed lanes to get around a tractor. "We have about five million in Ireland and another two million in Northern Ireland."

"Northern Ireland? Is there a reason you specify this separately? Is Eire no longer divided into five regions?"

Their host let out a chuckle. "People still use the general region names. Ulster, Connacht, Munster, Leinster, and Meath. But we divide those into counties, and the area of Ulster is claimed by England."

The car grew silent as Colin held his breath. Komie remembered there was a great deal of angst about Northern Ireland being part of the UK but had no idea how the Dagda would see such a foreign occupation.

"England. That is the island to the east?"

"In simple terms, yes. It's held the northern counties for almost a thousand years."

"Hmm."

Used to Macha's mercurial mood and outspoken manner, Komie was almost disappointed by the Dagda's restraint. But she felt grateful to finally be attached to someone with a more reasonable temper. Komie supposed someone who could calm the masses with a magical harp must have some diplomatic skill.

The Dagda stared out of the window with intense curiosity as they entered the city proper. They found parking at Leinster House and climbed out of the car.

The Good God spun in a circle, taking in the surrounding buildings, people, and bustle. "This is incredible! Yes, there is death of the trees. I can feel their sorrow beneath my feet. But the people thrive! Humans are spending their day without working in the fields or at the loom. Music is coming from the drinking houses, their voices rising in song and instruments caressing their ears. There's bounty and leisure here. That speaks of great wealth and comfort. The people of this time have done well for themselves, Colin Byrne. I am pleased."

That was one hurdle leapt, then. Now for the next. They led the Dagda through the ornate doors of the governmental building and down the hall. He insisted that they stop for each painting on the wall, the line of Taoiseachs since Ireland's independence. "These are your leaders?"

Colin nodded, a wry smile on his face. "They are."

"But you have no women?"

"None elected Taoiseach. We've had women presidents, though."

The Dagda stopped at the one of the last paintings. "What is the difference between your president and your Taoiseach?"

With a chuckle, the Irish man said, "The president is ceremonial, and elected with a direct vote from the people. The Taoiseach does most of the work and is selected by the party in power."

The god shook his head. "That sounds complex. How do they handle disagreements? Do they fight?"

"There are rules but yes, they can fight. With words, rather than weapons but there have been some spectacular debates. The Irish still love a good fight, when they can find one. Some things don't change."

He clapped the Irish man on his shoulder. "This is good! I approve. Now, where is Lugh hiding? It's unlike him not to seek the spotlight."

Colin led the Dagda to a conference room. Bintou and Ciara sat along one side of a table, while Lugh stood at the head.

Lugh rose, his arms wide. "*Eochaid Ollathair!* It has been much too long since I laid eyes upon your face!"

The two gods hugged each other tight, with all the affection of brothers, and the air seemed to seep out of the room. Komie slid into the chair next to Bintou, while Colin greeted Ciara with cautious side glances to the two gods.

Komie kept her voice low. "Bintou, how are things?"

"Well enough, when we can keep this one out of trouble. That's a job." She gave Komie a grin and gestured toward Lugh.

She was glad Bintou seemed in a better mood. She'd rarely smiled after Martin died, but now her face lit up with humor. "Did you pass on the Dagda's questions?"

Bintou shook her head. "I figured it would be easier to let them discuss things face-to-face rather than risk something, well, lost in translation."

They both turned to watch the old gods. They'd fallen into ancient Irish. Bintou could understand every word, but Komie was lost. She didn't even understand any modern Irish.

She still couldn't make head or tails over which gods could speak English. Each seemed to have different abilities at languages, much like humans. Komie had never been good at learning languages outside of English and her native Wolostiquey.

Komie recognized a name and her head perked up. They were talking about Manannán mac Lir. Her gazed passed back and forth between the two gods, wondering what they were planning. Then she exchanged a glance with Bintou, vowing to ask the Malian woman about it later.

***Latest CNN Update:** PHAE enclaves in Greece and Peru have entered negotiations with their respective national governments to work towards a reconciliation plan to integrate their populations. However, reports have come in of violence and riots in Peru, and there's a possibility that the promise of negotiation was simply a ruse to lure the Unhidden from their protective walls. More information as we learn new details about the conflict.*

*The United Nations has begun discussions about forming autonomous enclaves for Unhidden locations, but most national governments so far queried have refused to answer.*

*There are still no new developments in Omsk, and the barrier remains impenetrable to all efforts to date. The government of Russia has requested a representative to discuss negotiations, but no one has been sent out.*

*On Hawai'i, a humanoid form emerged from the largest active volcano, Mauna Loa. Witnesses say the form seems to be made of lava. The state Governor has sent a liaison, but so far, no communication has been verified.*

**Qacha:**

Qacha was determined to get out of this fairy land and to the real world, but she must move cautiously. She had no wish to make an enemy of this goddess.

So far, Brigit had been a kind hostess, catering to her needs with kindness. She even asked Qacha to cook while Brigit worked at the forge.

Cooking was always her greatest joy, but she was also so used to the steps, it freed her mind to form a plan.

They had no meat in Faerie, but she found several shelves with vegetables and mushrooms. Using the chopping board, she cut up turnips, mushrooms, greens, and prepared a stir fry.

When Brigit came inside and washed the soot from her hands, Qacha filled two wooden bowls, placing them at the table.

Brigit peered at the meal and gave a single nod, taking a bite. She raised her eyebrows. "This is quite tasty. Your cooking skill is impressive."

A warm flush heated her cheeks. Qacha was never one to solicit praise, but she had to admit, it did feel nice to get it from a goddess. "Thank you. I would like to cook more interesting meals for you, something from my homeland. To show you the full extent of my talents."

"I would welcome new tastes."

After a few bites, Qacha said, "There are several spices and other ingredients I am lacking. I would have to fetch them from the human world."

She held her breath while Brigit ate several more mouthfuls. Then the goddess gave a shrug. "Very well. We shall go after the meal. There are places in your world I should like to explore, as well."

Letting out a soft sigh, Qacha relaxed her bunched shoulders. Had it really been that easy? But she'd need to be careful not to squander this chance.

Once they were ready to go, Brigit asked, "Where must you obtain your ingredients?"

Qacha searched her mind but came up blank. "I'm not certain, but we should be able to find information about an international grocery store. If we go to Leinster House, Ciara can help us. She knows everything in Dublin."

"Leinster House. That is the large building on the square, in front of the park?"

Qacha gave a nod. Without further preamble, Brigit grabbed her hand, pulling her from the stool. Her empty bowl clattered to the ground, spilling the last bit of liquid on the flagstones.

Everything went gray and her stomach wrenched, the stew threatening to come back up. And then they were standing on a Dublin street in the midst of a crowd of angry protestors.

They shouted and carried signs. Qacha had seen similar groups of protestors many times now, and she'd grown bored with their xenophobic demands. *Unhidden go home* or *Pure humans only.* The cynic in her wondered how much they were being paid for their outrage.

Brigit shoved their way through the mass of people until Qacha spied the entrance gate for Leinster House. Once they got free of the mob, Brigit cast a haughty glance over her shoulder. "Who are these lawless rebels? Where is the chieftain's guards to quell them? It is ridiculous to allow such criminals here!"

"They are allowed to protest. This country has a guarantee of free speech."

Brigit shook her head as Qacha brought her through the gate and into the quiet halls. "We should be able to find Ciara quickly. If she's not here, someone will know where to find her."

She began to stride toward one of the conference rooms, but Brigit grabbed her arm. "Wait. This is where your rulers live, correct?"

Qacha gave a shrug. "Ireland's rulers work here, yes."

"I wish to meet them. And I want to see the modern Ireland. You will show me."

The Mongolian woman blinked. "I am only a recent arrival myself. I am not qualified to show you the country. Besides, you'll need governmental approval for many places."

"How do I obtain such approval?"

"Again, Ciara is our best resource. Please, allow me to search for her."

Brigit pursed her lips and crossed her arms. "Very well. Show me to this Ciara."

After they found the room where Ciara and the others were waiting, the goddess walked straight to Lugh and they clasped forearms.

Qacha drew Ciara aside. "I was able to escape under the guise of finding Mongolian spices to cook with, but Brigit wants to tour some places."

With sidelong glances at the powerful goddess, Ciara spoke in a fierce whisper. "This isn't the time to go playing tourist, Qacha. After the crisis is over, we can send all the PHAE and their gods around for a grand holiday, fit for a Victorian noblewoman, but right now, we've got more important things to deal with."

Qacha glanced at Brigit again, her voice growing harsher. "Do you wish to tell an Irish goddess no?"

The Irish woman shook her head with a rueful smile. "Of course not. But I can't tell her yes, either. Look, let me make some arrangements. Has she given any particulars of what she wants to see? Maybe she'd like to see the Guinness storehouse or the dockyards."

From the other end of the hall, Brigit raised her head. "You will show me your defense capabilities."

Ciara cursed under her breath. "She can hear us from here? Feck. Right, then. Let me see who I can call. Wait here."

The tall, elegant woman turned and strode toward the administrative offices, her stiletto heels clicking on the hardwood floor. Lugh and Brigit approached, a mischievous gleam in the goddess's eyes. "Will it be done?"

Qacha gave a shrug. "I have asked. That is the only thing in my power. It is now in Ciara's hands."

Lugh placed his hand on Brigit's shoulder and squeezed. "Ciara gets things done. She is a worthy seneschal. She would make any chieftain of our time proud."

Brigit let out a snort. "Then why does she torture herself with those knives on her feet? It seems like some painful conceit, like those Christ-worshippers were. Only interested in their pain."

Lugh let out a hearty laugh which echoed down the empty hallway. Qacha hid a smile herself, as she'd never truly understood the allure of high-heeled shoes herself.

Of course, being a woman over six feet tall, she had no desire to make herself taller, even if the shoes were comfortable, and they definitely weren't. High heels were impractical in the kitchen, even dangerous, and she'd spent most of her adult life working in one.

A twinge of nostalgia gripped her heart, missing her time as a chef. Even in that horrible corporate hotel kitchen, when she'd been delegated to a sous-chef role. At least she'd been cooking.

A door slammed somewhere, but no one appeared. Footsteps faded away from somewhere else. A roar came from outside, perhaps a plane flying overhead.

When Ciara finally returned, she wore a bemused expression. "The Minister of Defence, *An tAire Cosanta*, has agreed to a tour of our Defence Forces Headquarters in Newbridge."

The Irish goddess gave a single, gracious nod. "Where is this Newbridge?"

"Less than an hour's drive from here. I'll accompany you on the tour. Lugh, do you wish to come as well?"

He exchanged a cryptic glance with Brigit. Literal sparks flew from their eyes and Qacha's blood chilled.

Then, the goddess said, "That is something Macha would be more interested in. I wish to see where you create the weapons."

"Create them? Like a manufacturing factory?"

Brigit shook her head, glancing at Lugh again. "No, that's not the right word. Where you *discover* how to create things."

Qacha asked, "Experiments? Research and development?"

Brigit grinned wide and nodded. "Yes. Take me to those places. I wish to see your technology. Is that the word?"

Lugh patted her on the shoulder. "You are learning this modern world quickly. The Dagda will be proud."

Ciara tapped a finger on her lips. "I can take you on a tour of our research facilities here in Dublin. I don't need additional clearance for that."

Brigit made a noise in the back of her throat but gave a curt nod. "That will suffice for now."

They climbed into a minivan jitney and the entire trip, Qacha tried to puzzle out what Lugh and Brigit were trying to learn about modern science. Were they just assessing Ireland's capabilities? Or something more sinister?

When they first manifested, the gods had made the offer to help with military might if the PEM invaded again. Perhaps they just wanted to know what they might be up against.

Qacha, however, had always been pessimistic, and this didn't seem likely, even when viewed in the kindest light.

Brigit was no shrinking flower. The red-headed goddess had massive upper arms, and even if she had no god-like powers, would surely be deadly in a fight. Lugh had a sculpted muscular chest and arms. Together, they could rip mere humans apart with their bare hands.

Qacha meant never to allow herself to be in that situation. And hopefully, she wouldn't let anyone she cared for be there, either. That list of people had grown longer than ever. She wasn't sure that was an entirely bad thing, but it made her decisions more complex.

They traveled to a laboratory housed in a military research complex and greeted by a young, nervous man named Gerald. "We have a regular tour group coming through in two hours. Would you like to wait for that?"

Brigit gave him a haughty stare. "We will not wait."

He cleared his throat several times before continuing. "Right, then. Just wait, uh, I need to get badges. I'll be right back."

Once Gerald returned with four green harp badges, and they showed Brigit and Lugh how to attach them to their clothing, he took them down a long hallway, peeking into each lab room.

Gerald described what projects they were working on at each station. Brigit had several clarifying questions, some of which Gerald could answer, and some of which the laboratory workers could help with. A few were beyond either resource.

After they'd touched upon each room, Gerald took them back to the first room they'd visited and pulled aside one of the research technicians.

"Patik, can you do some of your splashy demonstrations, the sort you give to students who are considering a career in chemical research?"

The technician gave a pleasant grin and proceeded to pour some chemicals from one beaker into another, resulting in a colorful mass growing at a rapid rate.

The demonstration was a big hit, and once Brigit discovered the capabilities of chemistry, it was difficult to get her away from the laboratory.

Pitak went on to explain that this facility had been created to manufacture new explosives during the Civil War, but now worked on refining existing munitions.

Once she got the structure fixed in her mind, Brigit demanded her own experiment station. "I will need assistants that are familiar with your procedures and materials. I will bring in my own assistants to learn the process. Lugh, fetch Goibniu, Luchtaine, and Creidhne. They have the intelligence and curiosity sufficient to learn the modern process."

Gerald looked like someone had killed his puppy, but after Ciara gave him a solemn nod, he rushed away to find an empty station and some assistants. Qacha hoped he also assigned a more senior member, to keep an eye on whatever the goddess wanted to do.

Ciara had needed to return to the bunker, but left Qacha in charge of the goddess. Lugh disappeared in a flash of light, presumably to fetch the gods Brigit had listed, as Qacha followed Brigit around, trying to keep her out of trouble.

Qacha didn't like this assignment one bit. Yes, she had some martial training, but that was with tactics, strategy, and horseback archery, not modern munitions or explosives.

Still, she probably had a better military background than anyone else she'd met in PHAE, other than Max, so she resolved to do her best. But her only experience with actual chemistry was in baking.

By the time Lugh returned with three new Irish gods in tow, Brigit had wrangled a room assigned to her, along with three lab assistants. Each one looked terrified of the Irish goddess, though one had gray in his beard and looked slightly less frightened.

The lab dispatch provided the new arrivals with lab coats, safety gear, and required them to attend a safety training lecture and sign protocols and waivers. Nervous Gerald had long since disappeared, probably to guide that other tour group.

Goibniu, Luchtaine, and Creidhne remained silent as Brigit grilled her lab assistants. Qacha studied the newcomers, trying to get their measure.

Goibniu was the eldest, a beefy man with massive shoulders, even more so than Lugh. His longer hair and beard made seem rougher. Luchtaine looked more slender, almost delicate in comparison, with thin fingers and brown eyes. Creidhne was also thin and scowled as the assistants explained modern lab procedures and the safety gear they must all wear. Qacha wondered how well any of them understood modern English.

A harsh cry cut into her musing. Brigit held her right wrist, and her hand was open wide. "What did you burn me with? What was in that container?"

The lab assistant backed away, shaking her head. "N-n-nothing, Miss Brigit. Truly! The beaker was empty!"

The goddess' hand looked red and swollen, tiny blisters already forming. Qacha searched the floor and saw nothing but a plastic beaker on the ground.

Another lab assistant bent to pick up the beaker while keeping his eyes on Brigit. He placed it back on the counter, but Brigit didn't attempt to touch it. Instead, she directed him to mix the substances they'd been explaining. As the two liquids mixed, a hissing, angry foam bubbled out from the beaker.

Qacha stared at the beaker and pursed her lips. *Very interesting.*

# Chapter Five

"Neither gods nor men can foresee
when an evil deed will bear its fruit."
– Bodhidharma

*Latest CNN Update: As part of our ongoing series, we're bringing you news of protests against the Unhidden in several major cities throughout the world.*

*Demonstrations are ongoing in Beijing, Lima, Cairo, Ankara, Berlin, and Hong Kong, and they are intermittent in Hanoi, Addis Ababa, Mexico City, Tehran, and Rome. Several cities across larger countries, such as the United States, Australia, Russia, and the United Kingdom have reported violent outbreaks. The response to each of these outbreaks have been dependent on the country, with the worst atrocities reportedly occurring in Russia and China.*

*World leaders are meeting to discuss this worldwide crisis at an emergency peace conference in Buenos Aires this weekend. We will bring you updated news on that conference as it happens.*

**Hiroki:**

Hiroki wrung his hands. He wasn't looking forward to this arranged meeting in the slightest. In fact, he'd rather meet with his father than this

Macha, this Irish war goddess. He couldn't calm his racing heart and might even run away as soon as she spoke.

He glanced at Paul and Ciara, who'd agreed to accompany him. The gods had insisted that they hold this meeting in front of Leinster House, and then they would go on their tour.

The ever-present protesters were thin today, a mere dozen weary people holding up their vitriolic signs. Hiroki was almost used to them now, though he still felt a wave of shame every time he saw them.

Oghma had promised that Macha wouldn't harm him. And Hiroki had to trust a god's word. But Oghma seemed like a peaceful god, one more fascinated by knowledge and history than in weapons and fighting. So how could he understand what a war goddess might do?

Lugh stood in the center of the city square with his arms open wide. Then, a russet glow formed next to him, shifting like a dark rainbow in the summer sun.

As Macha manifested, her eyes glowed like embers, full of fire and anger. Something like a vengeful *Onryō*, a Japanese ghost bent upon redressing the wrongs done by the living world. The protesters didn't even notice.

Hiroki asked, "Is that her? The war goddess?"

Ciara rolled her eyes. "Who else would she be? Santa Claus?"

He scowled at the Irish woman, his fists clenched, but now was not the time to get into an argument.

The goddess wore her dark hair in tight braids against her head and her skin was milky white, almost as pale as Masaaki's. She wore practical armor, with leather and bronze decorations that wouldn't hinder her movement. A massive sword hung in a scabbard on her back. As she strode along beside Lugh, her long legs kept easy pace with the tall god.

Hiroki wanted to run so fast and so far, that this frightening entity would never find him, even though that was a foolish notion. She was a goddess, and if she wished to hunt him for pleasure, there was little he could do to prevent her.

But then again, maybe there was. He had the power of persuasion, didn't he? Would his Unhidden talent work on the gods?

Paul patted his shoulder and gave it a squeeze. "It'll be grand, Hiroki. We're both here with you, now."

He gave the Irish man a nod, but he didn't really believe either of them were truly with him. They stood beside him, but they'd probably leave if any true danger appeared.

Hiroki stepped forward, and with all the confidence he didn't have, gave a respectful bow from the waist. "I greet you, goddess Macha, on behalf of the Protectorate for unHidden Advancement and Education. You are welcome."

Macha's red eyes bore into him, as if she was drilling into the inner recesses of his soul and found him wanting. Then she released his gaze, turning to Ciara. "I have seen you before."

Ciara gave a nod with all the elegance and grace that Hiroki envied. "I was with Nokomis Nicholas when she spoke to you once. However, we haven't been formally introduced. I'm Ciara Doherty, also with PHAE. While Hiroki is our honored spokesperson, I can arrange things that you might require."

The Irish goddess gave a curt nod and turned to Paul. "And why are you here?"

A huge grin spread across his face, and he opened his arms wide. "Are you kidding? A chance to meet an actual goddess? This is bonkers! I've dreamt about this my entire life!"

Hiroki was horrified at Paul's disrespect, but the corner of Macha's mouth twitched so slightly, Hiroki decided he must have imagined it. She turned toward the car. "I am to be given a tour. We shall begin now."

Just as Paul opened the door, the sound of running feet made everyone turn. His best friend, Masaaki, was running toward them. As he got close, he slowed, his breath coming in rasping pants. "I thought I'd missed you! Sorry I'm late."

Lugh and Macha exchanged glances at his arrival. Lugh asked, "Is this a fae? I don't recall seeing this color skin amongst humans. Are there more variations we haven't been informed of?"

Masaaki leaned forward, bracing his hands on his thighs as he struggled to catch his breath. "I'm not a fae. This coloring is my Unhidden power."

Macha pursed her lips. "That is not a useful talent."

Masaaki cocked his head and gave her a shrug. "Not everything has to have a use."

Again, Hiroki thought his friend should be more respectful to actual gods. He tried to catch Masaaki's eyes, but his friend paid no attention to Hiroki. A true friend would have noticed his disapproval.

After they piled into two cars, they were driven to the Department of Defense in Newbridge. The cityscape faded to suburbs before they pulled into the Newbridge town centre.

They passed a sign for *An Roinn Cosanta*, with a stylized man holding a spear and a hint of a harp on his body, and then pulled into a series of long buildings. Hiroki appreciated the design while still being confused about the purpose of the shapes.

As soon as they entered and the door closed behind them, a brass military band played a tune Hiroki didn't recognize. By the way Ciara and Paul straightened and mouthed some Irish words, he guessed it might be the Irish national anthem. It had that slow, ponderous pomposity that many anthems carry.

Lugh grinned at the music and began dancing, pulling a reluctant Macha into a spin and horrifying the nearby military aide in her sharp uniform.

When the performance finished, the aide stepped forward and gave them a wide smile. "Hello and welcome to our facility. I'm Lieutenant Crowley, and I'm to show you around."

She brought them past several large rooms, filled with cubicles and people bent over their computers. "This is the main administrative hub of our armed forces. We are in charge of the raising, training, organization, maintenance, equipment management, discipline, and regulation of our troops."

With a haughty expression, Macha waved her hand. "I am not interested in watching scribes write. They are not warriors."

Lieutenant Crowley cleared her throat and led them to another room. "This is our intelligence centre. These researchers perform background checks of key personnel, potential threats, and counter-sabotage initiatives."

Macha raised one eyebrow. "But they are also scribes?"

"They work mostly on computers, yes, but they are highly trained individuals with top security clearance."

Lugh wrinkled his nose. "These are not exciting either, Macha."

A bell rang, and crowds of people flooded the hallway. Hiroki backed up against the wall to avoid them.

Crowley glanced at her mobile phone. "Ah, that will be lunch. Please, we are honored to host you for a meal."

By the time they reached the cafeteria, Hiroki's fear of the goddess had morphed into boredom. Military things didn't excite him nearly as much as, say, a film studio tour might. His stomach growled in hunger, though, and he was gratified for a meal break.

Without much thought, he grabbed a tray and pulled several plates of food from the items on offer. A bowl of beef stew, roasted potatoes, a green salad, and a cup of tea. He found a table as the others got their food.

Just as he took his first sip of tea, Macha's angry voice rose, and she stood with her feet apart and her hands braced on the sneeze-shield at the buffet.

Masaaki murmured something to her that Hiroki couldn't hear, but his words didn't mollify her, and she growled at him, her eyes literally sparking. Hiroki sprang to his feet and hurried over to find out what happened.

"This food is an insult! I will not be treated like the lowest tacksman."

Hiroki blinked, trying to puzzle out the unfamiliar term. *What is a tacksman?*

Ciara came to his rescue. "This is the way they serve all their guests, Macha, no matter what the rank. It allows each guest to choose the food they wish to eat."

He glared at Ciara. She ought to have used a more diplomatic tone. Was she trying to anger the goddess?

"Only a peasant would eat this way!" The goddess pushed down on the plexiglass and suddenly, it cracked, large pieces shattering and falling into the food, onto the floor, and one bouncing and hitting Hiroki in the shin.

Hiroki jumped back and put out his hands, palms down, in a placating gesture. His skin tingled as he drew in his power. "You should remain calm. I'm certain if the food is not to your standards, we can find some way to improve it." Hiroki glanced at Paul and cocked his head, gesturing toward the kitchen doors.

Paul gave a hasty nod and ran off, presumably to find someone in charge. Hiroki continued in his calm voice. "If you would please take a seat while we make arrangements, I will get you something to drink in the meantime. Would you like tea?"

His Unhidden power put impetus behind the suggestion, and tingling covered his skin.

Masaaki placed a hand on Hiroki's forearm. "I think she'd enjoy whiskey more, don't you?"

Macha's eyes narrowed, but she stepped away from the broken sneeze guard, allowing several cafeteria staff to start cleaning up the mess. "Whiskey? What is whiskey? I've heard it spoken of but haven't tasted it."

Hiroki led her to the table where he'd left his own food and continued in his calm tone. "Certainly, we can let you try some whiskey. Masaaki, would you go in search of some?"

The other Japanese man pulled Lieutenant Crowley aside and together, they left the cafeteria.

Ciara turned to the goddess with a wide smile. "I think you'll enjoy whiskey. It's an alcohol distilled to great strength and flavor. Many have termed it a drink fit for the gods."

Macha grunted as she finally took her seat. Lugh still wore a bemused grin as he settled next to the war goddess. Then they waited.

Hiroki dared to take a sip of his tea, but despite his rumbling stomach, he didn't dare eat in front of Macha before she had any food of her own.

His stew congealed as they waited some more. He glared at Ciara for her fumbling attempts at communication which had led to this delay. He ought to be the one speaking directly to the gods. He was the one with the Unhidden talent for that. And Oghma was teaching him ways to use his talents, but they didn't know that.

Paul returned first, a tray in his hand, and a kitchen worker followed him with a second tray. With proper pomp and circumstance, Paul placed the steaming plate in front of Macha, while the other man placed his before Lugh. Sizzling steaks with steamed broccoli, potatoes, and carrots smelled delicious.

Suddenly, Hiroki's congealing beef stew seemed pitiful, and his growling stomach lurched.

Macha gave an approving nod and Paul slapped the kitchen worker on the shoulder as he removed the empty trays. Paul went to fetch food for himself and Ciara as the gods took their first bite.

Someone must have already shown Macha how to use modern cutlery, though she sawed at the steak with the dull knife. But as soon as she swallowed the first bite, she closed her eyes and a smile played across her face. "It has been centuries since I tasted something so delicious. Your headwoman is skilled."

Lugh stuffed a huge bite into his own mouth and mumbled agreement as he chewed. Hiroki finally felt able to eat his own lunch, though he grimaced at the cold chunks of fatty beef.

Just as the gods cleaned the last morsel from their plates, Masaaki finally returned with Lieutenant Crowley. She held a bottle of amber liquid and a stack of shot glasses.

Hiroki's simmering resentment morphed into delighted anticipation of the gods' reaction to whiskey.

Lieutenant Crowley caressed the bottle of Teeling Single Malt with reverence. "You have never tasted whiskey, correct?"

Macha nodded. "I have been told I might enjoy this beverage. Describe it."

Ciara's mouth quirked up on one side. "Its name comes from *uisce beatha*. I presume you know what those words mean?"

Hiroki gave her a scowl. Of course, the gods would understand actual Irish words. Was she deliberately trying to make them angry?

Lugh's grin widened. "The water of life. A grandiose name. Does the beverage live up to its name?"

"You'll have to tell me if it does." Crowley set out seven shot glasses and poured a measure for each of them. Once every glass was full, she held hers up. Ciara clinked her shot glass, then Paul, and each of them followed suit.

Lieutenant Crowley said, "*Slainte!*" and tipped her shot back. Everyone else followed suit.

The warm, potent alcohol warmed Hiroki's bones and he savored the rich drink as it trickled down his throat. He let out a sigh of satisfaction.

Macha let out a whoop that echoed in the nearly empty cafeteria. Lugh added a maniacal laugh. "This *is* the drink of the gods! More!"

He slammed the shot glass on the table so hard, Hiroki marveled that it didn't shatter. Macha did the same. Hiroki placed his own down more carefully, near enough to the others so that the Lieutenant would refill his with theirs. She complied with a wry smile but didn't refill her own.

The three of them drank their second shots, and Hiroki's heart stopped racing as liquid courage filled his blood.

"Another!" Lugh slammed his glass down. This time, it did shatter.

Ciara placed a hand on his arm. "I thought you were interested in the rest of the tour?"

Macha scowled at the lieutenant. "We have seen very little except chambers and furniture and boring scribes. Take me to your military leader."

The Lieutenant looked distinctly uncomfortable, but she gave a nod. "Please wait here. I will see if the Deputy Chief of Staff has some time for you."

As she left the bottle, Macha poured another generous shot for her and, using the lieutenant's glass, one for Lugh.

She didn't offer one to anyone else, and though he loved whiskey, Hiroki felt glad. He didn't want to have to choose between turning down an offer by this frightening goddess and drinking more. His head already buzzed with the strong alcohol, and he'd be unsteady on his feet.

Footsteps echoed on tile floors and Hiroki turned as a man in a pristine military uniform approached. He was a middle-aged Caucasian with a trim build and graying hair, wearing several military decorations on his dress uniform.

As he approached, a smile played across his lips and he held out his hand. "Welcome to our facility. My name is Frank Hughes, and I'm the Minister of State at the Department of Defence."

Hiroki stood out of respect, as Masaaki and Ciara hastily followed his lead. Lugh and Macha didn't rise.

Ciara gave him a firm handshake. "I'm Ciara Doherty, a member of the Protectorate for unHidden Advancement and Education. My companions," she turned first to Macha, "are the goddess Macha, the god Lugh. And these are Masaaki Kimura, Hiroki Kubo, and Paul Finglas, also members of PHAE."

Hughes' smile slipped a notch, and Hiroki suspected he'd not been properly briefed on the nature of his guests.

Lugh finally rose and gripped the other man's forearm. "I greet you."

Macha lifted her chin. "You are the war chief?"

He frowned and glanced around. "I am one of them, and the ranking person at this facility. Will that do?"

She gave a curt nod. "It will do for now. I will review your troops."

Hughes cleared his throat again. "As it happens, they'll be performing some drills, known as the Screed, in less than an hour. I can bring you outside to watch them practice. In the meantime, I can show you some of our weaponry."

The goddess asked, "Will they be carrying arms?"

"They will have rifles, yes. But this isn't an arms drill, just a formation drill."

Macha gave a dignified nod. "That will suffice. For now."

After murmuring to his aide, Hughes led them down the hallway, past more rooms full of cubicles. Macha fired off several questions. "How many troops do you have?"

"Approximately 7,000, including infantry, cavalry, engineers, and medical corps."

"And what weaponry are these troops trained in?"

"Mostly rifles, pistols, machine guns, and grenade launchers."

Macha and Lugh exchanged a glance before she asked her next question. "Demonstrate these weapons. I want to see their range and power."

Hughes glanced at Ciara, and she gave a bare nod in response. He shrugged and said, "Please follow me to the shooting range."

Ciara must have cleared this access ahead of time. While Hiroki admired the woman's forethought, he also questioned the wisdom of giving the gods access to actual weapons of war. Still, Hiroki had to admit he was also curious about what the Irish had.

Hughes led them behind the main rank of buildings. Several wooden towers rose above them, offering views of open fields. A tall bank of hills almost surrounded the field, ideal for catching bullets.

Hiroki glanced back at the entire town of Newbridge spread out behind the armory, almost like a toy town for a model train set.

They climbed the stairs of the first tower. A sandy-haired young man in fatigues stood at attention next to several guns mounted on shooting stands. Hughes patted one of them. "Now, this is our most common weapon, the Steyr. It's a high-powered, semiautomatic weapon. Sean, here, will demonstrate what it's capable of."

After Hughes passed out earplugs and explained how to wear them, the soldier knelt behind the gun, took his sighting, and squeezed the trigger. Hiroki, despite anticipating the sound, flinched at the weapon's report. Macha and Lugh stared in fascination at the shredded target at the far end of the field.

The Irish goddess grinned. "Most effective, indeed. Better than any bow I've seen. What else?"

Hughes demonstrated their pistols and rifles, but the Steyr held her fascination. "You will give me twenty of these, to begin with."

The man shook his head. "I'm afraid that's quite impossible. We're not authorized to provide you weaponry, merely demonstrate."

Everyone grew silent. Hiroki held his breath as the goddess' face turned red. "Repeat your words."

All the previous slights and insults seemed enormous now.

Hughes looked distinctly uncomfortable at her steely tone. "We cannot provide you with weapons."

Macha exchanged another glance with Lugh and let out a grunt. "If you will not provide weaponry, then show me where we may craft our own from this knowledge. You will teach us the technology."

Hughes shook his head and glanced down at the side of the closest building. Hiroki peered in that direction and noticed a woman on her phone. Was she calling for assistance? "We cannot provide that, either. We have treaties in place not to share certain levels of weapon technology. In fact, due to international treaty and neutrality status, fully fledged weapons systems cannot be manufactured in the Republic of Ireland."

Hiroki waited for Macha's temper to explode and blast the man into nothingness, but nothing happened. Instead, the goddess stared out at the horizon for several moments.

Finally, she gave a single nod. "Then show me your troops drilling."

They followed him back down the tower and to the parade field where groups of soldiers dressed in fatigues were lining up into squared ranks. Each one stood to attention as they found their spot.

Hughes led them to a set of bleachers and while the PHAE people sat, Macha and Lugh stood next to the Minister of State. The Lieutenant excused herself and returned to the barracks building.

The sun beat warm upon Hiroki's head, and he wiped the sweat off his brow, wishing for Ireland's habitual clouds to cool the fierce heat.

A corporal called out a series of commands, but Hiroki didn't know the words. They sounded Irish.

As the soldiers complied with each directive, Macha studied them carefully. Suddenly, she strode toward the nearest rank of soldiers. The closest man's eyes grew wide as she plucked the rifle from his hands.

He glanced nervously toward his drill instructor, but that man looked just as confused. Macha examined the weapon, put her hand on the trigger, aimed at a hill in the distance, and squeezed. It clicked and her face turned angry red. "What is this toy? Why did the weapon not work?"

Hughes had hurried to catch up with her, his face flushed. "These are not loaded. As I said, this is not an arms drill."

Hiroki and the others followed more slowly, coming close to hear the conversation.

The goddess crossed her arms, her eyes flashing. "Load them. I wish to see your capabilities."

He shook his head. "We don't have arms drill scheduled today. Perhaps you can arrange for a tour next week."

She gripped the barrel of the rifle so hard, it creaked. Hiroki backed up, unsure what she might do when angry. Ciara's brow was furrowed, and she had her mobile out.

Macha's voice dropped to a dangerous tone. "You will show me now."

Lugh let out a laugh and clapped the goddess on her back. "Now, Macha, Manannán told us to have patience with these modern people."

She shrugged him off and gave him a glare that might melt iron. "They will show me now!"

Hiroki held back his angry words. *Let her do what she likes!* He didn't want to be destroyed by a frustrated goddess. If he got out of this situation, he would have to re-examine his relationship with people making these foolish choices.

Lugh exchanged a glance with Ciara. The PHAE representative pursed her lips. "Perhaps it would be safer to comply with her wishes."

The Minister of State crossed his arms and shook his head. "No, it is quite impossible. We have other things on our schedule this afternoon. She'll just have to wait."

The previously clear sky suddenly turned dark. Storm clouds blocked the summer sun and Hiroki backed further away. Angering a god didn't seem wise in the slightest.

Then he remembered his own capabilities and pulled the tingling sensation up as he spoke. "Macha, perhaps it *would* be better to wait. That way, they can prepare a stronger demonstration of their might. It will be more impressive if they have time to get ready."

She cocked her head at him, and the full impact of her regard hit him like a punch to the face. For a moment, she looked as if she might relent, but then turned back to Hughes. "Now."

He shook his head as thunder rolled across the field. The sun had disappeared, and it was so dark, it seemed like dusk. *Is this man a complete fool? Doesn't he notice?*

The loud caw of a raven made Hiroki flinch. One swooped down and alit on Macha's shoulder, then stared at Hughes. The raven cawed again, then the sound of wings surrounded them. Dozens, no hundreds of ravens flew in and landed on the ground, in a thick ring around the Minister of State.

Hughes had turned pale, with sweat forming on his brow as he glanced at the birds. "I… I can't change our schedule. Not now. Maybe tomorrow morning?"

Macha pursed her lips, and a bolt of lightning struck the ground at Hughes's feet. Her ravens exploded into a flurry of black feathers.

The Minister of State jumped back with a shout. The crack of thunder made Hiroki's bones ache. A hundred ravens attacked the military man. His green uniform was covered with black as he stumbled back, lifting his arms to shield his face.

The soldiers stood in nervous formation with worried expressions as Hughes's shrieks filled the air. He fell to the ground, still trying to protect his face. They backed away from his form writhing on the grass. No one of any rank stood close enough to tell them how to deal with this bizarre attack.

Hiroki searched frantically for someone of authority to help but found no one. Instead, he cried out, "Stop them! Stop!"

He tried to pull the power through his body, to put the Unhidden command into his voice. But his skin didn't tingle in the slightest, and his words fell upon deaf ears.

His command was nothing compared to Macha's power. Any advantage he might have had was useless against her.

They watched in horror as the ravens pecked at Hughes's face, arms, and neck, anywhere they could find skin. They ripped bits of his uniform, tearing off the shiny rank pins and flying away with their gruesome prizes. More ravens arrived, replacing those who fled.

Hughes stopped screaming and grew still.

As other officers finally came running to help, the remaining ravens scattered. Hiroki's heart thumped fast as he stared at the ruined, bloody mess.

Macha wore a satisfied smile.

**Bintou:**

After Hiroki handed the report to her, Bintou read about Macha's attack on Hughes several times, not wanting to believe her eyes. While she wished she could have been there to prevent this horrid disaster, at the same time, she was glad she hadn't witnessed the gory attack. A shiver ran down her spine.

Now Ciara, Paul, and Hiroki were meeting with her to decide how to respond to this tragedy. They were to discuss the event with the Taoiseach and the Chief of Staff for Defence Forces, the Lieutenant General.

She read through the report again. Hiroki had tried to use his persuasive power on Macha and failed. Their Unhidden powers were obviously utterly inadequate against the gods. How were they going to rein in these entities if they had no power over them?

More and more of these ancient gods were arriving, not just in Ireland, but all over the world. And they might be helpful or harmful, depending on individual whim and circumstances.

Right now, Bintou wanted to flee, back to the cozy little world of academia she'd left months ago. Back to the University in Mali, where she'd worked with perfect contentment, translating ancient manuscripts. The delightful aroma of medieval scrolls, ink, and dust. The thrill of discovering a new piece of literature, a new account of some momentous event, or even the day-to-day tally of trade goods on a piece of papyrus.

134

Each of those projects had given her a thrill of discovery, of finding out something about the world's past that had been hidden for hundreds, even thousands of years.

Now, what was her purpose? To play nursemaid to an arrogant Irish god who looked like he belonged on the cover of a cheesy medieval romance novel? He didn't even need her anymore. He'd grown fluent in modern English in record time and no longer needed her translations for everyday speech.

Lugh still called on her when he encountered new slang or jargon, but fewer times each day.

Approaching footsteps made her glance at her phone and note the time. She gathered up the report, straightened the pages with a few taps on the table, and hurried down the hall.

The conference room inside the bunker seemed larger than it should be, deep beneath Dublin streets. The harsh fluorescent lights shined on the dull beige concrete walls. Bintou shivered again as she entered the cold, impersonal space.

Hiroki was already sitting next to Ciara, wearing a frown. Just as Bintou entered, so did the Taoiseach, an older woman with a severe bun in her gray hair. They exchanged polite nods and sat at the circular table.

Hiroki fetched them both tea while Bintou fidgeted with her papers. They were still waiting for the Chief of Staff.

When he entered, they rose as one. The Taoiseach stepped forward to shake his hand. "Thank you for coming on such short notice, Tom. Did you read the report?"

"I did. I've met Ciara, but not you two. I'm Tom O'Donnell, Chief of Staff. And you are?"

Bintou got to her feet, shaking his offered hand. "Bintou Sissoki, from PHAE. This is my colleague, Hiroki Kubo."

Hiroki shook hands but shot Bintou a glance. She couldn't read his expression, but he seemed resentful. Of what? That she introduced herself first?

She sat back down and took a sip of her tea as O'Donnell spoke. "We have to do something in response to this attack. Yes, we need their help, but we simply cannot sanction this sort of violence without repercussions. What sort of precedence would that set?"

Precedence? They were worried about precedence? What about the man's life? Bintou glanced at Hiroki, but he was staring into his mug and wearing a downtrodden expression. Ciara stared at her lap, her fingers intertwined.

The Taoiseach droned on about protocol and formalities, and Bintou just couldn't take it any longer. She placed her hands on the table and swallowed. "Did the Minister survive?"

Startled, the Taoiseach nodded. "Ah, yes. He has, so far. Hughes is in intensive care at the moment, but he should recover, with time. He'll have scars for life."

Bintou let out a breath. At least he was alive. That was something. Hiroki was frowning again. Had he wished the man to die? That seemed so unlike Hiroki, she must be mistaken.

The door flung open, and brightness burst forth as Lugh strode in wearing a frown. "What is this meeting? Why was I not included?"

Bintou jumped to her feet, falling instantly into her diplomat role. "We're discussing how best to approach you about the recent incident. We meant no insult, I assure you. We just wanted to be prepared—"

He cut her off with a raised hand. He glared at first Ciara and then the Taoiseach. "I don't wish to hear your excuses. What are your intentions?"

Bintou glanced at the Chief of Staff. They hadn't come to any conclusions in their discussions yet, but she couldn't speak for them, not without a plan of action.

The Taoiseach crossed her arms. "Lugh, please understand that we are bound by duty to do everything in our power to ensure the safety of our people, even in light of all you and your fellow gods have done to help us."

Lugh's brow furrowed. "And we continue to help and heal your people. That is not the question here. Does your Minister require healing? I can arrange that. Dian Cecht can come."

Bintou held out her hands, palms down in a calming gesture. "And we appreciate that help greatly. The Minister is currently at our best hospital. However, we must ask for certain assurances from you." She glanced back again at the others.

The Chief of Staff stepped forward. "In the future, we will require a vow that our people are not to be harmed unless we offer physical harm to one of your people. Does that sound reasonable?"

Lugh pursed his lips but then gave a curt nod. "Those terms are fair, and I regret that such a resolution is necessary. I will speak to the others to ensure they agree to this stricture. What else?"

The Taoiseach cleared her throat. "We must impose some sort of penalty upon Macha for her violent action. That's the only way we can maintain a rule of law. Do you agree on that necessity?"

He clenched his jaw. "What sort of penalty?"

She lifted her chin. "Normally, this sort of attack would require a criminal trial. It would warrant time in prison."

Lugh straightened his shoulders with a scowl and the fluorescent lights above flickered. "Macha was unaware that such an act would be unacceptable in your society. The consequences for the man's intransigence and rudeness would have been well known in our time."

O'Donnell crossed his arms. "Ignorance of the law is no excuse. Everyone within our country must follow the law."

The god glanced between Bintou and Ciara before asking, "How long of an imprisonment are you proposing?"

The Minister of State shared a long look with the Taoiseach. "As I said, this would normally follow a fair trial of her peers. However, such a trial might be difficult to arrange and garner too much unwanted media attention. We are willing to discuss the possibility of commuting such a sentence in exchange for, say, community service."

Bintou gritted her teeth. Even if they were to sentence Macha to jail, she doubted a prison existed that would hold her. This entire discussion seemed moot.

Lugh cocked his head as he furrowed his brow. "Community service? Is that not what we are doing for the people of Ireland now? Giving a service to the community?"

O'Donnell nodded with a wide smile, his shoulders relaxing. "Of course, you are. You all are. And we greatly appreciate everything you've all done to help us. That's why we've discussed commuting any sentence upon Macha. Luckily, the man will live, so we don't have to worry about a murder charge. But the term *community service* also means a penalty for a wrongdoing, a form of restitution."

Lugh tapped his lip, his gaze on the ceiling. "Restitution? What is the man's worth? She can pay the *Éraic* in gold or silver, if you tell us his price."

Bintou recognized the Irish word as a fine charged upon murder, similar to the Anglo-Saxon term of *weregeld*. She didn't think there was an English equivalent.

O'Donnell conferred with the Taoiseach in low voices as Lugh turned to her. "Is the *Éraic* no longer part of your culture?"

"Not in Ireland, that I'm aware of. Usually, a murder is punishable by life in prison in this country. Other countries have death penalties for murder. Sometimes a lesser sentence is granted if there are extenuating circumstances, like self-defense or the defense of others."

Bintou wondered about the offered *Éraic*. Where did the gods store their wealth, this gold and silver Lugh mentioned? Where did they actually live? Was it a physical place in this realm, some Otherworld, a different dimension, or through a portal?

She'd opened her mouth to ask Lugh when the Taoiseach spoke. "We will not ask for any monetary compensation. It's against our philosophy for a criminal to buy their way out of a crime. However, we do ask that Macha help us with a project in payment for her actions."

Lugh gave a tentative nod, gesturing for the Taoiseach to continue.

"We are constructing low-income housing in a development south of Dublin, a project that was destroyed in the bombing. Would Macha be willing to lend her power to the rebuilding project? That would involve moving heavy materials and manual labor."

A slow smile spread across Lugh's face. "I will consult with her. However, I believe she would accept such a compromise. She has no need to perform such manual tasks with her physical body. She has the power to move such materials without her hands."

*Latest CNN Update: Reports of a divine attack upon a member of the Irish Defense Ministry have been confirmed. Though the victim has survived, he will suffer permanent injuries from this attack. We are still waiting for further details.*

*In a public statement, the PHAE have expressed their horror at this attack and have vowed to do everything in their power to prevent further violence.*

*In response, the PEM have vowed to get to the bottom of this tragedy and are calling on volunteers from all over the world to join their organization and assist their efforts. They are accusing the PHAE of a conspiracy to cover up their uncontrollable Unhidden members and of crafting a clever lie to hide their acts of violence.*

**Bintou:**

That evening, Bintou related the details of the meeting to Hiroki and Masaaki as they ate their dinner in their Dublin bunker rooms.

Hiroki's eyes grew wide as she finished the tale. "They're asking Macha to be a construction worker? The goddess of war? How can they do such a thing? She might get angry at such a demeaning task."

Bintou frowned and ate the final bite of her sandwich. After she finished chewing and swallowing, she said, "That is one point of this sort of community service, to humble the person who committed the crime. To get them to understand that we are all the same, all upon an equal level."

He leapt to his feet and began pacing, throwing his hands up in frustration. "But she isn't a *person*. She's a goddess! This is an insult to her, even to the other gods! We aren't on an equal level, by any measure."

She gritted her teeth in frustration at his obtuseness. "They may be gods, but they must abide by human law and custom. They cannot be allowed to flaunt those laws at will, can they? We need them to comply in order to fit into this society."

Masaaki drank his Coke in silence, watching the conversation bounce between his two friends. Hiroki halted, his expression hardening. "They'll never fit into this society. In fact, I think it's insulting of us to even ask them to. They're powerful beings, and deserve our respect."

Hiroki nodded to his friend. "Masaaki is correct. We must not mistake compliance with friendship. They are too powerful. One insult, and they can destroy us."

Bintou frowned at the Japanese man. "Even powerful beings cannot just take what they want. They must learn that there are consequences to their actions."

Hiroki refilled his teacup. "And what if they don't care about consequences? What if they simply take what they want? How are we to stop them?"

She leapt to her feet and clenched her fists. "We can't let them do that! We are the only ones who can!"

Masaaki spoke up. "Hiroki has an excellent point. If they don't seek our approval, what's to stop them from simply taking over the world? They have enough power that they could enslave us all if they really wanted to."

Bintou chewed on the inside of her lip, trying to formulate an answer to that question that didn't sound ridiculous. "Then why didn't they enslave everyone back in ancient times? Presumably, they had more power then. There were more of them, and fewer humans, right?"

Masaaki shook his head. "I don't know. Maybe they tried and failed. Maybe they are more powerful now. Maybe they didn't want to bother then."

Bintou chewed on her lower lip. "We need some sort of contingency plan, in case the gods take it into their head to exercise their full power over humans."

Hiroki shook his head. "You're foolish if you think any sort of plan can stop them."

The woman growled, "Stop calling me foolish! Are you going to just call me names, or do something about it!"

Hiroki locked gazes with her, and for a moment, no one else moved. He knew then that he could no longer rely upon her to make wise decisions.

At least now he knew who not to trust.

Bintou dropped her eyes first, pacing around the room. Hiroki sat back down, his anger simmering on a slow boil.

Masaaki cleared his throat. "According to the news reports, other pantheons have already tried to take over their areas of the world."

Throwing up her hands, Bintou asked, "How can mere humans stop them? Regular humans can't do it, not unless they use horrific weapons. Even those might not work. Tanks, grenades, automatic weapons, are all physical weapons, and the gods have plenty of physical strength."

She paced a few more times. "No, the only option is for the Unhidden to defend regular humans, to act as a shield between humans and gods. It must be us. We're the only ones with any power over the gods, no matter where in the world they are. We have to create a plan."

Hiroki's laugh was tinged with hysteria. "You think that will work? You think that even the Unhidden will be able to stand against ancient gods? My talent didn't even touch Macha. I have a great deal of respect for you, Bintou. You are a highly educated and intelligent person. But that's just the height of folly. Or maybe hubris."

That made Bintou glare at him. "Hubris? Us? More like desperation. I don't have any confidence in our superiority. But have more resources than vanilla humans do. Therefore, it falls upon us to protect them. The powerful should guard the weak. That's the way society should work."

Hiroki shook his head. "It's not the way society has ever worked in the past. I thought you'd read historical records?"

She scowled at his obtuseness. "I did say *should.*"

Masaaki grabbed another Coke from the minifridge and took a long swig. "And if Macha, or any of the other Irish gods, decides that we're no longer worthy of their kindness? If she tries to take power for herself? What can we actually *do* about it?"

Bintou let out a patient sigh. "We just need a decent plan. Maybe we can find something they don't like. Isn't iron harmful to them? Ciara can help us. Do you think her ability to dampen Unhidden powers will work on gods?"

***Latest CNN Update:*** *We have just received breaking news that the PHAE groups headquartered in Finland, Sweden, Denmark, and Norway have shifted their home base to Iceland, an area deep into the interior called Landamannalaugar.*

*This is a particularly difficult area to access, as there are no paved roads to the compound, and no easy place to land planes. It is assumed that they're building a more defensible location.*

*In other news, the Beijing contingent of PHAE has completely disappeared. We have a few unconfirmed reports that some Unhidden who had*

*previously lived there have escaped to either the Siberian enclave or the one in*
*Pakistan, but we have no confirmation of that information.*

*Stay tuned for more details as they come in.*

**Bintou:**

Masaaki, Hiroki, Bintou, and Ciara stayed up all night, working out several possible plans, counterplans, and disaster contingents.

Masaaki brought a handful of miniatures, the sort used in table-top gaming, to represent each god and each Unhidden in their group. Then, Ciara mapped out a grid, one edge being actions by the gods, and the other edge being reactions by PHAE.

They moved the figurines around on the table during each scenario, trying to block out what might happen with each choice.

Even after all that, they came to the conclusion that if the gods moved to take control, the Unhidden and the humans would have little say in the matter.

The television droned on the background during the whole night. When the announcement about the Chinese PHAE enclave disappearing was made, they all fell silent, staring at the screen.

Hiroki leapt to his feet to turn it off. "I'm no longer interested in CNN. They aren't giving balanced news."

The others gaped at him, but he sat back down, a scowl marring his face. Bintou scowled as he sipped his tea, but he said nothing further.

Bintou leaned forward, tapping the Macha figurine. "What if Macha and Taranis are just one political faction? We might be able to fight just them, if the other gods don't join in. There might be many factions amongst the gods. How can we know which way any scenario might play out if we don't know the politics behind their relationships?"

Ciara wrinkled her nose. "But how can we find out? Manannán seems reasonable enough, from what Anna says. But I'm not afraid to admit that Macha scares it right out of me."

Masaaki let out a snort. "And Taranis is a jerk. I'll tell you that for free."

Hiroki opened his mouth, but then shut it again. Had he met another that he hadn't mentioned? Or maybe he was just thinking of the Dagda.

The Good God seemed reasonable as well, but not very dignified. *Leaders ought to have dignity, and therefore Manannán seemed a more suitable leader than the Dagda.*

Afterwards, they all crept to their beds to catch a few hours of sleep. Bintou was scheduled to meet with Lugh the next morning and had no wish to play tour guide on a sleepless night.

The next morning, she rubbed her face hard, trying to get her mind going. Bintou was due to walk him through classes today, lectures on how modern Irish government worked, and she needed to be alert.

Lugh had requested this information and Paul had gotten them passes into a series of lectures at Trinity College. Bintou was to act as an interpreter for any terms he didn't understand, and to explain things when he got confused.

Oddly enough, she was looking forward to the classes themselves. Different cultures had always fascinated her, both modern and ancient. She wanted to understand more of her newly adopted country.

As she chose her clothing for the day, she decided she'd had enough of Irish fashion and chose something bright and bold, a pattern from her home country. The brown, red, and yellow geometric shapes were strong, and the dress hugged her curves comfortably, unlike the binding sleeves and slacks she'd been using.

Since she'd be out of the bunker for most of the day, the boring practical clothing could be upgraded for garb that delighted her senses. She did remember to bring a sweater, for even in the summer, this land could be damp and chilly.

Thus clothed, Bintou strode into the meeting room a few minutes early. Lugh was standing next to a whiteboard, studying terms Ciara had written down, Irish words for different levels of government, including Oireachtas, Dáil, Fianna Fáil, and Sinn Féin.

She'd already taught Lugh these words, and they'd been using them for weeks.

The god turned when she entered, a broad smile across his face. "Bintou! I am delighted to see you. And in such stunning colors!"

Before she could react, he enveloped her in a hug, his arms warm and strong. Despite her surprise, she enjoyed the strong embrace.

It had been a long time since a strong man had hugged her. Ever since Martin had died. Her breath caught in her throat at the memory of the man she'd loved and lost to the diseases rampaging across Ireland.

Lugh pulled back and looked at her, his hands on her shoulders. "Bintou? Have I injured you?"

She shook her head. "No, no. I merely had a memory of someone I cared for. Nothing you've done."

"That makes me glad! I would be grieved to hurt you. Is this garb from your homeland? The colors become you, they make you shine. You should always wear such brilliant decorations."

Her cheeks grew warm, and she was aware that he still held her shoulders. Bintou wished someone else would arrive. But, at the same time, she worried that they'd be interrupted. She didn't know which would be worse. Suddenly, despite all the thousands of words she knew in as many languages, she couldn't think of any.

A slow smile crept across Lugh's face as he stared into her eyes. His tone grew quiet. "Bintou, you are too delightful to stay here, working in this dark, depressing place. Will you come with me?"

She let out a nervous laugh, able to talk again. "Of course, I'm coming with you. We're due at Trinity College in an hour."

He moved his grip from her shoulders to grasp her hands, bringing them both to his lips. "I don't mean to this college. I mean, after we are done here, with this current crisis."

Bintou stared at their hands. "This current crisis. I haven't been able to think past it."

"There *will* be an end to it. It has been seen. And when it is over, I want to show you my home."

Excitement at visiting the home of the gods stirred within her, despite the accompanying fear and caution. She looked up into his eyes again. "Where do you live?"

Letting go of one hand, he swept his arm in a grand gesture. "In a palace beneath the hills, where the apples are honey-sweet and light shines upon us without a cloud. I can show you, if you like."

She let out a sigh just as the door opened, and Ciara and Paul entered. Bintou pulled her hand away from Lugh's instantly, though Ciara's glance flicked toward her. The Irish woman raised an eyebrow, and Bintou gave a casual shrug, as if it was nothing. She could tell by Ciara's expression that she didn't think it was nothing.

If she visited Lugh's home, she could search for some weakness, some way to stop the gods if they decided to seize power. She almost believed that rationalization herself.

When Hiroki arrived, he wore a huge smile, almost like his old self, back before his father had disowned him. He practically bubbled with excitement.

"I have thought of many ideas! Things we can show the gods. Lugh, would you like to see the ancient Stonehenge? Or the Eiffel Tower?"

He turned to Bintou, his face glowing. "What if we showed them the Great Wall of China? Or Burj Khalifa? Wouldn't that impress them all?"

None of this was part of either the official plan set forth by the Taoiseach and the PHAE, nor the secret plan they'd worked out against the gods growing power. Where had he gotten all these new ideas?

Lugh cocked his head. "What are these wonders that you speak of? Are they to do with the Irish armed capabilities?"

Bintou shook her head. "No, nothing to do with war. They are impressive monuments humans have built over the years."

Hiroki's enthusiasm dimmed and he gave a shrug. "Then we should show him the Port of Dublin, at least. To see how our supply chain operates."

Ciara tapped the table, a frown on her face. "Why should we be showing them the supply chain? That isn't on the approved list."

Hiroki gave a shrug. "I'm told that they wish to see where the supplies arrive in the Port of Dublin. Is this a big secret? It's only a few blocks that way. They can see it in passing."

Her gaze flicked to Lugh, who had crossed his arms. Then she turned back to Hiroki. "Not a secret, no. But we've been asked to keep information shared to a minimum, you should know that. We mean no offense, Lugh, but I'm sure you understand the need for caution."

Hiroki gave a shrug and turned with another brilliant smile, this time to Lugh. "It seems they don't want to show you everything."

What was he up to? His actions didn't seem in line with the Hiroki she'd come to know.

Lugh shrugged. "This was not a request that I made. Perhaps a different god is more interested. I would guess the request comes from Manannán mac Lir. He is obsessed with boats. He says they itch his skin when they're on the water."

**Bintou:**

Bintou was in yet another meeting with Ciara, in one of the conference rooms, and she was thoroughly sick of them. No one got anything actually done, just gathered again and again and discussed options *ad infinitum,* without ever actually affecting any action.

Her tea was growing cold in her cup, but she had no desire to drink it.

*Out of the frying pan and into the fire.* It was a phrase Ibrahim had used, and Bintou found it horribly appropriate to her situation. She'd shifted from being a liaison to Lugh to being a spokesperson for the entire human government to the gods.

She didn't understand how that had happened, nor how to reverse it, but she didn't like it one bit. She'd never been comfortable with power over others.

Ciara asked her something, but she hadn't heard it. To cover her gaffe, she cleared her throat. "I'm sorry, could you repeat that?"

"I asked if there was any way you could arrange a visit to where the gods live when they aren't manifested in our world."

Bintou's mind raced with fear and longing. Lugh had said he wanted to bring her home. She was riddled with curiosity but at the same time, afraid of leaving this world. And if she visited him, could she resist his obvious seduction?

Could she even survive loving a god? It must be possible. Mythology was riddled with demigods, even Irish mythology.

But what if he didn't let her return? Would she be content to stay with him for the rest of her life? To never see the human world again?

Bintou gave a carefully noncommittal shrug. "I might be able to convince Lugh to bring me for a visit. What should I look for?"

"Something, anything, we might use to combat them if we need to. The members of the Dáil are growing concerned about the gods' increasing influence upon our people and the human world. They want some sort of ace in the hole, a weapon or weakness we can use if they turn recalcitrant."

She let out a cynical snort. "Recalcitrant. Is that really the best description we have for angry gods?"

Ciara chuckled. "That's fair. Do you prefer power-mad overlords? But if you have a way to go on a mission, you might find something."

Frustration and fear made Bintou snap, "I'm not a spy, Ciara. I'm not a soldier of any type. Have I not made my position on that clear in the past?"

The Irish woman rubbed her temples and let out a long-suffering sigh. "We aren't asking you to do any soldiering. You aren't to hurt or attack anyone. No violence of any sort."

"Well, that's good. Because even if I wanted to hurt someone, I have absolutely no training. Nor do I have any training in spying."

Ciara placed her hands flat on the table, entreaty in her eyes. "We simply need information, and you're one of our most highly educated and trusted personnel. Your intelligence is needed for this mission."

Even though she'd already gotten the invitation from Lugh, Bintou needed to push back on this request. She didn't know why, but something within her balked. "Then why not send Colin? He has far more knowledge of Irish fairy lore than I do. He'd be much more likely to spot a weakness."

Ciara gave her a half-smile. "Ah, but Colin hasn't caught the wandering eye of one of the gods, has he?"

Bintou's cheeks blazed, and she stared at her hands. She didn't think she'd feel such an attraction for anyone so soon after Martin died, but Lugh had a particular power to make her feel cherished.

Her attraction to the god was even stronger than when she first dated Ibrahim, back in her college years. Her skin tingled just thinking about Lugh's caress.

The other woman folded her hands and let out a deep sigh. "Look, Bintou, I realize we're asking a lot of you. We discussed several options, including asking Colin, but he'd be much too star-struck to find out anything of value."

That made Bintou let out a snort and take a sip of her cold tea. She wrinkled her nose.

"We even discussed asking the gods to withdraw from our world on their own accord. But we can't afford to do that yet, not until we have contained the diseases, and we know what the PEM plans are. Or whatever they're calling themselves these days. Until we've neutralized that threat, we may need to call upon the gods' help. That's an unfortunate fact."

Bintou gave a scowl. "We're playing with fire."

Ciara pursed her lips. "Yes, we are, and we have no choice. The only other option is to freeze to death. But that doesn't mean we must fan the flames blindly. If we can find something, anything that will help us in the future against them, we need that information. And you're our diplomat."

Bintou held up her hands, shaking her head. "No, I'm your translator. I've never been trained for diplomacy."

"Fine, then, you're a translator. And that means you can listen to whatever they say in Old Irish. We only have a handful of people even trained to read that language, and their accent is different from what they imagined, so they're fair useless at the finer points."

Bintou narrowed her eyes. "That's fair. But—"

This time, Ciara held up her hand. "But nothing. You've caught Lugh's affection, and if you can go to where they live, you might be able to find a vital secret. Or more than one."

She swirled her tea, wishing it was still warm. "And how am I to get that information back to you? Or get back myself?"

Ciara bit her lip. "I admit, we haven't ironed out that detail yet. You'll have a mobile with you…"

Bintou let out a bitter laugh. "A mobile! Since when do they have cell towers in the Otherworld, or Faerie, or wherever they live?"

"Well, as I said, we're still looking for a solution. We have a recruit who might have some telepathic powers, so that's a possibility. I'll have to introduce you."

"A telepath? That's handy. What's their name?"

"Lee. They're from New Zealand, but just arrived a few days ago."

**Komie:**

Komie sat at the bunker table with Colin and Bintou, her mouth hanging open. She stared at the instructions Colin had just handed to her.

How could they even think of moving everyone in PHAE to another country? There must be hundreds, even thousands of Unhidden in Ireland now. The country had been a public sanctuary ever since the talents emerged last year.

Ireland should have been safe, but it wasn't. Bombs were smuggled in and they'd destroyed many lives in Galway, Belfast, and Dublin, both from the initial blasts and the weaponized diseases they'd carried.

A month later, Ireland was still reeling from the death and destruction. Only with the help of the gods were they beating back the pandemic.

But to move that many people to Iceland? Sure, it would be an even more difficult place to bomb. But Iceland had fewer armed forces than Ireland.

She turned to Colin, confusion on her face. "Are we supposed to go as well? Or just the vulnerable Unhidden, those with no defensive talents?"

He gave a shrug. "They haven't really given us any details. But I suspect they'll move the children and most vulnerable first. The rest of us will stay to hold the fort."

Komie shook her head, a shiver running down her spine. "I don't like it. You should keep the weakest where the strongest can protect them."

Bintou piped up. "And why are the Icelandic people letting us in? We still have a raging pandemic here."

Colin glanced at the papers he'd received. "The refugees are to be held in quarantine on the island. The PHAE compound is a very isolated place, away from all the cities."

Bintou frowned, rubbing the space between her eyes. "Are they moving by boat? By plane? They're going to have to be so careful with anyone they come in contact with."

Komie pursed her lips. "And Iceland has no army, is that right?"

"No army, but they have navy and air force. We're requesting help from the gods for both the transportation and defense of our people there. One of them has a magic boat, it seems."

Water transportation must mean Manannán mac Lir, Anna's god. He seemed one of the more reasonable gods, or the least prickly. Not so given to wanton war, death, and destruction as Macha or Taranis, at any rate.

Bintou shuddered. "I understand it's even colder there than it is here."

Colin let out a rueful chuckle. "Yes, it's definitely colder in Iceland. The name sort of gives it away, doesn't it? But there's also gorgeous landscape there, and no way to come in undetected."

She snorted. "I thought there was no way to come to Ireland undetected. That turned out to be a lie."

Colin let out a long sigh. "We learn from our mistakes. We have to, or we won't survive."

**Anna:**

Ever since her confrontation with Taranis, Anna had felt powerful. Sure, she'd barely tickled the god with her attack, but even that bit gave her confidence that she had more control over things than she'd ever had in her life.

Manannán had taught her how to use her power and control the finer aspects of it. And that gave her a new swagger.

In the past few weeks, he'd taken her through a hundred different drills, honing her finesse, and she loved both the exercise and the power flowing through her body. Only when Carlos had come to take her away from her teacher did she realize how far she'd come.

Now Carlos was driving her to Dublin, to talk to a group of politicians. She didn't want to do this at all, but Manannán had insisted she attend as his spokesperson.

But Anna didn't want to be a spokesperson, or a representative, or any of that. She just wanted to work with her beloved water, to shape and spin and swim forever. Like the god had taught her.

Her mind drifted with the memory of soft mist cooling her scaly skin as they drove down the highway. She didn't see the farmlands of the Curragh shift into the suburbs of Kildare and then Dublin. She didn't notice when they got off the highway and headed toward the port, to the entrance of the underground bunker that housed PHAE mission control.

Only when Carlos parked and pulled her car door open did her mind return to the present. He offered his hand, helping her from the vehicle with a warm smile.

As they descended the stairs into the bunker, he said, "You got this. No need to be nervous around these stiffs, I promise you. You can do so much more than they'll ever be able to do. Remember that! I have every faith in you. And be strong."

His sentiment was kindly meant, but despite her confidence, she didn't feel strong in the slightest, not in this horrible underground tomb. In the sea, yes, but not here. She hated the cold, dark, echoing tunnels. They pressed in on her. Not like claustrophobia, but like being completely cutoff from any source of water.

No water, no power, no strength.

Anna ached to be swimming in the bay, despite all the pollution around a busy city port. Her skin itched and burned whenever she was out of the water, though it was better now that her scales had stopped growing. They covered her legs and arms and a bit on her belly, and were pretty in the sun, iridescent and glinting.

Carlos grasped her hand as they walked through into the conference room. She flashed Bintou a grin and nodded to Hiroki. She sat next to Ciara, with Paul, Lugh, and the Taoiseach on the other side.

Anna felt the least of them, tiny beside giants. She wanted to crawl into a hole and hide. Carlos squeezed her hand again before letting go, whispering into her ear, "You're strong."

She took a deep breath before she delivered her memorized message. "Manannán mac Lir, god of the waves, has sent his compliments and has an offer. He understands you wish to move people to Iceland, and he would offer the use of his boat for the transportation."

The Taoiseach looked thoughtful, but Hiroki let out a snort. That seemed unlike him, but she knew something he didn't. Manannán's boat was an artifact out of legend, and it would grow to whatever size needed. And, of course, it would never capsize, not with the god of the sea keeping an eye on it.

After the Taoiseach pulled Ciara aside to confer, Lugh spoke to her. "You are learning a lot from Manannán, I see."

Anna unconsciously straightened her shoulders, not sure she wanted the regard of any other god. Before she could form a suitable answer, Carlos said, "She's doing fine, and we're all proud of her."

Her heart warmed at his defense. Carlos was a sweet man, no doubt about it, and he believed in her.

Brendan had believed in her, too, but where was he now? She'd visited him every day at the hospital and he'd never even called her after he got better. In fact, he seemed to have disappeared. Had he been sent on another mission? Or did he just not want anything to do with her anymore?

She'd probably turned into too much of a fish for his taste. It didn't matter. Anna had morphed into a different person after her time with Manannán, and maybe she was no longer fully human. She might not even want to date a land-bound man now. He'd never be able to live with her in the sea, and she wasn't comfortable on the land. Such a match seemed doomed, like something out of Aesop's Fables.

Anna cleared her throat as the Taoiseach and Ciara stopped whispering in the corner. The leader stood with her hands flat on the table. "We accept the sea god's generous offer, Anna. You may relay that information to him and find out where he would like us to send our first shipment of refugees. Also, please ask what supplies or personal goods they may bring with them, and how many he can handle on each trip."

Anna gave a grin. "They can bring whatever they can carry. I already asked him that. As many as want to come are welcome. And if they could gather in Galway port, that would be best. It's got the largest harbour on the west coast."

**Tiberius:**

As his secretary dropped another stack of newspapers on his mahogany desk, Tiberius glared at her. "Sharon, what the hell are these?"

"News reports. You said you wanted anything about the PHAE, didn't you?"

"Who the hell uses print newspapers anymore? Can't you just send me a curated news file?"

Sharon sniffed, her nose turned up. "I read printed newspapers, Mr. Wilkinson. Every day."

He let out a sigh. "I didn't mean to insult you, sweetheart. Now can you please take these away and compile something for me? I need it organized so I can drill down into a headline if it's interesting, but that I don't have to scroll through a dozen stories that aren't."

She pursed her lips. "Very well. Your ten o'clock is waiting outside."

He downed the dregs of his coffee and rose to refill. "Send 'em in."

As the police detective entered, Tiberius cursed under his breath. He'd forgotten about this appointment, and he'd meant to postpone it again. But that might make them too suspicious. No, it was best to deal with this man and get him off the scent. He didn't want the authorities digging too deep into his affairs, not at this time.

Luckily, he knew this man. He'd known him a long time. Hell, their mothers had been in the same sorority. "How can I help you, Officer Morris?"

The detective settled into the comfortable guest chair. "That's Detective Morris, please. And I sent you a list of the questions we're investigating. Didn't y' get it?"

He cast his mind back but couldn't remember it at all. "It may not have made it to my desk. Can you resend it? Or just ask the durned things. I can talk for hours, you must know that." He put on his most charming, backwoods hick grin. That usually worked on anyone, disarming and guileless.

The detective cleared his throat. "Very well. The first question is in regards to your investment with a security company, Allied Securiguard. They're out of Kenya, is that true?"

Tiberius nodded and rose, walking to the sideboard. "That's what their website says. Would you like something to wet your whistle?" He held up a crystal decanter, half-filled with bourbon.

"No, thank you. I don't drink on the job. And you've got how much invested in them?"

He let out a chuckle and poured himself a splash. "Now, that isn't public information, officer. The fact that I own some shares, that's well known. But how much, now, that's my own durned business. Unless you came with a warrant?" He raised his eyebrows.

The detective frowned and let out a snort. "No warrant, at least not at the moment. Then how about your shares in Tactitron International?"

He gave another charming half-smile, this time with a shrug as he sat back in his executive chair. "I'm a Texan. We like guns."

"Tactitron manufactures far more than guns, Tiberius."

His smile dropped into a neutral expression, and he spoke in a flat voice. "That's Mr. Wilkinson."

The detective cleared his throat. "Very well. That's far more than guns, Mr. Wilkinson. Tactitron makes grenades, launchers, even bombs."

He leaned back, steepling his fingers. "And your point is?"

The detective's voice grew flinty. "My *point* is that your political activities are raising a great many red flags, and I've been charged with making sure that your political activities and your investments aren't connected, *Mister Wilkinson.*"

Suddenly, he was tired of dancing around the truth. He jumped to his feet, clenched his fists, and leaned forward. "That's none of your durned business, *Detective Morris.*"

He got the satisfaction of seeing the detective flinch, even if only a little. Tiberius was a big man, wide-shouldered, six-foot-three. He had plenty of experience intimidating others, even the police. Even a detective he'd known for nigh onto twenty years.

The lights in the office flickered as they stared at each other like two gunfighters at sundown in a wild west town.

His phone buzzed. Tiberius cursed the secretary for ruining a perfectly tense moment. "Yes, Sharon?"

"Just calling to remind you that you've got that group of investors coming in a few minutes."

"Right, thanks, sweetheart."

He raised his eyebrows at the detective. "Are we done here? I've got people coming."

With a scowl, Detective Morris rose to his feet. "We're done, for now, Mr. Wilkinson. But we'll be back."

As the disgruntled detective left, he told Sharon to call the electrician to check out his office overhead lights and wondered if things were getting too hot for him here. If the detective actually had anything on him, he could get a warrant, and then Tiberius would have to do some serious finagling.

Maybe he should look into moving his headquarters elsewhere. He glanced at the stack of newspapers and let out a humorless chuckle. *If I was a real A1 asshole, I'd move my HQ to Ireland.* He let out a mirthless chuckle at that idea.

While it sounded ridiculous, the notion had some twisted merit. He'd heard too many conflicting reports about who was doing what, to whom, and with what power. He absolutely hated relying on rumor and scuttlebutt.

If he was going to enact true change, he needed true information. And as good as his spy network was, they'd already let him down too many times. Hell, they'd even allowed a couple of PHAE spies to steal some physical records over in the UK a few weeks ago.

If he *did* move to Ireland, he'd have the advantage of first-hand experience and no delay in enacting his plans. He could tell what was true and what was inflated garbage, fake news.

Now, Tiberius was no stranger to fake news. Hell, he created a lot of it himself, for his own propaganda machine. But he needed to know the facts in order to subvert them properly. He didn't want to get caught out in any lies.

Or in any investigations.

# Chapter Six

"For she is beautiful, intelligent, and deeply in love with you.
Hence, we are confident that you will be much happier with her
than you would ever have been with a lady of loftier birth."

– Giovanni Boccaccio


**Bintou:**

Bintou glanced across the conference room at Lee, the young person she'd just met. They were about twelve years old and touched Bintou's mind as a test.

She gave a discrete nod, to show that she'd received their message. Hopefully, they'd be able to contact her again, once she was at Lugh's home.

Lugh kissed her fingers, and a shiver ran down her back. With a great deal of trepidation, Bintou took Lugh's hand. He promised to take her to his home, wherever that was.

Lugh's hand felt warm and dry in her own. Despite that, her own were cold and clammy, nerves getting the better of her.

Bintou adored traveling. Her greatest joys were visiting other countries and going on shopping sprees. Why should this trip be any different? And yet, it was. She was traveling to another world, another existence, however she wanted to label it.

Lugh had described it as a land under the hills, but that seemed like poetic license, something the monks would say. They'd just been transcribing ancient fairy stories and labeled the home of the fairies that way. She doubted they'd ever actually visited.

Would she ever get back? Most of the stories described returning from the otherworld as incredibly difficult. Or fraught with danger. Why had she agreed to this?

Lugh stepped forward, pulling her along. "Close your eyes, my sweet Bintou. And we will arrive before you can open them again."

Steeling her spine, Bintou squeezed her eyes shut so tight, geometric patterns flashed in the darkness. She gripped hard to his hand and took a step forward, almost stumbling. Then he tugged again, and she took another step. And another. A wash of cool, moist air caressed her skin, and she smelled sweet roses mixed with rotting moss.

Lugh spoke in a triumphant tone. "Now, open your eyes and behold the glory of Fairy!"

When she did as Lugh commanded, her eyes grew wide. Bintou took a full turn, staring at everything in a grand sweep. He'd let her hand go, holding his arms out. "Is this not everything I promised?"

There was no sun, but everything glowed with spectral light of shifting rainbow colors. Some things pulsed while others held a steady shine.

The trees were nothing like those she'd seen on Earth. They swayed in the nonexistent wind, leaves of purple, orange, pink, and white waving at her.

Tinkling music surrounded them, music without melody or form. And a sweet aroma, a mix of floral perfume and buttered popcorn, filled her nose.

Bintou took in a deep breath and closed her eyes again. This place felt like a warm hug from her mother.

As she let the breath out, her skin tingled and Lugh swept her into his arms, twirling her with a shout.

She let out a laugh, and he laughed with her. This place completely enchanted her, and she couldn't resist his kiss when he pressed his soft lips to hers. "Come, I will show you where we will live."

Bintou hadn't agreed to live with him, had she? But he must have presumed, since she came with him. How could she say no? Any wish to say no, to anything Lugh suggested, shed away with each step she took.

As they passed a tree, the branch twisted in a way that reminded her of the garden entrance on the Byrne farm. With great difficulty, she focused her mind on the real world, the world she'd been born into.

It took concentration to not only remember that place, but to recall that she was supposed to reach out to Lee, the telepath. She sent a questing thought, and felt it grabbed by someone. It hurt, pounding in her brain. Had she gotten through?

*I hear you*, came Lee's mental voice. Bintou let out a sigh. At least she could contact the outside world.

But did she really want to?

Lugh led her down a sparkling path through tall trees and swaying bushes. Water gurgled nearby and music played everywhere.

Lugh pulled her around a bend, and she came into full view of a soaring tower. Glittering white stone shone in the light, and Bintou could have sworn the tower itself swayed as the trees did.

She'd fallen into a true fairytale.

Glee lit Lugh's features. "I can't wait to show you inside!"

Bintou noticed he looked larger, stronger, even more impossibly handsome here. The human world had faded him into a pale copy.

As she entered the pointed arch, pale pinks and greens surrounded her in a circular room with translucent walls. A spiral staircase hugged the wall, and her eyes traveled up, wondering where they led.

Lugh clutched her hand. "Would you like to see it all? Or would you like to eat?"

That aroma of buttered popcorn intensified, though still with that thread of sweet perfume. Her stomach rumbled, making Lugh laugh. "Food it is!"

He snapped his fingers, and several beings appeared, bearing platters of food and drink. The creatures stood no taller than her knee, gnarled and twisted, like little bushes without leaves.

They set up a table and chairs in the center of the room, the walls pulsing slowly in ambient light, in time to the music.

Picking up a morsel and holding it near her lips, Lugh whispered, "Eat, my sweet Bintou. Take your fill of all the delights I offer you."

He said the last with a sly grin. Lugh popped the food into her mouth and kissed the back of her hand. Lightning shot through her blood, and there was no mistaking the double meaning of his offer, but her physical hunger overrode her other urges. For now.

She chewed the morsel, something sweet like honey, but crunchy with a hint of nut flavor.

As she sat in a cloud masquerading as a chair, a flash of memory intruded upon her bliss. Colin Byrne, telling stories by the peat fire at the farm, relating a tale about a human being who wandered into the land of fairy. "He ate but three bites of the food, but those three bites were his downfall. He had to stay for three days because of them. And when he returned to his home, three years had passed. His wife had given up on him and married another. His son had moved away, apprentice to a carpenter in another town. His life had been shattered for that brief pleasure."

Bintou had been reaching for the bright purple fruit in a wooden bowl, but she halted. Lugh let out a laugh so loud, it hurt her ears. "Surely you don't believe the tales?"

Another story nagged at her, one she'd read in childhood. Persephone had eaten six pomegranate seeds in the underworld and was held six months under the ground each year. Even tales about eating the fruit of knowledge of good and evil had severe consequences.

Bintou pushed through the glamor and the mind-fog and asked, "Are you sure? All the tales warn against accepting Fairy food."

Lugh took her hand and placed the purple fruit in her palm. "Eat. I promise that you can leave any time you ask."

But would she *want* to ask if she ate more food? Or if she stayed too long? For some reason, the span of three days stuck in her mind, perhaps from one of Colin's tales. "Can you promise me that you will return me to my home in Ireland, three days after I left?"

A flicker of something flashed across his face, but he gave a gracious nod. "I can promise you that."

"Then please do so."

Now the flash solidified into a frown, but he nodded again. "I so promise you. I will return you to your home in Ireland, three days after you left." Then he caressed the back of his hand on her cheek. "But you do not wish to leave right now, do you?"

Bintou's skin burned where he touched. He turned her wrist over, caressing the soft skin on the inside of her arm. She shivered with delight and anticipation, and then bit into the purple fruit.

While the juice and flesh of the fruit was tangy and sweet, everything she craved, her hunger faded as she locked gazes with the Irish god.

The bed was even softer than the chair had been, and her stomach was full of sweet fruit juices and sharp cheese. They washed it all down with honey-wine, and birdsong serenaded their lovemaking.

When she finally woke, sated in every way possible, Lugh still slept beside her, beautiful even in his repose.

Bintou wanted to touch every inch of his glowing, hot skin, to trace the lines of muscles now free of any clothing. Sweat glistened on his skin, and that surprised her. Fairies sweated? Her own dark skin shone with her efforts, and she rose to find something to wipe it away.

On bare feet, she padded into the next chamber. The walls still pulsed with their low light. The floor seemed solid but sprang slightly as she stepped, like a yoga mat.

Bintou found a basin with clear, cool water and a flaxen cloth. She dipped the cloth, wiping her face, arms, and chest, and anywhere else she'd sweated. This place, wherever it was, seemed much warmer than Ireland.

Even in summer, that land was cold and wet. This was much more like the warm clime she'd grown up in, despite the humidity.

Belatedly, she searched for clues, as Ciara had asked. Something that might give some indication of a weakness. But how would she be able to tell?

The rooms were almost bare, except the furniture and a few things for comfort. A bed, a wash basin, a shelf with food. She wandered into another chamber, searching for something else, though she didn't know what. Bintou glimpsed a servant, a tiny pixie of a creature, bipedal, more like a tree than a human, with bark and leaves instead of skin and hair.

The creature gave her a polite nod and went about their business, clearing away fruit rinds and pits, replacing it with more fruit.

Would they eat nothing but fruit, cheese, and mead here? As much as she loved them, her digestion might complain of such fare. But what else had she expected of the food in Fairy?

Her stomach rumbled, but she wasn't hungry. She'd just stuffed herself with fruit and cheese a few hours before. Maybe her body already craved meat already.

Then she recalled tales of time working differently in the otherworld. Would her body run on this time or real time? What if Lugh didn't honor his promise? Would he find a loophole after all?

Colin had coached her how to negotiate with the fae, but there was always the chance she'd missed something.

If she were kept here for years, all the goals, conflicts, and worries would be past. She might experience three days, but only return to the human world years later.

That idea both made her blood chill and held a certain charm. If she came back years later, then the current war would be over. She'd have avoided all that fighting.

On the other hand, she might come back to a world ruled by the PEM, after they'd eradicated all the Unhidden.

If that happened, she'd be far better staying in the land of Fairy with Lugh.

Bintou shook her head. She had a mission to complete, and she needed to concentrate on that. She must find something to fight against the ancient gods.

With renewed purpose, Bintou considered each object, comparing it to what she might have in her world. The walls weren't made of metal, wood, or plastic. Perhaps some sort of bone?

Bintou placed her hand on the surface, trying to identify the substance. She remembered a scrap of trivia, that archaeologists licked artifacts to see if they were bone or stone. Bone was porous, and their tongue would stick. Self-consciously, she bent forward and licked the pale pink glowing surface.

"Bintou, my darling creature, what in the name of Anu are you doing?" She spun to find Lugh leaning in the doorway wearing nothing but an amused smile and the shimmer of sweat. "If you're hungry, my luscious love, I can call for more food."

Embarrassed, she ducked her head. "I was just trying to figure out what the walls were made of."

"By eating them? I assure you, they aren't made of gingerbread. You've read too many fairy stories."

Bintou wanted to laugh out loud at the irony of that statement but gave a sheepish smile instead. "So, what *are* they made from?"

He caressed the wall beside him. "They are stone, but with such fine workmanship that the surface is as soft as butter. We have avoided metals in our construction, though we use some in our weapons and armor."

Bintou caressed the wall, marveling at the way the stone felt almost alive. "I thought you didn't care for iron?"

He let out a chuckle. "That has been true in the past, though we're not been so sensitive to it in this time. That change has allowed us to re-emerge in your world, did you not know? Iron doesn't burn now. It's not pleasant, not in the slightest, but it is tolerable."

That answered one of their questions. If the others thought iron would be an effective weapon against the gods, they'd be disappointed.

Bintou wanted to ask more, but Lugh stepped closer, removed her hand from the wall, and placed it on his chest.

His warm muscles throbbed beneath her palm. He cupped her cheeks in his hands and kissed her on the lips.

She closed her eyes at his velvet touch, a shiver running down her spine. All thoughts of her mission fled as desire exploded within her heart.

**Bintou:**

Sweet birdsong woke her from somnolent pleasure this time. Once again, Lugh slept beside her, stunning in his relaxed repose. Bintou rose and splashed sweet water on her face, once again in command of her purpose.

She hadn't been able to think about anything but pleasure when Lugh touched her. It was like a madness, a mental spell.

Maybe Lugh actually did have glamor to cloud her mind, relegating her thoughts to animal lust. Bintou grinned at the memory of their lovemaking, their wanton desires and the way he made her body erupt in pleasure.

She'd never been so daring before, so eager to try new things. So full of lust and recklessness. Without thinking, she stepped back into the sleeping chamber.

Bintou slapped her cheeks and backed out again. No, she must concentrate. She dressed and walked out to the garden, surveying the countryside.

The tower stood on a gentle rolling hillside covered in green grass. Butterflies and songbirds flitted between the swaying trees. Gurgling water was still hidden somewhere, and Bintou decided she must find it. Perhaps she'd find a clue there.

Strolling through the trees, she tried to find the source of the gurgling. It grew louder as she pushed through some bushes to find the burbling brook. Clear water tumbled over colorful stones, and flashes of fish shone with their own light, like everything else in this place. She bent to take a sip of the water, and it tasted like the sweetest honey.

Nothing here suggested any clue about the gods' weaknesses, and she was about to return to the tower. But she heard a new sound, a mewing cat.

Curious, she searched through the bushes until she found the source. A creature very similar to Qacha's cat, Manol peeked from behind some river reeds. What would Qacha's cat be doing in Fairy?

She stooped to speak with the cat. "Are you Manol? You look like him."

The cat stood on his hind legs and shook their head, speaking in a high, gravely voice. "No, but Manol is my friend. I like him."

Bintou fall backwards on into the wet grass. "You can talk!"

The creature morphed into something vaguely cat-like, but no longer resembled Manol. "I talk, but I don't do it much. Sometimes my head hurts."

Bintou pulled herself back up and crouched next to the creature. "What should I call you? And how do you know Manol? Isn't he in... the other world?" She had no idea how to describe her world to a denizen of this one.

"You can call me Beagan. It means small, and I am small. He is not here, he is there. I visit him often! I also visit his servant."

She furrowed her brow. "Please call me Bintou. Manol has a servant? Who is that?"

"The fire woman. Do you not know her?" Beagan cocked their head in a comical pose.

The fire woman. That might be Qacha. "A woman taller than me? With very short hair and skin lighter than mine?"

"Yes! That's the servant!"

Bintou hadn't seen Qacha in ages and felt guilty for not knowing what had happened to her. "Is she here? Or with Manol?"

"She is in Brigit's home, just like you are in Lugh's home."

Possibilities swam in Bintou's mind. Was Qacha close enough to visit? She would enjoy seeing her again. She always admired the woman's strength and clarity.

Besides, they could compare notes. Maybe Qacha had seen something that might help them in a battle against the gods. "Is the fire woman close? I would like to speak with her."

Beagan cocked their head, and then their gaze flicked to Lugh's home and back to her. "I can ask. Stay here!"

The creature faded in a shower of sparks.

**Qacha:**

Qacha had just finished a swim in the pond when Beagan returned to her, their tail quivered with excited anticipation. Brigit had left hours before, and Qacha was enjoying the free time.

In her life, she'd rarely known the luxury of so much time to relax, and she delighted in the leisure. At the same time, boredom was creeping in. Speaking with Beagan offered a relief to that boredom.

With a ghost of a smile, Qacha sat cross-legged. "And did you find Manol? Is he doing well?"

"I found him! He's fat and happy. The girl servant feeds him delicious treats every day."

Qacha had never fed her cat human food or treats, but he deserved some pampering since she'd left him with a stranger. Still, when the current situation resolved, she'd have to get him used to his normal lifestyle again.

"I have other news! There is a human who wishes to see you."

Qacha sat up, abruptly wary, her eyes darting to the path. "A human? Here in Fairy? Or where Manol is living?"

Beagan shook their head. "Here in Fairy! Not far. They are visiting Lugh. The human's skin is very dark, like tree bark."

Could the Fae mean Bintou? Or Ibrahim? She couldn't think of anyone else with that description who would know she was here. Come to think of it, *they* wouldn't even know she was here. "What is their name?"

Beagan sat on their haunches and used their hind paw to scratch at their ear. "She told me. Something like be-too?"

"Bintou?"

The fairy creature leapt up and down in excitement. "That's it! That's what the human said. Her voice is silky and soothing."

But why had the Malian woman come to Fairy? Qacha had been brought here against her will, but she'd been free from pain since she arrived, so was in no hurry to return to the real world.

Had Bintou come willingly? She suddenly ached for human company. "I would like to speak to her."

Beagan faded into sparks without a response. Qacha wasn't certain if they were fetching Bintou or just left. She stood just as a noise came from Brigit's roundhouse.

Frowning, she hurried to investigate. The goddess had said she wouldn't return for a while, something about meeting Macha.

Qacha yearned to ask her more details, but the goddess wore a haughty expression that prevented even Qacha of being so bold.

Instead, she'd kept herself busy straightening the roundhouse and examining Brigit's forge. That's where the sound came from now.

A large barrel next to the forge held water, used for quenching and cooling objects after they were worked on the anvil. Qacha peered into the water, noting ripples on the surface. Something was inside.

As a Daughter of Fire, water was not her friend. She frowned at the black shining depths, trying to discern what was inside without touching it. With a flash of inspiration, she grabbed a long-handled ladle and stirred.

An eruption of water flew at her face. She stumbled away and landed on her back, a huge frog-like being on her chest.

Another Fae creature? She was getting tired of them just appearing out of the blue. "What are you?"

It let out a mighty croak and hopped toward the reeds, disappearing with a rustle. Perhaps it hadn't been a Fae creature after all, just a normal frog. Did normal animals live in Fairy?

Beagan popped back into view next to her. "I found her! I will bring you to her." They started to run up the path and with a final glance back toward where the frog disappeared, Qacha hurried to catch up.

The fairy creature ran faster than she'd expected, darting in and out of the reeds, and she lost sight of them several times. "Beagan! Stay on the path."

"But that is boring! I like to swerve."

"It's difficult for me to follow."

They sighed. "Very well. I will try."

The path branched several times, and Qacha tried to keep track of the route. Just to be cautious, she broke branches at each fork.

She might have followed the fairy creature for ten minutes. It may have been ten hours. Qacha had no way to tell how time passed here, and no measure of distance, as the countryside all looked the same.

Finally, a white tower soared above the trees. That must be where Bintou was.

Beagan winked in and out of existence, evidently eager for the meeting. "She's close! We're close!"

Qacha pursed her lips at the creature's antics as she strode toward the door. But before she reached it, Bintou appeared in the doorway, dressed in bright colors that set off her dark skin. Qacha felt unexpected relief and joy flood through her.

Qacha had never had close friends. Her life had been mostly solitary, working as a chef in top restaurants before she self-destructed her career.

But the few weeks she'd spent in PHAE had allowed her to forge strong bonds, and she greeted Bintou with a fierce hug. The other woman's eyes grew wide before she hugged back.

When they let go, Bintou gave her a happy grin. "I couldn't believe it when I heard you were here. Are you well?"

Qacha gave a single nod. "I am well enough. I see you are still a collector of beautiful things."

Bintou chuckled and glanced over her shoulder. "Yes, you can definitely say that."

In a low whisper, Bintou asked, "Ciara has sent me on a mission. We're worried about the gods having too much power over us. Have you found any weakness that might help?"

Qacha thought about the scene in the laboratory and gave a quick nod. "I may have discovered something."

Lugh emerged from the structure, wearing nothing but a loincloth and glistening muscles. His lazy smile and possessive arm around Bintou's waist told Qacha what they'd been doing.

Bintou cleared her throat. "This is Qacha. She's my friend."

An unexpected flush of warmth rose in Qacha's cheeks. Lugh gripped her hands. "You are Qacha! I have heard of you. I am told that you are a fierce warrior!"

Qacha felt much more comfortable being described as a warrior than as a friend. She straightened her spine and squared her shoulders. While her battles had been in the practice field or kitchen, they were still battles. "I have fought, yes."

"And you've won! Macha is eager to meet you. Brigit has been bragging about your exploits so much, she's already composed a bard's song."

Qacha had rarely flushed so much in her life. The gods had been gossiping about her? And writing songs? Both pride and concern flooded her.

Lugh snapped for his servants, and they prepared a meal for three. Then they wasted time with idle chatter. She must find a way to get Bintou alone, so they could discuss her discovery.

As if she read Qacha's mind, Bintou turned to Lugh. "I would like to take a walk with my friend. We haven't seen each other for a while and must catch up." Without waiting for his response, she grabbed Qacha's hand, and they strode for the path.

Qacha glanced back, but Lugh wore a bemused expression, not an angry one. They kept walking until they were out of sight of the tower.

She wasn't sure if she could fight a bemused god, much less an angry one. So far, Lugh seemed even-tempered, certainly more so than Brigit or Macha. And obviously so full of lustful energy that Bintou practically glowed with her own light after their dalliance.

Qacha was relieved she felt no attraction to the man. She'd finished with being attracted to men, anyhow. Too many heartbreaks and betrayals. This one seemed nice enough, unlike Taranis. Even the gods must have different personalities. That didn't mean she would trust any of them.

As the path curved, Qacha whispered in Bintou's ear. "Do they have ways to listen to us?"

Bintou shrugged and sat on a rock beside the path, speaking in perfect Mongolian. "I'm not certain, but they have just learned English. We know other languages."

Qacha gave a sly smile and answered in her native tongue as she sat next to her friend. "So we do! I've always admired your cleverness."

"Have you?" The other woman glanced down at her clasped hands. "You said you'd discovered something. That sounds clever to me."

"When we toured a laboratory in Kildare, Brigit cried out when she touched a plastic beaker. It's possible that they cannot stand the touch of that substance. After all, plastic is artificially crafted with polymers. They are fabled to be sensitive to iron, but they seem to have found a way around that."

"Lugh mentioned iron, and something about the magnetic pole shift. They still don't like to touch it, but it doesn't hurt them."

"Hmm. Maybe iron was a recent invention back when they were alive? And now it's older, they can bear it. But plastic is new."

Bintou tapped her lip. "That's logical. Not that the gods are required to be logical."

Qacha halted, staring at something rustling in the grass. But when nothing appeared, she continued. "But how do we get this information to PHAE?"

Bintou glanced back down the path, but no sign of Lugh's tower peeked through the trees. "I have a contact. Can you keep watch for a moment?"

The Mongolian woman scanned the surrounding area while Bintou closed her eyes and clenched her fists. Then she bowed her head, rubbing her temples. She squeezed her eyes shut even harder, then let out a gasp.

When she looked up, her eyes were red, as if she were drunk. "Maybe I don't have a contact. It hurt before, but now I can't seem to get through."

Qacha remembered Manol and his new friend. "I might have a way to send a message. But it involves the creature that brought me here. We would have to use your language skills, though."

Bintou raised her eyebrows. "Oh?"

"I can write a message to Manol. No one at the Byrne farm or at PHAE can read Mongolian, but if you coded a message in, say, Japanese, Hiroki or Masaaki could read it."

A slow smile spread across Bintou's face. "You're definitely being clever today. I'll need writing tools."

174

Qacha rose to her feet and offered her hand to help Bintou. "We can get some at Brigit's place. She writes poetry, so she keeps vellum and ink."

They wandered back toward Brigit's home to maintain the illusion of a casual stroll. Qacha thanked her foresight in breaking reeds and branches along the path. One fork had no branch broken. Qacha peered down each path, tapping her lip. "I swear I broke something at each turn."

Bintou scanned the ground and pointed. "There, what's that?"

Qacha bent to examine the bit of branch and nodded. "That's recently broken, but I don't see where it came from."

"Maybe it's growing back already?"

Qacha frowned as she examined the branches more closely. New growth was budding even as she watched. "You're right! That means my previous hints won't work on the way back."

She straightened, staring down the path with a growing foreboding.

Bintou placed a hand on her forearm. "I have been counting the turns. I think I can find my way back. Besides, once I have his tower in view, I will be able to find it."

Qacha wasn't so certain, but she was grateful Bintou had thought of it. Just in case, though, she broke new branches at each fork. This time, she actually broke them off and placed the bit pointed in the correct direction.

They made it through the twists and turns and finally found Brigit's home.

Qacha rifled through Brigit's supplies, coming back with several bits of scrap vellum, ink, and a sparkling purple quill. She had no idea what bird might have provided the feather, but it was nothing natural to the human world.

Bintou painted kanji script in elegant calligraphy. She really was a brimming font of beautiful things. Qacha had never really held true affection for anyone other than her grandfather, and even that had been more duty than love.

She'd had lovers, but they'd been all physical attraction and very little emotional involvement. Of course, that meant it should have hurt less when they inevitably left, but that wasn't true.

Now, this partnership, this friendship, she'd formed with Bintou from Mali made her feel warm and safe. In basic terms, Bintou made her smile, and she rarely smiled.

Of course, Max made her smile, but that was because he was just as harsh, cuss-headed, and angry as she was. That wasn't a partnership, more like a meeting of kindred spirits. She certainly held no physical affection for the Australian man.

But her feelings for Bintou were undergoing an odd shift. Did she have latent affection for the woman? Qacha had never explored such feelings and wasn't sure how to deal with them. Mongolia was not a safe place to express such feelings for another woman.

Was this why she'd never truly felt a connection with her male lovers? But Bintou seemed to prefer men and had given no hint that she wanted anything else, so she should put the notion from her mind. Besides, Qacha valued their friendship too much to risk it with an unwise advance.

Bintou pushed away from the table with a sigh. "There! Finished. Now, will you call for your Beagan? Or should I?"

"I will call him."

As they waited for the Fae creature to return, Qacha asked, "If I get this note to Manol, then Fiona will find it, that's certain. And you've labeled the note with Hiroki's name, correct?"

Bintou grinned. "That should be enough for her to tell her parents, and they can get the note to Hiroki. He's seldom far from Ciara, as they both work out of the Dublin bunker. It might take a while, though."

Qacha let out a long breath. "I hope that's enough. There are many things that might go wrong."

The younger woman gave a shrug. "The information is being sent. There's little else we can do from here. I'll try to contact Lee again later, in case it goes through this time. But I'm not even sure we can leave here without the gods' permission."

They fell to silence at that prospect just as Beagan faded into sight. "Did you call for me? I was visiting Manol. He is lonely."

Qacha crouched next to the small creature. "If he is lonely, then it would be best if you returned to Manol. Can you bring this with you? It's a note for Fiona, the young human who cares for him. I would like to thank her for all her efforts."

She glanced at her friend before continuing. "But before you go, can you bring Bintou back to Lugh's dwelling?"

He nodded with vigor. "Yes! I can do this. I will do this well. You will be proud of me."

**Qacha:**

Beagan and Bintou left, and Qacha waited. And waited. She got bored with waiting.

The goddess still hadn't returned, so Qacha decided to write something, to hide the fact that some of the vellum was missing. She had no talent for poetry, but she wrote a few mediocre lines, just to have something to show.

Then she grinned and wrote lines from a heavy metal song. How would Brigit know it was not her own work? Besides, the rage in the words pleased her.

The goddess arrived just as she finished the stanza. Qacha glanced up as Brigit came in, her clothing scuffed in several places but wearing a pleased grin.

Brigit peered over her shoulder. "You have been busy! What have you created?"

"I tried to write a poem. This is my latest attempt, but I'm still not happy with it."

Qacha put the vellum to one side. "Did you enjoy your day?"

Brigit settled into a chair and crossed her arms. "My afternoon has been filled with interesting information from the human world, as well as some revelations in the chemical laboratory they've given me. I am ready for something else. Read your lines to me."

Qacha cleared her throat. "'Til the bottle runs out or the clouds roll away, it's just whiskey and rain, like my soul's on fire."

Brigit blinked a few times and gave a belated nod. "I appreciate the rage, and the words suit your spirit. But it is well you aren't happy with it. More work is to be done on that. This whiskey, that is a drink that Macha has sampled. She approves of it."

"I can well imagine she approves. It's a powerful drink, and appropriate for a warrior."

Brigit cocked her head to one side with a frown. "I wish to sample it."

Qacha gave a shrug. "Well, I can't conjure any here. We'll have to get some from the other world."

"We will do that. Where should we go?"

Almost not daring to hope, Qacha's mind raced. Perhaps she could find a way to arrange a meeting with Ciara, or another way to get a message to the PHAE.

Suddenly, the long, convoluted path Bintou's note must take seemed much too complex.

"There is a distillery in Dublin, from the Jameson brand. It's best to obtain the drink at its source."

As Brigit stared out the window, a finger to her lip, Qacha clenched her fists and tried not to say anything to change Brigit's mind.

However, the goddess sprang into action with a suddenness that belied her human form and grabbed Qacha's hands, yanking her to her feet. The surrounding roundhouse and blacksmithy faded into gray and Qacha's stomach wrenched in protest.

A busy Dublin street surrounded them. A few people stared, but then kept walking, intent on their errands. Someone bumped into Qacha, cursing her clumsiness. Qacha rounded on the rude person, but then scanned the street. She didn't recognize any of the buildings. "Where are we?"

Brigit shrugged. "We are in Dublin, but I am not familiar enough to know where. I have been to that building."

The goddess pointed across the street, and Qacha recognized Leinster House. "That's where the government meets, but I'm not sure how to get to Jameson Distillery from here. We should ask directions."

With a purposeful stride, she walked toward Leinster House. If she could get inside, she might have a chance of staying in this world, out of Brigit's power.

But she had barely gone a few steps before the goddess gripped her arm, halting her. "No. We will get transportation. I have seen these used." She held her hand up, and a black cap pulled near them. Qacha's hopes fell but she resolved to try again later.

The cabbie stuck his head out of the car window. "Where to?"

With a glance back at Brigit, who was watching with interest, Qacha said, "How far away is the Jameson Distillery?" Then she remembered she had no money or credit cards, and certainly Brigit would have none. "Wait, we must do something else first. Thank you."

Brigit scowled as the cab drove away. "Why did you dismiss that servant? He seemed willing to take us where we wish to go."

She shook her head. "We have nothing to pay him with. I'm not sure where my own purse disappeared to, but for such services, we need money. The PHAE in Leinster House can provide us with either money or a tour."

This time, Brigit didn't halt her. With each step, Qacha's hopes climbed a notch. But just as they reached the massive double doors, a soulful screech ripped across the sky, like sandpaper across raw nerves.

Qacha clapped her hands to her head, trying to block out the painful sound. Brigit strode through the doors, apparently unaffected by the horrible noise.

But the sound was like a physical assault, and Qacha fell to her knees on the threshold, her head pounding like a thousand drums on a Mongolian plain.

The goddess stopped when she realized her human pet wasn't following and stepped back outside. Letting out a whimper, Qacha curled into a fetal position as the wail undulated into a sonic assault. A police siren added to the chaos, then an ambulance.

Brigit shone with an internal light, and she sang out her own call, something more soothing, calming, but it didn't make a dent in the wail. Other notes joined hers, forming an ethereal harmony, battling the shrieking cacophony.

More shining forms appeared in the square, becoming several of the gods. Macha, Manannán, Taranis, a hefty god Qacha didn't recognize, and Lugh, with Bintou in tow.

Bintou was also holding her head and ran to Qacha. The Malian woman pulled her to her feet, and they embraced, gripping each other with fierce relief. It helped to cut the pain.

Macha's mouth was open wide, her jaw looking unhinged as her scream cut across the air, filling all the quiet corners of the city with rage. Green summer leaves swirled in the wind, forming eddies in the city square. They withered to brown and crumbled to dust in moments. The gale whipped dust and debris against Qacha's skin, almost scouring it like a sandstorm.

One of the protestors used their sign as a weapon, hitting someone on the head. Then another protestor punched the man next to him. And a woman slapped her companion.

Across the square, several men in sports shirts were brawling with abandon.

Something within Qacha made her furious. Her blood boiled and she wanted to rip someone apart, limb by limb. Instead, she held tight to Bintou, not trusting herself without her friend.

Manannán placed a hand on Macha's shoulder and Brigit's song caressed her. Finally, Macha's noise decreased and the rage faded from Qacha's mind, and she could think again.

She stood in front of Bintou, inserting herself between the human and the gods, should she need protection. Qacha whispered, "Stay close to me. We'll move into the building, away from the gods."

Bintou's eyes grew wide, and her gaze flicked to Lugh, but he spoke with Manannán in urgent tones. With the gods preoccupied, they inched back, closer to safety.

Then fierce wind blew the doors shut with a slam. Frantic, Qacha tried to open them, but they wouldn't budge.

Finally, Macha closed her mouth and the horrid sound faded to nothing. The gale-force winds died to a summer breeze, and the remaining leaves floated to the ground, some halfway to rot.

Manannán addressed the other gods. **"We cannot act without consideration. Our relations must be honored."**

Macha's mouth twisted into a nasty smile. **"They have already betrayed our trust. We have no patience nor consideration for traitors."**

Taranis growled, clenching his fists. **"Destroy them all! They deserve no quarter given!"**

Thunder rolled across the clear sky. Every muscle in her body tensed and she grasped Bintou's hand as they stood with their backs against the doors to Leinster House.

Where was Max? He was the only one who had experience with this thunder god, as far as she knew. But she had no idea where the Son of Air had disappeared to.

She'd been so out of touch with the other Unhidden. Other than Bintou, she didn't know where anyone else was now. Was Anna still learning from Manannán? Qacha didn't see her. And where was the native woman, Komie? Or Róisín? *What in the name of all things is going on here?*

Manannán marched to within a few inches from the thunder god's face. **"You will not destroy anyone, Taranis. You will obey me."**

**"You have no control over me! Your only domain is the sea. I am the sky!"**

The strange god, with wide shoulders and a round belly, stood next to Manannán. **"I have control over you, Taranis. You will listen to Manannán's commands as if they were my own."**

Macha growled out, **"In this? Or in everything?"**

The door behind them burst open, and Komie stared at everything with worry and confusion.

While the sea god and the newcomer exchanged glances, Taranis let out a howl. **"No! I will not listen to either of you!"**

He raised his hands and dark storm clouds swirled overhead, once again making gale-force winds in the city square. A new flurry of leaves, dust, and debris scoured them all as the clouds swirled in a whirlwind. Taranis rose on this column of storm clouds and disappeared into the sky.

Then, a deluge pelted them, making everyone run for shelter.

Qacha grabbed Bintou's arm to pull her into the safety of Leinster House, but Lugh appeared beside them and grabbed the other. He spoke in an implacable tone. "She is not going with you."

Channeling her warrior ancestry, Qacha yanked back. "She damn well is!"

The god's face turned dark, and his voice took on the odd resonance of the others. **"I have laid claim to her, and she is mine."**

**Komie:**

Komie rushed to the doors of Leinster House to discover the source of that awful noise. At first, the door seemed jammed, but she unlatched the lock and shoved it with her shoulder.

When she burst upon the open city square, she halted in her tracks, trying to take everything in as she gripped the doorway. Several gods stood on one side of the square. Bintou and Qacha were in front of the doors, though Qacha gripped Bintou's hand.

Rolling thunder made her look up into the clear, summery sky. This couldn't be a natural occurrence, could it? Ireland's weather was usually mild.

One of the gods shot into the air on a column of storm clouds and a downpour pounded them. Komie stepped toward Qacha and Bintou to help them back to shelter. But Lugh had grabbed one of Bintou's hands, and a battle of wills was sparking between him and Qacha.

Qacha and Lugh held Bintou between them like a wishbone, each pulling on an arm. Komie placed a hand on each of theirs, yelling, "Stop! Both of you!"

Lugh dismissed her almost immediately and yanked Bintou from Qacha's grip. **"As I said, she is mine."**

Qacha screamed, "No!" And lunged toward the Malian woman, but Lugh and Bintou disappeared in a flash of lightning, and Qacha fell to the concrete with a grunt.

Komie helped her to her feet. "What happened?"

The other woman rounded on her. "You distracted me! I almost had her safe!"

Backing away, Komie wiped the rain from her eyes. "You almost had her split in two! Did you think you could win tug of war with a god?"

Qacha let out a howl of frustration and stalked toward the building with clenched fists. Komie followed her, and once they were safely out of the storm, she hurried to the meeting room where Ciara and Hiroki had been discussing the latest developments with her. The Mongolian woman growled as she followed.

As they both entered, Ciara asked, "What happened out there?"

Trying to squeeze the worst of the wet off her clothes, Qacha said, "A fight between the gods. Macha let out this skull-splitting scream, Brigit tried to calm her."

Ciara let out a snort. "Obviously that didn't work. What else?"

Komie continued. "I think Macha and Taranis have gone off the deep end. Manannán has wrested back some control, and the Dagda helped, but there's definitely a rift forming."

Qacha glared at her. "The Dagda? Is that the new god?"

She nodded. "He's an all-father type. A bit silly at times, but he seems reasonable. Ciara, I saw Bintou, but only for a few moments. Lugh took her against her will."

Qacha crossed her arms and glowered at Komie. "She and I had a plan to escape. I tried to help her, but I was interrupted."

Ciara leaned forward with interest. "You were able to plan with Bintou? Were you both in the same place? We've been trying to find you for days. We had a telepathic contact with Bintou, but Lee fell ill with a fever, unable to use their talent."

"Yes, we were both in Fairy. She was with Lugh, and I was with Brigit. Did you receive my note?"

The Irish woman cocked her head. "Note? What note?"

Qacha glanced at Hiroki, but he remained silent. "We crafted a note, but it was only recently sent. It may still be on the way. This doesn't matter now, as we have information about the gods' possible weakness. It is time to craft a battle plan against the ancient gods of Ireland."

Nothing but heartbeats and the slow drip of water broke the resulting silence. Then Hiroki jumped to his feet and burst into frenzied laughter. "You are joking! Of course, you are. Your command of English is getting better. I almost did not recognize the humor."

Qacha leveled a glare at the Japanese man. "I am not joking. They are unpredictable and unreliable. They represent a clear and present danger to us in Ireland and the world. We must determine a way to stop them."

He shook his head and began pacing. "You cannot be serious. They've done nothing but help us! Dian Cecht has healed half the nation. They helped us fight off a submarine attack in the middle of the night. They are our only chance of surviving!"

Qacha pursed her lips. "There is no way to control this storm god. And Macha is a goddess of battle. Their tempers are too volatile. They will be our downfall. We cannot trust them."

Ciara tapped her lip. "I have to admit that Qacha has an excellent point. Even if we don't use the plan, it would be wise to formulate a strategy. We've already discussed this with the Taoiseach and the Dáil. Qacha, you said you had information to share about a weakness?"

**Hiroki:**

Hiroki hated everything about this plan. He hated the idea of even having to make a plan. Why would they want to betray their own allies this way? Betrayal of trusted allies was the most dishonorable thing. His skin itched at how much disgrace he was being part of.

Oghma had been kind to him, and had taught Hiroki fascinating techniques of communication, turns of phrase to craft the best speech, even making them poetic.

Though Hiroki was Japanese and not Irish, the god had taken him under his wing. Oghma could speak ancient Irish, of course, but he had yet to find a language the god of communication didn't already know better than Hiroki himself.

So, as Hiroki was commanded by the Taoiseach to craft a declaration of war against the ancient gods, his very nature rebelled.

He'd agreed to help PHAE in their speeches, and that was his job. He believed in the PHAE's mission. But when they'd sent him across the country, making speeches to assure the population that everything was fine, that had bothered Hiroki very much. Lying to anyone was bad; lying to an entire country was horrible.

Now, this was in an entirely different realm of betrayal. He didn't want to do it, but defying PHAE would take more courage than he had.

Could he create such a draft so poorly that he was taken off the assignment? He detested the inherent deceit in such a ploy, but that seemed to be his only option. His stomach clenched at the idea of deliberately not doing his best work.

Hiroki's only other course of action was to refuse. But how could he refuse to do his job? He couldn't even quit in good conscience. He was here in Ireland as a guest and employee of PHAE. If he were to quit, he'd have to find a way to return to his home in Japan or become an illegal resident.

Even if his father hadn't already disowned him, he'd be returning in disgrace.

Hiroki had to admit that he had no honorable choices left. The best he could do was be honorable to himself, which meant doing the best he knew how, even if the task itself had no honor.

With a sigh, Hiroki bent to his work, creating the declaration of war against his allies. When Oghma learned of this, he'd cut off Hiroki's apprenticeship, and he'd be adrift without a mentor. Again.

Ciara burst in, her face a mask of agitation.

He and Masaaki exchanged a glance, and Hiroki asked, "What has happened?"

Instead of answering, she turned on the news on the wall screen.

A red-haired news reporter spoke in urgent tones. "Reports are coming in now of a rogue storm hitting villages across the Irish countryside.

186

While Ireland has very few, rare tornadoes, a massive F5 storm has formed without warning and is cutting a swath of destruction from central Dublin, west through Kildare. It's now moving southwest toward Carlow."

The reporter's gaze shifted nervously. "Residents are urged to evacuate if they can or to find underground shelter. Do not go outside, repeat, do not go outside! This storm is almost a kilometer across, full of teeming rain and winds of more than 200 kilometers per hour."

The reporter paused to swallow, her face ashen. "Further reports of outbreaks of senseless violence are coming from the north of Dublin. People are bursting into murderous rampages, attacking other people with whatever they can get their hands on. Everything from umbrellas to downed branches are being used as weapons to hurt others."

The news anchor asked, "Has anyone said why they are doing this?"

"The few survivors we've spoken to have said their mind just went blank, and they woke up standing over bloody bodies of their victims."

She glanced to one side and gave a faint nod. "We believe that both these incidents are connected to the ancient Irish gods who have recently come forth to help Ireland in her hour of need. We've received confirmation that two of the gods, Taranis and Macha, were recently seen in Leinster Square, arguing loudly. Our research team has told us that Taranis is the god of thunderstorms, while Macha is a goddess of war and destruction."

The reporter paused, glancing off screen a second time. "Again, we urge all residents to remain in their homes if they live north of Dublin. We are not certain where these gods are headed, or if there is a pattern to their path. Authorities are working on a way to halt their progress."

Hiroki clasped his hands under the table in an effort not to fidget. "The authorities. Do they mean us?"

Ciara nodded. "We're the only ones who have a chance of stopping them."

But Hiroki didn't want to stop them. Yes, he wanted to stop the destruction, but they needed to find a way that didn't upset the gods. Not all of them were murderous chaotic beings.

He wanted so badly to tell Ciara about Oghma. About all the things he'd taught, all the plans he'd shared. Maybe Oghma could help against Macha and Taranis?

But his Irish mentor had extracted a promise from Hiroki to stay silent about his very existence. He couldn't honorably break that promise. Besides, god or not, Oghma was a scholar, not a warrior.

Oghma had assured him everything would be fine. He'd said there would be chaos before there was calm, but that the gods had a grand plan, a scheme to make everything work.

Still, this was worse than chaos. This was more like Armageddon. Hiroki reminded himself that he must trust in this information. He must have faith in Oghma.

Hiroki *had* to trust Oghma, as he had no one else to trust.

# Chapter Seven

"Anybody depending on somebody else's gods
is depending on a fox not to eat chickens."
– Zora Neale Hurston

**Max:**

One moment, Max had been standing next to Anna, Róisín, and Carlos, facing the terror of an angry thunder god. Max had been bloody terrified, but he was damned if he was going to abandon his friends.

Max was no deserter. He might not have a snowball's chance in hell of beating the thunder god alone, but with this team, he might have a chance.

He was so bloody wrong.

The next moment, after a flash of lightning and a punch in the gut, he blacked out.

When he finally woke, he lay in darkness. He tried to open his eyes and realized they were already open. Max felt around him, but only felt cool, packed dirt under him. He lifted himself into a sitting position, and his head spun, which made his stomach churn and gurgle. His chest hurt like a mother fucker.

Max patted his shirt, and singed fabric crackled beneath his hand, then felt sticky. Everything ached, and that might be blood. Gingerly, Max rose to his feet, but his dizziness made him fall back on his butt almost immediately.

**"Do not move."**

*Bloody hell, that's Taranis.* Max held his breath. If the thunder god had him alone, away from any protection or moderating force, Max was a dead man, no doubt about it. He let his breath out again, as the dizziness almost made him pass out.

**"You have been insolent for the last time."**

A second rumbling tickled the dirt, and Max hoped against hope that one of the other gods was coming to rescue him. He had to keep Taranis talking, so he asked in a light, conversational tone, "Let's talk real talk here. Why do you hate me so much?"

**"You are insolent."**

"Yeah, you said that. Is that your favorite word or something? Or do you know others?"

The air around him growled, and Max thought maybe his diplomacy could use a bit of work. That had never been his strong suit. "So, Is the Dagda your boss or something?"

**"He is not in charge of me."**

"I thought he was a father-god? Or am I getting the information wrong?"

**"He is *an* all-father. He is not *the* all-father."**

That was actually like useful information. Max lost a bit of his caution and asked, "Is there a god in charge of everyone, then? Or is it pretty much a free-for-all?"

**"I am in charge of myself."**

Back to square one, then. But then Max tried a new tactic. "How many gods are there? Have all the ancient gods come back to life here and now? Or are there still some sleeping?"

Taranis didn't answer at first, and Max thought he must have pissed him off again, but eventually, the thunder god spoke in a quieter voice. **"Some of our brethren are gone forever. Some still slumber. Some are awake but powerless. Some have more power than they ever had."**

Just as Max opened his mouth to ask more details, thunder vibrated the earth. Taranis boomed, **"Enough! You ask too many questions."**

190

He shut up and hoped he hadn't dropped himself into the shit once more. The rumbling grew louder, and Max struggled to his feet. He fell down, but this time not because he was dizzy.

This time, the ground itself betrayed him. It shook like an earthquake. Without any light, Max couldn't tell what was happening, but he was willing to bet Taranis was having another temper tantrum, and Max would suffer for it.

Footsteps pounded closer. Max clenched his fists, ready to fight any way he could. Belatedly remembering his own power, he quested his mind to the local winds, but no answer came.

Taranis had probably taken him to some hidden pocket of the otherworld, to play cat and mouse with him until the god tired of playing.

Well, Max didn't feel like waiting around for that. He could think of few things worse than being perpetually tormented by some petty god with the mother of all anger management issues. His name was Max, not Prometheus. "Fine! Give me what you got, Thunder Boy! Hit me!"

The rumbling grew so loud, Max's ears ached. The sound pounded on his brain, making everything tingle. He clenched his fists and his stomach was doing flip-flops so hard, he was surprised it didn't invert. The stench of dank earth and scorched skin tickled his nose.

More footsteps added to the rumbling, and Max let out a scream. His already-black world disappeared.

**Róisín:**

While Anna did battle with the thunder god, Róisín dragged Max's unconscious body away from Taranis' reach and into the hospital. With the help of two nurses, she wrestled him into a cot.

Róisín drew her healing power up through the earth, into her legs, her body, out through her arms and tingling fingers. A blue glow enveloped Max, and she shouted with triumph.

However, while his skin was no longer scorched and gaping wounds got smaller, that was all. She just didn't have the power she used to when Dian Cecht lived in her body.

Róisín let out a cry of frustration and tried again, but the power flowed even less the second time. And the third time it was barely a trickle.

The burns across his body looked like a road map, branches of lines across his veins where lightning had traveled through his blood. Those, she could heal after a few sessions, though she had to rest several hours after each.

She repeated this cycle, heal, rest, heal rest, several times. Each time, Max healed a little more.

Róisín had to keep reminding herself to concentrate on Max, and pay no attention to the others in the ward. No one here was in any serious danger, and Max was her friend.

But no matter how much she tried to heal him, nothing seemed to help much.

It was several days before she could even get Max to moan in his sleep. Róisín wasn't sure if his unconsciousness was from his physical injury, a mental injury, or sheer blood-mindedness on the Australian's part, but Róisín was determined to get through to him.

Max wouldn't even open his eyes, though she sensed his mind was working overtime, wherever he really was. His eyes moved beneath his eyelids in rapid movement, signs of life that encouraged her.

Each time Róisín slept, she woke up later and later. These healing efforts were exhausting her, but she refused to give up on Max. She'd gotten so used to the easy healing power Dian Cecht gave her that her own Unhidden talent seemed horribly weak.

This time, Max groaned as she worked, and Róisín clutched onto a faint hope that he'd actually wake, but he fell back into slumber.

Shattered, she stumbled to her bunk to sleep and spiraled into intense, hyper-realistic dreams of another land.

Róisín stood in a clearing surrounded by standing stones, each reaching almost twice her height and pulsing with a preternatural yellow glow. Trees inside the stone circle seemed to dance without wind. The air sang, but there were no birds. Water gurgled, but she couldn't see a river.

Max's voice cried, "Róisín!"

She spun a full circle but couldn't see anything except slivers of pale light peeking through the gap between each stone and a blank glowing sky above. "Max! Max, I'm here! Where are you!"

Silence thundered through the clearing. Her heart raced as she ran to the largest stone, grabbing the edges to climb. But the surface of each was too smooth and the edges were too close together for her fingers to get any purchase. She was trapped within them.

After falling three times, she let out a howl of frustration. "Max! Are you still out there?"

No answer came. Had he fallen asleep again? Or had he disappeared? Where was she? She didn't recognize this circle, and she was familiar with most of them in Ireland.

Her father had made it a point to visit as many as he could find, a sort of folklore pilgrimage, and she'd accompanied him on many of those trips. But this didn't seem like anywhere in Ireland.

Dian Cecht's voice whispered in her ear. "You are my apprentice."

She jumped and spun, searching for her patron god. "Then where have you been? You left me. You took your power away."

"You turned away from me, but you are still mine. I claim you."

A shiver run down her spine. She rubbed the goosebumps from her arms. "Show yourself!"

Sparks appeared in front of her, swirling, dancing in a spiral and forming a shining shape. Her stomach roiled with fear, and she backed up against the nearest stone. Eventually, the shining subsided into Dian Cecht's smiling face. He opened his arms to hug her.

Róisín didn't want to be hugged, but her body reacted without her control. Dian Cecht enveloped her in his arms, a warm, comforting sensation, like when her Mam hugged her as a child. An embrace she never wanted to leave.

But she must, if she wanted to survive. Róisín had no idea where that notion came from, but the truth of it spiked through her mind-fog.

Róisín tried to pull away from Dian Cecht's arms, but he held her tight. She wriggled and twisted, pushed at his arms, tried to squeeze down and out, to no avail. His arms locked around her body, an inescapable cage.

She cried out, "Let me go! Let go!"

**"You are mine."**

**Hiroki:**

Hiroki slept fitfully, tossing and turning. He'd finally gotten used to the utter lack of outside sounds in the bunker, but he still didn't sleep well without city noises.

Cars passing on pavement, dogs in neighboring yards, the whoosh of airplanes overhead. These had been the background of his life in Tokyo, and he missed them whether he was sleeping at a rural farm or in an underground tunnel.

In addition to that discomfort, visions haunted him. All the possible permutations of what Oghma would do once he learned of the PHAE's secret plans. And, by extension, the other gods. Hiroki couldn't even get his head around all the ways things could go horribly wrong.

Why were the PHAE betraying the gods? His grandfather had been betrayed in the second world war and lived most of his life as a prisoner of war in the Soviet Union. The PHAE wouldn't escape punishment and worse, they'd deserve whatever punishment they incurred.

A bang woke him, and he shot to his feet, glancing around in alarm. He couldn't see anything in the darkness, so he flicked on his light, blinking in the sudden brightness.

His simple room held only a bed and a chest of drawers. There wasn't room for much more. But the simpleness appealed to him.

Hiroki couldn't figure out what caused the noise, so he crept out of his room and into the office area he shared with Bintou.

The darkness held an odd, cotton quality, like he had to push through resistance as he walked. Bintou had disappeared with Lugh, so the suite was empty.

He spared a glance toward her empty room, the woman who had been a friend to him, but even she had betrayed him. She'd attached herself to Lugh and left Hiroki behind. She was a slave to her own ambitions and desires. Bintou had no honor, either.

Hiroki peered down the hallway, now more curious than alarmed, but he nothing stirred. Then something glowed at one end, floating toward him. As it came closer, he could tell it was no human. Oghma's shining form stepped forward, his hands out. "Hiroki. You heard my call."

Hiroki gave the god a respectful bow, keeping his face emotionless. "You called me?"

"You were sleeping, and I called. I am pleased to find you awake and waiting." The god held out both his hands, palm up.

Hiroki swallowed and took Oghma's hands. The god clasped them so tightly that they hurt. "We have made great progress in our plan. Your help has been noted and appreciated."

Appreciated by Oghma? Or someone else? The phrasing was odd, and Oghma always used precise wording. A seed of doubt took root within Hiroki's mind, but he had nothing concrete to base it on, just a vague feeling of unease.

Oghma pulled him down the hall. "Come. We have work to do."

Hiroki resisted, pulling his hand away. "I should get dressed first."

The god looked him up and down. "Your clothing looks comfortable. Why do you need to change it?"

"These are pajamas, clothing designed only for sleeping. They will do little against the weather. And I have no shoes on."

With a roll of his eyes, Oghma gave a bored shrug. "Very well. You may change to more suitable clothing. But do not dawdle. I detest dawdlers."

As Hiroki hurried back to his room, he thought he should wake Ciara and let her know where he was going. But what would he tell her? That he was being taken away by the gods?

That sounded insane, even to someone who knew that the gods existed. Besides, waking her would mean telling her of Oghma's existence, and he'd vowed to keep him a secret.

Besides, she was the main architect of the plan against the gods. A dishonored person didn't deserve the respect of communication.

And Oghma might consider that dawdling.

Once Hiroki changed into sturdier clothing, he exited his room and took Oghma's hands again. The god led him down the hallway whence he'd come and into a shining portal.

They didn't even have to walk, as Oghma floated them along. Hiroki had to shut his eyes against the brightness, trusting Oghma to lead him into the light.

When they halted, Hiroki opened his eyes, then turned in a slow circle.

A thriving medieval European-style fairy city surrounded him. Soaring towers of glittering white stone, constructed with impossible spider-web décor.

The buildings glowed with their own light, a pulsing, relaxing, almost meditative rhythm, and Hiroki wanted nothing more than to curl up next to one and fall fast asleep, safe under Oghma's approval and protection.

196

**Tiberius:**

Tiberius let out a mighty yawn, still exhausted from the overnight flight. As often as he'd flown overseas, he'd never gotten used to sleeping on the plane, and was always a zombie the next day.

Luckily, his secretary set everything up at an office in Cork. She'd leased the premises, ordered furnishings and supplies, and gotten his paperwork in order.

Once he'd made the decision to move to Ireland, he'd chosen Cork as a big enough city to allow for decent infrastructure, but far enough away from PHAE headquarters in Dublin.

He could also escape from a coastal city much more easily than anything inland. Not that Ireland had much that qualified as inland. The tiny island was an eye-speck compared to Texas. But it should prove easy enough to fly under the radar here. Or sail under the radar, as the case might be.

Tiberius glanced at his passport and wrinkled his nose at the stupid fake name, Leonard Stone, but it had gotten him through customs and border protection. And more importantly, wouldn't raise any red flags at PHAE.

His own name was much too unusual and memorable. He'd had a love/hate relationship with his first name most of his life, but his mother had loved some campy show in the sixties. Thus, he was saddled with Tiberius, but at least he'd managed to make the name part of his personality.

Now he just had to settle into his new digs and get some quality information on the local political climate.

After the plane landed, he gathered his luggage, picked up the rental car, and drove into the city. It was an odd mixture of quaint and modern, with industrial buildings cozied up to stone walls.

It took a while for him to get used to driving on the left. The narrow streets made him already homesick for the wide Texan highways. He had to slam on his brakes, and then his horn, as someone swerved around him. He must be driving too slow for the locals.

After locating the address, Tiberius managed to find parking along the street in front of his new place. Glancing up, he noted the windows on the third floor looked secure enough. He entered the lobby and then grumbled at the lack of an elevator.

The office itself was controlled chaos as the movers were still bringing in furniture and hooking up equipment.

Sharon was directing them. "Hey, boss."

He gave her a nod. "D'ye need my help?"

Shaking her head, she gave him a half-smile. "You'd just be in the way, can you come back in a few hours?"

He gave a chuckle and, after he changed from his traveling clothing to a clean shirt and sports jacket, he escaped to stroll down the main road. Colorful houses out of a damned postcard lined the streets, and he smiled despite himself. He had to admit, Ireland had charm out the durned wazoo. Too much charm, maybe. Anything this pretty made him suspicious.

As he walked a few more blocks to the retail district, his stomach let out a massive growl. He noticed a sign for the "English Market" and entered, hoping he could find some lunch.

Once inside, a carnival of aromas and colors assaulted him, but he didn't mind. Tiberius drew in a deep breath, trying to extract the different smells, but then gave up.

He wandered from stall to stall, tasting samples and taking in the variety. This, this he could get used to! All the best bits of real farm food and none of the bullcocky.

Tiberius found a bench outside and ate a sandwich made with local pork sausage, smoked cheese, and sliced figs. He might have found a bit of Heaven, right here on earth.

Just as he ate the last bite and licked his fingers, a screech came around the corner.

A sports car going way too fast for this tiny coastal town skidded around a corner and careened through the one-lane street. A pretty young woman pushing a stroller was in its path.

Tiberius leapt to his feet and yanked her out of the street. He managed to get her to safety, but the car clipped another woman.

The driver sped off as Tiberius made sure the mother and baby were fine. Then he knelt next to the injured girl. "Hey, sweetheart! What's your name? Someone, call 911!"

Someone talked into their cell phone while he tried to assess the woman. Both her legs were sticking out at bad angles, and her skirt was already soaked with blood. Her face looked as pale as a sheet. "Where are you hurt, hon'?"

She mumbled something and then went limp in his arms. "Help! Someone, help her!"

Another woman knelt on the other side of the victim, about half his age with light brown hair. "I'm a healer. I can help."

Tiberius glanced up, startled. "A healer? D'you mean a doctor?"

"No. A healer." She placed her hands on the woman's body and closed her eyes, like some faith healer from some revival meeting.

Tiberius squinted. "She needs more than some praying, hon'. Did someone call 911?" Sirens in the distance answered his question.

She didn't open her eyes and spoke in a calm voice. "I am healing her. Now either shut your gob and let me work or go away."

When the woman's hands glowed blue, his eyes grew wide. "What in the actual hell?"

Suddenly, his skin tingled, and turned blue like hers. Tiberius fell back on his butt, but he still glowed. The healing woman arched her back, lightning crackled around her.

The victim gasped and sat straight up, her eyes wide and frightened, darting back and forth.

The healer sat back on her heels and nodded to him. "Thanks for your help. I have to admit, I don't have a lot of power, but whatever you did sure helped."

"Whatever I did? Hon', what in tarnation are you babbling on about?"

By that time, paramedics had arrived with an ambulance. They shooed both Tiberius and the healer away, strapped the victim to a gurney, and loaded her in their vehicle. All through that process, the injured woman was alert and talkative, a far cry better than when she'd lain in his arms.

*Whatever he'd done.*

Tiberius wandered back toward his office in a daze, thoroughly confused by the afternoon's events. As he got close to the office building doors, he spied a woman waiting outside. He narrowed his gaze as he walked forward, certain he recognized her from somewhere.

She rose and put out her hand as he approached. "I can't say it's a pleasure to meet you, Mr. Wilkinson, but I had to come by to introduce myself."

He shook her hand without thinking and raised his eyebrows. "And you are?"

"Ciara Doherty. May I come in?"

Tiberius recognized the name, and now the face clicked. She was one of the PHAE's representatives.

A flash of his daughter's face, a daughter he'd never hold again, made anger and grief boil in his blood, and he resisted the urge to throttle her right there.

Instead, Tiberius clenched his fists and growled, "You've got more guts than you can hang on a fence, coming to my office. What in the hell are you doing here?"

Ciara gave him a calm nod. "I might ask the same of you, but I appreciate I might be the last person you want to see. I wanted to ensure that you knew we're aware of your presence in Ireland. And that there are some things that we must discuss."

The last thing he wanted to do was sit down and parlay with the enemy. Tiberius wanted nothing more than to punch her, push her, do anything to get her away from him. Anything to help assuage his grief.

None of that would bring his family back.

She didn't seem to be the least bit concerned and folded her hands as she sat. "You put on quite a show this afternoon, Mr. Wilkinson. May I ask you some questions?"

He raised his eyebrows. "A show? I'm no rock star, sweetheart. You must have gone to the wrong stadium."

The woman let out a chuckle. "You are the colorful personality, aren't you? But you're well aware of what I'm referring to."

He stared at her, refusing to give ground. Normally, folks got nervous when no one spoke.

However, this Ciara seemed to take it in stride. A wide grin spread across her face. "You have a network of informants, Mr. Wilkinson. You know a great deal about our organization. However, what you may not know is that we are aware of your informants and have a lovely network of our own. We know quite a bit about you. Things you might not even know about yourself."

He settled back with a scowl, steepling his fingers. "Like what, precisely?"

"You helped to heal that woman."

Now Tiberius laughed. "Now, I know you're nuts. I'm not one of your pet magicians. I don't cater to the devil."

Ciara leaned forward, her expression intent. "We are not of the devil, Mr. Wilkinson. In fact, we are rather cozy with several gods."

He gaped at her. She couldn't be serious, could she?

"I see you are skeptical, and that's understandable. But haven't you paid attention to the news? Ancient gods are coming to life in all the corners of the world. And we've got our own batch, here in Ireland."

"And?"

"And they're working with us."

Shock kept his tone flat. "You're putting gods on the payroll."

The Irish woman rolled her eyes. "Not quite. But they are helping us. Your terrorist attacks, with the plagues? They killed a lot of innocent people. The gods are healing us."

Healing magic, like the woman on the street. That lightning had been no parlor trick, and that other woman had definitely had two broken legs. And despite that, she'd been trying to walk even as they took her to the ambulance.

The healer woman must have used magic, and he'd done something to help her. He just had no idea what.

His world seemed to be folding in new ways, and he didn't know how to keep his balance. "Was that woman on the street a god?"

"No, she was one of our Unhidden talents. She can heal people, though she isn't our strongest healer. She shouldn't have been able to heal the victim so quickly, not without serious help. You provided that help."

He still couldn't get his head around it, but that would take time. "Let's table that for now, sweetheart. Whatever happened out on that street isn't what you came here to talk to me about, because you couldn't have known it would happen. So, why are you here, exactly?"

**Tiberius:**

After the PHAE woman left, Tiberius stewed in his office for several hours. Sharon came in and set up a coffee machine, then left again without a word.

He went through the motions of fixing a cup and drank it while staring out the window. His mind spun with so many ideas, it felt like a Friday rush hour traffic jam on I-610.

202

This office was too quiet. He needed to walk to work this out. With a wave to Sharon, he hurried down the stairs to the street.

Dusk was just settling, and he drew in a deep breath. It grew quieter after the business day was over, here in this part of the city. People were shuffling off to their homes, to eat supper and spend time with their families.

His family was gone, though.

Tiberius wandered down the block, trying to work this out. That PHAE woman had given him a lot to think about, but he wasn't sure how much he could trust. Sure, he could verify some of the facts behind her information, but not many.

Most of what she told him hadn't been in the news, or on any sort of leaked video. Not even his spies had passed on a glimmer of that information. Of course, that's why he'd come here in the first place.

He turned a corner, onto another near-empty street. One pub was full of people, fiddle music leaking out, but he didn't want to drink with strangers. He still needed to think.

Ciara did convince him that he had some sort of talent. Some PHAE power. He'd tried to argue against her, but that woman was so strong, she'd make Samson look sensitive. He rather admired that sort of strength in a woman, and a handsome woman, at that. He shook his head against that notion.

That meant he was one of them, the Unhidden. One of the godless heathens who were causing chaos in the world. And now they were calling on him to help them.

He passed another pub, and a guy coming out almost knocked him over. Tiberius growled at the man and stalked away. To avoid more pubs, he turned down a dark alley.

The silence felt almost oppressive now, as he picked his way down the narrow passage, stepping over bits of stinking garbage.

Something cried out. A cat? No, a child. Tiberius searched in the dark, then took his phone out and turned on the flashlight app. "Hey! Who's out there?"

Tiberius searched up one side of the alley, and down the other, and finally saw something squirm away from the light. He steadied his hand, and saw a boy cowering from him, sniffling between a brick wall and a garbage can.

He could keep walking. This child had nothing to do with him and wasn't his responsibility. He was about to turn away, but then he heard his grandmother's voice in the back of his memory.

*"Whoever closes his ear to the cry of the poor will himself call out and not be answered."*

Tiberius cleared his throat and stared at the child. His grandmother might be watching from heaven right now, and there was no way he could disappoint her.

Speaking with a gentle voice, he put out his hand. "Hey, there, little man. I won't hurt you. Are you lost?"

The boy had dark skin, maybe middle eastern. His clothing was clean, but he had a dark smudge across one cheek. He nodded.

"What's your name, son?"

"Ammar."

"Here, Ammar, take my hand. Let's go find your parents."

As the child grasped his hand, Tiberius remembered his daughter. She'd been about six, the same age as this kid. His throat grew tight, and he swallowed back a surge of tears.

"So, you're lost, Ammar? Do you live nearby?"

The child nodded and wiped his nose with the back of his hand. Tiberius dug into his jacket pocket and pulled out a tissue, handing it over.

"Do you live in a house or an apartment?"

The child shrugged and sniffed again. He mumbled something.

"Sorry, son. I didn't hear that. Can you speak up?"

In a heavy accent, the child said, "I don't live in a house."

"Okay, apartment, then. Let's duck into this pub and find out where the closest apartments are."

They walked around the corner to the pub where he'd almost gotten knocked over. Tiberius put his hand on the door, and it burst open again. This time, a woman almost ran into him.

Her hands flew to her mouth in surprise, then she knelt next to the child, grabbing him close for a fierce hug. "Ammar! There you are. I was worried sick for you! Where did you go?"

Tiberius gave a smile. Mothers everywhere were the same, desperately worried for their children.

Then she glared at him. "Who are you? Why did you take Ammar? What did you do to him?" Her voice got more shrill with each question.

He backed away, his hands up in defense. "All I did was bring him here to help find his parents, sweetheart. I swear!"

"Get away from us!" She dragged the child away, glaring over her shoulder several times until they turned a corner.

Why had she been so angry? He had only been trying to help the poor kid. Tiberius let out a deep sigh. She'd been frightened, he understood that. She'd just been worried and lashing out in pain.

Just like he'd done after his family was killed.

It took Tiberius two full days to digest these events. Two full days to come to terms with the fact that he was one of *them*. One of the evil bastards who had caused his daughter's death, his wife's death, and his son's death.

Well, he'd find a way to make it less godless. Somehow.

Once he'd finally accepted that mission, the Irish woman visited again. This time, he invited her in and gestured toward her chair. "Hello again, sweetheart. Can I get you some coffee?" He turned to the sideboard, but she waved him away.

"I'm here to offer you a proposal. Don't answer at first but hear me out."

He steepled his fingers, studying her as she described an incredible plan.

First, there were ancient gods in Ireland, walking around and doing things. She'd mentioned that before, but he'd discounted that as ridiculous. At the very least, rampant exaggeration. Now, here she was, saying it was true.

Second, a few of the gods had gone off the rails, and needed reining in, maybe even imprisonment.

Third, she needed his help.

Tiberius sat forward, leaning on his hands. "Now, wait just a minute there, sweetheart. What sort of help d'you think I can offer? How could I possibly help in a battle with the gods?"

The first commandment echoed in the back of his mind, spoken in his wife's voice. *Thou shalt have no other gods before me.*

"Remember that power you had? Your ability to elevate someone else's power? Sort of a gestalt, a boost."

Tiberius waved his hand dismissively. "You don't really know that's what I did. You're only guessing."

She crossed her arms and leaned back, a calculating look on her face. "I supposed you didn't see it from the outside. It was patently clear that you were funneling in power to the healer, and then into the victim. She was almost dead, Mr. Wilkinson. Anyone could see that. And then she practically walked to the ambulance afterwards."

Tiberius barked out a laugh. "Fine. Assuming you're right, then what?"

"Well, I would like to experiment, to see if you can enhance anyone's power, not just Angie's."

"Help the PHAE." He sat back again, steepling his fingers. His mind was racing, but he couldn't let her know that. "Hon', are you sure you aren't high on something?"

**Anna:**

Standing in Galway's concrete harbour, Anna steeled herself to not run away. A bright sun beating down from a blue sky made the day warm and bright, but all the people crowding around made her want to scream and dive into the beckoning water.

Anna had never particularly cared for crowds, even before she'd started growing scales. Now she positively hated the teeming masses of humanity surrounding her, shoving her, talking, laughing, and breathing her air. They made her sweat and pant, and her heart raced.

So far, over a thousand people had answered the call to move to Iceland. A thousand Unhidden and their families, worried for their lives.

Like those fleeing the Great Hunger almost two hundred years before, they came with all their worldly possessions in luggage and carts, trunks and backpacks.

Some from the Galway area had very little, as their homes had been destroyed in the bombing. Others had grief etched on their faces, having already lost loved ones to the plague or the bombs.

All of them wanted to escape.

The Atlantic Ocean sang to her. *Come with me. Live within my waves. Swim beneath my surface. Sing with the tides.*

Anna inched toward the pier's edge, bunching her legs to dive in, when Carlos grabbed her hand. "Hey! You're not supposed to go off and leave this lot! Didn't Manannán say he'd meet us here with some magical boat of his?"

She mumbled out, "The *Sguaba Tuinne*."

"Yea, that. Wave-Sweeper, or some such?"

Anna nodded, still staring at the horizon. The song of the sea still caressed her ears, and she tried to block out the horrid noise of the crowd. Would she have to travel with all these people? She'd go mad in minutes.

A hush settled on the gathering. Anna glanced around, wondering what had finally shut them up. Her skin itched, and she rubbed her arms to calm herself.

Then she felt *him* approach, her blood surging with his proximity. The water in the center of the harbour rose. Higher and higher it grew, swelling into a massive bubble two stories tall.

Sounds of "Ooh!" and "Aah!" peppered the air, like the reactions at a fireworks show. Carlos squeezed her hand just as the bubble burst with an enormous splash, revealing the massive form of Manannán mac Lir The sea god, her mentor, raised his arms in a heroic pose.

The people lining the pier grew utterly silent, and for that, Anna sighed with gratitude.

Next to Manannán, a boat appeared, rounded at the ends like an ancient coracle. It looked tiny, with maybe enough room for six people.

Someone laughed, which set off a wave of whispers and giggles. Anna pursed her lips at their ridicule. But she knew this boat was magic and would grow to whatever size needed.

In his deep, velvet voice, Manannán addressed the crowd. "All will be welcome upon my vessel."

The laughter rose again, along with a heckler. "What? On top of each other? That's nothing but a rowboat!"

The sea god glared at the man, a middle-aged blond man with a paunch. Manannán spoke with quiet strength. "You doubt my power, human?"

Suddenly serious, the man backed up, stumbling into two women, his eyes wide.

Carlos held his hands up. "Okay, folks! I need you to form a line. Anyone who shoves or pushes or tries to cut in will not be allowed on this ride, and I mean it. Manannán can see each of you from up there, so no shenanigans!"

A general grumble answered him, but those closest to Anna shuffled into an orderly queue. She stepped to one side, trying not to get between them and the boat. Carlos typed each person's name into his pad, which checked it against the PHAE database.

He stopped one young blonde woman with his arm. "Hold on, I don't see your name on our list."

She gave him a sweet smile. "Sure, and it'll have my maiden name. I just got married a few days ago. Check under Meera Quinn."

She smiled up at the tall black-haired man behind her, who scowled at Carlos. "Her name better be on there."

Ignoring the implicit threat, Carlos nodded. "Right, there it is. On you go."

As they worked through the line, Anna watched the boat, which had already grown large enough to hold the eighty people they'd processed.

They didn't want to break up families, so only one member had to be part of PHAE. If one parent had Unhidden talent, the children would likely develop a special ability, even if they didn't normally show up until after puberty.

After the tally passed two hundred, the passengers began to squirm. To be fair, the wooden benches didn't look all that comfortable, and processing had already taken over an hour and a half. Anna realized the open boat had no bathroom facilities and wondered how that would work.

After a few more minutes, Manannán held up one hand. Carlos had logged in two hundred and fifty passengers so far. "I will take the first group. Those that remain can wait. I will return in two hours."

Carlos's eyes grew wide. "Two hours? Iceland's almost nine hundred miles away. Even traveling at fifty knots, that's like eighteen hours each way."

Manannán could keep the seas as calm as he needed to, but he must have something else in store for the refugees.

She glanced at the sea god, in case he wanted her on this trip, but Manannán didn't meet her gaze. He lifted the boat, water dripping from its keel. Then the ancient deity vanished, taking the boat with him.

Gasps swept across the remaining refugees. Even Anna felt her stomach twist with worry for all those people. She trusted the sea god implicitly, but he was still one of the ancient gods, and therefore not human.

Many of the onlookers murmured with alarm, and one girl screamed. Carlos raised his hands again. "No screaming allowed! No one needs to panic! This is the only way he'll get them to Iceland so quickly. Once they're safely on land, he'll come back, and we'll get the next group on. If you need a bathroom break, or to grab something to eat, go do that. Be back in two hours."

Someone yelled out, "What if we miss the boat?" That pun earned a few chuckles.

Carlos gave a saucy grin. "Then there will be another after that. And another. Until either no one else is waiting or we collapse from fatigue."

Anna was grateful Carlos was dealing with all these administrative tasks. She didn't have the patience for it, not any longer. Once she did, when she was a teacher, but even then, it was a necessary evil. Now, she just wanted to get into the water.

The song grew loud in her mind, calling to her with open arms, but Carlos tucked her hand into the crook of his arm. "Fancy some dinner?"

**Komie:**

Komie's head still ached from Macha's scream, and she needed a way to recover her spirit, some time alone with the gentle earth. But she was still stuck in a PHAE meeting. That seemed to be all these people did. Meet and talk, talk and meet. And what was accomplished?

She just needed to get away from everyone for a while. To speak to the trees, to feel her toes in the grass.

Komie hated Dublin's teeming stress. The city felt soulless to her, lacking in the spirits of the land. She longed for her home in the woods of Maine, on the slopes of Mount Katahdin, with her ancestors. Or even the dusty desert of Arizona. At least there, the land resonated with the Great Spirit.

But this was Ireland, and Komie was working for the PHAE, so she must remain. She didn't have to like Dublin to stay there, at least until the crisis had resolved one way or another. And in order to help resolve that crisis, she needed some help.

And to get help, she must seek the counsel of her people, the Great Spirit, and her ancestors. An underground bunker was no place to do that.

As the meeting with Hiroki, Ciara, Qacha, and Paul broke up, she drew Ciara aside. "I need some sort of escape, a place I can speak with my ancestors. Trees, park, forest, anything like that. Is there such a place in Dublin?"

Ciara's brow furrowed. "I don't think it's a grand idea for you to be wandering alone in the city at the best of times, especially right now. Can I send Paul with you? He can show you Phoenix, it's not far from here."

She gave a grateful grin. "Paul's company would be welcome, he has a kind soul. This is a city park? Does it have many trees?"

The Irish woman laughed out loud. "Sure, and it's got over seven hundred hectares of trees! You'll be spoiled for choice there."

Komie was surprised such a large green space existed inside the city, but she wasn't about to look a gift horse in the mouth. "Then that would be perfect. Can we go now?"

As Paul led her out of the tunnel and into his car, she asked, "I thought Ciara said it was close by?"

"Ah, but *close by* is a relative term in Dublin. It's near as the crow flies, but still a twenty-minute drive in traffic. And there's the destruction to contend with. What part of the park would you like to see? There's a zoo, the president's house, the Papal Cross, even a castle."

"The thickest forest area, if you can."

"Sure, and that'd be near the Glen Pond then. I can take you to the Car Park, now."

Office buildings, churches, and Georgian row houses passed by as Komie tried to compose her questions for the ancestors.

Calling upon the ancestors had its dangers, as did any power. But she trusted her ancestor spirits far more than these ancient Irish gods and their mercurial tempers.

What, exactly, was she hoping to get? Advice? Assistance? Approval? Normally, she'd simply provide a place they'd be comfortable, and wait for them to notice her. She'd burn white sage and open her mind to their visit. If they wished to give advice, they might. If they just wished to be in her presence, they'd do that.

This time, she'd have to ask them for more. Something more immediate. More physical. More protective.

As Paul pulled through a white stone arch complete with mock crenellations, Komie hid a smile. The Irish did love their medieval roots. At least they had pride in their history, as well as in their fierce independence. They'd fought for almost a thousand years to get that freedom back.

She had to admire that dogged determination, while she wished her own ancestors had fought for as long.

They continued through the park, passing green meadows, buildings, monuments, and clusters of trees. Not the old-growth woods of Maine, of course, but the trees seemed happy enough.

Finally, Paul pulled into a lonely car park on the far end of a vast copse of trees. Komie stepped out and breathed deep. She could smell the surrounding trees more strongly than the city beyond it. That should be enough to make contact.

Komie wished she could use the sweat lodge Colin and Michelle had built for her, but her people had needed to be resourceful for millennia.

212

She must get the ancestors' attention without all the trappings. They'd come to her once here in Ireland. Calling them a second time should be easier.

Paul cocked his head. "D'ye want me to come with you?"

Komie waved his offer away. "No, I'll be fine on my own. I shouldn't take too long, maybe an hour. Can you wait for me?"

He gave her a jaunty salute and sat on a bench, pulling his phone out.

Komie strode to the nearest tree, placing her hand on the trunk. The rough bark warmed beneath her fingers. She reached into the earth, communing with the roots. The tree shuddered, the bark cracking and growing.

She hadn't meant for that to happen and dropped her hand. She'd just wanted to speak with the land, to request permission for her to work her own summoning.

Letting out a sigh, she glanced over her shoulder. Paul still sat on his bench bent over his phone. She turned back toward the forest and walked further in.

Once Komie found a small clearing, barely enough for her to sit cross-legged, she did so, placing her hands flat on the grass. The ground vibrated in response to her touch. This was also something new, a reaction before she'd drawn any magic through the soil.

With measured breathing, Komie concentrated on her ancestors, her people, and of the *Gici Niwaskw,* the Great Spirit.

She visualized the animal spirits, such as Bear, Raccoon, Badger, and Wolf. She called to them across the ocean, across time, and across the veil between their worlds.

*Help me, my ancestors. Help me find my way in this faraway land. Help me protect those who are my found family.*

Voices whispered in the back of her mind, all speaking at once. She closed her eyes, trying to discern the words. Her name floated through the mumbling, and she managed to pick out a few phrases.

*Growth.*

*Coming to you.*

*New purpose.*

*Danger.*

Danger? She concentrated on that last word, zeroing in on who might have said it.

Standing on his hind two legs, Bear nodded at her. *Yes, daughter. There is danger. It comes for you.*

Bear had never directly addressed Komie before, but she felt the intense honor of his attention. "Danger from whom?"

*From those who would use you. You need protection against them.*

"Will you protect me? *Can* you protect me?"

Bear crossed his arms, giving a solemn nod. He glanced down at Badger, Raccoon, and Wolf, and they added their agreement.

Komie released her breath, a calmness rushing through her. "How will I call you when you're needed?"

*Call with your spirit and the earth and we will come. We are not strong here in this foreign land, but we will lend you what strength we have.*

**Bintou:**

As Qacha yanked on Bintou's left arm, Lugh gripped her right arm. They pulled and Bintou screamed. She had no desire to be ripped in two like a wishbone. She gave Qacha a pleading look, and the Mongolian woman, her face screwed in an angry scowl, released her.

She and Lugh faded into Faery, and he finally let go of her. Being wrenched from the human world made her stomach churn. Bintou rubbed her arms where they'd held her, her skin reddened from their grips. "You hurt me, Lugh."

His face instantly transformed into contriteness as he put his fingers under her chin, lifting it so their gazes met. "Ah, my fair flower, I did not mean to injure one inch of your silky skin. Will you forgive my clumsiness?"

Bintou's heart melted at the depths in his blue eyes. His caress traveled up along her jawline and down her neck. She closed her eyes as it moved to her shoulder, her waist, and her hips. Then he grabbed them both and drew her up against him. His need pressed hard in her belly, and her own body responded to that need.

Suddenly, his mouth was on hers, and any concern over Qacha, the PHAE, or the other world fled in the face of undying, urgent passion. He carried her into the tower and into his bedroom as her hands grabbed greedily for him.

After they finished exploring each other's bodies again, Bintou lay, panting and shimmering in sweat, as Lugh slept. How could she keep doing this? It's as if he worked a glamour on her, making her forget everything but him.

Perhaps he *was* casting some spell. Even when she'd been head over heels in love with Ibrahim, she'd always managed to keep her senses about her. Well, mostly.

But Lugh had some irresistible ability to keep her attention to the exclusion of everything else. She had no control over her own reactions. And that lack of control frightened her.

Bintou crept from their bed, and pulled on a dress with blue and green triangles, one of her favorites. She stepped out of the sleeping chamber and into the main room. Then she strode outside, determined to escape whatever spell he had on her.

She caught a glimpse of something in the reeds. When she walked closer to investigate, she found the cat-like creature, Beagan, and knelt beside them. "Hello, little friend. I see you there."

"Hello! Manol brings his greetings."

Manol. Qacha. The names flooded back into her memory. How could she have forgotten them so quickly?

She glanced back at Lugh's home and shook her head. He must be working a spell on her. "I would like to send greetings back to Manol. And his companion, Qacha. Can you reach Qacha with messages, as well? Do you know where she is now?"

They gave an eager nod.

"Then please tell her I am safe, but don't have a way to return. I may need her help to get free."

As the creature skittered away, Bintou wondered if her message would get to Qacha, if there was anything Qacha could do to rescue her, or if she'd sealed her own fate by entrusting a Fae creature with a message about escaping the Fae.

Then she glanced back at the white tower, shining and glowing in the dimly lit world, and a shudder at the memory of sweet pleasure rushed through her.

Or if she really wanted to escape.

**Qacha:**

Qacha paced with increasing agitation in front of the conference table. The Defence Minister and PHAE officials asked her yet another question. "I do not know the answer to that! I've told you everything I observed."

"I'm sorry, Qacha," Ciara said, "but you're the only one who has noticed this anomaly. If we don't discover the limits of their aversion to plastic, we could be wasting our one chance to build something to combat them."

"Combat them!" Qacha whirled, her eyes blazing. "You actually expect to craft some sort of weapon out of plastic? What will you make? A child's toy?"

Ciara pursed her lips. "A child's toy? Qacha, we can make guns out of polymer."

With a dismissive wave, Qacha returned to pacing. "Yes, you can make a gun from plastic. And how much good will that do? Is the bullet plastic? No, only the firing mechanism."

The man next to Ciara, someone from the Ministry of Defence, cleared his throat. "We make plastic bullets."

"For what, riot control? Those are meant to hurt, not kill. We need cannons. Grenades. High-powered automatic rifles. These are ancient gods we're fighting! You don't bring a plastic gun to a war."

Someone giggled, but when Qacha turned to discover whom, she couldn't pick out a guilty face. It didn't matter. These people were deluded if they thought they could build anything offensive out of plastic.

That made her halt her pacing and turn to the others. "What if we thought defensively rather than offensively? What if we crafted cages from the polymer?"

Ciara exchanged glances with the other PHAE people and the Defence Minister. The latter shrugged. "It's possible. If we can find a way to capture the gods, placing them in a polymer cell might work. But what if it doesn't? We have no way to test such a construction."

Qacha wondered idly if Manol's little friend would be willing to help them test the theory, but then realized the creature would be much less powerful than the gods and wouldn't be a valid test subject. Though a weak test subject might be better than no test subject.

Ciara furrowed her brow. "We still don't even know if they *are* going to attack us, or if we need such measures."

The Defence Minister shook his head. "Are you willing to gamble the safety of every human in Ireland on that assumption? Besides, you just saw Macha lose her mind out there. She has no control over her temper and might go off again any moment. We don't know what set her off this time, or how to keep that from happening again."

Qacha cleared her throat. "I might at least be able to find out what upset her."

They adjourned the meeting, and Ciara showed Qacha to Bintou's bunker. "You can stay in her room until we can find her again."

She gave a silent nod as Ciara left. The door closed with a solid *thunk*. Qacha didn't want to be here, in this cold place. It reminded her of a prison. She'd had enough prisons to last her a lifetime.

She dimmed the lights and crouched. "Beagan! Are you listening? Will you come visit?"

A mass of sparks formed beside her and when the creature popped into being, she gave them a nod. "Thank you for coming."

"Manol sends his greetings!" The creature licked his paw. "I don't like this place. The odd stone makes my skin itch."

Qacha didn't hide her grin. She missed her cat and wished she could return to him. But he must be patient until she finished this crisis.

"Can you tell me why Macha was so angry earlier today? Did we do something to upset her?"

They bowed their head, shame apparent on their features. "Yes. I did it."

"You upset her? How?"

Their voice turned to a raspy whisper. "She found the note I carried."

"Did      she      understand      what      it      said? Qacha frowned. *How could Macha read a note in Kanji?*

Beagan held their tail and stroked it nervously. "No, but she took the note to Oghma. He can read it. He can read anything."

*Fuck a goat.* Qacha hadn't heard of this god, but if he had a talent like Bintou's, then she understood Macha's rage.

"Oh! I almost forgot." Beagan's sorrow turned to excitement. "The Dark One also sends her greetings."

218

"The Dark One?" Visions of the Christian devil flicked through her mind. "Who is that?"

"The woman with the dark skin."

Qacha let out a breath. "Bintou? She is safe?"

The creature glanced around. "She says she doesn't know how to get back. She says she needs help."

Qacha's shoulders tensed. "Is Bintou in danger?"

Beagan stroked their tail again and shook their head. "No, she is in a nice place. It's pretty and peaceful and full of food. She wants to leave but doesn't want to leave."

She didn't know how to interpret that, but before she could ask if Beagan could bring Bintou out, the creature disappeared in a shower of sparks.

# Chapter Eight

"All gods are homemade, and it is we who pull their strings,
and so, give them the power to pull ours."
– Aldous Huxley

**Max:**

Max tried to scream but no noise came from his throat. He groped around, trying to find anything to hold on to, anything to pull him away from the pain that rooted through the center of his soul, but the only thing he could feel is the hot, sticky air pressing down on him. Footsteps approached, but he didn't care. He just wanted to get away from the pain.

**"What are you doing, Taranis?"**

The pain stopped so suddenly, Max let out a sob from the relief. And that wasn't Taranis's voice.

**"I am doing nothing involving you."**

Both male voices spoke in Max's mind. Taranis spoke with an undertone of a growl, almost grating the words across sandpaper.

The other voice, one Max didn't recognize, almost sang in baritone. It wasn't Manannán's voice nor Lugh's, but it had that echoing resonance he only heard from the gods.

The newcomer let out a huge belly laugh. **"Taranis, you are fooling yourself if you think this doesn't involve me. Everything involves me. Haven't you learned that by now? But you were never a quick study, were you?"**

**"Dagda, leave me to my work."**

Max had heard about this bloke, a father-god, like Odin or Zeus. Someone who might be able to stop Taranis from torturing him to death, at any rate. Or so Max hoped.

He tried to sit up, but every muscle in his body hurt, and all he managed was a weak moan.

**"Release this human, Taranis. He is not yours to torment."**

**"Oh, you want to torment him? Be my guest. I'd be happy to watch. In fact, I'd relish it."**

**"I will return him to his family."**

This time, Taranis laughed. **"He has no family! This is a lone soul, my favorite kind to feed upon."**

Since when did the Irish gods feed on souls? He hadn't heard any stories like that from Colin. He tried to move toward the Dagda's voice, but Taranis gripped so hard on his forearm, Max felt the bones grind. Another moan escaped his lips.

**"Release him now. I will not ask you again."**

**"Do your worst."**

The world lit in a painful flash, and the grip on his arm loosened, but didn't let go. It ripped at his flesh, and Max let out a howl.

Taranis rumbled and grumbled like faraway thunder before a crescendo of booms pelted Max's ears.

**"You aren't strong enough to banish me alone. You never were!"**

But the Dagda wasn't alone. Max had power, didn't he? He should help with his own rescue, damnit.

Max dug deep into his own power and tried to lend strength to whatever the Dagda was attempting.

The Dagda's power pulsed visibly in the near darkness, flashing toward Taranis's voice. Max simply shoved whatever he could toward the same spot. He had no idea if what he did made any difference.

Then the grip on his arm slipped away.

The flashing light faded into more reasonable levels, and Max blinked until he could finally focus on the god's form.

A large man with a big beer belly, massive shoulders, and red hair and beard stood looking over him, with fists on his hips. If he was wearing a red suit, he'd look like an Irish Santa Claus. **"You are safe now, Maximilian Hurley. I have come to return you to your people."**

Max coughed a few times to clear his throat after his screams. "That's great, mate, and I'm grateful as hell."

**"As you should be."**

Max let out a snort, now that his throat was usable again. "But what happens when Taranis gets pissy again?"

The Dagda gave a grin. **"He is always pissy, as you say."**

"Fair, but how do I fight him off next time? He's not here to fuck spiders, you know. He means business."

**"There will not be a next time. Taranis is forbidden from harming you again."**

"Yeah, well, he doesn't really need to touch me, does he? He can make the wind do that. And the wind is my only power. If he uses that against me, I'm useless again."

**"He will not harm you. You have my word."**

The word of a god. Max didn't have enough experience with these blokes to know if that was worth bugger-all. Not that he had any faith in anyone's word, human or otherwise. Too many people had broken faith with him to trust anyone. And that included himself.

**"You have a role yet to play in this world. I have seen the truth of that. I will not allow him to destroy you until your purpose is finished."**

*Nothing like a little pressure, then.*

**Róisín:**

After Dian Cecht had taken Róisín, he brought her… someplace. Someplace filled with fog and the cry of seagulls. Someplace with moss-covered rocks, and ocean waves breaking on a cliff face.

A lonely place.

When they arrived, he let go of her arm. She stumbled away, her blood boiling. "What do you think you're doing?"

He scowled and crossed his arms. "You are being disrespectful. You have devoted yourself to me, and therefore, you are mine to command."

Róisín returned his scowl. "That is not acceptable. I'm a human being with free will. While I've agreed to be your apprentice, that doesn't give you ownership of me! Now take me back."

He chuckled and turned away.

Róisín grabbed his arm. "Hey! Don't you walk away from me!"

Dian Cecht spun around, his eyes glowing with orange light. "Never dare to speak to me so!"

She pulled back from this fury, her heart leaping in her chest. But despite the fear coursing through her veins, she must be strong. Mam would never forgive her if she gave in to this bully. She needed to hold her ground, refusing to let him intimidate her. "I'll speak how I damn well please!"

A momentary twinge of guilt at swearing passed through her, but she shoved that away. Even Mam would have to admit this warranted some heartfelt cursing.

His eyes glowed brighter, and Róisín figured she'd just defied herself into a painful death. But she didn't feel afraid, just oddly bemused.

Funny, she'd always figured Max would do that, not her. Róisín wished Max was with her. He'd always managed to insert himself between her and any danger. It was rather sweet of him.

But she had to do this herself. Komie had tried to warn her, back at the beginning, but she thought she could handle an actual god living inside her.

Well, Róisín was no longer willing to be used. Not anymore. Now, she had to be strong, and demand her own independence, her own humanity, back. Even if she died in the process, just like her ancestors in the Easter rising.

Despite her fear of being incinerated on a whim, she clenched her fists and steeled herself for instant destruction. "Take. Me. Back. Now."

Dian Cecht's eyes flashed brighter and sparks fell like rain. Róisín was on the inside of a giant firework display, the surrounding mist glowing as the embers fizzled out before reaching her.

Puzzled, she peered up. They *were* fizzling. None of them came within a foot of her body before snuffing out. She narrowed her eyes at Dian Cecht, trying to figure out what he was playing at, who looked as confused as she was.

Dian Cecht's voice used to be the warmest velvet, smooth and soothing. It healed with every syllable. Now, it was harsh and rough, gritty and angry. "Very well. It seems I must return you. But there is a price for your brazen defiance, and I will have my due."

**Hiroki:**

As Oghma led him into the magical fairy village, Hiroki tried to absorb every details, but the scene shifted even as he stared at it. Walls faded into trees, and figures might look human one moment, and something entirely different the next.

He stumbled along after the Irish god, his head swiveling from one sight to the next. Finally, they entered what looked like an oak grove with a giant clearing in the center.

How had they arrived at a forest? They'd been in the middle of a town. Hiroki shook his head, trying to figure out what was happening.

Maybe this was all some illusion, a glamour as the tales described. He'd have to be very careful about what he believed.

Then Oghma turned to smile at him. "You have done very well. You have kept my existence secret. I appreciate your loyalty. Today, you will be granted a special reward for your trustworthiness."

Hiroki's heart swelled, and he instantly forgot about being careful. Finally, he'd get the approval he always craved.

While Oghma wasn't his father, he had taken Hiroki under his wing, taught him tricks of rhetoric, the structure of debate. Much like his teacher in college, he'd crafted Hiroki into a better version of himself.

And all he'd asked in kind was fidelity. Hiroki could be steadfast. He loved being loyal and it matched his own most treasured values. He'd proven himself, and now he would reap that reward.

They stood in grove's center now with the trees around them sparkling in the dim glow. There was no sun, but everything pulsed with beautiful, low radiance, like the time just before the sun rises, a perpetual twilight.

Bells tinkled in the back of his mind, with the faint sound of horns, as if someone had started a medieval fox hunt.

Subtle, not-quite-music rose around him, making him want to dance, but Hiroki never danced. He'd never had the courage to learn how. Despite this, his feet moved against his will, prancing around the edge of the circle. Other lights frolicked with him, miniscule fairies and sprites weaving through the stones.

Oghma nodded, a smile on his face. "Yes, yes, exactly like that. You are doing well."

Was this his reward? A compulsion to dance? Hiroki didn't understand it but knew very well never to question a gift from the fairies. He'd read too many tales, both in his own culture and others, to know the foolishness of such a course.

But the dance was exhilarating, despite his confusion. Joy traveled through his blood as he twirled around the circle, skipping and cavorting.

226

A heady sweetness swept through his body, intoxicating and delightful. He let out a laugh of pure ecstasy.

Hiroki's legs were already growing tired as he pranced around the tree line, his steps getting faster as the music grew louder. The sparks shone amongst the tree trunks, tiny creatures moving in an undulating spiral, leading his dance.

His joy was fading now, turning to alarm. He wanted to stop, to rest his aching muscles, but he was unable to do anything but dance.

The magical procession skipped in front of him. They moved faster than he could, and yet his legs tried to keep up. Hiroki couldn't catch his breath and sweat ran down his face.

He stumbled on a root and gripped the trunk to keep from falling. The bark scratched his hands, but he had to keep moving.

The music grew so loud, he could hear nothing else. Hiroki's head pounded with the beat, the bells, the horns, and inhuman voices rising to a crescendo of ecstasy and energy that he'd never known.

Fear rushed through him, replacing his ecstasy with dread. What if he could never stop? What if he died dancing with the fairies?

With a final flourish, the song finished, and the Japanese man collapsed, utterly exhausted. As Hiroki sucked in air and tried to keep his heart from bursting from his chest, the dancers gathered around and giggled, pointing at him lying in the dew-wet grass.

Oghma shushed them. "Do not poke fun at the human, children. He is new to this land."

When he could finally breathe almost normal, Hiroki turned to the god. "Was that my reward?"

"It was indeed. You have never known the bliss of complete abandon. I wanted to gift it to you."

Hiroki swallowed, trying to find a way to say he didn't like it and remain polite. "I had no control."

"That is exactly why it is a gift. Removing societal control is a delightful thing, but very few humans appreciate the treasure that it is."

Hiroki tried to absorb Oghma's words, but any understanding dangled just out of his grasp. Maybe Oghma didn't understand humans as well as he thought he did. Maybe none of the gods truly understood humans.

He shook his head and rose to a sitting position. "Is this the reason you brought me here?"

"It is not the *only* reason. We are meeting others, but I wanted to give you my gift before they arrived." He waved his hand at the tiny dancers. "Away, children! The rest will be here soon. They need no help in wanton abandon."

As the tiny dancers faded into darkness, the grove's light dimmed as well. Only a few heartbeats later, footsteps shuddered the ground. Hiroki glanced around wildly, trying to determine who or what approached. He scrambled to his feet to meet the new threat, despite his aching muscles and burning lungs.

**Anna:**

Anna stared at the slice of pizza on a paper plate, grease congealing as it cooled. When had she lost the taste for food?

That wasn't entirely fair. She loved mussels, clams, and fish, but what happened to her love affair with pizza? With garlic bread? With cheese? How could she no longer like cheese? Was she even human anymore?

Carlos cocked his head as he wiped his mouth. "What's wrong, Anna? Is your stomach hurting?"

She scowled and stared at her slice.

"C'mon. Something must be bothering you. You've been as quiet as a mouse ever since we left the harbour. Is it this place? Do you not like pizza?"

"No, the restaurant's fine. It's just been a long time since I ate pizza, I guess."

He jumped to his feet. "Not to worry! I'll get something else. Let's see." He ran his finger down the menu. "Pasta? Maybe with meat sauce? Or maybe something sweet. Oh, they have a Nutella pizza, how about that?"

Her stomach churned as she pushed the plate away. "No, nothing, please. I have to go to the bathroom."

Anna rushed into the back room and shut the stall door, poised over the toilet. She wasn't sure she had to vomit but wanted to be ready just in case. As her stomach decided which way it wanted to go, she measured her breaths, trying to calm her heart.

This might be yet another sign of her changing into a sea creature, further away from her human self. Anna wanted it to stop. She had the scales and the water magic, and that was great. She could breathe underwater and that let her swim as long as she liked.

But not being able to eat the foods she loved cut into her sense of self. Would she even be able to drink tea now? She had no idea what else might change in her body and wasn't sure she wanted to find out.

On the other hand, she had no way to stop it. Could Manannán halt whatever she was turning into? Did she dare ask? And if she did somehow muster up the courage to ask that question, would he help? Or would he consider it a betrayal of her loyalty to him and the sea?

Her stomach finally stopped roiling, so she rose, washed her face and hands, and returned to the blue plastic booth. Carlos looked worried but she gave him a reassuring smile, sat, and took a bite of her cold pizza.

It took forever to chew and swallow the greasy piece of bread and cheese. Her gut rumbled but didn't completely rebel, so she took another.

She finished half the slice and Carlos's concerned expression eased. Then he broke into a disarming grin. "Hey, want to get some dessert? We still have time. I remember you like cinnamon, and they've got something they call churros. I don't have any hope that they taste like *real* churros, mind you. I haven't had real churros anywhere in Ireland, and this is a pizza joint, not a Spanish restaurant. But they probably make something tasty, crunchy, and cinnamon-y."

Anna had to return his smile, even if she didn't share his enthusiasm. It was his smile which had first made her heart flutter when they'd met, though she was with Brendan at the time. But Brendan had basically abandoned her.

No, that wasn't fair. They'd gotten into a fight, and she'd left him to live in the ocean. But he never came to find her, while Carlos had.

Despite her affection for the American man, she felt the tug of the sea like a constant wind, threatening to blow her over. Anna peered out the window to catch a glimpse of waves in the bay.

Carlos had sung her a song about Galway Bay, homage to the fisherfolk who went out each day into the ocean. Which brought her back to Manannán's boat. He ought to return soon for another load of passengers to Iceland.

Carlos came back with the not-quite-churros. They were fried and absolutely drowning in cinnamon and butter, which would make dogshit delicious. She licked her fingers to get every crumb.

Anna and Carlos both reached for the last one, their hands touching. She giggled and he gestured with an open hand for her to take the lone treat. She broke it in half and offered him one.

"You are ever graceful in your victory." He then bit it straight out of her hand. "Hey, let's clean up here. Manannán should be back soon."

Carlos took her hand and kissed her fingers before they returned to the pier. It felt natural and comfortable. He flashed her another of those sweet smiles, and her cheeks grew warm as she returned a grin.

People were milling around the pier, no longer in the neat line they'd been in when Manannán left. Carlos raised his hands. "Okay, folks! You know the drill. Form an orderly queue, and we'll take names as you board. Remember, there's no need to fret, as we'll just keep doing this until everyone who wants to go has made the trip."

The crowd grumbled but seemed tranquil enough. Anna glanced at the harbour, but the water was calm, lapping against the pleasure vessels moored along the pier. She wondered if Manannán would fashion a similar entrance to his last one, or just arrive without fanfare. He did like his dramatic entrances.

Bubbling caught her attention, and she stared as a white mound of water rose. Manannán had chosen drama again, then. He had a new audience now that the previous group had cleared the pier.

With a surprising lack of drama, the Irish sea god repeated his description of the voyage process, and they got another two hundred and fifty passengers on board without much fuss.

Carlos said, "Alright, folks, that's it for this trip! Come back in two hours, and we'll get the next group aboard."

The boat disappeared as a general growl ran through the crowd, and someone yelled, "If the boat is magic, why can't we all get on it?"

Carlos glanced at Anna with a shrug as he put his pad back into its case. He didn't really understand Manannán's boat or its limitations.

Neither did she, but thinking quickly, she said, "It's not a limitation on the boat, but on our facilities in Iceland. They can only process so many people coming in at one time. And the pier there has limited amenities, like food or toilets. You don't want to have to hold it for hours, right?"

Her poor attempt at a joke didn't quell the grumbling, and someone started pushing. Someone else shoved back, shouting at the other to back off. A man with a huge suitcase stumbled out of the way and knocked into a young woman, who fell on her back with a scream and covered her head.

Soon, the mass of people was shouting and pushing and yelling. While there were a few Gardaí in the back, there weren't nearly enough to help against a violent mob.

Anna's heart raced with panic, and her eyes darted around for some way to escape the throng of angry people. Then, someone stumbled into Carlos, and he fell into the bay with a big splash.

Without a thought, Anna jumped in and pulled him to the surface. He spluttered and coughed, trying to breathe.

She was going to push him back up on the pier, but now it boiled with unhappy people, all fighting to be next in line.

They exchanged a glance, and she said, "Take a deep breath!"

Anna put her arms around him and dove under the pier, coming out on the other side. She swam until she reached the sandy beach along the Claddagh.

The call of the sea was so strong, Anna almost didn't get out of the water with him, but she wanted to make sure he was safe. As Carlos wrung out his sopping clothing, he shook his head. "I hope that lot calms down before the next run."

"They'll calm down when Manannán returns."

"Yeah, I bet it's hard to riot in the face of a sea god."

They shared a laugh and watched as the crowd fought on the pier. She didn't want to go back, and there was no need to until the boat came back for the next batch.

So, they basked in the late afternoon sun for about an hour. When they approached the pier, the rioters had either calmed back down or left, and they both heaved a sigh of relief.

But the number of people milling about to board had swollen with more refugees arriving all the time, and now thousands waited.

As soon as the sea god rose again from the water, everyone grew silent. And once again, Carlos and Anna helped each one check in and get on board.

As the number of passengers reached two hundred and fifty, unrest quickly morphed into anger. Again, it happened after Manannán disappeared.

Someone in the back shouted, "This is all a scam! These PHAE arses are just trying to get us out of Ireland! We'll end up in some jail cell, never to be seen again!"

232

Anna's blood boiled at this outright lie. "You are more than welcome to stay here! In fact, we don't want you in Iceland. Go away!"

Then he grew quiet, and another voice spoke, talking similar trash.

The crowd surged toward Carlos, the man with the passenger database. Anna reached for him, but would-be passengers separated them.

She screamed at the top of her lungs as they pushed her away. "Carlos!"

They rushed toward them until she fell off the pier. When she bobbed to the surface, she scanned the crowd, desperate to find Carlos. Anna found him near the shore, his hands held high.

He turned to her and nodded. "Go!" he mouthed. For a moment, she hesitated, loath to leave him to this rabble, but he motioned again, before she lost sight of him, swimming in an ocean of humanity.

The sea embraced her and approved of her return. It called her, it loved her, it needed her. Carlos didn't need her like the water did. The ocean's call was too strong now for her to ignore. She dove into the bay and left the pier, and the teeming crowd of angry humans, behind.

**Komie:**

As Paul drove Komie back from Phoenix Park, she placed a gentle hand on his arm. "Must we go back down into that bunker? Can't we do whatever else needs doing in Leinster House? Or anywhere above ground."

"D'ye not like it down there?"

"I can't hear the earth or smell the trees down below. The concrete interferes with both."

He gave a shrug. "Ciara called for a meeting in the conference room, so sure. Lugh's bringing some of the others."

For some reason, that news made goosebumps on her arms. "The others? You mean other gods?"

He gave a shrug, flipping his long hair back. "Not sure which ones, now. Hopefully not that Macha lass. She's a right terror."

While he lacked respect, Komie couldn't argue with his assessment. She'd worked closely with the goddess of war and never wanted to have to do that again.

At first, Komie thought she could work with her, after hearing Colin's tale of Macha running a footrace while about to give birth to twins. Anyone who could do that deserved kudos, goddess or human. But her temper was, as Paul said, a right terror. And after that race had finished, she'd brought down a horrific punishment on the people who made her run it.

As they entered Leinster House, Komie felt her connection with the natural world snap, a pain in her spirit.

They walked down the hall, their footsteps echoing on the characterless tiles. The room was empty except for Ciara, sitting in a corner and reading on her pad. She glanced up and waved at them, then returned to her reading.

Paul gestured toward a table with snacks and drinks before leaving again. Komie had just poured herself a cup of coffee and stirred in sugar as footsteps approached. She sat at the round table, cradling her warm cup in her hands.

Lugh entered with a shining smile across his face, as if he was the cat who ate the canary. A shiver ran down her spine and she wondered where Bintou was. Didn't the Malian woman usually trail behind the god as his translator?

The Dagda followed Lugh, his bulk and his grin both wide. Komie nodded to them. Their presence was a powerful force, almost oozing tangible charisma.

Ciara put down her pad and approached them with a quiet greeting. No one else arrived, and Komie glanced around. Had they specifically asked for her to be here? Or was this a general meeting?

Paul returned and sat on her other side, patting her shoulder for reassurance.

Lugh placed his hands on the table and leaned forward while the Dagda settled into the largest chair, which creaked under his weight. He glanced at each of the three humans. "We have a plan and would like to share it with you."

Komie spoke up. "Why just us? Are you not interested in the rest of the government knowing this information? And where's Bintou?"

A shadow of a frown passed across Lugh's sunny face, and he glanced at the Dagda. The father-god gave a solemn nod. "Those are all excellent questions. We would like to share the plan with you three, as trusted advisors. Then we will expand the information. Bintou is doing well. She's at your home, is she not, Lugh?"

The blond god pressed his lips together. "She is there and relaxing in the lap of luxury. She has earned a holiday, don't you think so?"

Komie pursed her lips. What would ancient gods know about taking holidays?

The Dagda tapped the table. "First, we would like to form a plan to educate young Unhidden on basic control. Things like how to discover their potential."

Ciara gave a solemn nod, and Komie could find no fault in that initiative. Education of the young was usually an excellent idea. PHAE had already set up a system of education, but any plan could be improved.

"Next, we would like to suggest a hierarchy within your organization."

Komie glanced at Ciara at the last suggestion, as she'd been in charge of crafting PHAE into what it was today, but the Irish woman's expression remained bland.

No one mentioned the current problem but broaching that subject would remind the gods of their offer to help fight off the PEM. They didn't want to open that can of worms if they could help it. As long as the PEM didn't attack again, they could afford that conceit. For now.

Ciara steepled her fingers. "That all sounds reasonable. I can't give you an answer myself, but I can pass it on to PHAE. What else?"

The Dagda cleared his throat and sat back. "I have another request for your leaders. One considerably more difficult, I think."

That set her imagination running wild. For the first time since Komie had met him, the Dagda looked uncomfortable. His gaze flicked to the doorway and then to the table. "We would like sanctuary."

Now Ciara's face flushed. Komie had never seen her so flustered. What would cause a god to want sanctuary? Especially the father of the gods?

Komie exchanged an incredulous glance with Paul and Ciara before asking, "Sanctuary? From whom?"

The Dagda scowled. "From the other immortals. There is a rift growing between us, and we may need a place to escape once the dust has settled."

**Bintou:**

Bintou relaxed in the pond, arms outstretched, and floating on her back. She wished the sun would shine in this strange other land, but at least the air was warm, and she had plenty of food and drink. As long as she stayed away from mead and wine, she could do as she liked in this paradise.

In her Islamic belief, paradise was an infinite garden with lush greenery and full of shade. Streams of milk, honey, and wine. Whatever meat one desires. And this place came very close to that description.

Even with Lugh gone, she felt a comfortable bliss, as if his physical touch lingered on her skin, even inside her body. Just thinking about him made her writhe in anticipatory ecstasy. Memory of his caress brought the woman out of her even as she floated alone in the tepid water.

Birdsong intruded upon her solitude, and she tried to identify the species. Not that she recognized any of the birds either in Ireland or in Fairy. Still, their song was sweet, and it added to her somnolent joy.

*Somnolent joy.* For some reason, this phrase reminded her of Martin's smile. She hadn't thought of him in much too long. A tear rolled down her cheek, meeting the water without a sound. His low, liquid chuckle, his bright smile, his soft hug. They all made Bintou long for home.

Not her home in Mali. That had been a temporary flat where she slept when she wasn't working, though she'd lived in that city for years.

Not her home in Cairo, before her parents moved. She'd only been a child there.

Not her home in Ireland, as that was nothing but a cold, soulless bunker with concrete walls.

For Bintou, her only true home had been Martin's embrace, warm and unjudging, full of laughter, sweetness, and a hint of his beloved whiskey.

A crack appeared in the glamour Lugh had cast over her. A widening rift through which she could see herself as she really was, and not what Lugh wanted her to see.

Bintou waded to shore, dried off, and wrapped a colorful sari around her generous curves.

The song of Lugh's bed called as if he waited there, beckoning to her with a knowing smile. But she kept a firm grip on Martin's image that helped to block the magical allure. She found her shoes and walked away from the tower.

Bintou had no idea of how she would bridge the magical passage between this land of Fairy and her own world. But if she didn't peel herself away from the sexual pleasure spell that Lugh had so carefully crafted upon her, she'd never have the strength to leave. Memory of Martin seemed to be the only thing that fought against that hold.

She marched down the path, through winding tall grass and swaying trees. Birds continued to sing as she passed, calling to her, begging her to stay and enjoy all that life in Fairy had to offer. Hunger gripped her belly, aching to be filled with the sweet fruit and cheese of Lugh's dining table.

That last urge was strong, but she shook her head and pushed through the mind-fog, intent upon breaking free.

This path might lead her deeper into unknown terrain. Could she follow broken branches to Brigit's home, and enlist Qacha's help?

But the Mongolian woman wasn't there any longer, as she'd escaped to the real world. Bintou wished she could be with Qacha in Dublin. She always felt safe in the other woman's presence. Protected, cherished. A feeling of home.

She needed a vantage point to get the lay of the land. Then she could picture the map in her mind and follow it to wherever she wanted to go. If she could recognize a gate back to the real world. If such a gate even existed for her to recognize.

With no hills nearby, Bintou chose a tree, its bark pliant and soft, unlike any tree she'd ever touched. She grunted as she dragged herself into the branches, trying to see something in the landscape that she might recognize, understand, or use to travel.

Undulating hills with tall grasses and clumps of oddly colored trees surrounded her. Lugh's tower rose in the distance. Nothing else.

What could she possibly do? She might call for help, but who would answer her, but a Fae creature? They'd be loyal to the Irish gods, and no help to her.

She might call on Allah, but she had never been a very good Muslim.

Then she recalled a visitation from her own goddess of wisdom, Orunmila. An image of her draped in green and yellow robes, telling her that Ireland was her home. She'd come to Ireland. Could she come to this Faery world?

Bintou focused her mind on that image, trying to call the Orisha to her. A deity who had existed before the creation of humanity, a sage, one who interceded on the behalf of humans.

But as much as she called to Orunmila, no one answered.

When she descended, full of disgust and disappointment, a voice called out. "Where are you going, mortal creature? Did you call for help?"

Bintou whirled to see a woman with skin like swirling rainbows.

**Qacha:**

Qacha cursed again for being so stupid. She should have realized Macha would get hold of their note. But she'd had the hubris to believe a mere language would protect them. But how was she to know that they'd be able to read Japanese?

But she should have known. Qacha had strategic training and should have realized the flimsiness of their plan. The only other person in their group with more training was Max, and she had no idea where he'd disappeared to.

She was thankful that Macha—along with that horrible, destructive shriek—had disappeared. The goddess's rage must be related to that damned note. Qacha needed to talk to Ciara and the others about the implications of this discovery, but before they could discuss anything, she spied Brigit through the window. The goddess had returned.

Qacha hurried down the hall but stayed hidden around a corner. She detested skulking, but this situation called for clandestine information however she could obtain it.

The goddess entered Leinster House with a thunderous expression. The poor receptionist at the front desk bore the brunt of her impatience. "I demand to be taken to the Minister of Defence immediately!"

The receptionist gave an amazingly patient nod. "Please have a seat and I will inform him you have come."

Brigit did not sit. She loomed over the woman with growing ire.

After a whispered phone call, the receptionist ignored the goddess. That didn't seem smart, but then a door down the hall opened, and the Minister of Defence walked toward Qacha.

He grabbed Qacha's arm as he passed, pulling her into the lobby. Then he spoke in a deliberate, pleasant voice. "I'm delighted to see you again so soon, Brigit. How can I help you today?"

The Irish goddess tried to loom over the Minister, and Qacha had to admit, she did a decent job. She was powerfully built, for a human, a goddess, or whatever type of measure she required.

But the Minister refused to be cowed. His expression and body language remained pleasant.

"I have been told of a particular technology you possess. You will show me."

"And what technology is this?"

"Something called fusion power."

Qacha almost choked. The Minister's bland façade slipped a notch. "Fusion power? I'm afraid that technology is only permitted for national governments. It's not for personal use. The equipment and materials are heavily regulated, incredibly expensive, and wildly dangerous in the wrong hands."

Brigit's scowl deepened as he spoke with frustration in her voice. "And does Ireland have this power?"

"Alas, we do not."

She growled and paced in the lobby, mumbling under her breath. Suddenly, she turned. "What leaders possess this power?"

He blinked a few times. "I believe the United States, the United Kingdom, France, and China are the only ones who currently use fusion, though several other countries are building reactors."

Brigit pursed her lips. "Then what technology does Ireland have? I've become bored with these mechanical guns and cannons. I need something more."

Qacha raised her chin. "I can give you a history of different weapons used over the time since you've been... asleep. There may be something within the past that you can use now without breaking international laws."

The goddess let out a long-suffering sigh. "I suppose that will have to do for now."

Before Qacha could blink, Brigit had snatched her hand and they disappeared into the gray mist. Her stomach churned as they shifted worlds.

When they coalesced in Brigit's workshop in Fairy, Qacha rounded on her. "I do not appreciate being taken like that! You should ask someone's permission before moving them."

Just as the words came from her mouth, Qacha realized she should have been more diplomatic with this volatile goddess.

Brigit stood over her. And while she was not easily intimidated, Qacha found her heartbeat racing. Still, she stood her ground. "This is common courtesy in modern society. We have bodily autonomy. We are not slaves."

Brigit continued to loom, her scowl deepening. "You are not one to complain. You have already betrayed our trust once."

*Fuck a goat! She must be talking about the damned note.* "Betrayed your trust?"

"There is no need to play coy. You know exactly what I speak of. Did you think a creature of the Fae would not be loyal to us? I thought you less foolish than that."

This reminded Qacha of the dressing down she'd received at her last chef position. Her temper boiled, and she struggled to keep control. Like fire, her ire was difficult to quench once lit. "If you hadn't taken each of us away without permission, then we wouldn't have to send notes to escape!"

Her head exploded in agony. Qacha didn't see the punch, but her cheekbone cracked with impact. She fell to the ground, scraping her hands as she tried to stop skidding across the gravel.

Qacha jumped to her feet, pulling power into her body. She wouldn't be caught unaware again.

Brigit's eyes lit with eager anticipation as she assumed a power stance, weight balanced on the balls of her feet, hands out.

They circled each other warily, neither attacking, but both assessing their opponent. This was Brigit's home base, and even if Qacha won the engagement—whatever that would look like—she'd have no way of returning home. And Brigit's power was strongest in Fairy.

Still, she didn't exactly have a choice.

She feinted to one side, but Brigit wasn't so easily fooled. Qacha wished she had a weapon, any weapon. Preferably her grandfather's horse bow. Or better yet, a Kalashnikov. A cannon. Even a nuclear warhead. Anything that might prove more powerful than this goddess.

Brigit raised her arms and faced the sky.

Qacha took the opening. Just like she had with the drones, she aimed as if holding a bow and arrow and targeted her fire at the goddess.

A fireball struck Brigit in the chest, and she staggered back, her eyes wide in surprise. "How can you do that here? You should have no power in my demesne!"

Qacha shrugged. "I never received a copy of the regulations."

They squared off again.

**Komie:**

After their meeting, Komie wanted to talk to Ciara, but she held up a hand. "Michelle and Colin are arriving, so we can discuss this with them. Come, they should be here any minute."

They exited Leinster House and entered the square. Thankfully, the constant protestor presence had thinned lately. Komie didn't relish crossing the picket lines again, not after having to quell an angry mob out on the west coast. Those PEM people turned nasty quickly and had very little sense or reason.

Komie thought she caught a glimpse of a familiar face in the crowd and shuddered. Was that Joel? Anger shot through her from the last time she'd seen the American man, as he tried to get a mob to kill her and Roísín.

She steadied her gaze, but it wasn't Anna's brother, just someone who looked like him. Komie was opposed to violence, but she wouldn't shed a tear if Joel was dropped off a cliff.

They hurried to the entrance to the PHAE bunker, not far from the Dublin docks. Just as they arrived, a car pulled up and Colin and Michelle climbed out.

Komie peered to see if any of their children had come, but Fiona must still be at home with the twins. They'd be safer there, as long as there was an adult to keep them from burning down the house.

Ciara shook Colin's hand and opened with, "We have a new situation."

He raised his eyebrows and reached for Michelle's hand. They exchanged a glance and she said, "What happened?"

Komie pursed her lips. "There's a rift forming between the gods. Two of them asked for sanctuary terms should things go pear-shaped."

Michelle gasped. "Sanctuary? From whom?"

"The Dagda and Lugh asked for it. Macha and Taranis are out of control. She might go off on a rampage."

Colin's face lost all color. "Macha on a rampage is no laughing matter. She has the power to destroy all of Ireland. Hell, she might even destroy the world, if she's upset enough. She wouldn't care."

A voice behind Komie said, "You are correct. I would not care."

She spun to see Macha, her red eyes flashing with rage. The goddess's muscular body quivered like a compressed spring, ready to burst at any moment. "Your people have betrayed mine, and you must pay for that betrayal. We do not tolerate disloyalty amongst our subjects. Prepare to be destroyed!"

Komie glanced around to ensure that no one else was in immediate danger, then put every ounce of reasonableness into her voice, wishing she had Hiroki's talent. "I'm sure we can come to some compromise."

Macha threw her head back and let out a laugh that chilled Komie to the bone. "There is no compromise. Only vengeance."

Still, she must try. Komie stepped forward, her hands out, palms down, in a placating gesture. "I'm sure no one meant to betray anyone, Macha. Let's talk about this. Can you tell me what exactly happened?"

Komie's arms tingled, but she wasn't calling her power. She glanced toward Ciara, who gave a bare nod.

Ciara must be using her own power to damp other people's magic. They didn't know if it would work on the goddess, but they had to try.

In the depths of her mind, Komie called to her spirit guides and ancestors. *Please, I need your help now. Can you come?*

The faint echo of Bear answered her. *We will come.*

Komie took a step closer, her hands still out to placate the goddess.

Macha threw her head back in a mad laugh. She began to grow, and not just in height. Her shoulders spread wider, her legs thicker, until she stood at twice the height and mass as her previous human form.

Her clothes didn't grow with her, and they ripped and split. She looked like something out of a Hulk movie, with the muscles and the rage to match. Several onlookers had the sense to scurry away.

The goddess let out a shriek that ripped across the city. It came with a gale-force wind, whipping fabric, roof tiles, even people from where they stood.

Colin, Michelle, and Ciara ducked and covered their ears. Komie was the only one standing between Macha and a destructive storm.

She cried out in her mind, *Bear, I need your help now!*

*We are far from you. We cannot be there yet. It will take time.*

Their help had been her only chance. *Dammit.*

Ciara stood slowly, her hands dropping from her ears. She wore a blank expression, as if watching something in the distance. She stepped forward, almost stumbling, closer to Macha.

Colin and Michelle both stood as well, taking the same zombie stance. They stepped forward as one.

Komie's gaze darted around frantically, but then her attention suddenly focused on the goddess. She had the incredible urge to join them. It would be so easy to join them. To come to Macha, and be part of her destructive army, and take over the land. To take over the world. To be the conquering heroes.

She shook her head. Since when did she have such thoughts? Komie was a peaceful person, a member of the Council of Mothers. Her vocation was to spread wisdom, not violence. Such thoughts must be from Macha's magic.

Komie drew upon her ancestors to give her strength to resist this sorcery. Even if Bear and the other spirits couldn't help yet, she still had her own power to draw on.

Ciara was no longer dampening anything, so she could use her magic. Komie searched around frantically for any plants she might call upon, but this concrete-covered part of the city had little to offer, just a few potted trees or window boxes.

She stared at the water past the docks, but nothing living stirred beneath. No seaweed or coral echoed her call, only dead rocks and sand.

If she couldn't hurt the goddess, she might at least pull her friends back from certain destruction.

Komie grabbed Colin and yanked him away from the goddess. He shook his head, his eyes glassy. "What? What happened?" He covered his ears again and winced.

"She's making some magical call, a thrall. We've got to break it!"

Colin lunged for his wife just as Komie grabbed Ciara. Both women fought their grip, trying to join Macha. Komie swore she saw the hint of a smile in Macha's screeching face.

Finally, she'd had enough. Putting all the power of a grandmother into her voice, Komie shouted, "Macha! Silence!"

If Macha could laugh and scream at the same time, she surely would. But Komie tried again, channeling the Council of Mothers through herself, all the authority of the matriarchs. "Silence! You will not enthrall us!"

With deliberate slowness, Macha's scream faded. Komie's ears throbbed from the cessation of sound, which morphed into ringing. Macha's gaze rested upon her, and her mouth spread into a wicked, horrifying smile.

Komie was able to take only a few pain-free breaths before Macha let loose another scream.

This time, the sound hit her like a cannon ball. She jerked back and clapped her hands over her ears, trying to block the horrific sound.

Bricks in the surrounding buildings shuddered as the sound ripped through the Dublin streets. A man ran away, but his skin ripped from him in bloody strips. That set more people screaming, a counterpoint to Macha's screech.

Komie caught a glimpse of Ciara, cowering next to another man, but her face was scrunched up in concentration. She must be trying to dampen the scream with her Unhidden talent. She didn't know if it was working, but one moment, the screaming filled the air, and the next, Macha vanished.

They all glanced around, the dust from her destructive call still settling, but the goddess had completely disappeared. Everyone took a collective breath of relief at the blessed silence.

Komie's heart sank as she realized the goddess might have gone anywhere and would wreak chaos and death wherever she went.

# Chapter Nine

"Art is the final cunning of the human soul which would rather do
anything than face the gods."
– Iris Murdoch

**Hiroki:**

As Hiroki sat cross-legged on the ground, surrounded by forest, Oghma was across from him in a classic Buddha meditation pose. For several long moments, they waited in sublime silence, communing with the surrounding nature and each other.

Their breaths were in rhythm. Their hearts beat as one. Birdsong danced in their ears in exquisite harmony. Even the swaying leaves seemed to caress his soul in sweet tenderness.

At that moment, Hiroki felt a part of something bigger than himself, more than ever before.

Then, something discordant shattered this bliss. Footsteps crunching on the grass, making the earth beneath them tremble.

Hiroki's eyes flew open and Oghma's expression changed. Instead of peaceful serenity, the god's brow was now furrowed, and his gaze flicked to the edges of the clearing.

The god rose to his feet and offered Hiroki a hand to help him rise. "They are coming."

"Who is coming?"

"The others."

Hiroki wrinkled his nose at this deliberate evasion, especially from a god of communication, but all he needed to do was wait and he'd know the truth.

The footsteps came closer and the birds flew away in a flurry. The absence of their song felt like a shot to the heart. Trees still swayed, but their fluttering leaves seemed lonely without the birds.

A glow shone through the trees to the right, then another to the left. A third shone in the middle. Three gods, then. Hiroki's heart began to race, as there was no way to escape whatever came for them.

As the lights came closer, he recognized the war goddess, Macha. Then Taranis's angry form appeared. And the final form resolved into Brigit. None of the three looked pleased.

Brigit barely spared him a glance before tearing into Oghma. "They've utterly betrayed us. They will not adhere to their promises! I've asked over and over again for their technologies and they outright refuse!"

Macha bared her teeth. "They've sown sedition against our plans and control. We must destroy them now, before they devise a plan!"

Taranis cut in. "They are incapable of being worthy of us."

Hiroki could barely breathe. He shouldn't be here. He shouldn't be witness to this meeting, not as a mortal.

He backed up a step, trying to fade into the background as Oghma tried to calm the others. "We have a plan, Brigit, and we hold true to it. Therefore, we need patience, not violence."

The god of communication turned to Hiroki, shattering his hope of disappearing from danger. Hiroki swallowed, knowing that Oghma wanted him to use his persuasion power on the others.

He cleared his throat and pulled his power inward. His skin tingled as the magic flowed through his blood, and he poured all the calm and verity he could into the words. "Humans in our modern society are excellent at compromise, and we will find a way to accommodate your needs, I'm certain. But sometimes we balk at what must be done. We just need time to consider the options."

While his skin tingled, he didn't think his magic had had any effect upon the gods. He tried again. "Much of modern diplomacy take months to work out the details, so that each party is satisfied. I know you are in the midst of several negotiations. The wisest course is to wait until those are complete before you make any decisions."

Brigit put a finger to her lips as if she was considering his suggestion, and Hiroki dared to hope his powers had worked. But then Taranis let out a roar and punched a tree, which split in two. The ground shuddered at the impact. A chunk of bark spun toward Hiroki, making him duck and lose his balance, stumbling back several steps.

Macha tilted her head back and roared so loud, Hiroki's eardrums pounded at his skull. He covered his ears and scuttled behind a large tree to hide from her wrath. Brigit let out a roar as well, and suddenly, the three of them disappeared, leaving Hiroki and Oghma in stunned silence.

Hiroki peeked out from behind the tree as Oghma sat with his face in his hands.

When the god finally looked up, tears streaked his cheeks. "We failed."

**Caoimhe:**

As Caoimhe dragged herself from an exhausted sleep, she rubbed her face and moaned. She needed far more than the three hours of rest she was getting each night, but there was no end in sight.

She simply didn't have enough folks with talent to guard the coast, not with Ireland's wimpy physical defenses and three thousand kilometres of coastline.

And now something dangerous was stirring within the land. Something Caoimhe couldn't put a finger on, but that definitely needed to be dealt with.

For a moment, she rebelled against her needing to be the responsible party. She hadn't run for political office. These weren't her children. She wasn't a leader of anyone. She wanted to just bugger off to some island off the west coast and shun everyone. No internet, no phone, just a thatched cottage, a few cats, and herself.

But there was no one else with her background and experience to coordinate their defenses, and if the PEM didn't get in, someone else would. And if that happened, she wouldn't be safe, even on her isolated island.

Caoimhe let out a long-suffering sigh and shoved herself to her feet to wash and dress. Once she left her bedroom in the lighthouse, instead of heading up to the gallery, she descended to the ground floor.

That earlier earth shake had her curious, and she wanted to discover what had happened.

Walking off the pavement, she lay down on the grass, to better feel the land itself. She closed her eyes and let the ground speak to her, ignoring the misty soft rain caressing her face. Breathing in and out, she let herself feel the story of her island.

Ireland sobbed.

Caoimhe shot up to a sitting position, panting, every inch of her skin pebbling with fear. She searched for something else that might have made that heart-wrenching noise, but nothing was nearby.

Dawn was barely beginning in the east, and even her fellow guards weren't awake yet. A lone night watchman on the lighthouse gallery stood at his post. She glanced up, but he didn't even see her, as he concentrated on the ocean horizon.

Swallowing, the *draoi* lay down again, bracing herself for more cries. They came almost as soon as she closed her eyes, pounding in her head and making her eyes tear.

Forcing herself to listen beyond the obvious, she dug deep into the source. Why did the land of Ireland weep? What was causing this pain?

A ponderous footstep trembled beneath her, then another. Someone was walking. Not a casual stride down the pavement, but a momentous stomp that could be felt throughout the island. The walk of a god or goddess, then, someone of the Old Blood. Someone of divine consequence.

Caoimhe swallowed again, afraid that she knew the answer already, and not wanting to verify. But that was literally her job as a guardian of Ireland, to discover what threatened the land and the people. And if Ireland was already crying, then the threat had already arrived.

A threat she'd have to deal with. Because who else could do it? Sure, the PHAE had power, but did they have enough to defend against a rogue god, now?

On the other hand, as much as she hated to admit it, Caoimhe couldn't combat a god on her own, even a small one. She could call up power, yes, but any power she possessed was from the grace of her patron goddess, Macha. If Macha decided she didn't want to grant that power, Caoimhe would be well fucked.

No matter which god was walking the land in a rage, Caoimhe would need all the help she could muster from the other guardians, from the PHAE, psychics, healers, whatever support she could get.

Maybe even the other gods, if the rogue entity had broken trust with the rest.

Caoimhe wrinkled her nose as she rose to her feet and wiped her hands on her jeans. By Danu's paps, she might even have to call in help from the Christians.

**Caoimhe:**

Two days after Caoimhe sent out the call, late in the afternoon, people gathered at the Hill of Uisneach, the spiritual center of the island of Ireland.

A sacred place for thousands of years, the hill was near the physical center, too, and commanded a stunning view of the surrounding counties.

Caoimhe's ancestors had held ceremonies on that hill since Neolithic times, and now she meant to hold another under the modern cloudless sky.

She'd sent out a summons to *everyone*. The druids, witches, seers, tarot card readers, psychics, healers, ministers, nuns, monks, even priests. Anyone who could wield any sort of power, influence, or magic. Caoimhe refused to fail now because her own prejudices or snobbery kept her from calling on rival clerics for help.

Those divine footsteps kept pounding in her head as she worked through the administrative details, shaking her bones and rattling her teeth.

Luckily, she'd set up a communication tree several years ago, back when that pandemic hit the world. She'd call five people, then they'd call five more each, and so on down the line.

It had worked in good stead when she needed to organize the perimeter watch, but now she needed everyone here at Uisneach. Caoimhe summoned everyone except today's coastal watch.

*Boom. Boom. Boom.* The footsteps were like someone hammering in her skull. She couldn't get rid of it. That made her think this must be Macha, but she didn't dare contact her goddess.

If Macha was raging, Caoimhe might be swept into the rapport and do violence for her patron goddess without even knowing it. She had to set up fail safes before she tried anything.

*Boom. Boom. Boom.* She glanced to the right, where the PHAE contingent clustered. Hiroki, Ciara, Bintou, Komie, she recognized all of them.

The tall older man might be that Max she'd heard about. He'd better keep hold of himself if Taranis showed up. Róisín stood next to him, looking worried and as tired as Caoimhe felt.

*Boom. Boom. Boom.* The hill shook with each step. Caoimhe did a full circle, searching across the landscape, but nobody approached other than vanilla humans like herself. Where were the footsteps coming from?

A primal screech cut across the hilltop, and everyone ducked, covering their heads. The sound made Caoimhe want to flee, to run away and hide in the darkest depths of her childhood bedroom, covered in blankets and clutching soft toys.

The sound awoke a visceral fear in her, so badly that she had to physically hold her legs to keep them from running down the hill and away to safety. Others started running, but then Ciara lifted her hands and screamed, "Stop!" and those fleeing slowed to a walk, then turned back toward the center of the Hill of Uisneach.

The screech halted.

That cessation of sound, both the footsteps and the shriek, felt a blissful relief, the removal of oppressive terror. A salve to her jagged soul.

A single point of red light burst forth in the center of the rounded hilltop. It shot out beams of red, white, and gold, as if someone moved torches inside a ball filled with holes.

Mist enveloped the hilltop, making the beams of light look like a laser show. A hum filled the air, like a thousand butterfly wings combined with a high-speed train.

The sound grew oppressive and heavy upon her shoulders. Caoimhe wanted to scream to rip off the audial burden. Just when she was about to burst, it stopped.

The flashing beams melted into a form. Then, Macha stepped from the light, her face and body covered in red, sticky blood, glistening in the late afternoon sun. She let out another screech, her jaw opening so wide, it looked unhinged, like a snake swallowing its prey. Caoimhe's skin crawled.

Chunks of dirt sprung up, as if bombs were falling. A huge stone burst into a thousand fragments, whizzing by people. One hit Caoimhe in the cheek, and she slapped her hand on it. Pulling away, she saw blood.

Several people, members of the PHAE as well as those in Caoimhe's paranormal group, finally gave up resisting their fear and fled.

As one woman reached the foot of the hill, the scream flayed her skin from her body. Chunks of bloody ribbons shot from her body, covering the people around her. They, in turn, screamed and ran. Another was flayed in the same way. Finally, everyone halted, evidently afraid of being next.

Now the *draoi* knew where that blood had come from, and for the first time in her life, true terror coursed through Caoimhe's veins.

She'd worked with Macha for decades, but she'd never seen the goddess manifest. And now, she was in full war mode. If they couldn't stop her, she was fully capable of destroying every human in Ireland.

Caoimhe turned to her closest cohorts, those mediums and witches who she'd worked with across the years. Compatriots in power, working at Rathcrogan, Emhain Macha, or Temhair. Folks who'd worked with the gods as she did, wielding their faint power across the millennia.

Another form stepped from the light beams. Taranis, his long hair sticking up as if electrocuted. His hair and beard were the color of storm clouds and lightning sparked from his eyes. Thunder crashed overhead and the clouds gathered in ominous darkness.

The gods had come to life, and humans must find a way to control their madness. At least, Macha's and Taranis's madness. She didn't see any others come from the light beams. Had these gods gone rogue? Could she count on the other gods to help?

No, she couldn't count on anyone else. Even her own people, here on the hill, were unreliable. Look at how many had tried to flee after the opening salvo.

Ciara stood next to her and grabbed her hand. She felt the PHAE leader's power tingle through her skin. She had the ability to damp other talents. Caoimhe hoped she was working against Macha and not her own magic.

Another man stood next to her, one she didn't recognize, wearing, of all things, a cowboy hat and boots. Caoimhe let out a snort at this typical American stereotype.

**Qacha:**

Qacha had no idea how long she'd battled against Brigit. Once, she had the fitness and stamina to work for hours in a busy kitchen, or ride horses while shooting arrows.

But she'd been too ill too long lately, and her muscles betrayed her. Brigit looked fresh and full of energy, despite being a bit singed around the edges from Qacha's fire attacks.

Brigit rose from Qacha's last attempt, a feral grimace on her face.

Qacha grunted and struggled back to her feet, despite the incredible fatigue shooting through every muscle. She must push through the fatigue.

The goddess wielded her massive blacksmith's hammer as if it was a toy, her thick arm muscles natural to the task. She lunged at Qacha's leg, aiming to smash her femur.

Qacha leapt out of the way, her leg muscles trembling with effort.

She didn't have the same power she might have in the real world, but Qacha had managed to score several hits on the Irish goddess.

In return, she'd shielded herself from the worst of Brigit's attacks, which had mostly been physical. While Qacha was glad of that reprieve, she worried that the goddess was holding back and would let loose with a more magical assault later.

Brigit lunged for another attack, and Qacha scooted to the side, stumbled, and fell painfully on her knee. She couldn't help but let out a whimper at the pain, and then hated herself for her own pathetic weakness. She turned it into a growl as she ducked again. The goddess was so quick!

Qacha roared in frustration. This wasn't how a warrior fought. This wasn't how a granddaughter of the greatest horse archer of the Mongolian steppes behaved.

A true warrior stood against the enemy, past the fear, past the pain, even unto death. Brigit feinted to one side, then the other, and then back to the first. Qacha struggled to keep up, but had to retreat several steps.

She had more strength than this. As she straightened her spine, she stared into Brigit's eyes. The goddess's gaze burned with rage, anger, and fire, something Qacha recognized all too well. Her own temper often flared with little reason, and she'd burned her own life to ashes more times than she could count.

Brigit was the same as herself, burning with an internal flame of determination and rage. They were both phoenixes, rising from the ashes again and again.

How does one fight fire with fire? As much as Qacha hated to admit it, she ought to use water to fight this goddess. Or the philosophical equivalent of water, logic.

Pulling her shoulders back, Qacha rose from her battle stance. Brigit narrowed her gaze at the unusual move.

Qacha dredged up memories about Brigit from Colin's evening stories but came up almost blank. A blacksmith, yes. A goddess of inspiration, creativity, fire. Healing, certainly. And maybe wisdom? Perhaps reason was her best weapon. She raised her chin. "It is illogical for us to battle this way."

Brigit's brow furrowed. "Why isn't it logical? You betrayed my trust. Your government is withholding access to vital technologies. You have broken our agreement and must pay the consequences. The logic is sound."

"But to what end? Would it not be more satisfactory to discover the reason behind these decisions? To learn more about the circumstances, and make a wiser, more informed judgment? I would think a goddess of wisdom would rather make her decisions with all the facts on hand."

The fire in Brigit's eyes flickered as she narrowed her gaze.

Qacha waited for a few heartbeats, but Brigit didn't renew her physical attack. "And once you do have all the information, if you decide that something else should be done, then you can act at that point."

The goddess of fire's eyes faded and she stood straight, her hammer hand dropping to her side.

**Tiberius:**

Tiberius still didn't like that Ciara woman, and he still didn't want to be part of this damned pagan PHAE group. However, Tiberius realized a lot more people than PHAE were on that hilltop. He even saw some priests and nuns. The Texan man exchanged a respectful nod with the closest minister.

The PHAE may represent godless heathens, but they'd evidently earned the respect of Christian leaders. Maybe they *could* work together to banish a literal evil force. He hoped.

Ciara pulled him aside. "Are you still on board with helping us? I don't want you backing out just when we need you most."

"I'm here, hon'. Never fear. I don't back out once I've given my word."

She raised her eyebrows. "I can appreciate that sort of steadfastness, even in a vulgar Texan."

Tiberius cocked his head. "And I can appreciate a woman who knows what she wants."

Ciara let out a chuckle. "Fine. What I want right now is for you to stick close to Max here. He's one of most powerful offensive talents we have, since Qacha disappeared. If you can boost his power, we might have a chance."

He'd given the older man the once-over, noting his lined face, haunted eyes, and gray ponytail. The PHAE man offered his hand, and they exchanged a strong shake. "G'day, mate."

"Howdy. What's your name? You sound Aussie."

"I'm from Oz, true enough. Max Hurley. You?"

"Tiberius Wilkinson."

The other man scowled. "Aren't you the bloke on the telly? The one calling for the whole bloody world to kill us in blood and fire?"

Giving a rueful half-smile, Tiberius gave a shrug. "That'd be me, alright."

Max let out a snort. "Well, hell in a bloody basket. What're you doing here?"

Sparing a glance to the ministers behind him and the priestess chanting in the center, he gave another shrug. "Evidently there's something more important to combat than you folks. At least, for the moment."

The Australian stared at him. "At the moment? And what the hell does *that* mean?"

Tiberius growled, "It means I am helping you now. That won't necessarily hold true after this crisis. Keep that in mind."

Max gave a slow nod. "Oh, no worries at all, mate. You better bet your boots I'll remember *that* little detail."

Tiberius snorted. "Don't dig up more snakes than you can kill, Aussie."

The priestess, a woman about Tiberius's own age with a long, gray braid and a frown, shot him an angry glare and increased the volume of her chanting. The others on the hilltop were chanting with her, speaking foreign words.

Well, he'd be damned if he started jabbering unknown words. He had no wish to meet Satan or any of his devils today. He glanced around at psychics in their colorful robes, priests, even ministers joining in.

Hell, did he *have* to help? Couldn't he just put his hands on their shoulders, or whatever he needed to do, to bolster their power?

Then he glanced over at Ciara, and suddenly, he wanted to do something to impress her. To make her admire him. She had some snap in her garters, no doubt about that. Hell, he hadn't felt *that* way about a woman since… well, since his wife had gone.

And here he was, helping out the very people who had killed her. But now that things were going to hell in a handbasket, he had to start punching for the other side. He swallowed away the pain and gritted his teeth.

Down the line, they gripped hands, sparks flying every time one touched. Person by person, they built a ladder of sparkling light. The sparks knitted together in an undulating mesh, forming a net.

He didn't chant the words, whatever they were, but he focused on the power they wielded. He could see it, physically in front of him, no illusion or hallucination. He didn't want to believe it, but there it was, clear as day.

The woman next to Max grabbed his hand, and the lightning snapped and crackled like a Tesla coil. Tiberius stared at the Aussie's hand when he offered it. He'd rather kiss a shark, but he gritted his teeth and took the hand.

A jolt of electricity shot through him, making every muscle in his body rigid for a moment, and then the crackling eased. He put his hand out for Ciara, and she took it.

Eventually, the circle closed with a snap, and the ladder of sparks became an actual net of electricity.

At first, the lightning was a knee-high corral inside the circle of people. Then it grew taller with each line of chanting. Eventually, the edges met at the top, a huge protective shield over the gods.

Then the nature of the chanting changed, coming more quickly, in short, sharp syllables. The net responded, contracting with each word, tightening around the prisoners.

He locked gazes with Ciara, and she gave him a nod. Tiberius took a deep breath and gripped Max and Ciara's hands, pushing into the shield with whatever he had.

At first, it pulsed white then yellow then orange, like a dying light. He pushed again, and it stayed white longer. Again, and he was almost able to sustain the color, like blowing on a sullen ember to keep a campfire strong.

Each time the net blazed, the shield grew thicker. At first, it was barely a fingertip wide. Now it was a handspan, maybe even a full foot wide.

Inside, the two gods screamed. At least, their mouths were open wide, and they looked like they were screaming, but no sound escaped their magical shield. He exchanged an incredulous look with Ciara. *They were doing it!*

Then lightning crashed around him, and the sky grew black.

**Caoimhe:**

Magic and pain battled inside of her. Her loyalty to the ancient gods, and to Macha in particular, demanded that she stop this immediately and bow before her patroness, begging her mercy after abject betrayal.

But when all was said and done, Caoimhe was human, and when the gods threatened the humans, she must choose her own people, no matter how much it hurt her soul.

Even though her own hold upon this logic, this determination, was tentative at best, Caoimhe passed that certainty through her hand into the next person, the Archbishop of Armagh.

Normally, she'd cross the street to avoid coming near the pompous primate, but his strength was a boon to their chain, this cage built against ancient power.

Once the magic passed to him and he felt her strength and determination, his eyes grew wide, and they shared a glance. Then he nodded and passed her strength to the next person.

As that tiny morsel of power passed from person to person within the chain, the shield around Taranis and Macha grew stronger, thicker, and more stable.

Then some American asshole with a bloody cowboy hat, of all things, funneled strength into the chain. Caoimhe felt the surge like a tide coming in, rushing forward with strength but precious little control. The power net sprang into tangible form, an actual cage made from white-hot iron.

Caoimhe had no idea how he'd done that. What sort of Unhidden talent did he have? It must have been one of them, because she didn't have anybody in her network like that.

She didn't know and frankly, she didn't care. Everyone knew that the ancient ones hated iron. That particular trait was so part of common knowledge that it had become a modern trope in books, movies, and songs.

Still, Caoimhe didn't notice any change in the gods struggling inside. They still screamed with silent rage, and storms roiled above them, the sky growing black.

It wasn't enough. Even with everyone with power helping, even with every heavy hitter from PHAE, even with the bloody damned Archbishop, it wasn't enough.

Maybe she should call the Pope.

**Hiroki:**

After the three angry gods disappeared, Hiroki and Oghma created a plan. It wasn't a good plan, but it was the best they could do.

Oghma would bring Hiroki to the gods with a planned speech, his best form of communication. Oghma would pour magic into Hiroki, to reinforce the power behind his Unhidden talent of persuasion.

Fear and anxiety flooded Hiroki. Why was it *his* duty to block these gods? He was no warrior. Besides, they had physical power. He only had words.

And if the gods decided to destroy the PHAE, why should he care so much? Everyone in the PHAE had turned their back on him. They hadn't helped him when he needed it most.

But Oghma insisted that they try. And after all, it was Oghma who had accepted him, taken him under his wing, and mentored him. It was Oghma who had granted him the approval he'd always craved from his own father. It was Oghma he must please, no matter what else he did in his life.

As the Irish god took Hiroki's hand, his heart pounded in his chest, and he broke out in a cold sweat. He wanted to run away into Fairy and never see the human world again. After all, what had the human world ever done but reject him?

But Oghma led, so he followed.

The world turned gray and Hiroki's stomach lurched. He had to swallow back vomit and coughed several times.

When they emerged from the fog of travel between worlds, they stood upon a massive hill. Hiroki turned in a full circle, taking in acres and acres of farmland and charming villages laid out before him. Hiroki had loved those European fairy tales, and this was exactly what he'd always imagined as the perfect part of Ireland. A scene belonging on a postcard.

But the hill was crowded with people. All of Ireland seemed to have gathered here. He recognized Ciara, Paul, and several other PHAE folks, such as Max and Komie. They were surrounded by strangers, people in all manner of dress, including priests in cassocks, nuns in habits, and hippies in colorful shawls.

He spied Macha and Taranis captured within a crackling cage of lightning and iron, screaming at the top of their lungs. The noise seared his brain, but not his ears. No physical sound escaped.

The gathered people held hands in a giant circle around the cage, then in another circle, and so on. At least six lines deep, though parts of the circle were squashed and uneven. This lack of symmetry bothered his sense of aesthetics.

Oghma turned to him. "Now is your chance. I can give you volume, but you must tell everyone what we discussed. Are you ready?"

Hiroki gathered his power, pulling upon whatever source fed his PHAE talent. His body, skin, and muscles tingled with energy and magic, and he took a deep breath, ready to deliver his carefully crafted speech.

Then he caught a glimpse of Ciara with the others. And Bintou. He remembered her anger with him. Hiroki let out the breath as doubt flooded him. Macha and Taranis had the strength of warriors. Warriors had subjugated weaker humans to their will for millennia.

How could mere humans fight against such strength? He had no reason to trust that they would do what he wanted. Humans were fickle and capricious, just like his former friends. How could mere humans triumph over actual, living gods?

He turned to the Irish god, his skin still tingling and full of persuasive power. "Macha and Taranis seem to be the true power behind the gods. They'll win this battle. Therefore, we should join them or be destroyed with the others."

The crowd grew hushed, and Hiroki realized that Oghma had indeed amplified his voice. So, despite his desire to speak quietly to the god, everyone heard him. And he'd just told Oghma, and everyone on the hill, to support Macha and Taranis.

At first, shame washed over him, as if he stood in front of a school assembly stark naked. A scene out of so many nightmares in his life.

But then, as Hiroki glanced at Oghma's expression of fear, he realized he had spoken the truth. He stood behind his words. He meant it. Power was power, and Macha and Taranis obviously wielded it with strength of purpose.

Hiroki was tired of being the perennial underdog, always on the losing side. For once, Hiroki wanted to be on the winning side, dishonorable or not. He wanted to be a warrior.

**Róisín:**

True to his word, Dian Cecht brought Róisín out of Fairy and into a chaotic mob. Róisín fought the urge to scream as noise assaulted her after the quiet peace and solitude of Fairy.

They stood on a hill, several circles of people holding hands around a sparkling iron cage. One face in particular she hadn't seen in too long, Max. She rushed to him and tackled him with a long hug.

She felt his body tremble. "Róisín? Where did you spring from, luv?"

Róisín gave him a half-smile. "From my mother, where else?"

He rolled his eyes and gave Dian Cecht a sidelong glance. "And what's your bloke over there doing? Which side is he on?"

She glanced from Dian Cecht to the other two gods on the hill, inside that iron cage. The humans surrounding them chanted, holding hands like some giant campfire sing-a-long, and the tension in the air crackled. "Side? What are you talking about? Max, what's going on?"

"Let's see, the two gods in the cage? They've gone utterly bonkers. They're trying to kill everyone. Or take over the world. Or something. I have no idea what, and we aren't bloody well letting them do it. I don't know if the other gods are behind them or against them or what. But we aren't taking any chances. So, is your bloke in with them, or in with us?"

As one, they turned toward Dian Cecht, who stood with his legs apart and his arms crossed. His gaze flicked from the gods trapped in the magical cage to the chanting circles of humans arrayed against them.

From her intimate connection with him, Róisín could feel his mind roiling, and she sent a prayer that he'd fall upon their side.

While Dian Cecht's mind sorted out the possibilities, Róisín fumbled for Max's hand and gave it a squeeze.

The god of healing had healed thousands. He'd worked through countless volunteers. He'd taught Róisín how to use and refine her own raw powers.

He'd touched the bodies and souls of more humans than any of the other gods. Surely that contact would convince him to support their side?

And still, Róisín felt his mind sway back to his own kind. Macha and Taranis, gods of rage, war, and anger. But they also had other aspects, like magic, sovereignty, and storms. No god was completely good or evil, just as no human was. But some fed upon chaos.

The Australian man said, "Oi, mate, what the bloody hell do you have to think about? The choice is obvious. You've been working with us for weeks now. Are you with us or not?"

The god glowered at Max, his eyes flashing to him and then back to the gods. Róisín prayed that Max would just shut the hell up. They needed a lot of things right now, but his mouth wasn't one of them.

Dian Cecht steadied his gaze upon the Australian man. **"Taranis is correct. You are insolent."**

Max gritted his teeth. "Oi, you owe me a favor, remember?"

**"I owe you nothing."**

Fear clutched at Róisín's throat as Max dropped her hand and stepped forward. "Yeah, well, insolence is all fine and dandy, but then there's destructive. And Taranis is destructive. I never took you for the destructive sort, mate. You're a healer, right? Healers help people. They don't destroy them."

**"Insolence must still be punished."**

Róisín clenched her fists as Dian Cecht's gaze shifted to her. His expression changed and by the gleam in his eyes, she knew his decision.

His countenance slid into anger, rage, and power. Dian Cecht let out a roar and lifted his arms toward her, as he'd done so many times to heal others.

But healing was just one side of the coin. The other side was harm. Róisín herself had wondered if she could use her healing power to harm others, but it went so utterly against her personal moral code, she'd refused to try, even to the point where she might die.

Dian Cecht didn't have such a moral stricture.

Power erupted from his outstretched hands, aimed straight for her chest. Róisín let out a cry and threw up a shield of healing magic, knowing that it would never be powerful enough to guard against the god's strength.

Max leapt out in front of the pillar of magic, intercepting the brunt of it. He let out a horrible shriek and landed with a thump. A splinter of power missed him, slamming into Róisín's shoulder, and she fell back with a cry.

Dian Cecht gathered his power for another attack, but Róisín had had enough. He might discard her completely when she was no longer useful.

But when it came to her friends, Róisín would die to defend them. And Dian Cecht had just attacked someone who had saved her many times before.

Róisín gathered her power, tingling potency down her arms. She had no practice in using her healing as an offensive weapon. She barely had any glimmer that she could.

But now, she'd just seen Dian Cecht do it, and he'd attacked *her*. The fact that he hit Max instead meant that not only had he hurt a friend, but the god had left her with enough power to fight back.

Róisín needed all the strength she could get. She pulled healing magic from the earth. It resisted at first, perhaps unsure of how she would use it, but then it flowed like never before. The magic flowed in through her feet and up her legs. It flowed through her torso and out to her arms, her hands, her fingers.

And then she blasted it into Dian Cecht's smug, smiling face.

The healing god reeled back from the impact, surprise clear in his wide-eyed expression. He hadn't expected her to fight back. He definitely hadn't expected her to have enough power to hurt him.

Before he could recover and retaliate, she gathered another volley. Róisín felt a hand on her shoulder and spared a look back.

Qacha wore a grim smile. "Do you need assistance?"

As Max groaned behind her, she spared him a glance. He lived, but was obviously in great pain, writhing on the ground. She locked gazes with Qacha. "Yes. Yes, I do."

Together, they faced Dian Cecht. Róisín let loose with her hurting power, crackling blue fire shooting like lightning from her fingertips, just as Qacha shot an arrow of fire from an invisible bow. Both hit Dian Cecht at the same time.

The god of healing staggered back but then let out a disdainful laugh. Still, Róisín spied a scorch mark on his torso, so she gathered another barrage.

Qacha held her hands up as if firing a bow again. Blue and red crackling flames flew and slammed into the god of healing.

This time, he fell. Then his human body, manifested out of his will, exploded into a thousand sparks, those motes flying into the sky like a campfire.

Róisín exchanged a glance with Qacha. "Did we just kill a god?"

Qacha's gaze panned across the hilltop, then pointed at the cage holding Macha and Taranis. "No! He's there!"

The hunched form of the god of healing crouched within the cage, curled up as if in pain. Róisín let out a sigh of relief. She didn't want to kill anyone or anything, even a god bent on destroying her.

Róisín dropped to her knees beside Max, still rolling on the ground, as the people on the hill chanted in the background and thunder rolled overhead.

Róisín pushed him onto his back. A huge black scorch mark covered his chest. His shirt had been completely burnt, and his skin bubbled with blisters down to his ribs. She drew in a deep breath and reached for her healing magic.

But only a trickle answered her call. She'd used all her power fighting Dian Cecht.

Max moaned again and tossed his head, and Qacha crouched next to her. "Can you heal him?"

She shook her head. "I'm all out of power."

Max let out a bone-shattering scream, chilling enough to scratch her nerves and ears raw. The scream of someone who had lost their grip on sanity.

**Max:**

Something intruded on Max's misery, some trickle of power, some blissful balm tickling his soul. A delicious caress, cool water on a blistering day.

But then it was gone, sputtering out to nothing, leaving him empty and alone. Was it Róisín? He cracked open his eyes but saw nothing.

Max couldn't breathe. He couldn't move. Every bone and muscle in his body ached, like a kangaroo had kicked him in the chest.

Dian Cecht's sneer flashed just before he slammed Max with his whammy. He tried to make sense of the images floating around him, but he couldn't hold on to any of them. They fluttered away, like sparrows always flying just out of reach. He wanted to grasp them, but his arms wouldn't obey.

*They weren't real.* Max kept saying that to himself. *Is any of this real?* A god of healing who tried to kill him. Tried to kill Róisín, but he got in the way. And The god would do it again if he didn't get his act together and stop him.

Max couldn't stand the idea of losing another young lady to fire. *Trina. Oh, Trina.* Tears burst forth and his chest burned, and he couldn't stop them. *Trina.*

His memory fled back over fifty years, back to the jungles, back to him holding the charred, flaking remains of Trina's body in his arms. *My fault. It's all my fault.*

He'd just been following orders. But he'd still destroyed the one human being he'd ever loved. Max howled in pain and regret, wanting nothing more than to erase the pain from his world.

He couldn't let that happen again.

Thunder rolled and rain dripped down. Heavy, fat drops plopped on his face. He tried to wipe them away, but more kept coming.

A crack of lightning made Max shoot up to a sitting position, despite his muscles all screaming.

Róisín and Qacha crouched next to him, surprise on their faces. The healer touched his shoulder with a tender hand. "Max? Are you okay?"

He glanced down at the scorched hole in his shirt, his burnt and flayed flesh, bubbling skin, and white-hot pain seared through him. He let out a growl. "I'm pretty fucking far from okay, darlin'!"

The rain grew into a deluge and wind gusted across the hill. People were still chanting and holding hands.

Max squinted at the sky, then to the gods still in the cage of lightning and iron. "Well, I guess Taranis isn't really held captive, is he? Not if he can still command the skies. But maybe I can do something about this."

With Qacha's silent help, he stumbled to his feet, took a deep breath, and asked for the winds. "Slow down! Don't listen to Taranis!"

He'd finally gotten to the point where he no longer had to make friends with them first. In fact, he no longer had to even speak out loud to them. But he liked doing that.

The gale fizzled out to a faint breeze, but the rain still pounded them. The grass-covered hilltop turned to squelching mud.

Max shouted at the black storm clouds. "Go away! Find some farm that needs you! We don't want you here!"

He couldn't tell if the rain lightened, but the clouds rolled and boiled, as if someone was stirring them with a giant spoon.

Max held his hands up and then shoved them apart, as if he was swimming. The storm clouds moved, but then flowed back together. He tried again, and then watched them come back. Again and again, each time parting the clouds a bit further. *Yeah, that's me. A modern-day Moses, parting the fucking Red Sea storm.*

A sliver of blue sky shone through the center as he shoved them apart again. Murmurs ran through the chanting crowd, and their voices faltered.

Max shouted, "Keep chanting! We're far from fucking clear!" He felt as if he were swimming through mud, or maybe through the rain itself, and perhaps that's exactly what he was doing.

He didn't have much strength left, and his skin felt on fire, but he kept swimming. Chunks of crispy flesh flaked off his torso, but he kept swimming.

Someone clapped a hand on his shoulder, and he turned to see a stranger. No, not a stranger, the bloke he'd met earlier, the PEM man. The one who had been on telly and screaming about fire and brimstone, and how all the PHAE were going to hell in a Texan handbasket.

Now this bloke, with his hand on his shoulder, gave him an encouraging nod. "Try again, Aussie. I'll boost your power."

Once again, Max shot his arms up, wincing as his shoulder muscles protested. He split the clouds and shoved his arms to the side. This time, with the Texan's power boost, the clouds flew apart, making a huge blue hole in the middle.

Encouraged, Max did it again and again, until the black clouds had flown to the edges of the horizon and his arms were numb.

# Chapter Ten

"I do not concern myself with gods and spirits,
either good or evil, nor do I serve any."
– Lao Tzu

**Bintou:**

Bintou stared at the rainbow goddess in awe. Her divine beauty surrounded Bintou in joy and warmth, but also terror. Like the stories of angels appearing to people in the Christian Bible.

The new goddess's skin was iridescent, her voice like a lost song from childhood. Bintou couldn't move from fear and love, frozen in contradiction.

The goddess spoke, her voice was the sweetest treacle, covered in cream. "You need have no fear, child. You are one of my own."

Bintou managed to swallow, the warmth flooding through her body like sexual ecstasy. "I am one of your own."

Was this a glamour, like Lugh's spell? Something cast upon her that made her unable to say no?

"I am Danu, and you must love me of your own free will, Bintou Sissoki. I compel no creature to my affection. That is a tool of the lesser gods, and unworthy of true devotion."

Bintou let out a long, shuddering breath. She wanted to believe this shining beacon. With every beat of her heart, she longed to believe. But she'd been betrayed by love and trust so many times, and was wary of another betrayal.

The goddess reached out her hand, gently caressing Bintou's cheek. "You may believe in me, my child. How may I prove my sincerity?"

Her first thought was for Lugh and his lovemaking. Bintou knew, intellectually, she shouldn't be thinking of him. She ought to be thinking of her friends, of PHAE, of the safety of the people of Ireland.

But her thoughts weren't her own as long as Lugh had his enchantment upon her. Shoving aside the glamour, she asked, "Can you break Lugh's spell?"

The goddess Danu gave a sweet smile and passed her hand across Bintou's heart. The stricture squeezing her fell away in shattered fragments, like shards of glass at her feet.

Bintou took a deep breath in, the first truly free breath she'd taken since she first met Lugh so long ago. Had it only been a few weeks? It seemed like a lifetime.

Memory of her real love, Martin, crowded into the vacuum, and she grasped onto that painful grief like a talisman against Lugh's fairy glamour.

Bintou tried to make sense of the world, now that she could think more clearly. Where were her friends? Who was still in danger?

Her last memory was Qacha, trying to keep her out of Lugh's control as Macha screeched. "Can you bring me to Qacha? The last time I saw her, she needed help."

Before she could blink, Lugh's peaceful glade disappeared, her stomach churned, and she stood amidst stormy chaos.

People swarmed over a muddy hilltop, chanting powerful words, with some flashing iron contraption in the center, holding three figures. Storm clouds raced away from them in all directions as if chased by a gale.

Searching desperately for a familiar face, Bintou spied Ciara near the central cage. She shouldered her way into the mass of people to get closer the PHAE woman. "Ciara!"

The PHAE leader turned, and her eyes grew wide. "Bintou! Thanks be to Mary, you're safe!"

"We need to thank Danu, not Mary." Bintou glanced back to where the goddess stood, but only saw a shimmering rainbow of light.

"Whoever's helped, I thank them."

A voice she recognized rasped out. "You're here!"

Bintou spun to find Qacha, and they shared a fierce embrace. Bintou didn't want to let the other woman go. A small measure of that joy she had felt in Danu's presence was in Qacha's protective hug and that was a spell she didn't wish to break.

And for a brief moment, she felt the peace and safety she had once known in Martin's embrace.

When they parted, Bintou gave her a grin and turned to Ciara. "What's happened here?"

The Irish woman stared at the cage, a frown on her face. "We've got them stopped for now, but we need help. We're in a holding pattern, but I can feel the rogue gods punching against their cage."

Bintou glanced around. "Is everyone else here? Who's doing what?"

"Max got hurt. Róisín's helping him. Anna's getting refugees to safety. Komie's here. We're not sure where Hiroki disappeared to. I'm doing my best to dampen their power, but even with all of us working together, it isn't enough."

A voice in the distance caught Bintou's attention, a voice she recognized. She squinted to make out Hiroki on the other side of the cage of light.

Then he spoke, his voice amplified as if he had a microphone and concert speakers. "You should not fight! The gods will help you all. They've already healed many of you, saved hundreds, even thousands of lives!"

This was Hiroki? Her friend? The shy, unassuming young businessman from Tokyo who was so eager to be liked, to please others?

"The best course is to stop fighting them, to accept their gracious leadership! They are on a noble mission to unite us all beneath their incredible power!"

He sounded like a different person. Someone who was pushing an agenda upon people who didn't want or need it. A missionary bringing *the good word* to the savages. Though she felt the strong urge to obey, she shoved through it.

Bintou wasn't sure why she could. When Danu broke Lugh's glamour, maybe a lingering effect helped her push through Hiroki's talent. She glanced at Ciara, who wore a bewildered expression. As did Paul and everyone she glanced at. Bintou seemed like the only one thinking clearly.

The only one who could stop Hiroki.

Bintou pushed her way around the circle, toward the cage. She wove through the still-chanting crowds, blank stares as she hurried past.

Eventually, she reached her Japanese friend.

When Bintou spoke to him, her own voice was amplified like his. "But we cannot beholden ourselves to such gods. They've proven unworthy of being our leaders."

Hiroki scowled, and held his arms wide, as if calling down manna from heaven. "They *are* worthy of us! They have shown their power and their might!"

She grabbed his arm, pulling it down. "And since when is power the only virtue we search for in a leader? A leader also needs compassion, care, and fairness."

Hiroki wrenched his arm from her grip and waved her away. "In this day and age, power is what speaks to all. A strong leader is better for the entire society."

Bintou felt his words press upon her, urging her to agree. She recognized his power, an inarguable compulsion. And yet, she could pull back from it. Not much, but enough to realize what he was doing.

Could Danu's release from Lugh's spell have lingered? "Hiroki, how can you say that? How can you stand there and tell me that *might makes right?* You *know* better! You've got a stronger conscience than that!"

He looked her up and down, an uncharacteristic sneer on his face. "I warned you there was no way to fight against this power. And you are just a weak person, a slave to your desires."

Bintou couldn't believe he'd just said those words and her temper boiled up. "A slave? You dare speak to me about slaves?"

She clenched her fists, aching to smack the expression from his face, despite her hatred for violence. The fact that Hiroki had been her friend made this descent into bigotry all the more painful. Was he being controlled by the gods? But his eyes looked crystal clear and full of judgment.

But she couldn't give in to her anger. That would only lead to being subsumed by these gods and their evil purpose. Bintou counted her breaths to get her temper back under control.

With measured words, she spoke to him, still amplified by Oghma to all assembled. "You used to be a good person, Hiroki. Please, come back to us. Be a kind soul again."

He held up a hand, his face full of haughty certainty. "That is impossible. You've had your chance to make the right choice. You have chosen poorly. Now the gods will destroy you for your failure, and that destruction will be glorious and full of honor."

**Max:**

As Hiroki and Bintou snapped at each other in front of the entire magical contingent of Ireland, Max's anger grew with each word. The winds responded to his mood, despite his earlier attempt to clear the sky.

Hiroki, who used to be so considerate and unsure of himself. Hiroki, who had helped Max get over his PTSD attack after the flight to Europe. Hiroki, who had been his friend, damnit. Hiroki, who had gone over to the side of evil.

In the back of his mind, Max still held tight to the hope that the young Japanese man might come to his senses, but then he spoke about glory and honor.

Those final sentences killed any hope in Max's heart. *Glory and honor* were catchphrases used by warmongers, intent upon sending people to their deaths. He needed to remove Hiroki from this place. Move him to someplace where he couldn't do harm.

Max raised his arms to call for power, despite aching muscles and shooting pain. Gusts grew to squalls. He'd chased Taranis's storm away, but now he created one of his own.

Howling wind wrenched Hiroki, making him stagger. Max concentrated that force into a miniature tornado, whipping around the Japanese man, raising him off the ground.

Oghma glanced up in alarm, and gasps spread through the crowd.

Max raised his arms as Hiroki lifted higher and higher from the ground, caught in the center of his cyclone. And for a brief moment, Max was ready to slam Hiroki into the earth, and damn to his *glory and honor*.

Bintou glanced back toward him, but it was Qacha's hand on his shoulder who made him stop short. "You are going to kill him?"

A tear fell down Max's cheek. "I don't want to. I just want to get him away, where his words aren't broadcast to the whole bloody crowd."

Qacha clenched her jaw. "His power is too strong. All he needs to do is talk, and the world turns against us. And then those gods will have control. You can't let that happen."

He turned to Qacha, pleading with his eyes. "I don't want to kill the bloke! He's my friend!"

Hiroki screamed from the air. "Max! Put me down, now!"

Resisting the pull of Hiroki's magic wasn't easy, and Max didn't want to kill yet another person he cared for.

The Mongolian woman shook her head. "You have no choices left, Maximilian. Hiroki chose to fight on the side of the powerful. We must defend the weak. That is the purpose of society."

Max shook his head and commanded the winds to fly Hiroki to someplace far away. He couldn't betray his friend.

Then, Qacha gripped his shoulder, spinning him around. "What are you doing? You know what must be done! You are a warrior! You need to do your duty!"

Max's concentration on the wind faltered and Hiroki dropped.

He watched with horrified eyes. He'd never forget of the sound the Japanese man's body squelching into the muddy mess on the Hill of Uisneach. Something cracked, a hollow sound, like someone knocking on a coconut. Stone hidden beneath the mud.

Now, Max let go of the winds. He could no longer hold back memories of Trina. They grabbed his heart and tore it out. Trina had Hiroki's face, and together, they ripped his soul apart.

Max fell to his knees and sobbed. The tornado now flew from his control, attacking everyone on the hill as he held his head and rocked.

He curled into a fetal position and fought his internal demons while everyone else fought his rogue tempest.

Screams echoed across the hilltop, and somewhere amidst the chaos, the cage fragmented.

Macha, Dian Cecht, and Taranis burst free and shared a sinister smile with Oghma.

**Komie:**

As Komie stared at the cage, she prayed that her spirit helpers would arrive soon.

Their heartbeats pounded within her own, stronger as they grew closer. Bear's was the loudest, then Wolf, Raccoon, and Badger.

When Bintou arrived with a ball of light, Komie thought she might not need the spirits' help, and almost sent them away, but the goddess accompanying the Malian woman did nothing to help.

*Thump, thump, thump.* The spirits came closer.

Then, Hiroki and Bintou fell into a shouting match, and the resulting chaos hammered at her senses.

So many people fought here with massive power, but it wasn't focused. Some were keeping the cage strong. Others were fighting each other. They needed a nexus, some place to direct their power. Right now, there was no hub, no leader.

Did she need to step up and lead?

*Thump, thump, thump.* The spirits came closer.

She had no loudspeaker, or whatever Hiroki was using to broadcast their conversation.

Ciara was arguing with a priest, while Qacha held Max on the ground next to Róisín. The healer was sitting cross-legged in the mud, her face in her hands, sobbing.

Bintou stood behind her, a hand on her shoulder, but Komie was too far away to hear what she said.

They could have used Anna's command over water to rid themselves of this pelting rain, but Komie didn't see her. The storm had gone mad, but Max looked too far gone to calm it.

The spirit heartbeats grew loud within her. The deluge shrouded her view, but a faint shimmering outline of a massive animal stood on the edge of the hill.

Hope leapt to her throat as she recognized Bear. Beside him stood the others. She beckoned them closer.

As Bear walked toward her, everyone stared at the ghostly white forms. They parted like the Red Sea before Moses and they walked down the open aisle.

Silence spread with each step. Eventually, as Bear, Wolf, Raccoon, and Badger stood around her, a universal hush fell across the hilltop, broken only by the whistling wind of Max's storm.

Nokomis Nicholas raised her arms for attention, not that she needed to with the spirits at her side.

She faced Macha, Dian Cecht, and Taranis, who also stared at the new arrivals. Would the spirits be strong enough to defeat these ancient gods?

Putting thousands of years of ancestors in her words, the native woman encouraged the earth below her to sing, to spread her magic to the entire island. Echoes of her spell spread across the land in rippling waves.

*Gazing into the approaching darkness*
*I lean upon my staff of hope.*
*Icy tendrils of dread caress my calves*
*Shooting pain cripples my resolve.*
*But still I stand.*

*Hatred hammers upon my ears*
*Bigotry and loathing, rage and fear.*
*Shouting, beating, thudding every day,*
*Drums of war with no relief.*
*But still I stand.*

*I scream against the death,*
*Part the waters of intolerance,*
*Yet the flood threatens to drown*
*Every soul which I hold dear.*
*But still I stand.*

*There may come an end to ire,*
*When strength and force*

*Fall to compassion and care.*
*A day may come when love prevails.*
*Until then, I stand.*

The entire hilltop shouted the last line with her, and then, no one breathed.

Macha opened her mouth and another scream burst forth, shredding peace and tension into shards of violence.

Now that the cage had disintegrated, she grabbed the closest person, a priest wearing his cassock, and tore him apart with her bare hands.

His body parts fell into quivering, bloody bits, gushes of red splattering everywhere. Taranis grabbed a dangling arm and shoved it into his mouth with a roar, while Macha tied the dead priest's head onto her belt, an acorn of the battlefield.

Komie's speech had only angered them further, rather than mollifying them into surrender. The pacifist within her shattered. *Very well. Battle it must be.*

Macha reached for the next person, one of the Traveler cunning folk, and the woman let out a heart-rending scream.

Badger leapt to her aid, biting Macha's calf so hard, it almost chomped through the muscle. The goddess dropped her prey and spun to confront this pain.

Raccoon jumped into the air and landed on her face, his claws tearing stripes. As the war goddess scrambled to remove claws from her skin, Taranis grabbed Badger.

But Bear slapped him with an enormous paw, making the storm god's head wobble. With a thunderous glower, Taranis growled at Bear, louder and more fiercely than any worldly bear.

But Bear was not of the earth. He was a Spirit, and he could match any god's growl. His roar rose from the depths of all the caves in Ireland, hollow and ominous. His kind once ruled this land, thousands of years ago, and the land remembered.

Wolf raised his hackles in a standoff with Oghma, while that god rose slowly to his feet. Wolf let out a low growl, a warning noise that no creature could ignore. The god crouched, his hands open as if ready for a grapple.

Wolf launched at Oghma, aiming for the throat, but the god dodged more quickly than any human could. The attacker swiveled quickly and chomped hard on the god's right hamstring. Oghma let out a howl of his own and pounded Wolf's nose with his fists.

While he let out a whimper, Wolf held fast, and soon he'd chewed through the hamstring, leaving Oghma writhing in pain. The god screeched as he faded away, the sound dying in the wind.

Wolf let out a yip as Dian Cecht grabbed the spirit animal by the scruff, but he was too slow. Wolf whipped around and bit his elbow and he let out a screech of pain.

Macha's screech cut across the battle sounds.

Badger was dragging his hind leg while Raccoon's right arm hung limp, a blossom of red dripping from his fur. Macha had some scratches, but nothing more. As Komie watched, Badger leapt at her belly while Raccoon bit her upper leg.

Macha let out a feral roar, and tufts of fur flew from both her attackers. They staggered back, and Raccoon fell to the ground, twitching.

Pain stabbed at Komie's heart and tears fell down her cheeks. Raccoon had been the kindest of them.

Bear roared at Taranis again. Several bursts of lightning fell from the sky, but Bear was too fast. He swiped a massive paw again, this time connecting with the god's torso, throwing him back.

The storm god landed on his side, a massive gash across his chest. His eyes grew wide as Bear lumbered forward, his arms open to crush his opponent.

Macha threw Badger to one side and joined Taranis to face off Bear. Worried that the two gods together would be enough to destroy Bear, Komie searched frantically for someone who could help.

Her gaze fell upon the light that had accompanied Bintou. It remained where it had appeared, not interfering, which made her angry. But if the gods refused to help, the humans would need to.

**Tiberius:**

Thunder and screaming made Tiberius spin, only to see the cage he'd worked so hard to create had faded into faint lines. And ghostly forms of wild animals battling the rogue gods.

Ciara approached, with the Irish priestess who led the chanting. "This is Caoimhe. Can you boost her network?"

He narrowed his eyes, suspicious of this new person. "What are they planning on doing with this power?"

Caoimhe threw up her hands. "Typical! And this is your so-called ace in the hole?"

Ciara crossed her arms and scowled at him. "Tiberius. We talked about this already. We need your help. Are you going to back out now?"

He did love a strong woman, he had to admit. "Fine. I'll be damned if I'm gonna let some ancient Irish wanna-be gods run loose."

The previous cage had been made of iron, but it still hadn't felt solid. He had no idea how he could judge what was solid or strong enough to hold an ancient pagan god, but something just felt off.

A tall, rangy Asian woman ran up to Ciara. She wore a no-nonsense scowl. "Plastic! Make a plastic bubble. They can't stand polymers."

Caoimhe yelled out the order. Tiberius had no idea what the mechanism for change was, and he didn't need to. He was there to boost the others, not to create anything himself.

Tiberius took a deep breath and boosted their crafting magic. He focused every ounce of his energy upon pouring this newfound talent into their magical construct.

Tingling turned to fire burning every inch of his skin, but he kept pushing. He was grunting with pain, then growling, then howling as the fire sunk into his muscles, but still he kept pushing.

Every bit of his body pulsed with pain, and he knew he'd pay for this later, but he'd be damned if he'd half-ass this.

A bubble enclosed the rogue gods, shining iridescent white in the afternoon light. The entire structure shrank to surround just the three gods.

The wounded spirit animals began to fade. The raccoon looked dead, the white outline of his body disappearing even as he watched.

Tiberius let out a grunt of pain. He hated those destructive assholes. But the bear looked the worse for wear, too, as it stumbled away. The wolf and badger had vanished among all the people chanting and holding hands.

Behind him, someone shouted. He glanced over his shoulder to see the black woman yelling at a form made of light. No matter how much he tried to make sense of that, he failed.

Then, his own pain took over and his world turned gray. As he lost consciousness, he fell into Ciara's arms.

**Bintou:**

Macha and Taranis tore their way through the priest, the Traveler woman, and then Komie's spirit creatures. Bintou's stomach churned at the blood and gore, and she turned to Danu. "Please, please, help us! We can't win without help! They'll get free and enslave or destroy us all!"

Danu, still clothed in dancing light and rainbows, gave her a beatific smile. She sang a single note, her voice still perfectly calm. The note grew loud as the crowd went quiet.

Macha's shriek died, drowned out by this single, lovely note. The gods were now completely enclosed in a slick, white plastic bubble.

The note died, and silence fell upon the Hill of Uisneach. The goddess turned to Bintou, her eyes iridescent and sad. "I cannot hurt them, Bintou. They are my own children. All of those beings upon this hilltop, upon this island, are my own children."

Qacha came to stand next to Bintou. She took the Mongolian woman's hand and gripped it hard. The chef stared at Danu for a moment, then said, "These may be your children. But if a child misbehaves, they should be punished. They are misbehaving."

The goddess opened her arms. "But they are beautiful. Would you hurt something beautiful?"

Qacha stepped in front of Bintou, shielding her from Danu. "Not everything that is beautiful is good. You should know that. This woman behind me, she is both good and beautiful. And precious few things in this world are both. When true evil shows its face, like those," and she pointed at the plastic bubble of rogue gods, "Then they must be punished. If not for their own sakes, for the detriment of others considering evil."

Danu frowned, glancing at the gods.

"If you will not punish them, we must find a way. And our way will be less gentle than yours. We cannot allow the ugly to conquer the beautiful." Qacha turned to Bintou, taking both her hands. "This woman is beautiful. She deserves more."

Bintou swallowed, her heart racing, and she forgot all her words, in all languages.

Danu floated to where Max still lay, cradled in Róisín's arms. The healer looked up, tears on her face. "Can you heal him? I used up all my magic. He's dying."

Max let out a pained moan. "No, don't waste any power on me."

The mother goddess held her hands above Max. "Will you take my healing, my son?"

He shook his head, but Róisín grabbed his arm. "Max! Stop being an arse. Take the healing, for my sake if not your own. Please?"

Max swallowed and his gaze shifted between the Irish woman and the rainbow goddess. Finally, he gave a single nod. "Just leave me my memories, aye? I need to remember Trina."

Iridescent light floated over his body, and the scorched hole in his torso curled and closed, healing the bone, the skin, and even the hairs on his chest.

His skin was whole, but Danu stayed in place. Sickly, gurgling popping came from inside his head. Max screamed and held his temples.

A black, oily thing oozed out of his mind and into the dirt. Komie shouted in protest, but the thing spread across the muddy grass and sank into the earth.

Max now wore a serene smile, as sweet as a sleeping child. He shut his eyes and fell into a dream. Róisín looked up, tears still running down her cheeks. "He's better? He'll live?"

Danu lifted Róisín's chin up. "He will live, and further, he will *want* to live. You have done well to nurture him in his pain, my daughter. I have only completed what you started. But you must rest, as well."

As the goddess touched her forehead, Róisín also fell into slumber.

Bintou finally broke her gaze with Qacha and caught her breath in alarm, wondering if they'd put too much trust in this goddess, that she might even now be betraying them, destroying them one by one under the guise of healing.

But then the goddess turned back to her. Harmony flowed through Bintou's mind and body, and she felt guilty for her doubts.

"There is one more I must heal, but she is not upon this hill. I must leave and tend to her. You have won the day, you humans of Eire. Your staunch hearts called to me, and I followed your need. Keep this victory in your soul, and remember that love, not hate, wins."

As she disappeared in a shower of rainbow sparks, so did the plastic bubble encasing the rogue gods. All fell silent upon the Hill of Uisneach.

**Anna:**

As she played in the waves, Anna might have missed Carlos, or even Brendan, if she'd remembered to think about them. But, with the ocean's caress on her skin, she couldn't bring any human to mind. Not them, not her parents, and certainly not her brother.

She'd completely forgotten about Manannán's task of bringing people to Iceland. It was difficult to keep anything in her mind other than swimming, playing amongst the waves, or diving down to commune with the creatures of the depths.

Anna was doing exactly that, touching noses to a minke whale, when a light shone above, sunbeams cutting in a cone all around her. Curious, she swam toward the light, admiring the beauty of the water in the beams, tiny creatures swimming in and out.

When she finally broke the surface, the iridescent form before her filled her with delight.

The musical voice said, "You have swum long enough, child. It is time to return home."

"But I am home!"

"The ocean is not your home. While you may feel comfortable here, you are a human, and you belong on the land."

Anna shook her head, memories of taunting and anger now intruding upon her bliss. "I don't want to be on the land. The creatures of the sea accept me as I am."

"Nevertheless, that is where you belong. I shall take you to the arms of someone who cares for you. And you will find joy in purpose there."

Anna didn't remember being plucked from the water. She didn't remember floating along the surface of the sea to Galway Harbour. She barely remembered the name of the young man with curly black hair who gasped when he saw her. "Anna!"

"C-Carlos?"

Anna wanted to hold him tight. But she also wanted the ocean. She stood, her eyes shifting between the man and the water.

Finally, Carlos placed a hand on her shoulder. "Anna? What if we find you a job you can be in the ocean for? We need someone here to study marine ecology. Or give tours. Or teach people swimming. That's what you used to do, right?"

Anna swallowed and turned back to Carlos. "That seems like so long ago."

He gave her a lopsided smile. "You can be whatever you want. *Do* whatever you want. I promise, I'll never get in your way. You're a force of nature, Anna! How could I?"

She couldn't help but smile back. She'd come a long, long way from that frightened teacher, running from an angry mob.

The shining goddess touched Anna's forehead with infinite gentleness. "You are safe now, daughter. You are all safe now."

# Epilogue

*__Latest CNN Update:__ Breaking news! We have verification that the gods in Ireland have signed a treaty with the government of Ireland and the PHAE. The treaty outlines several initiatives, including conflict resolution. Not all the gods have signed it, but the terms include a promise from the signatory deities to police those who refused to take part.*

*In China, all PHAE citizens have either fled or been killed, according to the national news reporters. We have not verified this information and will bring more news as we discover the truth.*

*The Omsk enclave has entered negotiations with the Russian government to relocate to a Siberian outpost, while the PHAE enclave in Iceland has promised to create a public education initiative, a tourist spot for people to come and learn about what the Unhidden can do for humanity.*

*The various groups known as the Pure Earther Movement, or PEM, seems to have fractured with the defection of their leader, Tiberius Wilkinson. He has joined the PHAE and is campaigning for the censure of the previous terrorist organizations.*

Bintou stared at the blank stationery. It had gorgeous scrollwork on the edge, and she almost hated using it, but she'd gotten into the habit of writing actual letters to her PHAE friends.

Taking up her pen, she began the letter to Anna. She'd moved into Carlos's B&B in western Ireland and spearheaded a marine ecological research initiative. On the weekends, she took tourists out to meet dolphins and whales. It seemed like a good compromise between the land she needed and the sea she loved.

Bintou finished that letter, and started the next, the one to Komie. She'd moved to Eritrea, of all places. The PHAE was contracting her out to help farmers to improve their crops, and she was moving from region to region, increasing arable land. She'd even brought her granddaughter, though the child was still a toddler. Bintou missed the native woman, but she must be loving her new job.

Speaking of jobs, she wrote next to Colin, Michelle, and their children. They still lived on their farm, but had stopped processing new immigrants for the PHAE. Colin still taught as a lecturer, though. And Róisín had gone back to school to become a physician.

Bintou sniffed back at the thought of Brendan. He'd never fully recovered from his illness. Two years later, and he was still an invalid. She made sure to write to him often, as he said he treasured her letters.

Max, on the other hand, had disappeared. He'd been pretty destroyed by Hiroki's death. They'd held a service for him, after all the dust and mud settled. And, despite Max's healing, he'd blamed himself for his friend's death.

Bintou had no idea how to get hold of him, though Róisín said she kept in touch with him. She said he had a plane and was flying, so he must be happy, wherever he was.

A growl at her feet made her glance down. Once he saw her looking, he gave a plaintive meow, full of pitiful entreaty. She chuckled at the manipulative creature. "Manol, I already fed you."

The door opened behind her, and she turned to smile as Qacha came inside, carrying several grocery bags. She jumped up to help her carry them to the kitchen, then kissed Qacha on the cheek. "Did you find everything you wanted for the meal tonight, dear one?"

The Mongolian woman shook her head. "I had to make substitutions. Paris has extensive stores, but not camel."

Bintou wrinkled her nose. "Camel? Please tell me you got lamb or goat instead?"

Qacha let out a chuckle. "Yes, my beautiful one. I got lamb instead. Do you think Ciara and Tiberius will like it?"

"Lamb is very common in Ireland. I'm sure Ciara will love it. Tiberius... I'm not so sure. But you're cooking, so it will be delicious."

As Qacha unpacked the groceries and began to prep for cooking, Bintou looked out of the flat's window, across the rooftops of Paris. She'd come a long way from the vaults beneath the university, poring through dusty volumes. She missed that. But she had found a home, and that was more important than anything.

*When the magical secrets of The Emerald Isle beckon,*
*will she survive answering the call?*

Pittsburgh, 1846. Valentia McDowell wishes she could rest. Plagued by nightmares of her grandmother's mysterious brooch lost in Ireland, the wealthy young woman grows more troubled when a fire ravages her family's business. But as she buries herself in the rebuilding efforts, she can't shake the sense that a powerful inheritance awaits her across the ocean... if she can weather the treacherous journey.

Can Valentia uphold a destiny she doesn't yet understand without losing everyone she loves?

**Start reading Legacy of Hunger to find a lost family treasure today!**

## Thank You!

Thank you so much for enjoying All's Fae That Ends Fae. If you've enjoyed the story, please consider helping others find Róisín, Hiroki, and the rest of the Unhidden by leaving a review.

If you would like to get updates, sneak previews, sales, and contests, please sign up for my newsletter.
Monthly Newsletter Signup and homepage:
www.greendragonartist.com

## See all the books available through

## Green Dragon Publishing at

http://www.greendragonartist.com/books

# Dedication

I'd like to thank my fantastic critique group for all their help keeping me on-genre and for some tough love regarding too many points of view, especially authors Mattea Orr and MA Hoyler. And sincere thanks go to my editors and beta readers, including Ian Erik Morris and Joseph Lau.

I also dedicate this series to those who face prejudice, hatred, and bigotry in any form.

# About the Author

Christy Nicholas writes under several pen names, including Emeline Rhys, CN Jackson, and Rowan Dillon. She is an author, artist, and accountant. After she failed to become an airline pilot, she quit her ceaseless pursuit of careers that begin with the letter 'A' and decided to concentrate on her writing. Since she has Project Completion Compulsion, she is one of the few authors with no unfinished novels.

Christy has her hands in many crafts, including digital art, beaded jewelry, writing, and photography. In real life, she's a CPA, but having grown up with art all around her (her mother, grandmother, and great-grandmother are/were all artists), it sort of infected her, as it were.

She wants to expose the incredible beauty in this world, hidden beneath the everyday grime of familiarity and habit, and share it with others. She uses characters out of time and places infused with magic and myth, writing magical realism stories in both historical fantasy and time travel flavors.

**Social Media Links:**
Blog: www.GreenDragonArtist.net
Website: www.GreenDragonArtist.com
Facebook: www.facebook.com/greendragonauthor
Instagram: www.instagram.com/greendragonartist9
TikTok: www.tiktok.com/@greendragonauthor

Milton Keynes UK
Ingram Content Group UK Ltd.
UKHW040742310723
426074UK00005B/652